Frances Fuller Victor

The New Penelope

And Other Stories and Poems

Frances Fuller Victor

The New Penelope
And Other Stories and Poems

ISBN/EAN: 9783743408135

Manufactured in Europe, USA, Canada, Australia, Japa

Cover: Foto ©Andreas Hilbeck / pixelio.de

Manufactured and distributed by brebook publishing software (www.brebook.com)

Frances Fuller Victor

The New Penelope

AND

OTHER STORIES AND POEMS.

BY

MRS. FRANCES FULLER VICTOR.

SAN FRANCISCO:

A. L. BANCROFT & COMPANY, PRINTERS.

1877.

PREFACE.

THIS collection consists of sketches of Pacific Coast life, most of which have appeared, from time to time, in the *Overland Monthly*, and other Western magazines. If they have a merit, it is because they picture scenes and characters having the charm of newness and originality, such as belong to border life.

The poems embraced in the collection, have been written at all periods of my life, and therefore cannot be called peculiarly Western. But they embody feelings and emotions common to all hearts, East or West; and as such, I dedicate them to my friends on the Pacific Coast, but most especially in Oregon.

PORTLAND, AUGUST, 1877.

CONTENTS.

STORIES.

POEMS.

STORIES.

The New Penelope and Other Stories and Poems.

THE NEW PENELOPE.

I MAY as well avow myself in the beginning of my story as that anomalous creature—a woman who loves her own sex, and naturally inclines to the study of their individual peculiarities and histories, in order to get at their collective qualities. If I were to lay before the reader all the good and bad I know about them by actual discovery, and all the mean, and heroiç, attributes this habit I have of studying people has revealed to me, I should meet with incredulity, perhaps with opprobrium. However that may be, I have derived great enjoyment from having been made the recipient of the confidences of many women, and by learning therefrom to respect the moral greatness that is so often coupled with delicate physical structure, and almost perfect social helplessness. Pioneer life brings to light striking characteristics in a remarkable manner; because, in the absense of conventionalities and in the presence of absolute and imminent necessities, all real qualities come to the surface as they never would have done under different circumstances. In the early life of the Greeks, Homer found his Penelope; in the pioneer days of the Pacific Coast, I discovered mine.

My wanderings, up and down among the majestic mountains and the sunny valleys of California and Oregon, had made me acquainted with many persons, some of whom were to me, from the interest they inspired me with, like the friends of my girlhood. Among this select number was Mrs. Anna Greyfield, at whose home among the foot-hills of the Sierras in Northern California, I had spent one of the most delightful summers of my life. Intellectual and intelligent without being learned or particularly bookish; quick in her perceptions and nearly faultless in her judgment of others; broadly charitable, not through any laxity of principle on her own part, but through knowledge of the stumbling-blocks of which the world is full for the unwary, she was a constant surprise and pleasure to me. For, among the vices of women I had long counted uncharitableness; and among their disadvantages want of actual knowledge of things—the latter accounting for the former.

I had several times heard it mentioned that Mrs. Greyfield had been twice married; and as her son Benton was also called Greyfield, I presumed that he was the son of the second marriage. How I found out differently I am about to relate.

One rainy winter evening, on the occasion of my second visit to this friend, we were sitting alone before a bright wood fire in an open fireplace, when we chanced to refer to the subject of her son's personal qualities; he then being gone on a visit to San Francisco, and of course very constantly in his mother's thoughts, as only sons are sure to be.

"Benton is just like his father," she said. "He is self-possessed and full of expedients, but he says very little. I have often wished he conversed more readily, for I admire a good talker."

"And yet did not marry one:—the common lot!"

Mrs. Greyfield smiled, and gazed into the fire, whose pleasant radiance filled the room, bringing out the soft warm colors in the carpet, and making fantastic shadows of our easy-chairs and ourselves upon the wall.

" Mr. Greyfield was your second husband?" I said, in an inquiring tone, but without expecting to be contradicted.

" Mr. Greyfield was my first, last, and only husband," she replied, with a touch of asperity, yet not as if she meant it for me.

" I beg your pardon," I hastened to explain: "but I had been told—"

" Yes, I can guess what you have been told. Very few people know the truth: but I never had a second husband, though I was twice married;" and my hostess regarded me with a smile half assumed and half embarrassed.

For my own part, I was very much embarrassed, because I had certainly been informed that she had lived for a number of years with a second husband who had not used her well, and from whom she was finally divorced. Doubt her word I could not; neither could I reconcile her statement with facts apparently well known. She saw my dilemma, and, after a brief silence, mentally decided to help me out of it. I could see that, in the gradual relaxing of certain muscles of her face, which had contracted at the first reference to this—as I could not doubt—painful subject. Straightening her fine form as if ease of position was not compatible with what was in her mind, she grasped the arms of her chair with either hand, and looking with a retrospective gaze into the fire, began:

" You see it was this way: the man I married the second time had another wife."

While she drew a deep breath, and made a momentary pause, I seemed to take it all in, for I had heard so many stories of deserted Eastern homes, and subsequent illegal marriages in California, that I was prepared not to be at all surprised at what I should learn from her. Directly she went on:

" I found out about it the very day of the marriage. We were married in the morning, and in the afternoon a man came over from Vancouver who told me that Mr. Seabrook had a wife, and family of children, in a certain town in Ohio." Another pause followed, while she seemed to be recalling the very emotions of that time.

"Vancouver?" I said: "that is on the Columbia River."

"Yes; I was living in Portland at that time."

In reply to my glance of surprise, she changed the scene of her story to an earlier date.

"Mr. Greyfield had always wanted to come to California, after the gold discoveries; but when he married me he agreed not to think of it any more. I was very young and timid, and very much attached to my childhood's home, and my parents; and I could not bear the thought of going so long a distance away from them. It was not then, as it is now, an easy journey of one week; but a long six months' pilgrimage through a wilderness country infested by Indians. To reach what? another wilderness infested by white barbarians!"

"But I have always heard," I said, "that women were idealized and idolized in those days."

"That is a very pretty fiction. If you had seen what I have seen on this coast, you would not think we had been much idealized. Women have a certain value among men, when they can be useful to them. In the old States, where every man has a home, women have a fixed position and value in society, because they are necessary to make homes. But on this coast, in early times, and more or less even now, men found they could dispense with homes; they had been converted into nomads, to whom earth and sky, a blanket and a frying-pan, were sufficient for their needs. Unless we came to them armed with endurance to battle with primeval nature, we became burdensome. Strong and coarse women who could wash shirts in any kind of a tub out of doors under a tree, and iron them kneeling on the ground, to support themselves and half a dozen little, hungry young ones, were welcome enough—before the

Chinamen displaced them. We had some value as cooks,
before men, with large means, turned their attention to
supplying their brothers with prepared food for a consideration below what we could do with our limited means. And
then the ladies, the educated, refined women, who followed
their husbands to this country, or who came here hoping
to share, perchance, in the golden spoils of the mines!
Where are they to-day, and what is their condition? Look
for them in the sunless back rooms of San Francisco board-
ing-houses, and you will find them doing a little fine sewing for the shops; or working on their own garments,
which they must make out of school hours, because the
niggardly pay of teachers in the lower grades will not allow of their getting them done. Idealized indeed! Men
talk about our getting out of our places where we clamor
for paying work of some kind, for something to do that
will enable us to live in half comfort by working more
hours than they do to earn lordly livings."

How much soever I might have liked to talk this labor
question over with my intelligent hostess at any other time,
my curiosity concerning her own history having been so
strongly aroused, the topic seemed less interesting than
usual, and I seized the opportunity given by an emphasized
pause to bring her back to the original subject.

"Did you come first to California?" I asked.

"No. I had been married little over a year when Benton
was born. 'Now,' I thought, 'my husband will be contented to stay at home.' He had been fretting about having
promised not to take me to California; but I hoped the
baby would divert his thoughts. We were doing well, and
had a pleasant house, with everything in and about it that
a young couple ought to desire. I deceived myself in expecting Mr. Greyfield to give up anything he had strongly
desired; and seeing how much he brooded over it, I finally
told him to be comforted; that I would go with him to

California if he would wait until the baby was a year old
before starting; and to this he agreed."

"How old were you at that time?"

"Only about nineteen. I was twenty the spring we
started; and celebrated my anniversary by making a general gathering of all my relatives and friends at our house,
before we broke up and sold off our house-keeping goods
—all but such as could be carried in our wagons across the
plains."

"You were not starting by yourselves?"

"O no. There was a large company gathering together
on the Missouri river, to make the start in May; and we,
with some of our neighbors, made ready to join them. I
shall never forget my feelings as I stood in my own house
for the last time, taking a life-long leave of every familiar
object! But you do not want to hear about that."

"I want to hear what you choose to tell me; but most of
all about your second marriage, and what led to it."

"It is not easy to go back so many years and take up
one thread in the skein of life, and follow that alone. I
will disentangle it as rapidly as I can; but first let us have
a fresh fire."

Suiting the action to the word, my hostess touched a
bell and ordered a good supply of wood, which I took as
an intimation that we were to have one of our late sittings.
In confirmation of this suspicion a second order was given
to have certain refreshments, including hot lemonade, made
ready to await our pleasure. When we were once more
alone I begged her to go on with her story.

"We left the rendezvous in May, and traveled without
any unusual incidents all through the summer."

"I beg pardon for interrupting you; but I do want to
know how you endured that sort of life. Was it not terrible?"

"It was monotonous, it was disagreeable, but it was not
terrible while everybody was well. There were compensa-

tions in it, as in almost any kind of life. My husband was strong and cheerful, now that he was having his own way; the baby throve en fresh air and good milk—for we had milch cows with us—and the summer months on the grassy plains are delightful, except for rather frequent thunder storms. The grass was good, and our cattle in fine order. Everything went well until the cholera broke out among us."

"And then?"

"And then my husband died."

"Ah, what have not pioneer women endured!"

" Mr. Greyfield had from the first been regarded as a sort of leader. Without saying much, but by being always in the right place at the right time, he had gained an ascendancy over the less courageous, strong and decided men. When the cholera came he was continually called upon to nurse the sick, to bury the dead and comfort the living."

"And so became the easier victim?"

My remark was unheeded, while my hostess lived over again in recollection the fearful scenes of the cholera season on the plains. I wanted to divert her, and called her attention to the roaring of the wind and beating of the rain without.

" Yes," she said; " it stormed just in that way the night before he died. We all were drenched to the skin, and he was not in a condition to bear the exposure. I was myself half sick with fever, and when the shock came I became delirious. When I came to myself we were a hundred and fifty miles away from the place where he died."

" How dreadful!" I could not help exclaiming. "Not even to know how and where he was buried."

"Nor if he were buried at all. So frightened were the people in our train that they could not be prevailed upon to take proper care of the sick and dying, nor pay proper respect to the dead. After my reason returned, the one subject that I could not bear to have mentioned was that of my husband's death. Some of the men belonging to the

train had taken charge of my affairs and furnished a driver
for the wagon I was in. The women took care of Benton;
and I lived, who would much rather have died. Probably
I should have died, but for the need I felt, when I could
think, of somebody to care for, support and educate my
child. My constitution was good; and that, with the
anxiety about Benton, made it possible for me to live."

"My dear friend," I exclaimed; "what a dreadful experience! I wonder that you are alive and sit there talking
to me, this moment."

"You will wonder more before I have done," she returned, with what might be termed a superior sort of smile
at my inexperience.

"But how did you get to Oregon?" I asked, interrupting her again.

"Our train was about at the place where the Oregon and
California emigrants parted company, when I recovered
my reason and strength enough to have any concern about
where I was going. Some of those who had started for
Oregon had determined to go to California; and the most
particular friend Mr. Greyfield had in the train had decided
to go to Oregon instead of to California, as he first intended.
Now, when my husband was hopeless of his own re-
covery, he had given me in charge of this man, with instructions to be governed by him in all my business affairs;
and I had no thought of resisting his will, though that be-
quest was the cause of the worst sorrows of my life, by
compelling me to go to Oregon."

"Why cannot people be contented with ruling while
living, without subjecting others to the domination of an
irrevocable will, when they are no longer able to mold or
govern circumstances. I beg your pardon. Pray go on.
But first let me inquire whether the person to whom you
were commanded to trust your affairs proved trustworthy?"

"As trustworthy as nearly absolute power on one side,
and timid inexperience on the other, is likely to make any

one. When we arrived finally in Portland, he took my
wagons and cattle off my hands, and returned me next to
nothing for them. Yet, he was about like the average ad-
ministrator; it did not make much difference, I suppose,
whether this one man got my property, or a probate court."

"Poor child! I can see just how you were situated.
Alone in a new country, with a baby on your hands, and
without means to make a home for yourself. What *did*
you do? did you never think of going back to your parents?"

"How could I get back? The tide of travel was not in
that direction. Besides, I had neither money nor a sufficient outfit. There was no communication by mail in those
days oftener than once in three months. You might perish
a thousand times before you could get assistance from the
East. O, no! there was nothing to be done, except to
make the best of the situation."

"Certainly, you had some friends among your fellow-
immigrants who interested themselves in your behalf to
find you a home? Somebody besides your guardian already
mentioned."

"The most of them were as badly off as myself. Many
had lost near friends. I was not the only widow; but some
women had lost their husbands who had several young
children. They looked upon me as comparatively fortunate. Men had lost wives, and these were the most wretched
of all; for a woman can contrive some way to take care of
her children, where a man is perfectly helpless. Families,
finding no houses to go into by themselves, were huddled
together in any shelter that could be procured. The lines
of partition in houses were often as imaginary as the paral-
lels of latitude on the earth; or were defined by a window,
or a particular board in the wall. O, I could'nt live in
that way. My object was to get a real home somewhere.
As soon as I could, I rented a room in a house with a good
family, for the sake of the protection they would be to me,

2

and went to work to earn a living. Of course, people were
forward enough with their suggestions."

" Of what, for instance?"

"Most persons—in fact everybody that I talked with
—said I should have to marry. But I could not think of
it; the mention of it always made me sick that first winter.
I was recovering strength, and was young; so I thought I
need not despair."

" Such a woman could not but have plenty of offers, in
a new country especially ; but I understand how you must
have felt. You could not marry so soon after your husband's death, and it revolted you to be approached on the
subject. A wife's love is not so easily transferred."

" You speak as any one might think, not having been in
my circumstances. But there was something more than
that in the feeling I had. I could not realize the fact of
Mr. Greyfield's death. It was as if he had only fallen
behind the train, and might come up with us any day. I
waited for him all that winter."

." How distressing !" I could not help saying. Mrs.
Greyfield sat silent for some minutes, while the storm raged
furiously without. She rested her cheek on her hand and
gazed into the glowing embers, as if the past were all
pictured there in living colors. For me to say, as I did,
" how distressing," no doubt seemed to her the merest
platitude. There are no conventional forms for the expression of the utmost grief or sympathy. Silence is most
eloquent, but I could not keep silence. At last I asked,
" What did she do to earn a living?"

" I learned to make men's clothes. There was a clothing
store in the place that gave me employment. First I made
vests, and then pants ; and finally I got to be quite expert,
and could earn several dollars a day. But a dollar did not
buy much in those times ; and oh, the crying spells that I
had over my work, before I had mastered it sufficiently to
have confidence in myself. Sancho Panza blessed the man

that invented sleep—I say, blessed be the woman that invented crying-fits, for they save thousands and thousands of women from madness, annually!"

This was a return to that sprightly manner of speech that was one of Mrs. Greyfield's peculiar attractions; and which often cropped out in the least expected places. But though she smiled, it was easy to see that tears would not be far to seek. "And yet," I said, "it is a bad habit to cultivate—the habit of weeping. It wastes the blood at a fearful rate."

"Don't I know it? But it is safer than frenzy. Why I used—but I'll not tell you about that yet. I set out to explain to you my marriage with Mr. Seabrook. As I told you, everybody said I must marry; and the reasons they gave were, that I must have somebody to support me; that it was not safe for me to live alone; that my son would need a man's restraining hand when he came to be a few years older; and that I, myself, was too young to live without love!—therefore the only correct thing to do was to take a husband—a good one, if you could get him—a husband, anyway. As spring came round, and my mind regained something of its natural elasticity, and my personal appearance probably improved with returned health, the air seemed full of husbands. Everybody that had any business with me, if he happened not to have a wife, immediately proposed to take me in that relation. All the married men of my acquaintance jested with me on the subject, and their wives followed in the same silly iteration. I actually felt myself of some consequence, whether by nature or by accident, until it became irksome."

"How did all your suitors contrive to get time for courtship?" I laughingly inquired.

"O, time was the least of their requirements. You know, perhaps, that there was an Oregon law, or, rather, a United States law, giving a mile square of land to a man and his wife: to each, half. Now some of the Oregonians

made this " Donation Act " an excuse for going from door
to door to beg a wife, as they pretended, in order to be
able to take up a whole section, though when not one of
them ever cultivated a quarter section, or ever meant to."

"And they come to *you* in this way? What did they
say? how did they act?"

" Why, they rode a spotted cayuse up to the door with a
great show of hurry, jangling their Mexican spurs, and making as much noise as possible. As there were no sidewalks
in Portland, then, they could sit on their horses and open
a door, or knock at one, if they had so much politeness. In
either case, as soon as they saw a woman they asked if she
were married; and if not, would she marry? there was no
more ceremony about it."

"Did they ever really get wives in that way, or was it
done in recklessness and sport? It seems incredible that
any woman could accept such an offer as that."

"There were some matches made in that way; though,
as you might conjecture, they were not of the kind made in
heaven, and most of them were afterwards dissolved by leg-
islative action or decree of the courts."

"Truly you were right, when you said women are not
idealized in primitive conditions of society," I said, after
the first mirthful impulse created by so comical a recital
had passed. "But how was it, that with so much to disgust you with the very name of marriage, you finally did
consent to take a husband? He, certainly, was not one of
the kind that came riding up to doors, proposing on the
instant?"

"No, he was not: but he might as well have been for any
difference it made to me," said Mrs. Greyfield, with that
bitterness in her tone that always came into it when she
spoke of Seabrook. "You ask 'how was it that I at last
consented to take a husband?' Do you not know that such
influences as constantly surrounded me, are demoralizing
as I said? You hear a thing talked of until you become ac-

customed to it. It is as Pópe says: You 'first endure, then
pity, then embrace.' I endured, felt contempt, and finally
yielded to the pressure.

"Why, you have no idea, from what I have told you, of
the reality. My house as I have already mentioned, was
one room in a tenement. It opened directly upon the street.
In one corner was a bed. Opposite the door was a stove
for cooking and warming the house. A table and two chairs
besides my little sewing-chair completed the furnishing of
the apartment. The floor was bare, except where I had put
down an old coverlet for a rug before the bed. Here in
this crowded place I cooked, ate, slept, worked, and received company and offers!

"Just as an example of the way in which some of my
my suitors broached the subject I will describe a scene.
Fancy me kneeling on the floor, stanching the blood from
quite a serious cut on Benton's hand. The door opens behind me, and a man I never have seen before, thrusts his
head and half his body in at the opening. His salutation
is 'Howdy!'—his first remark, 'I heern thar was a mighty
purty widder livin' here; and I reckon my infurmation was
correct. If you would like to marry, I'm agreeable.'"

"How did you receive this candidate? You have not
told me what you replied on these occasions," I said,
amused at this picture of pioneer life.

"I turned my head around far enough to get one look
at his face, and asking him rather crossly 'if there were any
more fools where he came from,' went on bandaging Benton's hand."

The recollection of this absurd incident caused the nar-
rator to laugh as she had not often laughed in my hearing.

"This may have been a second Werther," I remarked,
"and surely no Charlotte could have been more unfeeling
than you showed yourself. It could not be that a man coming in that way expected to get any other answer than the
one you gave him?"

"I do not know, and I did not then care. One day a man, to whose motherless children I had been kind when opportunity offered, slouched into my room without the ceremony of knocking and dropping into a chair as if his knees failed him, began twirling his battered old hat in an embarrassed manner, and doing as so many of his predecessors had done—proposing off-hand. He had a face like a terra-cotta image, a long lank figure, faded old clothes, and a whining voice."

"He told me that he had no 'woman,' and that I had no 'man,' a condition that he evidently considered deplorable. He assured me that I suited him 'fustrate;' that his children 'sot gret store by me,' and 'liked my victuals;' and that he thought a 'heap' of my little boy. He also impressed upon me that he had been 'considerin' the 'range-ment of jinin' firms for some time. To close the business at once, he proposed that I should accept of him for my husband then and there."

"And pray, what did you say to *him!*"

"I told him that I did not know what use I had for him, unless I should put him behind the stove, and break bark over his head."

This reply tickled my fancy so much that I laughed until I cried. I insisted on knowing what put it into her mind to say that.

"You see, we burned fir wood, the bark of which is better to make heat than the woody portion of the tree; but is never sawed or split, and has to be broken. I used to take up a big piece, and bring it down with a blow over any sharp corner to knock it into smaller fragments, and something in the man's appearance, I suppose, suggested that he might be good for that, if for nothing else. I did not stop to frame my replies on any forms laid down in young ladies' manuals; but they seemed to be conclusive as a general thing."

"I should think so. Yet, there must have been some,

more nearly your equals, attracted by your youth and beauty, loving you, or capable of loving you, to whom you could not give such answers, by whom such answers would not be taken."

"As I look back upon it now, I cannot think of any one I might have taken 'and did not, that I regret. There were men of all classes nearly; but they were not desirable, as I saw it then, or as I see it now. It is true that I was young, and pretty, perhaps, and that women were in a minority. But then, too, the men who were floating about on the surface of pioneer society were not likely to be the kind of men that make true lovers and good husbands. Some of them have settled down into steady-going benedicts, and have money and position. The worst effect of all this talk about marrying was, that it prepared me to be persuaded against my inner consciousness into doing that which I ought not to have done. My truer judgment had become confused, my perceptions clouded, from being so often assailed by the united majority who could not bear to see poor, little minority go unappropriated. But come, let us have our cakes and lemonade. You need something to sustain you while I complete the recital of my conquests."

I felt that she needed a brief interval in which to collect her thoughts and calm a growing nervousness that in spite of her efforts at pleasantry would assert itself in various little ways, evident enough to my observation. A saucepan of water was set upon the hot coals on the hearth, the lemons cut and squeezed into two elegant goblets, upon square lumps of sugar that eagerly took up the keen acid, and grew yellow and spongy in consequence. A sociable little round table was rolled out of its seclusion in a corner, and made to support a tray between us, whereon were such dainty cakes and confections as my hostess delighted in.

There was an air of substantial comfort in all the arrangements of my friend's house that made it a peculiarly pleasant one to visit. It lacked nothing to make it home-

like, restful, attractive. The house itself was large and
airy, with charming views; the furniture sufficiently elegant
without being too fine for use; flowers, birds, and all manner of *curios* abounded, yet were never in the way, as they
so often are in the houses of people who are fond of pretty
and curious things, but have no really refined taste to
arrange them. Our little ten-o'clock lunch was perfect in
its appointments—a "thing of beauty," as it was of palat-
ableness and refreshment. So strongly was I impressed
at the moment with this talent of Mrs. Greyfield's, that I
could not refrain from speaking of it, as we sat sipping hot
and spicy lemonade from those exquisite cut-glass goblets
of her choosing, and tasting dainties served on the loveliest
china: "Yes, I suppose it is a gift of God, the same as a
taste for the high arts is an endowment from the same
source. Did it never strike you as being absurd, that men
should expect, and as far as they can, require all women to
be good housekeepers? They might as well expect every
mechanic to carve in wood or chisel marble into forms of
life. But it is my one available talent, and has stood me
in good stead, though I have no doubt it was one chief
cause of my trouble, by attracting Mr. Seabrook."

"You must know," I said, "that I am tortured with curiosity to hear about that person. Will you not now begin?"

"Let me see—where did I leave off? I was telling you
that although I had so many suitors, of so many classes,
and none of them desirable, to my way of thinking, I was
really gradually being influenced to marry. You must
know that a woman so young and so alone in the world,
and who had to labor for her bread, and her child's bread,
could not escape the solicitations of men who did not care
to marry; and it was this class who gave me more uneasiness than all the presuming ignorant ones, who would
honor me by making me a wife. I know it is constantly
asserted, by men themselves, that no woman is approached
in that way who does not give some encouragement. But

no statement could be more utterly false—unless they determine to construe ordinary politeness and friendliness into a covert advance. The cunning of the "father of lies" is brought to bear to entrap artless and inexperienced women into situations whence they are assured there is no escape without disgrace.

"During my first year of widowhood my feelings were several times outraged in this way; and at first I was so humiliated, and had such a sense of guilt, that it made me sick and unfit for my work. The guilty feeling came, I now know, from the consciousness I had of the popular opinion I have referred to, that there must be something wrong in my deportment. But by calling to mind all the circumstances connected with these incidents, and studying my own behavior and the feelings that impelled me, I taught myself at last not to care so very much about it, after the first emotions of anger had passed away. Still I thought I could perceive that I was not quite the same person: you understand?—the 'bloom' was being brushed away."

"What an outrage! What a shame, that a woman in your situation could not be left to be herself, with her own pure thoughts and tender sorrows! Was there no one to whom you could go for advice and sympathy?—none among all those who came to the country with you who could have helped you?"

"The people who came out with me were mostly scattered through the farming country; and would have been of very little use to me if they had not been. In fact, they would, probably, have been first to condemn me, being chiefly of an uneducated class, and governed more by traditions than by the wisdom of experience. There were two or three families whose acquaintance I had made after arriving in Portland, who were kindly disposed towards me, and treated me with great neighborliness; especially the family that was in the same tenement with me. To them I sometimes mentioned my troubles; but while they were willing to do anything for me in the way of a common friendly service, like the loaning of an article of household convenience, or ·sitting with me when Benton was sick—as he very often was—they could not understand other needs, or minister to the sickness of the mind. If I received any counsel, it was to the effect that a woman was in every way better off to be married. I used to wonder why God had not made us married—why he had given us our individual natures, since there was forever this necessity of being paired!"

"Yet you had loved your husband?"

"I had never ceased to love him!—and that was just what these people could not understand. Death cut *them* loose from everything, and they were left with only strong desires, and no sentiment to sanctify them. That I should love a dead husband, and turn with disgust from a living one, was inexplicable to them."

"My dear, I think I see the rock on which you wrecked your happiness." For the moment I had forgotten what she had told me in the beginning, that Seabrook had married her illegally; and was imagining her married to a living husband, and loving only the memory of one dead. She saw my error, and informed me by a look. Pushing away the intervening table with its diminished contents, and renewing the fire, Mrs. Greyfield proceeded:

"It would take too long to go over the feelings of those times, and assign their causes. You are a woman that can put. yourself in my place, to a great extent, though not wholly; for there are some things that cannot be imagined, and only come by experience."

"Benton was two years and a half old; a very delicate child, suffering nearly all the time with chills and fever. I had occasional attacks of illness from the malaria, always to be met with on the clearing up of low-lands near a river. Still I was able to sew enough to keep a shelter over our heads, and bread in our mouths, until I had been a year in

Portland. But I could not get ahead in the least, and was often very low spirited. About this time I made the acquaintance of Mr. Seabrook. He was introduced to me by a mutual acquaintance, and having a little knowledge of medicine, gave me both advice and remedies for Benton. He used to come in quite often, and look after the child, and praise my housekeeping, which probably was somewhat better than that of the average pioneer of those days. He never paid me any silly compliments, or disturbed my tranquillity with love-making of any sort. Just for that reason I began to like him. He was twelve or fifteen years older than myself; and more than ordinarily fine-looking and intelligent. You have no idea, because you have never been so placed, what a comfort it was to me to have such a friend."

"Yes, I think I know."

"One day he said to me, 'Mrs. Greyfield, this sitting and sewing all day is bad for your health. Now, I should think, being so good a housekeeper, you might do very well by taking a few boarders; and I believe you could stand that kind of labor better than sewing.' We had a little talk about it, and he proposed trying to find me a house suited to the purpose; to which I very readily consented; for, though I was wholly inexperienced in any business, I thought it better to venture the experiment than to keep on as I was doing."

"How did you expect to get furniture? Pardon me; but you see I want to learn all about the details of so strange a life."

"I don't think I expected anything, or thought of all the difficulties at once."

"Which was fortunate, because they would have discouraged you."

"It is hard to say what has or has not been for the best. But for that boarding-house scheme, I do not believe I should have married the man I did.

"As I was saying, Mr. Seabrook never annoyed me with attentions. He came and talked to me in a friendly manner, and with a superior air that disarmed apprehension on that score. Mrs. ——, my neighbor in the next room, once hinted to me that his visits were indicative of his intentions, and thereby caused me a sleepless night. But as *he* never referred to the subject, and as I was now full of my new business project, the alarm subsided. A house was finally secured, or a part of a house, consisting of a kitchen, dining-room and bed-room, on the first floor ; and the same number of rooms above. I had a comfortable supply of bedding and table linen ; the trouble was about cabinet furniture. But as most of my boarders were bachelors, who quartered themselves where they could, I got along very well."

"You made a success of it, then?"

"I made a success. I threw all my energies into it, and had all the boarders I could cook for.

"Mr. Seabrook boarded with you?—I conjecture that."

"Yes; and he took a room at my house. At first I liked it well enough; I had so much confidence in him. But in a short time I thought I could perceive that my other boarders were disposed to think that we looked toward a nearer relationship in the future. Perhaps they were justified in thinking so, as they could only judge from appearances; and I had asked Mr. Seabrook to take the foot of the table, and carve, because I had so much else to do that it was impossible for me to do that also. Gradually he assumed more the air of proprietor than of boarder; but as he was so much older and wiser, and had been of so much service to me, I readily pardoned what I looked upon as a matter of no great consequence.

"It proved to be, however, a matter of very great consequence. I had been established in the new house and business four or five weeks, when one evening, Benton being unusually ill, I asked Mr. Seabrook's advice about him.

My bed-room was up stairs, against the partition which separated my apartments from those occupied by a family of Germans. I chose that room for myself because it seemed less lonely, and safer for me, to be where I could hear the voice of the little German woman, and she could hear mine. In the same manner my kitchen joined on to hers, and we could hear each other at our work. Benton being too ill to be dressed, was lying on the bed in my room, and I asked Mr. Seabrook to go up and look at him. He examined him and told me what to do, in his usual decided and assured manner, and went back to the dining room, which was also my sitting-room. As soon as Benton was quieted, so that I could leave him, I also returned to the lower part of the house to finish my evening tasks.

"There is such a feeling of hatred arises in my heart when I recall that part of my history that it makes me fear my own wickedness! Do you think we can hate so much as to curse and blight our own natures?"

"Undoubtedly; but that would be a sort of frenzy, and would finally end in madness. *You* do not feel in that way. It is the over-mastering sense of wrong suffered, for which there can be no redress. Terrible as the feeling is, it must be free from the wickedness you impute to yourself. Your nature is sound and sweet at the core—I feel sure of that."

"Thank you. I have had many grave doubts about myself. But to go on. Contrary to his usual habit, Mr. Seabrook remained at the house that evening, and in the dining-room instead of his own room. I was so busy with my work and anxious about Benton, that I did not give more than a passing thought to him. He, also, seemed much pre-occupied.

"At last my work was done, and I took a light to go to my room, telling Mr. Seabrook to put out the lights below stairs, as I should not be down again. 'Stop a moment,' said he, 'I have something to tell you that you ought to know.' He very politely placed a chair for me, which I took. His manners were faultless in the matter of etiquette—and how very far a fine manner goes, in our estimate of people! I had not the shadow of a suspicion of what was coming. 'Mrs. Greyfield,' he said, with great gravity, 'I fear I have unintentionally compromised you very seriously. In advising you to take this house, and open it for boarders, I was governed entirely by what I conceived to be your best interests; but it seems that I erred in my judgment. You are very young—only twenty-three, I believe, and—I beg your pardon—too beautiful to pass unnoticed in a community like this. Your boarders, so far, are all gentlemen. Further, it has been noticed and commented upon that—really, I do not know how to express it—that *I* have seemed to take the place in your household that—pray, forgive me, Mrs. Greyfield—only a husband, in fact or in expectancy, could be expected or permitted to occupy. Do you see what I mean?'

" I sat stunned and speechless while he went on. 'I presume your good sense will direct you in this matter, and that you will grasp the right horn of the dilemma. If you would allow me to help you out of it, you would really promote my happiness. Dear Mrs. Greyfield, permit me to offer you the love and protection of a husband, and stop these gossips' mouths.' "

"You do not think he had premeditated this?" I asked.

"I did not take it in then, but afterwards I saw it plainly enough. He pressed me for an answer, all the time plausibly protesting that although he had hoped some time to win my love, he had not anticipated the necessity for urging his suit as a matter of expediency. In vain I argued that if his presence in the house was an injury to me, he could leave it. It was too late, he said. I indignantly declared that it was not my fault that my boarders were all men. I was working for my living, and would just as willingly have boarded any other creature if I could have got my money for it; a monkey or a sheep; it was all the same to me. He smiled superiorly on my fretfulness; and when I at last burst into a passion of tears, bade me good night with such an air of being extremely forbearing and judicious that I could not help regarding myself as a foolish and undisciplined child.

"That night I scarcely slept at all. Benton was feverish, and I half wild. All sorts of plans ran through my head; but turn the matter over any way I would, it amounted to the same thing. The money I must earn, must come from men. Whether I sewed or cooked, or whatever I did, they were the paymasters to whom I looked for my wages. How, then, was it possible to escape contact with them, or avoid being misunderstood. In one breath I resented, with all the ardor of my soul, the impertinence of the world's judgment, and in the next I declared to myself that I did not care; that conscious innocence should sustain me, and that I had a right to do the best I could for myself and child.

"But that was only sham courage. I was morally a coward, and could not possibly face the evil spirit of detraction. Therefore, the morning found me feverish in body and faint in spirit. I kept out of sight of my boarders, except Mr. Seabrook, who looked into the kitchen with a sympathizing face, and inquired very kindly after Bennie, as he pet-named Benton. When my dinner was over that day, I asked the little German woman to keep the child until I could go on an errand, and went over to Mrs. ——, my old house-mate, to get advice.

"Do you know how much advice is worth? If you like it, you haven't needed it; and if you do not like it, you will not take it. Mrs. —— told me that if she were in my place, as if she *could be* in my place! she would get rid of all her troubles by getting some man to take charge of her and her affairs. When I asked, with transparent duplicity, where I was to find a man for this service, she laughed in

my face. People *did* talk so then, and what Mr. Seabrook
said was the unexaggerated truth. It did not occur to me
to examine into the authorship of the rumors; I was too
shrinking and sensitive for that.

"When I reached home I found Mr. Seabrook at the
house. A sudden feeling of anger flashed into my mind,
and must have illuminated my eyes; for he gave me one de-
precating glance, and immediately went out. This made me
fear I was unjust to him. That evening he did not come to
tea, but sent me a note saying he had business at Vancouver
and would not return for two or three days; but that when
he did return it would be better to have my mind made up
to dismiss him entirely out of the country, or to have our
engagement made known.

"That threw the whole responsibility upon me; and it
was, as he knew it would be, too heavy for my twenty-three
years to carry. To lose the most helpful and agreeable
friend I had in the country, to banish him for no fault but
being too kind to me, or to take him in place of one whose
image would always stand between us: that was the alter-
native.

"The next day an incident occurred that decided my des-
tiny. I had to go out to make some purchases for the
house. At the store where I usually bought provisions I
chanced to meet a woman who had crossed the continent
in my company; and she turned her back upon me without
speaking. She was an ignorant, bigoted sort of woman,
of an uncertain temper, and at another time I might not
have cared for the slight; but coming at a time when I was
in a state of nervous alarm, it cut me to the quick. With
great difficulty I restrained my tears, and left the store.
While hurrying home with a basket on my arm, almost
choked with grief, I passed a kind old gentleman who had
always before had a pleasant word for me, and an inquiry
about my child. He, too, passed me with only the slight-
est sign of recognition. I thought my heart would burst

in my breast, so terrible was the sense of outrage and shame—"

"Which was, after all, probably imaginary," I interrupted. "The insult of the ignorant, ill-tempered woman was purely an accidental display of those qualities, and the slight recognition of your old friend the consequence of the other, for your face certainly expressed the state of your feelings, and your friend was surprised into silence by seeing you in such distress."

"That, very likely, is the true explanation. But it did not so impress me then. You cannot, in the state of mind I was in, go after people, and ask them to tell you whether or not they really mean to insult you, because you are only too certain that they do. I was sick with pain and mortification. How I got through my day's work I do not remember; but you can understand that my demoralization was complete by this time, and that when Mr. Seabrook returned I was like wax in his hands. All that I stipulated for was a little more time; he had my permission to announce our engagement.

"My boarders and every one who spoke to me about it congratulated me. When I look back upon it now, it seems strange that no one ever suggested to me the importance of knowing the antecedents of the man I was going to marry; but they did not. It seemed to be tacitly understood that antecedents were not to be dragged to light in this new world, and that "by-gones should be bygones." As to myself, it never occurred to my inexperience to suspect that a man might be dishonorable, even criminal, though he had the outside, bearing of a gentleman."

"Did he propose to relieve you of the necessity of keeping boarders?"

"No. The business was a good one; and, as I have said, I was a success in this line. My constitution was good; my energy immense, in labor; my training in house-

3

hold economy good; and, besides, I had a real talent for pleasing my boarders. I was to be provided with a servant; and the care of the marketing would devolve upon Mr. Seabrook. With this amelioration of my labors, the burden could be easily borne for the sake of the profits."

"What business was Mr. Seabrook in?"

"I never thought of the subject at that time. He was always well dressed; associated with men of business; seemed to have money; and I never doubted that such a man was able to do anything he proposed. Women, you know, unconsciously attribute at least an earthly omnipotence to men. Afterwards, of course, I was disillusioned. But I must hasten, for it is growing late; and either the storm or these old memories shake my nerves.

"I had asked for a month's time to prepare my mind for my coming marriage. At the end of a week, however, Mr. Seabrook came to me and told me that imperative business called him away for an absence of several weeks, and that, in his judgment, the marriage ceremony should take place before he left. He should be away over the month I had stipulated for; and, in case of accident, I would have the protection of his name. My objections were soon over-ruled, and on the morning of his departure we were married—as I believed, legally and firmly bound—in the presence of my family of boarders, and two or three women, including Mrs. ——. He went away immediately, and I was left to my tumultuous thoughts."

"May I be permitted to know whether you loved him at all, at that time? It seems to me that you must have sometimes yearned for the ownership of some heart, and the strong tenderness of man's firmer nature."

Mrs. Greyfield looked at me with a curiously mixed expression, half of sarcastic pity, half of amused contempt. But the thought, whatever it was, went unspoken. She reflected a moment silently before she answered.

"I have told you that my heart remained unweaned from

the memory of my dead husband. I told Mr. Seabrook the same. But I admired, respected and believed in him; he was agreeable to me, and had my confidence. There can be no doubt, but if he had been all that he seemed, I should have ended by loving him in a quiet and constant way. As it was, the shock I felt at the discovery of his perfidy was terrible.

"My ears were yet tingling with my new name, when, everybody having gone, I sat down with Benton on my lap to have the pleasure of the few natural tears that women are bound to shed over their relinquished freedom. I was very soon aroused by a knock at the door, which opened to admit an old acquaintance, then residing in Vancouver, and a former suitor of mine. Almost the first thing he said was, 'I hear you have been getting married?' ' Yes,' I said, trying to laugh off my embarrassment, 'I had to marry a man at last to get rid of them!'

"You made a poor selection, then," he returned, rather angrily.

"His anger roused mine, for his tone was, as I thought, insolent, 'Do you think I should have done better to have taken you?' I asked, scornfully."

"You would at least have got a man that the law could give you," he retorted, "and not another woman's husband."

"The charge seemed so enormous that I laughed in his face, attributing his conduct to jealous annoyance at my marriage. But something in his manner, in spite of our mutual excitement, unsettled my confidence. He was not inventing this story; he evidently believed it himself. 'For God's sake,' I entreated, 'if you have any proof of what you say, give it me at once!' And then he went on to tell me that on the occasion of Mr. Seabrook's late visit to Vancouver, he had been recognized by an emigrant out from Ohio, who met and talked with him at the Hudson's Bay store. That man had told him, my informant, that he

was well acquainted with the family of Mr. Seabrook, and
that his wife and several children were living when he left
Ohio.

"Can you bring this man to me?" I asked, trembling
with horrible apprehensions.

"I don't know as I could," said he; "for he went, I
think, over to the Sound to look up a place. But I can
give you the name of the town he came from, if that would
be of any use." I had him write the address for me, as I
was powerless to do it for myself.

"I am sorry for you," he said, as he handed me the slip
of paper; "that is, if you care anything for the rascal."

"Thank you," I returned, "but this thing is not proven
yet. If you really mean well by me, keep what you have
told me to yourself."

"You mean to live with him?" he asked.

"I don't know what I shall do; I must have time to
think."

"Very well; it is no affair of mine. I don't want a bullet through my head for interfering; but I thought it was
no more than fair to let you know."

"I am very grateful, of course;—I mean I am if there is
any occasion; but this story is so strange, and has come upon
me so suddenly that I cannot take it all in at once, with
all its consequences."

"'I know what you think,' he said finally: 'You suspect
me of making up this thing to be revenged on you for pre-
ferring Seabrook to me. I'd be a damned mean cuss, to
do such a turn by any woman, would'nt I? As to consequences, if the story is true, and I believe it is, why your
marriage amounts to nothing, and you are just as free as
you were before!'

"I fancied his face brightened up with the idea of my freedom, and a doubt of his veracity intruded upon my growing conviction. Distracted, excited, pressed down with
cares and fears, I still had to attend to my daily tasks. I

begged him to go away, and not to say a word to any other mortal about what he had told me; and he gave me the promise I desired. That was a fatal error, and fearfully was I punished."

" How an error? It seems to me quite remarkable prudence for one in your situation."

" So I thought then; but the event proved differently."

"Pray do tell me how you bore up under all this excitement, and the care and labor of a boarding-house? The more I know of your life, the more surprised I am at your endurance."

"It was the care and labor that saved me, perhaps. At all events, here I am, alive and well, to-night. I sometimes liken myself to a tree that I know of. It was a small fir tree in a friend's garden. For some reason, it began to pine and dwindle and turn red. My friend's husband insisted on cutting it down, as unsightly; but this she objected to, until all the leaves were dry and faded, and the tree apparently dead. Still she asked for it to be spared for another season; and, taking a stick, she beat the tree all over until not a leaf was left on a single bough; and there it stood, a mere frame of dry branches, until everybody wished it out of the way. But behold! at last it was covered with little green dots of leaves, that rapidly grew to the usual size, and now that tree is the thriftiest in my friend's garden, and a living evidence of the uses of adversity. But for the beating it got, it would now be a dead tree! I had my child to live and work for; and really, but for this last trouble, I should have thought myself doing well. I had found out how I could make and lay up money, and was gaining that sense of independence such knowledge gives. Besides, I was young, and in good physical health most of the time before this last and worst stroke of fortune. *That* broke down my powers of resistance in some directions, I had so much to resist in others."

" Do you see what o'clock it is ? " I asked.

"Yes; but if you do not mind the sitting up, let's make a night of it. I feel as if I could not sleep—as if something were going to happen."

Very cheerfully I consented to the proposed vigil. I wanted to hear the rest of the story; and I knew she had a sort of prophetic consciousness of coming events. If she said "something was going to happen," something surely did happen. So the fire was renewed, and we settled ourselves again for " a night of it."

" What did you do? and why do you say that you committed a fatal error by keeping silence ?"

" By suffering the matter to rest, I unfortunately fixed myself in the situation I would have avoided. My object was what yours would have been, or any woman's—to save all scandal, until the facts were known to a certainty. I was so sensitive about being talked over ; and besides felt that I had no right to expose Mr. Seabrook to a slanderous accusation. It was not possible for me to have foreseen what actually happened.

" I took one night to think the matter over. It was a longer night than this one will seem to you. My decision was to write to the postmaster of the town from which Mr. Seabrook was said to come. *Now* that would be a simple affair enough ; the telegraph would procure us the information wanted in a day. *Then* a letter was five or six months going and coming. In the meantime I had resolved not to live with Mr. Seabrook as his wife; but you will see how I would, under the circumstances, be compelled to seem to do so. I did not think of that at first, however. You know how you mentally go over impending scenes beforehand? I meant to surprise him into a confession, if he were guilty; and believed I should be able to judge of his innocence, if he should be wrongly accused. I wrote and dispatched my letter at once, and under an assumed name, to prevent its being stolen. When that was done I tried to rest unconcerned ; but, of course, that was impossible. My mind ran on this subject day and night.

" The difficulties of my position could never be imagined;
you would have to be in the same place to see them. Everybody now called me Mrs. Seabrook, and I could not repu-
diate the name without sufficient cause. I was forced to
appear to have confidence in the man I had married of my
own free will. Besides, I really did not know, of a verity,
that he was not worthy of confidence. It seemed quite as
credible that another man should invent a lie, as that Mr.
Seabrook should be guilty of an enormous crime.

" Naturally I had a buoyant temper; was inclined to see
the amusing side of things; enjoyed frolicsome conversation; and in a general way was well fitted to bear up under
worries, and recover quickly from depressed conditions.
The gentlemen who boarded with me were a cheerful and
intelligent set, whose conversation entertained me, as they
met three times a day at table. They were all friends of
Mr. Seabrook, which gave them the privilege of saying
playful things to me about him daily. To these remarks I
must make equally playful replies, or seem ungracious to
them. You will see how every such circumstance compli-
cated my difficulties afterwards.

" You know, too, how pliable we all are at twenty-three
—how often our opinions waver and our emotions change.
I was particularly mercurial in my temperament before the
events I am relating hardened me. I often laid in a half-
waking state almost all night, my imagination full of horrible images; and when breakfast-time came, and I listened to
an hour of entertaining talk, with frequent respectful allu-
sions to Mr. Seabrook, and kindly compliments to myself,
these ugly visions took flight, while I persuaded myself that
everything would come out right in the end.

" A little while ago you asked me if I did not love Mr.
Seabrook at all?—did not long for tenderness from him?
The question roused something of the wickedness in me
that I confessed to you before; but I will answer the inquiry now, by asking *you* if you think any woman in her

twenties is quite reconciled to live unloved? I had not
wished to marry again; yet undoubtedly there was a great
blank in my life, which my peculiarly friendless condition
made me very sensible of; and there *was* a yearning desire
in my heart to be petted and cared for, as in my brief married life I had been.   But the coarseness and intrusiveness
I had experienced in my widowhood had made me as irri-
table as the 'fretful porcupine' towards that class of men.
The thought of Mr. Seabrook loving me had never taken
root in my mind. Even when he proposed marriage, it
had seemed much more a matter of expediency than of love.
But when, after I had accepted him as an avowed lover,
his conduct had continued to be unintrusive, and delicately
flattering to my womanly pride, it was most natural that I
should begin to congratulate myself on the prospect before
me of life-long protection from such wounds as I had received, with the great satisfaction of increased dignity in
point of social position; for then, much more than now,
and in a new country more than in an old one, a woman's
position depended on her relationship to men; the wife
of the most worthless man being the superior of an unmarried woman.   Accordingly I felt my promised importance, and began to exult in it."

"In short, you were preparing to become much more
subject to the second love than the first; a not infrequent
experience," I interrupted.   "You certainly must have
loved a handsome, agreeable, courteous, and manly man,
who would have interposed between you and the rude
shocks of the world; and you had begun to realize that
you could, in spite of your first love?"

"And to have a feeling of disappointment when the pos-
sibility presented itself that after all these blessings might
be wrested from me; of horror when I reflected that in that
case my last estate would be inexpressibly worse than the
first."

"There was a terrible temptation there!"

"No; that was the one thing I was perfectly clear about. Not to be dragged into crime or deserved disgrace, I was determined upon. How I should avoid it was where I was in doubt."

"I am very anxious to know how you met him on his return."

"There was no one in the house except myself, and Benton, who was now quite well again for the time. I was standing by the dining-room window, arranging some ferns in a hanging basket, and Benton was amusing himself with toys the boarders were always giving him. I heard a footstep, and turned my head slightly to see who it was. Mr. Seabrook stood in the door, regarding us with a pleased smile.

"How is my wife and boy?" he said, cheerily, advancing towards me, and proffering a kiss of greeting.

"I put up my hand to ward him off, and my heart stood motionless. I seemed to be struck with a chill. My teeth chattered together, while the ends of my fingers turned cold at once.

"Naturally, he was surprised; but thinking perhaps that the suddenness of his return, under the circumstances, had overcome me, he quickly recovered his tenderness of manner.

"'Have I frightened you, my darling?' he asked, putting out his arms to fold me to his breast. Not being able to speak, I whirled round rapidly, and hastened to place the table between us. Of course, he could not comprehend such conduct, but thought it some nervous freak, probably.

"Turning to Benton, he took him up in his arms and kissed him, asking him some questions about himself and toys. 'Could you tell me what is the matter with your mamma, Bennie?' he asked, seeing that my manner remained inexplicable.

"'I tink see has a till,' answered Benton, who by this time knew the meaning of the word 'chill' by experience.

" ' She has given *me* one, I know,' said Mr. Seabrook, regarding me curiously. I began to feel faint, and sat down, leaning my head on my hand, my elbow on the table.

" ' Anna,' said he, addressing me by my Christian name for the first time, and giving me a little shock in consequence—for I had almost forgotten I had ever been called ' Anna '—' if I am so disagreeable to you, I will go away again; though I certainly had reason to expect a different reception.'

" ' No,' I said, suddenly rousing up; ' you must not go until I have told you something; unless you go to stay— which would perhaps be best.'

" ' To stay! go to stay? There seems great need of explanation here. Will you be good enough to tell me why I am to go away to stay?'

" ' The reason is, Mr. Seabrook,' I answered, ' that your true wife, and your own children expect you at home, in Ohio.'

" I had worded my answer with the intention of shocking the truth out of him, if possible. If he should be innocent, I thought, he would forgive me. There was too much at stake to stand upon niceties of speech; and I watched him narrowly."

" How did he receive such a blow as that? I am curious to know how guilty people act, on being accused."

" You cannot tell an innocent from a guilty person," Mrs. Greyfield returned, with a touch of that asperity that was sometimes noticeable in her utterances. Then, more quietly: " Both are shocked alike at being accused; one because he is innocent; the other, because he is guilty. How much a person is shocked depends upon temperament and circumstance. The guilty person, always consciously in danger of being accused, is likely to be prepared and on the defensive, while the other is not.

" What Mr. Seabrook did, was to turn upon me a look

of keen observation, not unmixed with surprise. It might
mean one thing; it might mean another; how could I tell?
He always impressed me so with his superiority that even
in that moment, when my honor and life's happiness were
at stake, I was conscious of a feeling of abasement and
guiltiness that I dare accuse *him* to his face. Perhaps, he
saw that I was frightened at my own temerity; at all events
he was not thrown off his guard.

" ' Do I understand you to charge me with crime—a very
ugly crime, indeed?' he asked pointedly.

" ' You know,' I said, ' whether you are guilty. If you
are, may God so deal with you as you have meant to deal
with me.'

" I fancied that he winced slightly at this; but in my excitement could not have seen very clearly. He knitted his
brows, and took several turns up and down the room.

" ' If I knew who had put this monstrous idea into your
mind,' he finally said with vehemence; ' I would send a
bullet through his heart!'

" ' In that case,' I replied: ' you could not expect me to
tell you;' and I afterwards made that threat my excuse for
concealing the name of my informant.

" Mr. Seabrook continued to pace the floor in an excited
manner, stroking his long blonde beard rapidly and unconsciously. I still sat by the table, trying to appear the calm
observer that I was not. He came and stood by me, saying: ' Do you believe this thing against me?'

" ' I do not know what to believe, Mr. Seabrook,' I replied, ' but something will have to be done about this
rumor.' I could not bear to go on; but he understood me.
He leaned over my chair, and touched my cheek with his:

" ' Are you my wife, or not?' he asked. I shuddered, and
put my face down on my hands. He knelt by my side, and
taking my hands in his, so that my face must be seen,
asked me to look into his eyes and listen to him. What he
said, was this:

" 'If I swear to you, by Almighty God, that you are my true and only wife, will you then believe me?' "

Mrs. Greyfield was becoming visibly agitated by these reminiscences, and paused to collect herself.

"You dared not say 'yes,' I cried, carried away with sympathy, and yet, you could not say 'no.' What did you do?"

"I burst into a passion of tears, and cried convulsively. He would have caressed and consoled me, but I would have none of it.

" 'Anna, what a strange home-coming for a bridegroom!' he said, reproachfully.

" 'Go away, and leave me to myself,' I entreated; 'You must not stay here.'

" 'What madness?' he exclaimed. 'Do you wish to set everybody to talking about us?' Ah! 'talking about us,' was the bugbear I most dreaded, and he knew it. But I wanted to seem brave; so I said that in private matters we were at liberty to do as we thought right and best.

" 'And I think it right and best to stay where my wife is. Anna, what is to be the result of this strange suspicion of yours, but to make us both unhappy, and me desperate! Why, I shall be the laughing-stock of the town—and I confess it is more than I can bear without flinching, to have it circulated about, that Seabrook married a wife who cut him adrift the first thing she did. And then look at your position, too, which would be open to every unkind remark. You must not incur this almost certain ruin.' ⁕

" 'Mr. Seabrook,' I said, more calmly than I had yet spoken; 'what you have said has suggested itself to me before. Stay here, then, if you must, until I can take measures to satisfy myself of the legality of our marriage. You can keep your own counsel, and I can keep mine. I have spoken to no one about this matter, nor will I for the present. There is your old room; your old place at the table. I will try to act as natural as possible; more than this you must not expect of me.' This business-like tone nettled him.

" ' May I inquire, Mrs. Seabrook, how long a probation I may anticipate, and what measures you intend taking to establish my good or bad character? A man may not be willing to wait always for a wife.'

" ' Very well,' I replied to this covert threat; ' when you tire of waiting, you know what to do.' But my voice must have trembled, for he instantly changed his manner. There was more chance of winning me through my weakness than of intimidating me, coward though I was.

" ' My dear Anna,' he said kindly, ' this is a most mortifying and trying predicament that I am in; and you must pardon me if I seem selfish. I do not know how I am to bear several months of this unnatural life you propose; and in thinking of myself I forget you. Yet your case, as *you* see it, is harder than mine; and I ought to pity and comfort you. If my darling would only let me !' He stretched out his arms to me. It was all I could do to keep from rushing into them, and sobbing on his breast. I was so tempest-tossed and weary !—what would I not have given to lay down my burdens ?"

" That is where the unrecognized heroism of women comes in. How few men would suffer in this way for the right ! Had you chosen to ignore the tale that you had heard, and taken this man whom fortune had thrown with you upon this far-off coast, he might have been to you a kind friend and protector. Do you not think so ?"

"Very likely. Plenty of bad men, when deferred to, have made good husbands, as men go. But I, by resisting the will of one bad man, made infinite trouble for myself. Are you becoming wearied ?"

" No, no; go on."

" I must pass over a great deal; and, thank God! some things have been forgotten. Mr. Seabrook took his old room down stairs. As before, he sat at the foot of the table and carved, but now as master of the house. Servants not being easily obtained, it was not remarked that my duties prevented my sitting down with my supposed husband at meals. He marketed for me, and received the money of my boarders when pay-day came; and at first he did—what he failed to do afterwards—pay the money over to me.

"You are curious to know how Mr. Seabrook conducted himself toward me personally, and in particular. For a few days, well; so that I began to feel confidence that so honorable a gentleman would be proved free from all stain. But he soon began to annoy me with the most persistent courtship, looking, as I could see, to breaking down my reserve, and subjecting me to the domination of a passion for him. If I had ever really loved Mr. Seabrook, it would have been a love of the senses, of interest, of the understanding, and not of the imagination and heart. I was just on the eve of such a love when it was fortunately put in check by my suspicions. For him to endeavor to create a feeling now that might, nay, that was intended to subvert principle and virtue, appeared even to my small worldly sense, an insult and an outrage.

"When I talked in this way to him, he half laughingly and half in earnest always declared that I should get into the habit of forgetting our marriage before my 'proofs' came from Ohio, unless he every day put me in mind of it! and this willingness to refer to 'proofs' threw me off my guard a little. He designed very cunningly, but not quite cunningly enough. As time wore on and he feared the proofs might come before he had bent me to his will, his attempts lost even the semblance of love or decency. Many and many a night I feared to close my eyes in sleep, lest he should carry out his avowed purpose; for locks and bolts in a house in those days were considered unnecessary, and I improvised such defenses as I could. I used to threaten to call in my little German neighbor, to which he replied she would probably recognize a man's right to occupy the same apartment with his wife! Still, I think he was deterred somewhat by the fear of exposure from using violence."

The recital of such sufferings and anxieties as these; endured, too, by a young and lonely woman, affected me powerfully. My excited imagination was engaged in comparing the Mrs. Greyfield I saw before me, wearing her nearly fifty years with dignity and grace, full of a calm and ripe experience, still possessing a dark and striking beauty, with the picture she had given me of herself at twenty-three. What a wonder it was that with her lively temperament either for pain or pleasure; with her beauty and her helplessness, she had come out of the furnace unscathed, as she now appeared.

"How could you," I said, with a feeling of deep disgust, "how *could* you allow such a man to remain in your house?"

"How could I get him out? We were legally married, so far as anybody in Oregon knew, except himself. Everybody presumed us to be living amicably together. He was careful to act the courteous gentleman to me in the presence of others. If we never went out together, it was easily explained by reference to my numerous household cares, and Benton's frequent illness. As I before said, no one could understand the position who had not been in it. I could not send him away from me; nor could I go away from him. He would have followed me, he said, to the 'ends of the earth.' Besides, where could I go? There was nothing for me but to endure until the answer to my letter came. Never was letter so anxiously desired as that one; for, of course, I fully expected that whatever news it contained, would bring relief in some way. But I had made up my mind to his guilt, rightly judging that, had he been innocent, he would either have found means to satisfy me, or have gone away and left me altogether.

"It had been six or seven months since my marriage. I had a large family of boarders to cook for, and Benton giving me a great deal of worry, fearing I should lose him. Working hard all day, and sleeping very little nights, with constant excitement and dread, had very much impaired my health. My boarders often said to me: 'Mrs. Seabrook, you are working too hard; you must make Mr. Seabrook get you a cook.' What could I say in return, except to force a smile, and turn the drift of the conversation? Once, carried away with indignation, I replied that 'Mr. Seabrook found it as much as *he* could do to collect the money I earned!'"

"And you were set down at once as a vixen!" I said, smiling.

"Well, they were not expected to know how matters stood, when I had taken so much pain to conceal the truth. I was sorry I had not held my peace a little longer, or altogether. Men never can understand a woman's right to resent selfishness, however atrocious; even when they are knowing to it, which in this case they were not. I might as well have held my tongue, since every unguarded speech of mine militated against me afterwards."

"You allowed Mr. Seabrook to have all your earnings?"

"I could not prevent it; he was *my husband*. Sometimes I thought he meant to save up all he could, to take him out of the country, when the hoped-for proofs of his crime should arrive. And in that light I was inclined to rejoice in his avarice. I would have given all I had for that purpose. Oh, those dreadful, dreadful days! when I was so near insane with sleeplessness and anxiety, that I seemed to be walking on the air! Such, indeed, was my mental and physical condition, that everything seemed unreal, even myself; and it surprises me now that my reason did not give way."

"Did you never pray?"

"My training had been religious, and I had always

prayed. This, I felt, entitled me to help; and yet help did not come. I felt forsaken of God, and sullenly shut my lips to prayer or complaint. All severely tried souls go through a similar experience. Christ himself cried out: ' My God, my God, why hast thou *forsaken* me!'

" No wonder you felt forsaken, indeed."

" You think I was as tried as I could be then, when I had a hope of escape; but worse came after that—worse, because more hopeless."

" You were really married to him then?" I cried in alarm: "I thought you told me in the beginning, that you were not."

" Neither was I; but that did not release me. When at last I received an answer to my inquiries, confirming the statement of the immigrant from Ohio, it was too late."

" You do not mean!"—I interrupted, in a frightened voice.

" No, no! I only mean that I had committed a great error, in keeping silence on the subject at the first. You can imagine one of your acquaintances who had been several months peaceably living with a man of good appearance and repute, to whom you had seen her married, suddenly declaring her husband a bigamist and refusing to live with him; and on no other evidence than a letter obtained, nobody knew how. To *me* the proof was conclusive; and it made me frantic to find that it was not so received by others."

" What did he say, when you told him that you had this evidence? How did he act?"

" He swore it was a conspiracy; and declared that now he had borne enough of such contumelious conduct; he should soon bring me into subjection. He represented himself to me, as an injured and long-suffering man; and me, to myself, as an unkind, undutiful, and most unwomanly woman. He told me, what was true, that I need not expect people to believe such a ' cock and bull story;' and

4

used every possible means of intimidation, except actual
corporeal punishment. *That* he threatened long after; and
I told him if he ever laid a finger on me, I should certainly
shoot him dead. But we had not come to that yet."

"Long after!" I repeated. "You do not, you cannot
mean that this wretch continued to live under the same roof
with you, long after he knew that you would never acknowledge him as your husband?"

"Yes, for years! For years after he knew that I knew
he was *what he was*, he lived in my house and took my
earnings; yes, and ordered me about and insulted me as
much as he liked."

"But," I said, "I cannot understand such a condition
of things. Was there no law in the land? no succor in the
society about you? How could other women hold still, and
know that a young creature like you was being tortured in
that way?"

"The inertia of women in each other's defense is immense," returned Mrs. Greyfield, in her most incisive tone.
"You must not forget that Portland was then almost a
wilderness, and families were few, and often 'far between.'
Among the few, my acquaintances were still fewer; for I
had come among them poor and alone, and with all I could
do to support myself, without time or disposition to visit.
The peculiar circumstances I have related to you broke my
spirit and inclined me to seclusion. However, I did carry
my evidence, and my story together, to two or three women
that I knew, and what do you suppose they said? That I
'should have thought of all that before I married!' They
treated it exactly as if, having gone through the marriage
ceremony, I was bound, no matter how many wives Mr.
Seabrook had back in Ohio."

"They could not have believed your story," I said; not
being able to take in such inferior morality.

"What they believed I do not know: what they said I
have told you. I incline to the opinion that they thought

I might be a little daft—I am sure I must have looked so at times, from sheer sleeplessness and exhaustion. Or they thought I had no chance of establishing the truth, and would be better off to submit quietly. At all events, not one encouraged me to resist Mr. Seabrook; and to overflow my cup of misery, he contrived to find the important letter, which I had hidden, and destroy it."

"Did you never go to men about your case, and ask for assistance?"

"At first I was afraid to appeal to them, having had so many unpleasant experiences; and when I at last was driven to seek counsel, I was too late, as I before explained."

"Too late?"

"Yes; I mean that the idea of my being Mr. Seabrook's wife was so firmly seated in their minds that they could not see it in any other light. The fact of my having written and received a letter did not impress them as of any consequence. You will find this to be a truth among men; they respect the sense of ownership in women, entertained by each other; and they respect it so much that they would as soon be caught stealing, as seeming in any way to interfere with it. That is the reason that, although there is nothing in the wording of the marriage contract converting the woman into a bond-slave or a chattel, the man who practices any outrage or wrong on his wife is so seldom called to account. In the eyes of these men, having entered into marriage with Mr. Seabrook, I belonged to him, and there was no help for me. For life and until death, I was his, to do what he pleased with, so long as he did not bruise my flesh nor break my bones. Is not that an awful power to be lodged with any human being?"

"But," I said, "if they were told the whole truth, that the marriage had never been consummated, and why, would they not have been moved by a feeling of chivalry to interfere? Your view of their sentiments pre-supposes the non-existence of what I should call chivalry."

"There may be in men such a sentiment as you would
call chivalry; but I never yet have seen the occasion where
they were pleased to exercise it. I would not advise any
other young woman to tell one of them that she had lived
alone in the same house with a man reputed to be her husband, for seven months, without the marriage having been
consummated. She would find, as I did, that his chivalry
would be exhibited by an ineffectual effort to suppress a
smile of incredulity."

"Can it be possible," I was forced to exclaim, "that
there was no help for you?"

"You see how it was. I have outlined the bare facts to
you. Nobody wanted to be mixed up in my troubles, and
the worst of it was that Mr. Seabrook got more sympathy
than I did, as the unfortunate husband of a terrible terma-
gant, who made his life a burden to him. He could talk
in a certain way around among men, and put on an aggrieved
air at home before the boarders, and what was the use of
my saying anything. If it had not been for my little German neighbor, I should have felt utterly forsaken by all
the world. But she, whatever she thought of my domestic
affairs, was sorry for me. 'What for you cry so much all
de time?' she said to me one day. 'You makes yourself
sick all de time mit cryin'; an' your face be gettin' wite as
my hankershif. De leedle boy, too, he sees you, an' he
gets all so wite as you are, all de same. Dat is not goot.
You gomes to see me, an' brings de boy to see my Hans.
You get sheered up den.' And I took her advice for Benton's sake."

"What object had Mr. Seabrook in remaining where he
was so unwelcome? He certainly entertained no hope that
you would finally yield; and his position could not have
been an agreeable one, from any point of view; for whether
he was regarded as the monster he was, or only as a sadly
beshrewed husband, he must have felt himself the subject
of unpleasant remark."

"He could afford to be remarked upon when he was a free pensioner upon a woman's bounty, and in receipt of a fine income which I earned for him by ceaseless toil. I can see him now sitting at the bottom of the table, my table, flourishing his white hands, and stroking his flowing blonde beard occasionally as something very gratifying to his vanity was said; talking and laughing with perfect uncouncern, while he fattened himself at my expense; while I, who earned and prepared his dinner for him, gasped half fainting in the heat of a kitchen, sick in heart and body. Do you wonder that I hated him?"

"I wonder more that you did not kill him," I said; feeling that this would have been a case of 'justifiable homicide.'

"The impulse certainly came to me at times to kill him; or if not exactly that, to wish him dead. Yet when the opportunity came to be revenged upon him by fate itself, I interfered to save him. That was strange, was it not? To be suffering as I suffered at this man's hands, and yet when he was in peril to have compassion upon him?"

"You could not alter your nature," I said, "which is, as I told you before, thoroughly sound and sweet. It goes against us to suffer wrong; but it goes still harder with us to do wrong. Besides, you had your religious training to help you."

"I had the temptation, all the same. It happened in this way: One night I was lying awake, as I usually did, until I heard Mr. Seabrook come in and go to his room. He came in rather later than usual, and I listened until all was still in the house, that I might sleep the more safely and soundly afterwards. I had, however, become so nervously wakeful by this time that the much needed and coveted sleep refused to visit me, and I laid tossing feverishly upon my bed when I became aware that there was a smell of fire in the air. Rapidly dressing, I took Benton in my arms and hastened down stairs, to have him where

I could save him, should the house be in danger. There
was a still stronger odor of burning cloth and wood in the
lower rooms, but very little smoke to be detected. After
looking into the kitchen and finding all right there, I
feared the fire might be in the other part of the house, and
was about to give the alarm, when it occurred to me that
the trouble might be in Mr. Seabrook's room.

"Leaving Benton asleep on the dining-room table, I ran
to his door and knocked. No answer came; but I could
smell the smoke within. Pushing open the door I discovered him lying in a perfectly unconscious state, and half
undressed, on the bed, sleeping off the effects of a wine
supper. A candle which he had lighted, and left burning,
had consumed itself down to the socket, and by some
chance had ignited a few loose papers on the table beside
the bed ; the fire had communicated to the bedding on one
side, and to some of his wearing apparel on the other.
All was just ready to burst into a blaze with the admission
of fresh air, which I had the presence of mind to prevent,
by closing the door behind me.

"There I was, in the presence of my enemy, and he in
the clutches of death. I shudder when I think of the feelings of that moment! An evil spirit plainly said to me,
'Now you shall have rest. Let him alone ; he is dying by
his own hand, not yours—why do you interfere with the
decree of fate ?' An exulting yet consciously guilty joy
agitated my heart, which was beating violently. 'Let him
die !' I said to myself, 'let him die !'

"Very rapidly such thoughts whirl through the brain
under great excitement. The instant that I hesitated
seemed an age of cool deliberation to me. Then the wickedness of my self-gratulation rushed into my mind, making me
feel like a murderer. 'O, God,' I cried in anguish of spirit,
'why have I been put to this test?' The next instant I was
working with might and main to extinguish the fire, which
with the aid of blankets and a pitcher of water was soon
suppressed.

"Through it all he slept on, breathing heavily, an object of disgust to my senses and my feelings. When all was safe I returned to my room, thankful that I had been able on the spot to expiate my murderous impulses. The next day he took occasion to say to me, 'I shouldn't have expected a visit of mercy from you, Mrs. Seabrook. If I had known you were coming, I should have tried to keep awake!' 'If ever you refer to such a subject again,' I replied, 'I will set fire to you myself, and let you burn;' and either the threat deterred him, or some spark of generosity in his nature was struck by the benefit received, but he never afterwards offered me any annoyance of that kind."

"How did Mr. Seabrook usually treat your son? Was he kind to him?"

"He was not unkind. Perhaps you cannot understand such a character; but he was one who would be kind to man, woman, or child who would be governed by him; yet resistance to his will, however just, roused a tyranny that sought for opportunities to exhibit itself. Such a one passes in general society for a 'good fellow,' because 'the iron hand in the velvet glove' is scarcely perceptible there, while its ungloved force is felt most heavily in the relations of private life. If I had been in a position to flatter Mr. Seabrook, undoubtedly he would have shown me a corresponding consideration, notwithstanding his selfishness. It would have been one way of gratifying his own vanity, by putting me in a humor to pander to it. But knowing how I hated and despised him, he felt toward me all the rancor of his vain and tyrannical nature. It is always more dangerous to hate justly than unjustly, and that is the reason why domestic differences are so bitter. Somebody has always done wrong and knows it, and cannot bear to suffer the natural consequences—the disapprobation of the injured party, in addition to the stings of conscience."

"I suppose, then," I said, "it has been the perception of this truth that has caused the sweetest and purest women

in all time to ignore the baser sins of man, while calling
their own sex to strict account. And yet I cannot think
but that this degree of mercy is injurious to their own
purity and derogatory to their dignity. I remember being excessively shocked several years ago by having this
trait of *forgiveness* in woman placed in its true light by
an accidental publication in a New York paper, which was
intended to have just the opposite effect. It was headed
'A Model Woman,' and appeared in the *Evening Post*
—Bryant's paper. With a curious desire to know the
poet's model for a woman—though the article may have
never come under his eye—I commenced reading it. It ran
to this effect: A certain man in New York had a good wife
and two interesting little children. But he met and fell in
love with a handsome, dashing, and rather coarse girl; and
the affair had gone so far as to lead to serious expostulation
on the part of the wife. The writer did not relate whether
or not the girl knew the man to be married; but only that
the two were infatuated with each other.

"As the story ran, the wife expostulated, and the husband was firm in his determination to possess the girl at
all hazards, concluding his declaration with this business-
like statement: 'I shall take the girl, and go to California.
If you keep quiet about it, I will leave a provision for you
and the children; if you do not, I shall go just the same,
but without leaving you anything.' *The wife acquiesced in
the terms.* Her husband went to California with his para-
mour, and tired of her (it was in old steamer times), about
as soon as he got there. Very soon he deserted her and
returned to New York *a la prodigal*, and was received back
to the arms of his forgiving wife. The girl followed her
faithless lover to New York, and failing to win a kind word
from him by the most piteous appeals, finally committed
suicide at her hotel in that city. The wife continued to
live with the author of this misery upon the most affectionate terms.

"That was the whole story. Is it possible, I asked myself, that the writer of that article, whoever he may be, could have meant its title in anything but irony? Yet, there it stood on the front page of a most respectable journal, indorsed by an editor of the highest reputation. To my way of thinking, the wife was accessory to the crime; had no womanly self-respect, no delicacy, no Christian feeling for her husband's victim; was, in short, morally, as guilty as he was; and yet a newspaper of high standing made her out to be a model for wives. For what? Plainly for consenting to, or for forgiving three of the most heinous crimes in the decalogue, because committed *by her husband.* I confess that since that day I have been prone to examine into the claims of men to be forgiven, or the moral right of women to forgive them certain offenses."

"When you examine into the motives of women," said Mrs. Greyfield, "I think you will find there is a large measure of sordid self-interest in their mercy, as in the case you have just quoted. While some women are so weak, and so foolishly fond of the men to whom they became early attached, as to be willing to overlook everything rather than part with them; a far greater number yield an unwilling submission to wrongs imposed upon them, simply because they do not know how to do without the pecuniary support afforded them by their husbands. The bread-and-butter question is demoralizing to women as well as to men, the difference being that men have a wider field to be demoralized in; and that the demoralization of women is greatly consequent upon their circumscribed field of action."

"Do you think that the enlargement of woman's sphere of work would have a tendency to elevate her moral influence?"

"The way the subject presents itself to me is, that it is degrading to have sex determine everything for us: our employments, our position in society, the obedience we owe

to others, the influence we are permitted to exercise, all
and everything to be dependent upon the delicate matter of
a merely physical function.   It affects me so unpleasantly
to hear such frequent reference to a physiological fact, that
I have often wished the word *female* stricken from our lit-
erature.   And when you reflect, that we are born and bred
to this narrow view of ourselves, as altogether the creatures
of sex, you cannot but recognize its belittleing, not to say
depraving effect, or fail to see the temptation; we have to
seize any base advantage it may give us."

When we had canvassed this, to us interesting, topic a
little further, I begged Mrs. Greyfield to go on with the
relation of her history.

"I find I must be less particular," she said, "to give so
many and frequent explanations of my feelings.   By this
time you can pretty well imagine them, and my story is
likely to be too long, unless I abbreviate.

"I had been living in the way I have described, for two
years, and had learned to do a good many things in my
own defence, very disagreeable to me, but nevertheless very
useful.   I had gotten a little money together by asking some
of my boarders for pay before pay-day came, or by making such remarks as prompted them to hand the money to
me instead of Mr. Seabrook.   It was my intention to save
enough in such ways to take me to California, where I felt
confident, with the experience I had gained, I should be
able to make myself a competence.   This plan I had nourished in secret for more than a year, when I was tempted
to do a very unwise thing.

"I ought to say, perhaps, that with every year that had
passed since my arrival in Portland, the population had
increased, and with this increase there was a proportionate
rise in the value of property.   Hearing business topics discussed almost every day at table, I could not help being
more or less infected with the spirit of speculation; and it
often almost drove me wild to think how profitably I might

have invested my earnings could I have gained possession of them for myself.

"Having an opportunity one day to speak on the subject to a gentleman in whose honor I placed great confidence, I mentioned that I was tempted to buy some property, but that my means were so limited I feared I could not do so. He immediately said that he would sell me a certain very good piece of land in the best business locality, on the installment plan, and at a bargain, so that when it was paid up I could immediately sell again at an advance. Thinking this would accelerate the carrying out of my scheme of fleeing from my master, to a land of freedom, I eagerly accepted the proposition, and paid down all the money I had, taking a bond for a deed. The transaction was to be kept a secret between us, and he was to assist me in selling when it came the proper time, by deeding direct to my purchaser. I felt almost light-hearted in view of the fact that I should be able, after all, to achieve a kind of independence in the course of time."

"It seems to me," I said, "that I should have grown reckless before this, and have done something of a desperate nature—committed suicide, for instance. Did the thought never occur to you to end your bondage in that way?"

"My desperation never took that form, because I had my child to take care of. If I killed myself, I should have to kill him, too. But many and many a night I have felt it so impossible to be alive in the morning, and go right on in my miserable round of life, worn out in mind and body, with Benton always ailing—often very ill, that I have prepared both myself and him for burial, and laid down praying God to take us both before another day. But Death is like our other friends—he is not at hand to do us a service when most desired.

"I have told you that I used to cry a good deal. Weeping, though a relief to us in one way, by removing the pressure upon the brain, is terribly exhausting when excessive, and I was very much wasted by it. An incident occurred about the time I was just speaking of, which gave me comfort in a strange manner. I used sometimes, when my work for the day was done, to leave Benton with my German friend, and go out for a walk, or to call on an acquaintance. All the sights and sounds of nature are beautiful and beneficial to me in a remarkable degree. With trees and flowers and animals, I am happy and at home.

"One evening I set out to make a visit to Mrs. ——, my old neighbor, who lived at some distance from me. The path led through the fir forest, and at the time of day when I was at liberty, was dim and gloomy. I walked hurriedly along, fearing darkness would overtake me; and looking about me as I went, was snatching a hasty pleasure from the contemplation of Nature's beneficence, when my foot caught in a projecting root of some tough shrub, and I fell prostrate.

"In good health and spirits I should not have minded the fall; but to me, in my weak condition, every jar to the nervous system affected me seriously. I rose with difficulty, and seating myself upon a fallen tree, burst into tears, and wept violently. It seemed as if even the sticks and stones were in league to injure me. Looking back upon my feelings, I can understand how man, in the infancy of the race, attributed power and will to everything in Nature. In his weakness and inexperience, Nature was too strong for him, and bruised him continually.

"As I sat weeping with pain and an impotent resentment, a clear sweet voice spoke to me out of the dusky twilight of the woods. '*Don't cry so much!*' it said. Astonishment dried my tears instantly. I looked about me, but no one was near ; nor any sound to be heard, but the peculiar cry of a bird that makes itself heard in the Oregon woods at twilight only. A calm that I cannot explain came over my perturbed spirit. It was like the heavenly voices heard upon the earth thousands of years ago, in its power to move the heart. It may make you smile for me to say so; but from that hour I regained a degree of cheerfulness that I had not felt since the day of my marriage to Mr. Seabrook. I did not go to Mrs. ——'s that evening, but returned home and went to my bed without putting on clothes to be buried in!"

We talked for a little of well attested instances of similar incidents of the seeming supernatural. Then I said:

"And how did your investment turn out?"

"As might have been expected by a more worldly-wise person. After succeeding, almost, I was defeated by the selfishness and indifference of the man I had trusted to help me through with it. He sold out his property, including that bonded to me, when nearly the whole indebtedness was paid, without mentioning his design, or giving me an opportunity to complete the purchase. The new proprietor went immediately to Mr. Seabrook, who, delighted with this unexpected piece of fortune, borrowed the small amount remaining to be paid, and had the property decded to himself. A short time after he sold it at a handsome advance on the price I paid for it, and I had never one dollar of the money. The entire savings of the whole time I had been in a really profitable business, went with that unlucky venture."

"You were just as far from getting to California as ever? O, what outrageous abuse of the power society gives men over women!" I exclaimed with vehemence.

"You may imagine I was bitterly disappointed. The lesson was a hard one, but salutary. I took no more disinterested advice; I bought no more property. There are too many agents between a woman and the thing she aims at, for her ever to attain it without danger of discomfiture. The experience, as you may guess, put me in no amicable mood towards Mr. Seabrook. Just think of it! There were three years I had supported, by my labor, a large family of men, for that is what it amounted to. My money purchased the food they all ate, and I had really received nothing for it except my board and the clothes I worked in. The fault was not theirs; it was Mr. Seabrook's and society's."

"I will tell you what you remind me of," I said: "You are like Penelope, and her train of ravenous suitors, in the *Odyssey* of Homer."

"In my busy life, I have not had time to read Homer," Mrs. Greyfield replied; "but if any other woman has been so eaten out of house and home, as I was, I am sorry for her."

"Homer's Penelope, if we may believe the poet, was in much better circumstances to bear the ravages of her riotous boarders, than you were to feed yours gratuitously."

"Talking about suitors," said Mrs. Greyfield, "I was not without those entirely, either. No young mismated woman can escape them perhaps. The universal opinion among men seems to be that, if you do not like the man you have, you *must* like some other one; and each one thinks it is himself."

The piquant tone in which Mrs. Greyfield uttered her observations always provoked a smile. But I caught at an intimation in her speech. "Sometimes," I said, "you speak as if you acknowledged Mr. Seabrook as your husband, and it shocks me unpleasantly."

"I am speaking of things as they appeared to others. In truth, I was as free to receive suitors as ever I had been; but such was not the common understanding, and I resented the advances of men upon the ground that *they* believed themselves to be acting unlawfully, and that they hoped to make me a party to their breaches of law and propriety. I laugh now, in remembering the blunders committed by self-conceit so long ago; but I did not laugh then; it was a serious matter at that time."

"Was Mr. Seabrook jealous in his behavior, fearing you might fancy some one else?"

"Just as jealous as vain and tyrannical men always are when they are thwarted in their designs. No real husband could have been more critical in his observations on his wife's deportment, than he was in his remarks on mine. If I could have been guilty of coquetry, the desire to annoy him would have been incentive enough; but I always considered that I could not afford to suffer in my own estimation for the sake of punishing him. When I recall all these things, I take credit to myself for magnanimity; though then I was governed only by my poor uncultivated judgment, and my impulses. For instance, Mr. Seabrook fell ill of a fever not long after he appropriated my real estate. Of course, I was as bitter towards him in my heart as it is possible to conceive, but I could not know that he was lying unattended in his room, without offering assistance; so, after many struggles with myself to overcome my strong repulsion, I visited him often enough to give him such attentions as were necessary, but not more. I had no intention of raising any false expectations."

"I hope you took advantage of his being confined to his room, to collect board-money," I said.

"I found out, in time, several ways of managing that matter, which I would once have thought inadmissible. When I had begged some money from a boarder, Mr. Seabrook discovered it when payday came, very naturally. He then ordered me to do the marketing. Without paying any attention to the command, I served up at meal-time whatever there was in the house. This brought out murmurs from the boarders, and haughty inquiries from the host himself. All the reply I vouchsafed was, that what he procured I would cook. In this way I forced him to pay out the money in his possession, at the expense of my character as a good wife, and a polite one. He took his revenge in abusive language, and occasional fits of destructiveness in the kitchen, which alarmed my little German neighbor more than it did me. So long as he secured all

my earnings, and deceived people thoroughly as to his real
conduct, he maintained, before others at least, a gentlemanly demeanor. But this was gradually giving way to
the pressure of a constant thorn in his flesh, and the consciousness of his own baseness. He could swear, threaten,
and almost strike at slight provocation now. He never
really attempted the latter, but once, and it was then I told
him I should shoot him, if he dared it.

"I ought to say here, that in the last year I had two or
three families in the house for a short time. I don't know
what these real wives thought of me; that I was a terma-
gant probably; but they were not the kind of women I
could talk to about myself, and I made no confidences. A
plan was maturing in my mind that was to make it a matter
of indifference what any one thought. I had relinquished
the idea of getting money enough together to make a sure
start in California, and was only waiting to have enough
to take me out of the country in any way that I could go
cheapest. Another necessary point to gain was secrecy.
That could not be gained while I was surrounded by
boarders, nor while Mr. Seabrook was in the house, and I
resolved to be rid of both."

"Oh," I cried, delighted and relieved, "how *did* you
manage that?"

"I am going to tell you by how simple an expedient. *I
starved them out!*"

"How strange that in all those years you never thought
of that," I said laughing. "But, then, neither did Homer's
heroine, who kept a first-class free boarding house for twice
or thrice as long as you. Do tell me how you accomplished
the feat of clearing your house."

"It is not quite true that I had not thought of it; but I
had not dared to do it. Besides, I wanted to get some
money, if possible. Perhaps I should not have done it at
the time I did, had not a little help come to me in the shape
of real friends. I was all the time like a wild bird in a

cage, and the continual attempts to escape I was making, only bruised my wings. It occurred to me one day to go to a certain minister who had lately come to Portland, and whose looks pleased me, as did his wife's, and tell them my story. This I did.

"Instead of receiving it as fiction, or doubting the strange parts of it in a way to make me wish I had never spoken of them, they manifested the greatest interest and sympathy, and promised me any assistance they could give. This was the first recognition I had gotten from anyone as being what I was; a woman held in bondage worse than that of African slavery, by a man to whom she owed nothing, and in the midst of a free, civilized, and Christian community. They were really and genuinely shocked, and firmly determined to help me. I told them all the difficulties in the way, and of the expedient I had almost decided upon, to free my house from every one; for I thought that when his income stopped, Mr. Seabrook would be forced to go away, and seek some other means of living. They agreed with me that there appeared no better way, and I decided to attempt it.

"It did not take long, of course, to drive away the boarders, for they were there only to eat; and when provisions entirely failed, or were uncooked, there was nothing to be done but to go where they could be better served. I did not feel very comfortable over it, as many of them were men I liked and respected, whose ill opinion it was disagreeable to incur, even in a righteous cause; and then no woman likes to be the talk of the town, as I knew I must be. The 'town talk,' as it happened, in time suggested my further course to me.

"Pray tell me if Mr. Seabrook followed the boarders, or did he stay and compel you to cook for him?"

"He stayed, but he did not compel me to cook for him. That I peremptorily refused to do. Neither would I buy any supplies. If he wanted a meal, he must go out, get

5

his provisions, and cook them for himself. Then he refused
to buy anything to come in the house, lest I should share
his plenty. This reduced our rations to nothing. I used
to take Benton out and buy him good, wholesome food, myself eating as little as would support nature. Occasionally,
now that I had time on my hands, I spent a day out among
my few visiting acquaintances; and sometimes I took a
meal with my German friend. In this way I compelled my
former master to look out for himself.

"One night, there not being a mouthful in the house to
eat, I went out and bought a loaf of bread and some milk
for Benton's breakfast; for I was careful not to risk the
child's health as I risked my own. In the morning when I
came down stairs the bread and milk were gone. Mr. Seabrook had breakfasted. 'Bennie' and I could go hungry.
And that brings me back to what 'town talk' did for me.

"It soon became noised about that Mr. and Mrs. Seabrook, who had never got on well together, were now going
on dreadfully, and that probably there would be a divorce.
'Divorce!' I said, when my new friend, the minister,
mentioned it to me, 'divorce from what? How can there
be a divorce where there is no marriage?" 'Nevertheless,'
he replied, 'it is worth considering. If the society you live
in insist that you are married, why not gratify this society,
and ask its leave to be legally separated from your nominal
husband?'

"At first I rebelled strongly against making this tacit
admission of a relationship of that kind to Mr. Seabrook.
It appeared to me to be a confession of falsehood to those
few persons who were in my confidence, some of whom I
felt had always half-doubted the full particulars, as being
too ugly for belief. And what was quite as unpalatable as
the other was that my enemy would rejoice that for once,
at least, and in a public record, I should have to confess
myself his wife. My friends argued that it could make
little difference, as that was the popular understanding

already, which nothing could alter; and that so far as Mr. Seabrook was concerned his triumph would be short-lived and valueless. They undertook to procure counsel, and stand by me through the trial."

" What complaint did you purpose making ?" I interrupted.

" ' Neglect of support, and cruel treatment;' the general charge that is made to cover so many abominable sins, because we women shrink from exposing the crimes we have been in a measure partners to. My attorney assured me that, under the circumstances, Mr. Seabrook would not make any opposition, fearing we might prove the whole, if he did so; but would let the case go by default. This was just what he did; and oh, you should have witnessed his abject humility when I at last had the acknowledged right to put him out of my house !

" Up to the time the divorce was obtained, he kept possession of the room he had first taken, on the lower floor, and which I hired an Indian woman to take care of as one of the chores assigned her about the house. For myself, I would not set my foot in it, except on the occasions referred to; but the rent, and the care of it, he had free. Such was the moral degradation of the man, through his own acts, that after all that had passed, he actually cried, and begged of me the privilege to remain in that room, and be taken care of, as he had been used to be."

" What did you answer him ?"

" I told him never to darken my door—never to offend my sight again; that I should never be quite happy while his head was above the sod. O, I was very vindictive! And he was as mild as milk. He ' could not see why I should hate him so, who had always had so high a regard for me. He had never known a woman he admired and loved so much !' Even I was astonished at the man's abjectness."

" It is not uncommon in similar cases. Dependence

makes any one more or less mean; but it is more noticeable in men, who by nature and by custom are made independent. And so you were free at last?"

"Free and happy. I felt as light as a bird, and wondered I couldn't fly! I was poor; but that was nothing. My business was broken up; but I felt confidence in myself to begin again. My health, however, was very much broken down, and my friends said I needed change. That, with the desire to quit a country where I had suffered so much, determined me to come to California. It was the land of promise to my husband—the El Dorado he was seeking when he died. I always felt that if I had come here in the first place, my life would have been very different. So, finally, with the help of my kind friends I came."

"*I* should have felt, with your experience, no courage to undertake life among strangers, and they mostly men."

"On the contrary, I felt armed in almost every point. The fact of being a divorced woman was my only annoyance; but I was resolved to suppress it so far as I was able, and to represent myself to be, as I was, the widow of Mr. Greyfield. I took letters from my friends, to use in case of need; and with nothing but my child, and money·enough to take me comfortably to the mines on the American River, left Oregon forever."

"To behold you as you are now, in this delightful home, it seems impossible that you should have gone through what you describe; and yet there must have been much more before you achieved the success here indicated."

"It was nothing—nothing at all compared with the other. I proceeded direct to the most populous mining town, hired a house, bought furniture on credit, and took boarders again. I kept only first-class boarders, had high prices—and succeeded."

"Did you never have the mining-stock fever, and invest and lose?"

"Not to any dangerous extent. One or two parties, in

whose judgment I knew I might confide, indicated to me
where to invest, and I fortunately lost nothing, while I
made a little. My best mining-stock was a present from a
young man who was sick at my house for a long time, and
to whom I was attentive. He was an excellent young fellow, and my sympathies were drawn out towards him;
alone in a mining-camp, and sick, and, as I suspected,
moneyless. When he was well enough to go away, he confessed his inability to pay up, and presented me with several
shares in a mine then but little known; saying that it might
not be worth the paper it was printed on, but that he hoped
it might bring enough to reimburse my actual outlay on
his account; 'the kindness he had received could not be
repaid with filthy lucre.' A few months afterwards that
stock was worth several thousand dollars. I made diligent
inquiry for my young friend, but could get no news of him
from that day to this. I have been fortunate in everything
I have touched since I came to California. Benton grew
well and strong; I recovered my health; Fortune's wheel
for me seemed to remain in one happy position; and now
there seems nothing for me to do but to move slowly and
easily down the sunset slope of life to my final rest."

Mrs. Greyfield smiled and sighed, and remarked upon
the fact that the hour-hand of the clock pointed to two in
the morning. "It is really unkind of me to keep you out
of bed until such an hour as this," she said, laughing a
little, as if we had only been talking of ordinary things.
"But I am in the mood, like the 'Ancient Mariner;' and
you are as much forced to listen as the 'Wedding Guest.'"

"There is one thing yet I desire to be satisfied about,"
I replied. "As a woman, I cannot repress my curiosity to
know whether, since all the troubles of your early life have
been past, you have desired to marry again. Opportunities
I know you must have had. What I want to be informed
about is your feeling upon this subject, and whether any
man has been able to fill your eye or stir your heart."

The first smile my question called up died away, and an introspective look came over Mrs. Greyfield's still handsome face. She sat silent for a little time, that seemed long to me, for I was truly interested in her reply.

"I think," she said at last, "that women who have had anything like my experience, are unfitted for married life. Either they are ruined morally and mentally, by the terrible pressure; or they become so sharp-sighted and critical that no ordinary man would be able to win their confidence. I believe in marriage; a single life has an incomplete, one-sided aspect, and is certainly lonely." Then rallying, with much of her usual brightness: "Undoubtedly I have had my times of doubt, when I found it hard to understand myself; and still, here I am! Nobody would have me; or I would not have anybody; or both."

"One more question, then, if it is a fair one: Could you love again the husband of your youth; or has your ideal changed?"

Mrs. Greyfield was evidently disturbed by the inquiry. Her countenance altered, and she hesitated to reply.

"I beg your pardon," I said; "I hope you will not answer me, if I have been impertinent."

"That is a question I never asked myself," she finally replied. "My husband was all in all to me during our brief married life. His death left me truly desolate, and his memory sacred. But we were both young, and probably he may have been unformed in character, to a great degree, as well as myself. How he would seem now, if he could be restored to me as he was then, I can only half imagine. What he would now *be*, if he had lived on, I cannot at all imagine. But let us now go take a wink of sleep. My eyelids at last begin to feel dry and heavy; and you, I am sure, are perishing under the tortures of resistance to the drowsy god."

"The storm is over," I said. "I thought you felt that something was going to happen!"

"It will be breakfast, I suppose. By the way, I must go and put a note under Jane's door, telling her not to have it before half-past nine. There will be a letter from Benton, by the morning mail. Good night; or, good morning, and sweet slumber."

"God be with you," I responded, and in twenty minutes was sleeping soundly.

Not so my hostess, it seems, for when we met again at our ten o'clock breakfast, she looked pale and distraught, and acknowledged that she had not been able to compose herself after our long talk. The morning was clear and sunny, but owing to the storm of the night, the mail was late getting in, a circumstance which gave her, as I thought, a degree of uneasiness not warranted by so natural a delay.

"You know I told you," she said, trying to laugh off her nervousness, "that something was going to happen!"

"It would be a strange condition of things where nothing did happen," I answered; and just then the horn of the mail-carrier sounded, and the lumbering four-horse coach rattled down the street in sight of our windows.

"There," I said, "is your U. S. M. safe and sound, road-agents and land-slides to the contrary and of no effect."

Very soon our letters were brought us, and my hostess, excusing herself, retired to her room to read hers. Two hours later she sent for me to come to her. I found her lying with a wet handkerchief folded over her forehead and eyes. A large and thick letter laid half open upon a table beside the bed.

"Read that," she said, without uncovering her eyes. When I had read the letter, "My dear friend," I said, "what *are* you going to do? I hope, after all, this may be good news."

"What *can* I do? What a strange situation!"

"You will wish to see him, I suppose? 'Arthur Grey-

fied.' You never told me his name was Arthur," I remarked,
thinking to weaken the intensity of her feelings by refer-
ring to a trifling circumstance.

"Why have I not died before this time?" she exclaimed,
unheeding my attempt at diversion. "This is too much,
too much!"

"Perhaps there is still happiness in store for you, my
dear Mrs. Greyfield," I said. "Strange as is this new dis-
pensation, may there not be a blessing in it?"

She remained silent a long time, as if thinking deeply.
"He has a daughter," she at length remarked; "and Benton says she is very sweet and loveable."

"And motherless," I added, not without design. I had
meant only to arouse a feeling of compassion for a young
girl half-orphaned; but something more than was in my
mind had been suggested to hers. She quickly raised herself from a reclining posture, threw off the concealing
handkerchief, and gazed intently in my face, while saying
slowly, as if to herself: "Not only motherless, but according to law, fatherless."

"Precisely," I answered. "Her mother was in the same
relation to Mr. Greyfield, that you were in to Mr. Seabrook;
but happily she did not know it in her lifetime."

"Nor he—nor he! Arthur Greyfield is not to be spoken
of in the same breath with Mr. Seabrook."

The spirit with which this vindication of her former husband was made, caused me to smile, in spite of the dramatic interest of the situation. The smile did not escape
her notice.

"You think I am blown about by every contending
breath of feeling," she said, wearily; "when the truth is,
I am trying to make out the right of a case in which there
is so much wrong; and it is no easy thing to do."

"But you will find the right of it at last," I answered.
"You are not called upon to decide in a moment upon a
matter of such weight as this. Take time, take rest, take
counsel."

"Will you read the letter over to me?" she asked, lying down again, and preparing to listen by shielding her face with her hands.

The letter of Arthur Greyfield ran as follows:

"My Dear Anna: How strange it seems to me to be writing to you again! It is like conversing with one returned from another world, to you, too, no doubt. There is so much to explain, and some things that perhaps will not ever be explained satisfactorily to you, that I know not where to begin or what to say. Still Benton insists on my writing before seeing you, and perhaps this is best.

" To begin at the beginning. When I was left for dead by my frightened comrades on the plains, I had not died, but was only insensible; and I do not believe they felt at all sure of my death, for they left me unburied, as if to give me a chance; and deserted me rather than take any risks by remaining any longer in that place. How long I laid insensible I do not know. When I came to myself I was alone, well wrapped up in a large bed-quilt, and lying on the ground close by the wagon-trail. Nothing was left for my support, if alive, from which I concluded that they agreed to consider me dead.

" When I opened my eyes again on the wilderness world about me, the sun was shining brightly, and the wind blowing cool from the near mountains; but I was too much exhausted to stir; and laid there, kept alive by the pure air alone, until sunset. About that time of day I heard the tread of cattle coming, and the rumbling of wagons. The shock of joy caused me to faint, in which condition I was found by the advance guard of a large train bound for the mines in California. I need not tell you all those men did for me to bring me round, but they were noble fellows, and earned my everlasting gratitude.

" You can imagine that the first thought in my mind was about you and Benton. When I was able to talk about myself and answer questions, my new friends, who had laid by for a couple of days on my account, assured me that they should be able to overtake the California train, in which I supposed you were, before they came to the Sierras. But we had accidents and delays, and failed to come up with that train anywhere on the route.

" At last we arrived in the mining country, and my new friends speedily scattered abroad, looking for gold.

I was still too feeble to work in the water, washing out, or
to dig. I had no money or property of any kind, and was
obliged to accept any means that offered of earning a subsistence. Meanwhile I made such inquiry as I could under
the circumstances, and in such a country, but without
learning anything of any of my former friends and acquaintances, for two years. Before this time, however, my
health was restored, notwithstanding great hardships; and
being quite successful in mining, I was laying up considerable gold-dust.

"About this time a man came into our camp from
Oregon. As I was in the habit of inquiring of any new-
comer concerning you, and the people in the train you
were in, I asked this man if he had ever met a Mrs. Greyfield, or any of the others. He replied that he thought
there was a woman of my name living in Portland, Oregon,
a year or two before—he was sure he had heard of a young
widow of that name. I immediately wrote to you at that
place; but whether the letter was lost on the way, or
whether it was intercepted there (as by some intimations I
have from Benton, it might have been), no reply ever came
to it. I also sent a letter to Mr. ——, in whose care I had
left you, but nothing was ever heard from him.

"When I had waited a reasonable length of time I
wrote again to the postmaster of the same place, asking
him if he knew of such a person as Mrs. Greyfield, in
Oregon. The reply came this time from a man named
Seabrook, who said that there had been a woman of the
name of Greyfield in Portland at one time, but that both
she and her child were dead. This news put an end to
inquiries in that direction, though I continued to look for
any one who might have known you, and finally found one
of our original party, who confirmed the intelligence of
your having gone to Oregon instead of California, and so
settled the question, as I supposed, forever.

"You may wonder, dear Anna, that I did not go to
Oregon when I had the barest suspicion of your being
there. The distance and the trouble of getting there were
not what deterred me. I was making money where I was,
and did not wish to abandon my claim while it was pro-
ducing well, for an uncertain hint that might mislead
me."

"Stop there!" interrupted Mrs. Greyfield. "Do you

think *I* should have hesitated in a case like that? But go on."

" I knew you had considerable property, and thought I knew you were with friends who would not let you suffer—"

" Though they had abandoned him while still alive, in the wilderness! Beg pardon; please go on again."—

" And that Oregon was really a more comfortable, and safe place for a family than California, as times were then—"

Mrs. Greyfield groaned.

" And that you, if there, would do very well until I could come for you. I could not suspect that you would avail yourself of the privilege of widowhood within so short a time, if ever."

" Oh!" ejaculated my listener, with irrepressible impatience.

I read on without appearing to observe the interruption.

" To tell the truth, I had not thought of myself as dead, and that is probably where I made the greatest mistake. It did not occur to me, that you were thinking of yourself as a widow; therefore, I did not realize the risk. But when the news came of your death, if it were really you, as I finally made up my mind it must be—"

An indignant gesture, accompanied by a sob, expressed Mrs. Greyfield's state of feeling on this head.

" I fell into a state of confirmed melancholy, reproaching myself severely for not having searched the continent over before stopping to dig gold! though it was for you I was digging it, and our dear boy, whom I believed alive and well, somewhere, until I received Mr. Seabrook's letter.

" My dear Anna, I come now to that which will try your feelings; but you must keep in view that I have the same occasion for complaint. Having made a comfortable fortune, and feeling miserable about you and the boy, I concluded to return to the Atlantic States, to visit my old home. While there I met a lovely and excellent girl, who consented to be my wife, and I was married the second time. We had one child, a girl, now eighteen years of age; and then my wife died. I mourned her sincerely, but not more so than I had mourned you.

"At last, after all these years, news came of you from a reliable source. The very man to whose charge I committed you when I expected to die, returned to the States, and from him I heard of your arrival in Oregon, your marriage, and your subsequent divorce. Painful as this last news was to my feelings, I set out immediately for California (I had learned from him that you were probably in this State), and commenced inquiries. An advertisement of mine met Benton's eye only two days ago, and you may imagine my pleasure at the discovery of my only and dear son, so long lost to me. He is a fine, manly fellow, and good; for which I have to thank you, of course."

"You see, he appropriates Benton at once. Never so much as 'by your leave.' But Benton will not quit me to follow this new-found father," Mrs. Greyfield said, with much feeling.

"He may not be put to the test of a choice. You have a proposition to consider," I replied. "Let me read it."

"No, no! Yet, read it; what do I care? Go on.

"My daughter, Nellie, is the very picture of her mother, and as sweet and good as one could desire. Benton seems to be delighted with her for a sister. And now that the young folks have taken such a fancy to each other, there is something that I wish to propose to you. It cannot be expected, after all that has passed, and with the lapse of so many years, we could meet as if nothing had come between us—"

"Who suffered all this to come between us?" cried Mrs. Greyfield, much agitated.

"But I trust we can meet as friends, dear friends, and that possibly in time we may be re-united, as much for our own sakes, as the children's."

"Oh, how can I ever forgive him? Does it not seem to you that if Mr. Greyfield had done his duty, all this terrible trouble and illegal marrying would have been avoided? Do you think a man should consider anything in this world before his wife and children, or fail of doing his utmost in any circumstances for them? How else is marriage superior to any illicit relation, if its duties are not sacred and not to be set aside for anything? I could never have done as he has done, blameless as he thinks himself."

The condition of Mrs. Greyfield's mind was such that no answer was written or attempted that day nor the next. She sent a brief dispatch to Benton, asking him to come home, and come alone. I wished to go away, thinking she would prefer being left quite to herself under the circumstances, but she insisted on my remaining until something had been decided on about the meeting between her and Mr. Greyfield. Benton came home as requested, and the subject was canvassed in all its bearings. The decision arrived at was, that an invitation should be sent to Mr. Greyfield and daughter to visit Mrs. Greyfield for a fortnight. Everything beyond that was left entirely to the future. When all was arranged, I took my leave, promising and being promised frequent letters.

The last time I was at Mrs. Greyfield's, I found there only herself and her daughter Nellie.

" I have adopted her," she said, " with her father's consent. She is a charming girl, and I could not bear to leave her motherless. Benton is very much attached to his father. They are off on a mountaineering expedition at present, but I hope they will come home before you go away."

" Are you not going to tell me," I asked, " how you finally settled matters between Mr. Greyfield and yourself."

" He is a very persistent suitor," she replied, smiling, " I can hardly tell what to do with him."

" You do not want to break bark over his head? " I said, laughing.

" No; but I do almost wish that since he had stayed away so long he had never come back. I had got used to my own quiet, old-maid ways. I was done, or thought I was done, with passion and romance; and now to be tossed about in this way, on the billows of doubt—to love and not to love—to feel revengeful and forgiving—to think one way in the morning and another way by noon, is very tiresome. I really do *not* know what to do with him."

I smiled, because I thought the admission was as good as Mr. Greyfield need desire, for his prospects.

"I think I can understand," I said, "how difficult it must be to get over all the gaps made by so many years of estrangement— of fancied death, even. Had you been looking for him for such a length of time, there would still be a great deal of awkwardness in the meeting, when you came together again."

"Yes," said Mrs. Greyfield, "it is inevitable. The most artistic bit of truth in the *Odyssey* (you see I have read Homer since you called me PENELOPE), is where the poet describes the difficulty the faithful wife had in receiving the long-absent, and now changed, Ulysses as her true husband."

"But she did receive him," I interrupted, "and so will you."

"The minister will have to bless the reception then. And to confess the whole truth to you, we are corresponding with my friend of long ago in Portland. He has promised to come down to perform the ceremony, and as his health is impaired, we have invited him to bring his family, at our expense, and to remain in our home while Mr. Greyfield and I, with Benton and Nellie, make a tour to and through Europe."

"How much you and Mr. Greyfield must have to talk over! It will take a year or two of close association to make you even tolerably well acquainted again."

"No; the 'talking over' is *tabooed*, and that is why we are going to travel—to have something else to talk about. You see I am so unforgiving that I cannot bear to hear Mr. Greyfield's story, and too magnanimous, notwithstanding, to inflict mine upon him. To put temptation out of my way, I proposed this European excursion."

"You are commencing a new life," I said. "May it be

as happy as your darkest days were sad. There is one thing you never told me, what became of Mr. Seabrook."

"I saw his death in a Nevada paper, only a few days ago. He died old, poor and alone, or so the account ran, in a cabin among the mountains. 'The mills of the gods,' etc., you know?"

"Then I am not to see Mr. Greyfield?"

"O yes; if you will stay until Mr. —— comes from Portland. I shall be glad of your presence on that occasion. Mr. Greyfield, you must understand, is under orders to keep out of the way until that time arrives. You can be of service to me, if you will stay."

I staid and saw them off to Europe, then went on my way to Lake Tahoe, to meet other friends; but I have a promise from this strangely re-united couple, to spend a summer in Oregon, when they return from their trans-Atlantic tour; at which time I hope to be able to remove from Mrs. Greyfield's mind the painful impression derived from her former acquaintance with the city of my adoption.

A CURIOUS INTERVIEW.

VANCOUVER'S Island furnishes some of the finest scenery on the Pacific Coast; not grandest, perhaps, but quietly charming. Its shores are indented every here and there with the loveliest of bays and sounds, forming the most exquisite little harbors to be found anywhere in the world. The climate of the Island, especially its summer climate, is delightful. Such bright, bracing airs as come from the sea on one side, and from the snow-capped mountains of the mainland on the other, are seldom met with on either hemisphere. Given a July day, a pleasant companion or two in a crank little boat, whose oars we use to make silvery interludes in our talk, and I should not envy your sailor on the Bosphorus.

On such a July day as I am hinting at, our party had idled away the morning, splashing our way indolently through the blue waters of Nittinat Sound, the mountains towering behind us, the open sea not far off; but all around us a shore so emerald green and touched with bits of color, so gracefully, picturesquely wild, that not, in all its unrestraint, was there an atom of savagery to be subdued in the interest of pure beauty. It was a wilderness not wild, a solitude not solitary; but rather populous with happy fancies, born of all harmonious influences of earth, air and water; of sunlight, shadow, color and fragrance.

> "My soul to-day is far away,
> Sailing a sunny tropic bay,"

Sang Charlie, bursting with poetry. The next moment "Hallo! boat ahoy!" and into the scene in which just now we had been the only life, slipped from some hidden inlet, an Indian canoe.

"Isn't she a beauty, though?" said Charlie, laying on his oar. "Fourteen paddles; slim, crank, and what a curious figure-head! By George, that's a pretty sight!"

And a pretty sight it was, as the canoe, with its red and blue-blanketed oarsmen, was propelled swiftly through the water, and quickly brought alongside; when we had opportunity to observe that the crew were all stalwart young fellows, with rather fine, grand features, that looked as if they might have been cut in bronze, so immobile and fixed were they. Their dress was the modern dress of the Northern Indians, supplied by the Hudson's Bay Company, of bright colors and fine texture. But what most engaged our attention was the figure of the fifteenth occupant of the canoe, who acted as steersman. He was evidently a very old man, and instead of being dressed in blankets, had on a mantle of woven rushes, and leggins of wolf-skin. A quiver full of arrows hung at his back; his bow rested on his knees. On his grizzled head was a tall, pointed and gaily painted hat, made of braided grasses, which completely resembled a mammoth extinguisher. As the canoe shot past us, I imagined that I detected an expression of contempt upon the old man's face, though he never moved nor spoke, nor in any way evinced any interest in us.

"Eheu! what a funny-looking old cove," said Charlie, gazing after the canoe, "I should like to cultivate his acquaintance."

"Well, you have the opportunity," rejoined Fanny, the third member of our party. "They are going to land on that point just ahead of us."

We were all watching them, fascinated by the noiseless dexterity of their movements, when suddenly there was nothing to be seen of either boat or crew.

"Where the deuce have they gone to?" asked Charlie, staring at the vacant spot where the canoe had disappeared.

"Great heavens!" cried Fanny, who, like her brother,

6

used a very exclamatory style of speech; "why, they have all vanished into thin air!"

As I could not contradict this assertion, I proposed that we should follow, and examine into the mystery; but Fanny cried out, "O, for goodness' sake, don't! I'm afraid. If they have the power to make themselves invisible, they may be hiding to do us harm."

"It is only visible harm that I'm afraid of," answered Charlie, with his eyes still fixed wonderingly on the point of space where they had so lately been; "pull fast, Pierre, let us find out what the rascals are up to."

Thus urged, I threw what force I could into my oar-stroke (for I was but a convalescent), and very soon we came to the long sloping point of mossy rocks where we had expected to see the canoe's passengers land. I own that I approached it with some caution, thinking it possible that a whirlpool might have sucked the boat and its freight of fifteen lives out of sight, in some point of time when our eyes were for an instant averted. But the water was perfectly quiet, and the whole place, both on water and on land, silent, sunny, and not in the least uncanny or alarming. We dropped our oars and gazed at each other in amazement.

"Well, if that don't beat the Dutch!" was Charlie's comment; and I fancied that his brown cheek grew a shade less ruddy than usual. As for Fanny, she was in a fright, paling and shrinking as if from some terrible real and visible danger; and when I proposed to land and investigate the mystery, fairly mustered quite a copious shower of tears with which to melt my resolve.

"O, Pierre—Mr. Blanchett, I mean—oh, please don't go ashore. I am sure either that these dreadful savages are lurking here to destroy us, or that we have been deceived by some wicked conjuror. Oh, I am *so* frightened!"

"My dear Miss Lane," I answered, "I give you my word no harm shall come to you. Shall we let a lot of blanketed savages perform a conjurer's trick right before our faces that we do not attempt to have explained? By no means. If you are too nervous to come ashore with us, Charlie may stay with you in the boat, and I will go by myself to look into this matter." Whereupon Fanny gave me so reproachful a look out of her great brown eyes that I quailed beneath it.

"Do you think Charlie and I would leave you to go into danger alone? No, indeed; if you *will* be so rash, we will accompany you; and if *die* we must, we will all die together." That last appeal being made with a very touching quaver of a very melodious voice.

For answer, I assisted her out of the boat, which Charlie was already fastening by the chain to some bushes near the bit of beach; and tucking the little gloved hand under my arm, seized an opportunity to whisper something not particularly relevant to this story.

The boat being secured, we climbed a short distance up the rocky bank, stopping to gather wild roses and mock-orange blossoms, which, in spite of her alarm, engaged Miss Lane's attention to such an extent that Charlie had gotten fairly out of sight before we missed him. But as we turned to follow, he confronted us with a face expressive of a droll kind of perplexity.

"Not a red rascal in sight," said he, glancing back over his shoulder, "except that queer old cove that was sitting in the stern. *He's* just over there," jerking his head in the direction meant, "sitting on his haunches like an Egyptian idol, and about as motionless, and about as ancient."

"But their canoe," I said, "what could they have done with their canoe? It is not in the water, and there is no sign here of their having dragged it ashore."

"They didn't land, not in the regular way, I mean, for I was watching for them every instant; and how that old chap got there, and how that canoe got out of sight so quick, is too hard a nut for me to crack, I confess."

"Let us not go near the dreadful old thing," pleaded Fanny once more, her alarm returning.

Again I proposed to her to stay in the boat with Charlie, which had the effect, as before, to determine her upon going with us; which determination I strengthened by an encouraging pressure of the little gloved hand in my possession; and without waiting for further alarms pressed on at once, with Charlie for guide, to the spot where the "dreadful old thing" was understood to be.

And there, sure enough, he was, squatting on the ground beside a spring, where grew a thicket of willows and wild roses; alone and silent, evidently watching, if not waiting, for our approach.

"What will you say to him?" asked Fanny, as we came quite near, eyeing the singular object with evident dread.

"We'll ask him if he is hungry," said Charlie lightly. "If he is a live Indian he is sure to say 'yes' to that proposition; and Charlie actually produced from his pockets some sandwiches, in a slightly damaged condition. Holding these before him, very much as one holds an ear of corn to a frisky colt he wishes to catch, he approached near enough to offer them, Fanny still holding me back just enough to let this advance be made before we came up. To her great relief the mummy put out a skinny hand, and snatched the offered provisions under its robe.

"You see he is only a poor starving old Indian," I said.

"Me no poor—no starve; me big chief," retorted the old man, glancing disdainfully at us, with eyes that now appeared bright.

I exchanged telegraphic communication with Charlie and Fanny, seated her comfortably upon a mossy boulder, and threw myself at her feet, while Charlie disposed of himself also, within conversational distance.

"May I ask what is your name?" I inquired, insinuatingly.

"My name is Nittinat—this is my country; this water is mine; this earth, these stones—all mine that you see."

" Such a great chief must have many warriors—many people. I do not see any. Were those your people that I saw in the canoe ?"

"Nittinat's people all gone," answered the old man sadly, dropping his chin upon his rush-clad breast.

" But we saw a canoe with fourteen warriors in it, besides yourself," Charlie eagerly asserted. " Where are those young men ?"

" Me great medicine man; make see canoe—make see young men," responded the owner of the place, with a wan yet superior sort of smile.

Charlie glanced at us, then asked quite deferentially, " Can you make us see what is not here ?"

" You have seen," was the brief reply.

"Ask him why we are thus favored," whispered Fanny.

" This young cloochman (you see I must talk to him in his own tongue, Fanny), wishes to know why you opened our eyes to your great medicine."

" White man come to Nittinat's land, white man see Nittinat's power. White man ask questions !"—this last contemptuously, at which Fanny laughed, as asking questions was one of her reserved rights.

" You must be an old man, since these waters are named after you," suggested I. " Who was the first white man you remember seeing?"

" *Hyas tyee*, Cappen Cook. Big ship — big guns !" answered Nittinat, warming with the recollection.

" This is a good lead," remarked Charlie, *sotto voce;* " follow it up, Pierre."

" You were a child then? very little?" making a movement with my hand to indicate a child's stature.

" Me a chief—many warriors—big chief. Ugh !" said the mummy, with kindling eyes.

At this barefaced story, Charlie made a grimace, while he commented in an undertone: " But it is ninety-six years since Captain Cook visited this coast. How the old humbug lies."

At this whispered imputation upon his honor, the old chief regarded us scornfully; though how such a parchment countenance could be made to express anything excited my wonder.

"Me no lie. Nittinat's heart big. Nittinat's heart good. *Close tum-tum*, ugh!"

"White man's eyes are closed—his heart is darkened," said I, adopting what I considered to be a conciliatory style of speech. My friend cannot understand how you could have known Captain Cook so long ago. All the white men who knew the great white chief have gone to their fathers."

"Ugh, all same as Cappen Cook. He no believe my cousin Wiccanish see big Spanish ship 'fore he came."

"How did he make him see it at last?" asked Charlie, stretching himself out on the grass, and covering his eyes with his hat, from under the brim of which he shot quizzical glances at Fanny and I.

"Wiccanish showed Cook these," replied Nittinat, drawing from beneath his robe a necklake of shells, to which two silver spoons were attached, of a peculiar pattern, and much battered and worn.

"Oh, do let me see them," cried Fanny, whose passion for relics was quickly aroused. Charlie, too, was constrained to abandon his lazy attitude for a moment to examine such a curiosity as these quaint old spoons.

"Only to think that they are more than a hundred years old! But I cannot make out the lettering upon them; perhaps he is deceiving us after all," said Fanny, passing them to me for inspection.

I took out of my pocket a small magnifying-glass, which, although it could not restore what was worn away, brought to light all that was left of an inscription, probably the manufacturer's trade-mark, the only legible part of which was 17-0.

"Did the Spanish captain give these to your cousin?" I asked.

"Ugh!" responded Nattinat, nodding his tall extinguisher. "Wiccanish go on board big ship, see cappen."

"And stole the spoons," murmured Charlie from under his hat.

Fanny touched his foot with the stick of her parasol, for she stood in awe of this ancient historian, not wishing to to be made a subject of his powerful "medicine."

"And so you knew Captain Cook?" I repeated, when the spoons were hidden once more under the mantle of rushes, "and other white men too, I suppose. Did your people and the white people always keep on friendly terms?"

"Me have good heart," answered Nittinat rather sadly. "Me and my cousins Wiccanish, Clyoquot, Maquinna, and Tatoocheatticus, we like heap sell our furs, and get knives, beads, and brass buttons. Heap like nails, chisels, and such things. If my young men sometimes stole very little things, Nittinat's heart was not little. He made the white chiefs welcome to wood and water; he gave them his women; and sometime make a big feast—kill two, three, six slaves. White chief heap mean to make trouble about a few chains or hammers after all that!"

"Oh, the horrid wretch!" whispered Fanny: "Does he say he killed half a dozen slaves for amusement?"

"If he did, Miss Lane," I answered; "was it worse than the elegant Romans used to do? The times and the manners have to be considered, you know."

Fanny shuddered, but said nothing, and I went on addressing myself to Nittinat:

"How many ships did you ever see in these waters at one time?—I mean long ago, in Captain Cook's time?"

The old chief held up five fingers, for answer.

"And you and your cousins were friendly to all of them?"

"Maquinna's heart good, too,—*close tum-tum.* Sell land to one Cappen; he go 'way. Sell land to other Cappen; he go 'way, too. Bime-by two Cappens come back, quarrel 'bout the land. Maquinna no say anything. When one Cappen ask: ' Is the land mine?' Maquinna tell him ' yes.' When other Cappen ask: 'Is the land mine?' Maquinna tell him 'yes,' too, all same. O yes; Indian have good heart; no want to fight great white chief with big guns. He stay in his lodge, and laugh softly to himself, and let the white chiefs fight 'bout the land. Ugh!"

"The mercenary old diplomat!" muttered Charlie, under his hat. "Here's your 'noble savage,' Fanny. Burn a little incense, can't you?" But Fanny preferred remaining silent to answering her brother's bantering remarks; and if she was burning incense at all, I had reason to think it was to one who shall be nameless.

"Did you always have skins to sell to so many vessels?" I asked, returning to the subject of the trading vessels.

" Long ago had plenty; bime-by not many. White chief he heap mean. Skin not good, throw 'em back to Indian. My young men take 'em ashore, stretch tail long like sea-otter, fix 'em up nice; give 'em to other Indian, tell him go sell 'em. All right. Cappen buy 'em next time; pay good price; like 'em heap;" at which recollection the mummy actually laughed.

"How is that for Yankee shrewdness?" asked a muffled voice under a hat; to which, however, I paid no attention.

" You speak of the white chiefs fighting about land. Did they ever use their big guns on each other? Tell me what you remember about the white men who came here in ships, long ago."

"After Cappen Cook go 'way, long time, come Spanish ship, King George ship, Boston ship. Spanish Cappen no like King George Cappen. One day fight with long knives; (swords) and Spanish Cappen put King George man in big ship; send him 'way off. Many ships came and went; sold many skins. One time all go 'way but the Boston ships. Bime-by King George's ships came back and fight the Boston's."

"And you kept your good heart all the time? Never killed the Bostons or King George men?"

At this interrogation, Nittinat shuffled his withered limbs uneasily beneath his rush mantle, and averted his parchment countenance. Upon my pressing the question, as delicately as I knew how, he at length recovered his immobility, and answered in a plausible tone enough:

"Boston Cappen Gray, he build a fort at Clyoquot. My cousin Wiccanish sell him the ground, and Cappen Gray bring all his goods from the ship, and put them in the fort for winter. Our young men were lazy, and had not many skins to sell; but they wanted Cappen Gray's goods; they liked the firewater a heap. So the young men they say, 'kill Cappen Gray, and take his goods.' My cousin say, 'no; that a heap bad.' Nittinat say that bad too. But we tell our young men if they *will* do this bad thing, we will not leave them without a chief to direct them. So my young men came to Clyoquot to help their cousins take the big guns of the fort. But Cappen Gray find all out in time to save our young men from doing wrong. We tell him our hearts all good. He give us presents, make *close tum-tum*. No use kill Boston *tyee* when he give us what we want."

Charlie tilted up his sombrero, and shot an approving glance at the venerable philosopher that caused a smile to ripple Fanny's face at the instant she was saying, "The horrid wretch!" with feminine vehemence. To cover this by-play, I asked if Nittinat remembered the *Tonquin*.

"Oh, come!" ejaculated Charlie, starting up, "I say we have had enough of this artless historian's prattle; don't you?"

"Consider," I urged, "how rare the opportunity of verifying tradition. Compose yourself, my friend, while I continue my interviewing. Turning to Nittinat I asked: "Why did the Indians destroy Captain Thorn's vessel?"

"Cappen Thorn big chief; no like Indian; big voice; no

give presents; no let Indian come on board without leave;
Indian no like Cappen Thorn. He get mad at my cousin
Kasiascall for hiding on his ship; keep him all night prisoner, cause he no punish his young men for cutting the
boarding-netting. Kasiascall get mad. Next day no Indian go to trade with the ship; then Cappen Thorn he send
McKay ashore to say he is sorry, and talk to Indian 'bout
trade.

"Indian very good to McKay; say not mad; say come
next day to trade plenty. Kasiascall, too, tell McKay all
right; come trade all same. But McKay he look dark; he
no believe my cousin; think Indian lie. All same he tell
come to-morrow; and he shake hands, and go back to ship.
He tell Cappen Thorn, 'Indian say he trade to-morrow.'
Big Cappen walk the deck very proud. He say he 'teach
the damned Indians to behave themselves.'

"Next day six white men come ashore to visit our lodges.
My cousin treat white men well. Kasiascall and his young
men go to the ship to trade. Pretty soon Kasiascall come
back: say McKay look dark and sad; say Indian buy plenty
of knives and hide under their blankets; say I will see the
ship taken by the Indians in one hour. My heart was sad
for McKay. He good man. Indian like McKay heap.
But my cousin and his people want plenty goods; no like
Cappen Thorn; so Nittinat say nothing.

"Bimeby there was big noise like a hundred guns, and
the ship was all in pieces, flying through the air like leaves
on the wind. My cousin's people were all in pieces too;
one arm, one leg, one piece head. Ugh!"

"Served them right, too!" ejaculated Charlie. "Is that
the whole story, old mortality?"

But Nittinat was silent—overcome, as it seemed by these
sad reminiscences. He bowed his head upon his breast
until the extinguisher pointed directly at Fanny's nose, as
her brother mischievously made her aware. When I
thought that Nittinat had taken time to sufficiently regret

his cousin's misfortune in losing so many young men, I gently reminded him of Charlie's question.

"Kasiascall's heart was very little when he saw the destruction of his warriors, and heard the wailing of the women and children. To comfort him the six white men were taken and bound for slaves. When the days of mourning were past, my cousin laid the six white slaves in a row, their throats resting on the sharp edge of a rock, and set his Indian slaves to saw off their heads with a cedar plank. It was a very fine sight; our hearts were good; we were comforted."

As no one uttered an opposing sentiment, Nittinat, after a pause, continued:

"For many moons we feared the Bostons down on the Columbia would come to make war on us; and we went no more to trade with any ships. But after a time Kasiascall's heart grew big within him. He asked my advice. I said 'you are my brother. Go kill all the whites on the Columbia.' Then we danced the medicine dance; and Kasiascall went alone to the country of the Chinooks, to the fort of the Boston men. He told the chief of the Bostons how the *Tonquin* was destroyed, with all on board; but he kept a dark place in his heart, and his tongue was crooked. He said Kasiascall knew not of the treachery of his relations, and people, and he said nothing of the six white slaves. Then the Boston chief gave him presents, and he staid many days at the fort, until he heard that some Indians from Sooke were coming there. Fearing the Sooke Indians might have straight tongues, Kasiascall left the fort that day, and went among the Klatskenines, and stirred them up to take the fort and kill all the Bostons. But the chief discovered the plot, and my cousin fled back to Neweeta. Ugh?"

These events occurred a long time ago," I suggested. "Your hearts were dark then, but surely you have a better heart now. You would not kill the whites to-day if you could?"

A very expressive "Ugh!" was the only rejoinder.

"But the Indians I see about here look very comfortable and happy. They have good warm blankets, and enough to eat."

"Indian hunt furs to pay for blanket; Indian catch fish for eat. Bime-by furs grow scarce; white man catch fish, too. Bime-by Hudson Bay men go way; Indian go naked. Then come black-gowns (priests, or preachers). He say, 'Indian pray for what he want.' But that all d—d lie; pray one moon—two, three moons, nothing comes. White man say to Indian, 'work.' What can Indian do? Indian big fool—know nothing."

"He is making out a case," said Charlie; "but he don't look as if *he* need concern himself about the future."

"Ask him if he ever saw any white ladies, in that long ago time he has been telling us of," whispered Fanny, who could not muster courage to address the manikin directly. I considered how best to put the desired question, but Nittinat was beforehand with me.

"I have seen many things with my eyes. First came the big ships, with wings; and only men came in them. By and by came a long, black ship, without sails, or oars, but with a great black and white smoke. I went on board this vessel with one of my wives, the youngest and prettiest; and here I saw the first white woman that came to my country. I liked the white woman, and asked her to be my wife. She laughed, and said, 'go ask the Cappen.' I asked the Cappen, but he would not hear. I offered him many skins, and my new wife. He swore at me. I am sworn at and laughed at for wanting wife with a white skin. White man take Indian wife when he please. Nittinat has many wrongs; yet Nittinat has good heart, all same. Bime-by big medicine-man come and make all right. White man all melt away like snow on the mountain-side. Indian have plenty house, plenty blankets, plenty eat—all, everything, all the time. Good!"

" White wives included, I presume. Well," said Charlie, " I think this interview might be brought to a close. Hold fast to Pierre and I, Fanny, or the wizard may spirit you off to his wigwam, to inaugurate the good time coming that he speaks of."

So saying, Charlie rose to his feet, stretched his limbs lazily, and turned to disengage his sister's veil from a vicious thorn-bush in our way. Not succeeding immediately, I lent my assistance, and the delicate tissue being at last rescued with some care, turned to say farewell to the chief of all the Nittinats, when lo! I addressed myself to space.

" The old cove has taken himself off as mysteriously as he came. That is a confounded good trick; could'nt do it better myself. Does anybody miss anything?" was Charlie's running comment on the transaction.

" Can't say that I do, unless it is my luncheon. I'm ravenously hungry, and every sandwich gone. Could that dreadful old ghoul have eaten those you gave him, Charlie? Do you know, I could'nt help thinking he must be a ghost?"

" Well, the ghost of an Indian could eat, steal, and beg, I should think. I felt like rattling his dry bones, when he so coolly confessed to the most atrocious murders of white men."

" That is because you are not an Indian, I presume," said I, with a heavy sense of conviction about what I gave expression to. " Indian virtue is not white men's virtue, If it won you rank, and riches, and power, to become a mighty slayer, a slayer you would undoubtedly become. A man, even an Indian, is what his circumstances make him. The only way I can conceive to make a first-class man, is to place him under first-class influences. I am generalizing now, of course; the exceptions are rare enough to prove the rule."

" I wish I had those spoons," said Fanny, " they would be such a curiosity at home."

" The spoon I wish for is one of the vessel's forks, with a bit of roast beef on it. Here, Sis, jump in; we shall be late for dinner, and the Captain will call us to account."

In a few moments we were out of the little cove, and in open water of the sound, pulling back toward the harbor, where the steamer was lying that had brought us this summer excursion. As we came abreast of a certain inlet. Fanny cried out, "Look there!" and turning our eyes in the direction of her glance, we saw the canoe with its bronzed crew just disappearing up the narrow entrance, half-hidden in shrubbery.

Our adventure was related at dinner in the steamer's cabin, and various were the conjectures regarding the identity of Chief Nittinat. The captain declared his ignorance of any such personage. Most of the party were inclined to regard the whole affair as a practical joke, though who could have been the authors of it no one ventured to say. It was proposed that another party should repeat the excursion on the following day, in order that another opportunity might be given the mysterious medicine man to put in an appearance. And this, I believe, really was carried into effect, but without result, so far as solving the mystery was concerned. A canoe, similar to the one we had seen, had been discovered up one of the numerous arms of the Sound, but on attempting to overtake it, the pursuing party had been easily distanced, and the clue lost, so that all hope of clearing up the mystery was relinquished.

One evening, shortly after, Fanny and I sat together in the soft, clear moonlight, listening to the dance-music in the cabin, and the gentle splash of the waters about the vessel's keel. All at once, a canoe-load of Nootkans shot across the moon's wake, not fifty yards from our anchorage, and as suddenly was lost again in shadow. "Fanny," I said, " being the only invalid of this party, I feel a good deal nervous about these apparitions. They are usually regarded, I believe, as portentious. Without designing to take advantage of your too sympathizing disposition, I am tempted to remind you that if I am ever to have the happiness of calling your precious self truly my own, it ought to be before the third appearance of the ghostly presence; will you condescend to name the day?"

"I should prefer, Pierre, not to have any ghostly influences brought to bear on this occasion. Suppose we try a valse, which I think will tend to dissipate your melancholy forebodings."

I may as well own it here: the little witch could not be brought to make any final arrangements, although I did entreat her seriously.

"You must talk about these things when I am at home with my papa and mamma," she insisted; and I was compelled to respect her decision.

But we have been married almost a year, and we often refer to the strange interview we had with Chief Nittinat. Perhaps the Smoke-eller doctrine now popular among the northern Indians, and which corresponds to our spiritualism, may have some foundation in similar occurrences themselves. Who knows but Nittinat was talking to us through a medium?

MR. ELA'S STORY.

THREE or four years ago, my husband and I were making a winter voyage up the Oregon coast. The weather was not peculiarly bad: it was the ordinary winter weather, with a quartering wind, giving the ship an awkward motion over an obliquely-rolling sea. Cold, sick, thoroughly uncomfortable, with no refuge but the narrow and dimly-lighted state-room, I was reduced in the first twenty-four hours to a condition of ignominious helplessness, hardly willing to live, and not yet fully wishing or intending to die.

In this unhappy frame of mind the close of the second weary day found me, when my husband opened our state-room door to say that Mr. Ela, of ——, Oregon, was on board, and proposed to come and talk to me, in the hope of amusing me and making me forget my wretchedness. Submitting rather than agreeing to the proposal, chairs were brought and placed just inside the door-way, where the light of the saloon·lamps shown athwart the countenance of my self-constituted physician. He was a young man, and looked younger than his years; slightly built, though possessing a supple, well-knit frame, with hands of an elegant shape, fine texture, and great expression. You saw at a glance that he had a poet's head, and a poet's sensitiveness of face; but it was only after observation that you saw how much the face was capable of which it did not convey, for faces are apt to indicate not so much individual culture as the culture of those with whom we are habitually associated. Mr. Ela's face clearly indicated to me the intellectual poverty, the want of æsthetic cultivation in his accustomed circle of society, at the same time that it suggested possible phases of great beauty, should it ever become possible for certain emotions to be habitually called to the surface by sympathy. Evidently a vein of drollery in his nature had been better appreciated, and oftener exhibited to admiring audiences, than any of the finer qualities of thought or sentiment of which you instinctively knew him to be capable; and yet the face protested against it, too, by a gentle irony with a hint of self-scorn in it, as if its owner, in his own estimation, wrote himself a buffoon for his condescension. Altogether it was a good face; but one to make you wish it were better, since by not being so, it was untrue to itself. I remember thinking all this, looking out with sluggish interest from my berth, while the two gentlemen did a little preliminary talking.

Mr. Ela's voice, I observed, like his face, was susceptible of great change and infinite modulations. Deep chest tones were followed by finely attenuated sounds; droning nasal tones, by quick and clear ones. The quality of the voice was soft and musical; the enunciation slow, often emphatic. His manner was illustrative, egotistic, and keenly watchful of effects.

''You never heard the story of my adventure in the mountains?'' Ela began, turning to me with the air of a man who had made up his mind to tell his story.

'' No; please tell it.''

'' Well''—running his tapering fingers through his hair and pulling it over his forehead—'' I started out in life with a theory, and it was this: that no young man should ask a woman to marry him until he had prepared a home for her. Correct, wasn't it? I was about nineteen years old when I took up some land down in the Rogue River Valley, and worked away at it with this object.''

''Had you really a wife selected at that age?''

'' No; but it was the fashion in early times in that country to marry early, and I was getting ready, according to my theory; don't you see? I was pretty successful, too; had considerable stock, built me a house, made a flower

7

garden for my wife, even put up the pegs or nails she was to hang her dresses on. I intended that fall to get on my horse, ride through the Wallamet Valley, and find me my girl."

At the notion of courting in that off-hand, general style, both my husband and I laughed doubtingly. Ela laughed, too, but as if the recollection pleased him.

"You think that is strange, do you? 'Twasn't so very strange in those days, because girls were scarce, don't you see? There was not a girl within forty miles of me; and just the thought of one now, as I was fixing those nails to hang her garments on; why, it ran just through me like a shock of electricity!

"Well, as I said, I had about two hundred and fifty head of cattle, a house with a garden, a young orchard, and vegetables growing; everything in readiness for the wife I had counted on getting to help me take care of it. And what do you think happened? There came such a plague of grasshoppers upon the valley that they destroyed every green thing: crops, orchard, flowers, grass, everything! My stock died, the greater portion of them, and *I was ruined.*" (Deep bass.) "I considered myself disappointed in love, too, because, though I hadn't yet found my girl, I knew she was somewhere in the valley waiting for me; and I felt somehow, when the grasshoppers ate up every thing, as if I had been jilted. Actually, it pierces me with a pang now to think of those useless pegs on which so often my imagination hung a pink calico dress and a girl's sun-bonnet."

Knitting his brows, and sighing as he shifted his position, Ela once more pulled the hair over his forehead, in his peculiar fashion, and went on:

"I became misanthropic; felt myself badly used. Packing up my books and a few other traps, I started for the mountains with what stock I had left, built myself a fort, and played hermit."

"A regular fort?"

"A stockade eighteen feet high, with an embankment four feet high around it, a strong gate, a tent in the middle of the inclosure, all my property, such as books, feed, arms, etc., inside."

"On account of Indians?"

"Indians and White Men. Yes, I've seen a good many Indians through the bead of my rifle. They learned to keep away from my fort. There were mining camps down in the valley, and you know the hangers-on of those camps? I sold beef to the miners; had plenty of money by me sometimes. It was necessary to be strongly forted."

"What a strange life for a boy! What did you do? How spend your time?"

"I herded my cattle, drove them to market, cooked, studied, wrote, and indulged in misanthropy, with a little rifle practice. By the time I had been one summer in the mountains, I had got my hand in, and knew how to make money buying up cattle to sell again in the mines."

"So there was method in your madness—misanthropy, I mean?"

"Well, a man cannot resign life before he is twenty-one. I was doing well, and beginning to think again of visiting the Wallamet to hunt up my girl. One Sunday afternoon, I knew it was Sunday, because I kept a journal; I was sitting outside of my fort writing, when a shadow fell across the paper, and, looking up, lo! a skeleton figure stood before me." (Sepulchral tones, and a pause.) "Used as I was to lonely encounters with strange men, my hair stood on end as I gazed on the spectre before me. He was the merest boy in years; pretty and delicate by nature, and then reduced by starvation to a shadow. His story was soon told. He had left Boston on a vessel coming out to the northwest coast, had been wrecked at the mouth of the Umpqua, and been wandering about in the mountains ever since, subsisting as best he could on roots and berries. But you are becoming tired?"

"No, I assure you; on the contrary, growing deeply interested."

"The boy was not a young woman in disguise, or anything like that, you know"—with an amused look at me. "I thought you'd think so; but as he comes into the story as a collateral, I just mention his introduction to myself. I fed him and nursed him until he was able to go to work, and then I got Sam Chong Lung to let him take up a claim alongside a Chinese camp, promising to favor the Chinaman in a beef contract if he was good to the boy. His claim proved a good one, and he was making money, when two Chinamen stole a lot of horses from Sam Chong Lung, and he offered four hundred dollars to Edwards if he would go after them and bring them back. Edwards asked my advice, and I encouraged him to go, telling him how to take and bring back his prisoners." (Reflective pause.) "You can't imagine me living alone, now, can you? Such an egotistical fellow as I am, and fond of ladies' society. You can't believe it, can you?"

"Hermits and solitaires are always egotists, I believe. As to the ladies, your loneliness was the result of circumstances, as you have explained."

"Well, I should have missed Edwards a good deal, if it had not been for some singular *incidents* which happened during his absence." Ela always accented the last syllable of any word ending in e-n-t, like "incident" or "commencement," giving it besides a peculiar nasal sound, which was sure to secure the attention. The word incident, as he pronounced it, produced quite a different effect from the same word spoken in the usual style.

"A man came to my fort one day who was naked and starving. He was a bad-looking fellow; but a man naturally does look bad when his clothes are in rags, and his bones protruding through his skin. I clothed him, fed him, cared for him kindly, until he was able to travel, and then he went away. The next Sunday, I was sitting outside the stockade, as customary, reading some translations of the Greek poets, when, on raising my eyes from the book to glance over the approach to my fort—I was always on the alert—I beheld a VISION. Remember, I had not seen a woman for a year and half! She was slowly advancing, riding with superb grace a horse of great beauty and value, richly caparisoned. She came slowly up the trail, as if to give me time for thought, and I needed it. That picture is still indelibly impressed upon my mind; the very flicker of the sunlight and shadow across the road, and the glitter of her horse's trappings, as he champed his bit and arched his neck with impatience at her restraining hand——. Are you very tired?" asked Ela, suddenly.

"Never less so in my life; pray go on."

"You see I had been alone so long, and I am very susceptible. That vision coming upon me suddenly as it did, in my solitude, gave me the strangest sensations I ever had. I was spell-bound. Not so she. Reining in her horse beside me, she squared around in her saddle, as if asking assistance to dismount. Struggling with my embarrassment, I helped her down, and she accepted my invitation into the fort, signifying, at the same time, that she wished me to attend to stripping and feeding her horse. This gave us mutually an opportunity to prepare for the coming interview.

"When I returned to my guest, she had laid aside her riding-habit and close sun-bonnet, and stood revealed a young, beautiful, elegantly-dressed woman. To my unaccustomed eyes, she looked a goddess. Her figure was noble; her eyes large, black, and melting; her hair long and curling; her manner easy and attractive. She was hungry, she said; would I give her something to eat? And, while I was on hospitable cares intent, she read to me some of my Greek poems, especially an ode of one of the votaries of Diana, with comments by herself. She was a splendid reader. Well," said Ela, slowly, with a furtive glance at me, and in his peculiar nasal tones, "you can guess whether a young man, used to the mountains, as I was, and who had been disappointed and jilted as I had been, enjoyed this sort of thing or not. It wasn't in my line, you see, this entertaining goddesses; though, doubtless, in this way, before now, men have entertained angels unawares. You shall judge whether I did.

"What with reading, eating together, singing—she sang 'Kate Kearney' for me, and her voice was glorious—our acquaintance ripened very fast. Finally, I conquered my embarrassment so far as to ask her some questions about herself, and she told me that she was of a good New England family, raised in affluence, well educated, accomplished, but by a freak of fortune, reduced to poverty: that she had come to California resolved to get money, and had got it. She went from camp to camp of the miners with stationery, and other trifling articles needed by them; sold them these things, wrote letters for them, sang to them, nursed them when sick, or carried letters express to San Francisco, to be mailed. For all these services, she received high prices, and had also had a good deal of gold given to her in specimens. I asked her if she liked that kind of a life, so contrary to her early training. She answered me: 'It's not what we choose that we select to do in this world, but what chooses us to do it. I have made a competency, and gained a rich and varied experience. If life is not what I once dreamed it was, I am content.' But she sighed as she said it, and I couldn't believe in her content."

"You have not told us yet what motives brought her to you," I remarked, in an interval of silence.

"No; she hadn't told me herself, then. By and by, I asked her, in my green kind of way, what brought her to see *me*. I never shall forget the smile with which she turned to answer me. We were sitting quite close: it never was in my nature, when once acquainted with a

woman, to keep away from her. Her garments brushed my
knees; occasionally, in the enthusiasm of talk, I leaned
near her cheek. You know how it was. I was thinking of
the useless pegs in my house down in the valley: 'You
will be disappointed,' she said, 'when you learn that I
came to do you a real service.' And then she went on to
relate that, having occasion to pass the night at a certain
place not many miles away, she had overheard through the
thin partitions of the house, the description of my fort, an
account of my wealth, real or supposed, and a plan for my
murder and robbery. The would-be murderer was so described as to make it quite certain that it was he whom I
had fed, clothed, and sent away rejoicing, only a few days
previous. I was inclined to treat the matter as a jest; but
she awed me into belief and humility at once by the majesty with which she reproved my unbelief: 'A *woman* does
not trifle with subjects like this; nor go out of her way to
tell travelers tales. I warn you. Good bye.'

"After this she would not stay, though I awkwardly expressed my regret at her going. By her command I sad-
dled her horse, and helped her mount him. Once in the
saddle, her humor turned, and she reminded me that I had
not invited her to return. She said she 'could fancy that
a week of reading, talking, riding, trout-fishing, and ro-
mancing generally, up there in those splendid woods,
might be very charming. Was I going to ask her to
come?'

"I didn't ask her. A young man with a reputation to
sustain up there in the mountains, couldn't invite a young
lady to come and stop a week with him, could he? I must
have refused to invite her, now, mustn't I?"

The perfect ingenuousness with which Ela put these
questions, and the plaintive appeal against the hard requirements of social laws in the mountains, which was
expressed in his voice and accent, were so indescribably
ludicrous that both my husband and myself laughed con-

vulsively. "I never tell my wife that part of the story, for fear she might not believe in my regard for appearances, knowing how fond I am of ladies' society. And the struggle *was* great; I assure you, it was *great.*

"So she went away. As she rode slowly down the trail, she turned and kissed her hand to me, with a gesture of such grace and sweetness that I thrilled all over. I've never been able to quite forgive myself for what happened afterward. *She came back, and I drove her away!* Usually, when I tell that to women, they call me mean and ungrateful; but a young man living alone in the mountains has his reputation to look after—now, hasn't he? That's what I ought to have done—now, wasn't it—what I always say I did do. It was the right thing to do under the circumstances, wasn't it?"

While we had our laugh out, Ela shifted position, shook himself, and thridded his soft, light hair with his slender fingers. He was satisfied with his success in conveying an impression of the sort of care he took of his reputation. "Now, then, I was left alone again, in no pleasant frame of mind. I couldn't doubt what my beautiful visitant had told me, and the thought of my murder all planned out was depressing, to say the least of it. But, as sure as I am telling you, the departure of my unknown friend depressed me more than the thought of my possible murder. The gate barred for the night, I sat and looked into my fire for hours, thinking wild thoughts, and hugging to my lonely bosom an imaginary form. The solitude and the sense of loss were awful.

"This was Sunday night. Tuesday morning I received a visit from three or four mounted men, one of whom was my former naked and hungry *protege.* He did not now try to conceal his character from me, but said he was going down to clean out the Chinese camp, and proposed to me to join him, saying that when Edwards returned with the horses we would pay him the $400, as agreed by Sam Chong Lung.

I was on my guard; but told him I would have nothing to do with robbing the Chinese; that they were my friends and customers, and he had better let them alone; after which answer he went off. That afternoon, Edwards came in with his prisoners and horses. He was very tired, on account of having traveled at night, to prevent the rescue of his prisoners by other vagabonds, and to avoid the Indians.

"You will understand how the presence of the horses increased my peril, as there was no doubt the scoundrels meant to take them. It wouldn't do either to let Edwards go on to the Chinese camp; so I persuaded him to wait another day. We brought the prisoners, bound, inside the fort, and took care of the horses. I said nothing to Edwards of my suspicions.

"About dusk, my expected visitor came. He appeared to have been drinking; and, after some mumbling talk, laid down inside the fort, near the gate. I made the gate fast, driving the big wooden pins home with an axe; built up a great fire, and sent Edwards to bed in the tent. The Chinese prisoners were already asleep on the ground. Then I sat down on the opposite side of the fire, facing the gate, placed my double-barreled rifle beside me, and mounted guard."

" Had you no arms but your rifle?" asked my husband, anxiously.

" I wanted none other, for we understood each other— my rifle and I."

" What were you looking for; what did you expect? A hand-to-hand encounter with these men?" was my next inquiry.

" It seemed most likely that he had planned an attack on the fort. If so, his associates would be waiting outside for a signal. He had intended, when he laid down close to the gate, to open it to them; but when I drove the pins in so tight, I caught a gleam from his eyes that was not a drunken one, and he knew that I suspected him. After that, it was a contest of skill and will between us. He was waiting his opportunity, and so was I.

"You think I've a quick ear, don't you? You see what my temperament is; all sense, all consciousness. My hearing was cultivated, too, by listening for Indians. Well, by and by, I detected a very stealthy movement outside the fort, and then a faint chirrup, such as a young squirrel might make. In an instant the drunken man sprang up; and I covered him with my rifle, cocked. He saw the movement and drew his pistol, but not before I had ordered him to throw down his arms, *or* DIE."

It is impossible to convey, by types, an idea of Ela's manner or tone as he pronounced these last words. They sounded from the bottom of his chest, and conveyed in the utterance a distinct notion that death was what was meant. Hearing him repeat the command, it was easy to believe that the miscreant dared not do more than hesitate in his obedience. After a moment's silence—which was the climax to his rendering of the scene—he continued:

"I havn't told you, yet, how the man looked. He was a tall, swarthy, black-bearded fellow, who might have been handsome once, but who had lost the look which distinguishes men in sympathy with their kind; so that then he resembled some cruel beast, in the shape of a man, yet whose disguise fitted him badly. His eyes burned like rubies, out of the gloomy caverns under his shaggy eyebrows. His lips were drawn apart, so that his teeth glistened. The man's whole expression, as he stood there, glaring at me, was Hate and Murder.

"My eye never winked, while he hesitated. He saw that, and it made him quail. With my finger on the trigger, I kept my rifle leveled, while he threw down his arms —pistols and knife—with a horrible oath. With the knife in his hand, he made a movement, as if he would rush on me; but changed his purpose in time to stop my fire. His cursing was awful; the foam flew from his mouth. He demanded to be let out of the fort; accused me of bad intentions toward him, and denounced me for a robber and murderer. To all his ravings I had but one answer: To be quiet, to obey me, and he might live; dare to disobey me, and he should die.

"I directed him to sit down on the opposite side of the fire—not to move from that one spot—not to make a doubtful motion. And then I told him I knew what he was, and what he had meant to do. When he became convinced of this, he broke down utterly, and wept like a child, declaring that now he knew my pluck, and I had been the first man ever to get the best of him, he loved me like a brother!

"There was a long night before us, and I had got to sit there, with my rifle across my knees, till morning. I could move a little, to stir up or add to the fire; but he could have no liberty whatever. The restraint was horrible to him. One moment he laughed uneasily—another cursed or cried. It was a strange scene, wasn't it? Finally, to pass the time, I asked him to relate the history of his life. He wanted first to shake hands, for the love he bore me. Touching my rifle, significantly, I pointed to a stick lying across the fire between us. 'That is our boundary line; don't go to reaching your hands over that.' Then he sank into a fit of gloom and sullenness.

"We must have remained thus silent until near midnight. Several times I observed him listening to slight sounds outside the fort. But his associates must have given up the game and gone off, for, as the morning hours approached, he ceased to listen, and everything remained quiet. His head was bent forward, his chin resting on his breast, the shaggy beard spreading over it like a mantle."

"How horrible it must have been to keep such company. Why not call on Edwards?"

"The boy was worn out, and there was no need. I was very much strung up, too; so that the exhaustion of sleeplessness, fatigue, or excitement was not felt or noticed. But *he* suffered. He was like a hyena caged, though he showed it only by involuntary movements and furtive glances. Finally, he could bear it no longer, and entreated me piteously, abjectly, to give him him his freedom or blow out his brains. I told him he couldn't have his freedom just yet; but he knew how to get his brains blown out, if he desired it. Then followed more execration, ending in renewed protestations of regard for me. I reminded him that talking would relieve the irksomeness of his position, again inviting him to tell me his history. He replied that if he talked about himself, he would be sure to get excited and move about; but I promised to remind him.

"Once on the subject of himself, it seemed to have a fascination for him. What he told me was, in substance, this: He had been honestly raised, by good, affectionate parents, in the State of Missouri; loved a young girl in the town where he lived; and, wishing to marry her, had resolved to go to California, to make the necessary money, quickly. He was successful; returned full of joyful anticipations, and arrived at an old neighbor's, a few miles from his home, having hardly tasted food or taken any rest the previous twenty-four hours.

"While he hastily ate some breakfast and listened to the friendly gossip of his entertainers, one name, the name of her he loved, his promised wife, was mentioned. *She was married.* He staggered to his feet, asking the name of her husband; and when he heard it, he knew he had been betrayed by that man. He could recall a strange sensation in his brain, as if molten lead had been poured into it; that was the last of his recollections. Afterward, he learned that he had been weeks in a brain fever.

"When he had recovered, some of his old friends, thinking to do him honor, made an evening party for him. To this party came his love, and her husband; his betrayer. When she gave her hand to welcome him home, and looked in his eyes, he knew that she too had been betrayed. Again the molten lead seemed poured upon his brain. Turning to leave the room, fate placed in his path the man he now hated with a deadly hatred. With one blow of a knife, he laid him dead at his feet. A few hours later, in the desperation of trying to escape, he killed two other men. Then he eluded his pursuers, and got back to California. Since then he had reveled in murder, and every species of crime. Once he had seen, in the streets of Sacramento, the woman he loved. Up to that moment, it had never occurred to him that she was free. Following her to her home, he forced himself into her house, and reminded her of their former relations. She had denied all knowledge of him, finally calling upon her husband to satisfy him. The husband ordered him out of the house, and he shot him. Then the Vigilantes made it hazardous to remain in California. He fled to the mountains, where he was nearly starved out, when I took him in and fed and clothed him.

"Such was his story. My blood curdled in my veins, as I listened to the recitals of his atrocities. 'In God's name,' I said, ' who are you—what is your name?' 'I am BOONE HELM.' "

"Who was Boone Helm?" I asked.

"One of the greatest desperadoes that ever was on this coast. He met his fate, afterward, up east of the mountains."

"What did you do with him? What *could* you do with him?" .

"You ought to have shot him while you had him," my husband suggested.

"*I* didn't want to shoot him. He said, if I had been a coward, I would have killed him. To confess the truth, the wretch appealed to my sympathies. I don't think he had ever been sane since the time when he felt the ' molten lead poured into his brain.' I knew somebody was sure to kill him, before long; so, when morning came, I called

Edwards to open the gate; and, when it was unbarred, escorted my visitor out, telling him that there was not room enough in that part of the country for both of us, and that the next time I pointed my rifle at him it would be to shoot. I never saw him again."

"Then he did not molest the Chinese camp?"

"No. Edwards got his four hundred dollars, and went home to Boston."

There fell a silence upon us, and, through my open door, I could see that the cabin was nearly deserted. Ela seemed wearied—sighed, and made a movement, as if to go.

"What about your Guardian Angel?" my husband asked. "You have not told us about her second coming."

"I always say that she didn't come; or else I say that she came, and I drove her away. That is proper; isn't it, now?" glancing at me.

"But *I* want to know if you have seen her—if you never met her anywhere in the world—since that time. I have a right to be curious—yes, or no?" I urged, laughingly.

"How do you feel, now?"—with a light laugh and peculiar change of expression.

"O, better; a great deal better. To be perfectly cured, I only need to hear the sequel."

"I may as well tell it, I suppose. It has been running in my head all day. Wouldn't want my wife to know it. Didn't think of meeting her when I came down to 'Frisco. You see, I've been in Oregon a long while—never traveled on a railroad in my life—wanted to see something of the great outside world—and so, ran down to the great city to see the sights. The first thing I did, I went up to Colfax, on the cars; and while I was up there, the engineer invited me to take a ride on the engine—a special one. Now, I knew that he meant to astonish me, because he thought I was green; and I didn't know, really, how fast the thing ought to run. But we came down the grade with a speed that was ter-rif-ic!—more than a mile a minute, the engineer said. When we got to Lincoln, the fellow asked me, with his superior sort of smile, 'How I liked *that* rate of travel?' I told him I liked *that* pretty well; 'but, I suppose, when you want to make time, you can travel at a considerably *more* accelerated rate of locomotion?'"

How we laughed at the natural drollery of the man, the deliberate utterance, the unsophisticated air. While we laughed, he prepared himself to finish his story.

"It was only day before yesterday," he said, "that I met her. I happened to be in the parlor of the hotel when she came in. At first, I wasn't certain of its being her; but, as I watched her, I became certain of it. And she recognized me; I felt certain of that, too. It was in the early part of the evening, and I had to wait until the people in the parlor would disperse. She saw what I was waiting for, and stayed, too; she told me with her eyes that she *remembered*. After a while she went to the piano, and played and sang 'Kate Kearney.' Then I was satisfied that she would not leave me before I had spoken to her. As soon as the opportunity came, we confessed ourselves."

"Was she married? was she happy?"

"She was married, yes. Happy? she told me, as she had once before, that she was 'content.' She said it with a sigh, as she did the first time; and I doubted her as I did then. But they are putting out the lights. There is always, in this world, somebody going around, putting out our lights. Good-night."

"Good-night."

ON THE .SANDS.

I WAS summering at our Oregon Newport, known to us by the aboriginal name of Clatsop. Had a balloonist, uninstructed in the geography and topography of this portion of the Pacific coast, dropped down among us, his impression would have been that he had alighted in a military encampment, very happily chosen, as military encampments usually are.

Given, one long, low, whitewashed house enclosed by whitewashed pickets; a group of tents outside the enclosure and on the bank of a beautiful graveled-bottom, tree-shadowed stream, and you have the brief summing up of accommodations for summer visitors at Clatsop. The plentiful sprinkling of army buttons among the guests—for there are two forts within a three hours' ride of this beach—tend to confirm the impression of military possession. Besides, our host of the whitewashed hotel is a half-breed; and there is enough of the native element hanging about the place, picking berries and digging clams, to suggest an Indian family where a temporary station might be demanded. It would only be by peeping inside those tents where ladies and children are more numerous than bearded men, that one could be convinced of the gypsy nature of this encampment; though, to be sure, one need not press inside to find them, for the gay campers are sauntering about in all directions, ladies with their escorts, children with their nurses, parties returning from boating or fishing, or riding or bathing: everybody living out in the open air the whole day through on one pretense or another, and only repairing to the hotel at meal times, when the exquisite dishes prepared by French half-breeds suffer the most instant demolition— such hunger does open air inspire.

I had come here just invalid enough to be benefited by
our primitive style of living; not too delicate to endure it,
nor too robust to enjoy the utter vagabondism of it. There
had been no necessity upon us to ape fashionable manners;
no obligation to dress three times a day; no balls to weary
ourselves with at night. Therefore this daily recurring pic-
nic was just sufficient for our physical recreation, while our
mental powers took absolute rest. For weeks I had arisen
every morning to a breakfast of salmon-trout. French
coffee (*au lait*), delicious bread, and fresh berries; and
afterwards to wander about in the cool sea-fog, well wrapped up in a water-proof cloak. Sometimes we made a
boating party up the lovely Neah-can-a-cum, pulling our
boat along under the overhanging alders and maples,
frightening the trout into their hiding-places under the
banks, instead of hooking them as was our ostensible design. The limpid clearness of the water seemed to reflect
the trees from the very bottom, and truly made a medium
almost as transparent as air, through which the pebbles at
the greatest depth appeared within reach of our hands. A
morning idled away in this manner, and an afternoon spent
in seeing the bathers—I never trust my easily curdled blood
to the chill of the sea—and in walking along the sands with
a friend, or dreaming quietly by myself as I watched the
surf rolling in all the way from Tilamook Head to Cape
Disappointment,—these were my daily labors and recreations. The arrival of a bundle of letters, or, still better,
of a new visitor, made what variety there was in our life.

I had both of these excitements in one day. One of my
correspondents had written: "I hope to see you soon, and
to have the opportunity, long sought, of telling you some
of the experiences of my early life. When I promised you
this I had not anticipated the pleasure of talking over the
recollections of my youth while listening with you to the
monotone of the great Pacific, whose 'ever, forever' is more
significant to me than to most lovers of its music. I never

8

gaze upon its restless waves, nor hear the sound of their ripple on the sands, or their thunder on the rocks without being reminded of one episode in my life peculiarly agitating to remember; but perhaps when I have told it to you, you may have power to exorcise the restless spirit which rises in me at the recollection."

So here was promise of the intellectual aliment I had begun to crave after all these weeks of physical, without mental, action. I folded my letter with a feeling of self-congratulation, and turned to watch the movements of a newly arrived party for whom our half-breed host was spreading a tent, and placing in it rather an extra amount of furniture; for, be it known to the uninitiated, we had platform floors under our tents, real bedsteads, dressing-bureaus, rugs, and other comforts to match. That our new arrival exceeded us in elegant conveniences was, of course, duly noted by such idlers as we.

The party consisted of a lady, a little girl of ten, and a Kanaka servant. The lady's name, we learned, was Mrs. Sancy, and she was from the Sandwich Islands. More than that no one was informed. We discussed her looks, her manners, her dress, and her probable circumstances, as we sat around the camp-fire that evening, after the way of idle people. It occurred to me, as I glanced toward her tent door, illuminated by our blazing fire, and saw her regarding the weird scene with evident admiration of its picturesqueness, to ask her to come and sit with us and help us eat roast potatoes—roasted as they cook pigs in the Islands, by covering up in the ground with hot stones. The fact that the potatoes, and the butter which went with them, were purloined from our host's larder, gave a special flavor to the feast—accompanied as it was, too, by instrumental and vocal music, and enlivened by sallies of wit.

Mrs. Sancy seemed to enjoy the novelty of her surroundings, contributing her quota to the general fund of mirth and sparkling talk, and I congratulated myself on having acquired an interesting acquaintance, whose cheerfulness, notwithstanding the partial mourning of her dress, promised well for its continuance. Had she been sad or reserved she certainly would not have been sought as she was by our pleasure-loving summer idlers, consequently my chances of becoming intimate with her would have been greatly abridged. As she was, she soon became, without question, one of the chief social attractions; easily falling into our vagabond ways, yet embellishing them with so much grace and elegance that they became doubly precious to us on account of the new charm imparted to them. All the things any of us could do, Mrs. Sancy could do better; and one thing she could do that none of the rest of us could, which was to swim out and float herself in on a surf-board, like a native island woman; and seeing Mrs. Sancy do this became one of the daily sensations of Clatsop Beach.

I had known Mrs. Sancy about one week, and came to like her extremely, not only for her brilliant, social qualities, but on account of her native originality of thought, and somewhat peculiar culture. I say peculiar, because her thinking and reading seemed to be in the byways rather than the highways of ordinary culture. If she made a figure of speech, it was something noticeably original; if she quoted an author, it was one unfamiliar though forcible. And so she constantly supplied my mind with novelties which I craved, and became like a new education to me. One forenoon, a misty one, we were out on the beach alone, wrapped up in water-proofs, pacing up and down the sands, and watching the grey sullen sea, or admiring the way in which the masses of fog roll in among the tops of the giant firs on Tilamook Head, and were torn into fragments, and tangled among them.

"You never saw the like of this in the islands?" I said, meaning the foggy sea, and the dark, fir-clad mountains.

"I have seen *this* before;" she answered, waving her hand to indicate the scene as we then beheld it. "You look sur-

prised, but I am familiar with every foot of this ground. I
have lived years in this neighborhood—right over there, in
fact, under the Head. This spot has, in truth, a strong fascination for me, and it was to see it once more that I made
the voyage."

"You lived in this place, and liked it years ago! How
strange! It is but a wilderness still, though a pleasant one,
I admit."

She gave me a playfully superior smile: "We are apt to
think ourselves the discoverers of every country where we
chance to be set down; and so Adam thought he was the
first man on the earth, though his sons went out and found
cities were they learned the arts of civilization. So birth,
and love, and death, never cease to be miracles to us, notwithstanding the millions who have been born, and loved,
and died, before our experience began."

"But how did it happen," I urged, unable to repress my
curiosity, "that you lived here, in this place, *years ago?*
That seems so strange to me."

"My parents brought me here when a little child. It is
a common enough history. My mother was an enthusiast
with brain, who joined her fortunes to those of an enthusiast without brain, and emigrated to this coast, when it was
an Indian country, in the vain hope of doing good to the
savages. They only succeeded in doing harm to themselves,
and indirectly, harm to the savages also. The spirit of the
man became embittered, and the mean traits of his nature
asserted themselves, and wreaked their malice, as is customary with mean natures, on the nearest or most inoffensive
object. My poor mother! Maternity was marred for you
by fear and pain and contempt; and whatever errors your
child has fallen into, were an evil inheritance that only years
of suffering and discipline could eradicate."

As Mrs. Saucy pronounced the last sentence, she seemed
for the moment to have forgotten my presence, and stood,
looking off over the calm grey sea, with absent unrecogniz-

ing gaze. After a brief silence she turned to me with a smile: "Pardon my mental desertion. It is not good to talk of our own lives. We all become Adams again, and imagine ourselves sole in the universe."

On this hint I changed the conversation, and we returned to the hotel to lunch, after which, I saw no more of Mrs. Saucy for that day.

That afternoon, my correspondent, Mr. Kittredge arrived; and as it was bright and sunny after the fog, we took a boat, and pulled along under the alders that shade the Neah-can-a-cum. It was there that I listened to this story:

"While I was still a young man, nearly fifteen years ago, I floated on this stream, as we are doing to-day. My companion was a young girl whom I shall call Teresa. She was very young, I remember now with sorrow, and very beautiful; though *beautiful* is not so much the word to describe her as *charming*—magnetic, graceful, intelligent. A lithe, rather tall figure, a high-bred, sensitive, fine face, and pleasing manners. She seemed older than she really was, on account of her commanding physique and distinguished manner.

"I will not go over the details of our acquaintance, which ripened rapidly into love;—so I thought. This was a new country then, even more emphatically that it is now; new with the charm of novelty—not new because it had ceased to progress, as is now the case. Scattered around here within a radius of a dozen miles were half-a-dozen other young men like myself, who had immigrated to the far west, in the spirit of romantic adventure; and once here, were forced to do whatever came to our hands to gain a subsistence. I lived on a farm which I improved, keeping house quite by myself, and spending my leisure hours in study. Of course, the other young men, similarly situated, often visited me, and we usually talked over authors, or such questions of the day as we were familiar with or interested in.

"But one evening love was the theme of our conversation, and incidently, Teresa's name was mentioned among us. I don't know who first uttered it, but I observed at once, that the faces of all three of my companions betrayed an interest too strong and too peculiar to be attributed to an ordinary acquaintanceship with the subject of our remarks. For myself, I felt my own face flushing hotly, as a horrible suspicion seized my consciousness, becoming on the instant, conviction too painful to endure.

"You being a woman, cannot imagine the situation. I believed myself to be Teresa's accepted lover; and so I knew intuitively, did all my three companions; their faces revealing their thoughts to me, as did mine to them. Whatever you women do in the presence of your rivals, I know not. Men rage. It is not often, either, that a man encounters more than one rival at a time. But three!—each of us poor rivals saw three rivals before him. Whatever of friendship had hitherto existed among us was forgotten in the extreme anguish of the moment, and we sat glaring at each other in silence, with heaving chests and burning brows.

"All but Charlie Darling—darling Charlie, we used to call him—his face was deathly white, and his eyes glowed like a panther's in the dark. Yet he was the first to recover himself. 'Boys,' said he, ' we ought not to have brought a lady's name into the discussion; but since Teresa's has been mentioned, we may as well have an understanding. I consider the young lady as engaged to me, and you will please remember that fact when you are talking of her.'

"He said it bravely, proudly, though his lip trembled a little, but he eyed us unflinchingly. No one replied for some moments. Then Tom Allen, a big clumsy, good-hearted, but conceited fellow, lifted his eyes slowly, and answered with a hysterical laugh: 'You may be her darling Charlie, but I'll be d—d if I am not to be her husband!'

"This was the match to the powder. Charlie, myself,

and Harry King, each sprang simultaneously forward, as if we meant to choke poor Tom for his words. Again Charlie was the first to use reason:

"'Hold, boys;' cried he hoarsely; 'let us take a little time to reflect. Two of us have declared ourselves to be engaged to Teresa. Let us hear if she contemplates marrying King and Kittredge, also. What do you say, King?'

"'I say yes!' thundered King, bending his black brows, and bringing down his fist on the table by which he stood.

"'And *I* say, I contemplate marrying *her*,' was my answer to Charlie's challenge.

"Charlie flung himself into a chair, and covered his face with his hands. The action touched some spring in our ruder natures which responded in sympathy for our favorite, and had the effect to calm us, in manner at least. I motioned the others to sit down, and addressed myself to Charlie Darling. 'See here, Charlie?' I said, 'it seems that Teresa has been playing us false. A girl who could be engaged to four young men at once cannot be worth the regards of any of us. Let us investigate the matter, and if she is truly guilty of such falsehood, let us one and all quit her forever without a word of explanation. What do you say? do you agree to that?'

"'How are you going to investigate?' asked Tom Allen, roughly. 'Have not we each declared that she was committed to us individually, and what more can be said?'

"'It appears incredible to me that any girl, much less a girl like Teresa, could so compromise her self-respect as to encourage four suitors, each in such a manner as that he expected to marry her. It is so strange that I cannot believe it, except each man swears to his statement. Can we all swear to it?'

"I laid my little pocket-bible on the table, and set the example of taking an oath to the effect that Teresa had encouraged me to believe that she meant to marry me. King and Allen followed with a similar oath. Charlie Darling

was the last to take the oath; but as he did so, a gleam of
gladness broke over his pale, handsome face; for he could
word his oath differently from ours. ' I swear before these
witnesses and Almighty God,' said Charlie, ' that Teresa
Bryant is my *promised wife.*'

" ' That takes the wind out of our sails,' remarked Allen.

" ' Do you allow other men to kiss your promised wife?'
asked King, with a sneer.

" Charlie sprang at King, and had his hand on his throat
in an instant; but Allen and I interfered to part them. It
was no difficult matter, for Darling, excited as he was, felt
the force of my observations on the quarrel. I said: ' Shall
a trifling girl make us enemies, when she has so behaved
that no one of us can trust her. You, Darling, do not, cannot have confidence in her promise, after all you have this
night learned. You had best accept my first suggestion,
and join with the rest of us in renouncing her forever and
at once.'

" ' That *I* will not,' broke out King, vehemently. ' Her
word is no better than her acts, and I have as much right
to her as Charlie Darling, or either of you, and I'll not give
up the right to a man of you.'

" ' We'll have to fight a four-cornered duel,' remarked
Tom Allen, beginning to see the ludicrous side of the affair.
' Shall we choose up, two on a side?'

" ' I will withdraw my pretensions,' I reiterated, ' if the
others will do so, or even if King and Allen will quit the
field to Charlie, who feels himself bound by Teresa's promise to him.'

" ' I have said I would not withdraw,' replied King, sullenly. And thus we contended, hot-browed and angry-
voiced, for more than an hour. Then rough but practical
Tom proposed a scheme, which was no less than to compel
Teresa to decide between us. After long deliberation, an
agreement was entered into, and I hope I shall not shock
you too much when I tell you what it was."

Kittredge paused, and looked at me doubtingly. I glanced aside at the over-hanging trees, the glints of sunshine on the bank, a brown bird among the leaves, at anything, rather than him, for he was living over again the excitement of that time, and his face was not pleasant to study. After a little waiting, I answered:

"I must know the remainder of the story, since I know so much; what did you agree upon?"

"A plan was laid by which Teresa should be confronted with her four lovers, and forced to explain her conduct. To carry out our design it was necessary to use artifice, and I was chosen as the one who should conduct the affair. I invited her to accompany me to a neighboring farm-house to meet the young folks of the settlement. There was nothing unusual in this, as in those primitive times great latitude was granted to young people in their social intercourse. To mount her horse and ride several miles to a neighbor's house with a single escort, not to return until far into the night, was the common privilege of any young lady, and therefore there was no difficulty about obtaining either her consent or that of her parents to my proposition.

"We set off just at sunset, riding along the beach some distance, admiring the gorgeous western sky, the peaceful sea, and watching the sand-pipers skating out on the wet sands after every receding wave. I had never seen Teresa more beautiful, more sparkling, or more fascinating in every way; and my heart grew 'very little' as the Indians say. It was impossible to accuse her even in my thoughts, while under that bewitching influence. She was so full of life and vivacity that she did not observe the forced demeanor I wore, or if she did, had too much tact to seem to do so. As for me, guarded both by my hidden suspicions and by my promise to my friends, I uttered no word of tenderness or admiration with my tongue, whatever my eyes may have betrayed.

"The road we were going led past my house. When we

were almost abreast of it I informed Teresa that there were
some of our friends waiting for us there, and invited her
to alight. Without suspicion she did so. —— Don't look
at me that way, if you can help it. It was terribly mean
of us fellows, as I see it now. It looked differently then;
and we had none of us seen much of the world and were
rude in our notions of propriety.

" When she came inside of the house and saw only three
men in place of the girls of her acquaintance she expected
to meet, she cast a rapid, surprised glance all round,
blushed, asked, ' where are the girls?' — all in the most
natural manner. There was positively nothing in her deportment to betray a guilty conscience. I recognized that,
and so, I could see, did Darling. He made haste to hand
her a chair, which she declined, still looking about her with
a puzzled, questioning air. I was getting nervous already
over my share in the business, and so plunged at once into
explanation.

" ' Teresa,' I said, ' we four fellows have made a singular
discovery, recently, to the effect that we each believed himself to be your accepted lover. We have met together to
hear your explanation. Is there a man in the house you
are engaged to?"

" She gave one quick, scrutinizing glance at our faces,
and read in them that we were in earnest. Indeed, the
scene would have given scope to the genius of a Hogarth.
Alternate red and white chased each other in quick succes-
sion over her brow, cheeks, neck. Her eyes scintillated,
and her chest heaved.

" ' Please answer us, Teresa,' said Darling, after a most
painful silence of a minute, which seemed an hour.

" She raised her flashing eyes to his, and her tones
seemed to stab him as she uttered, ' You? you too?' Then
gathering up her riding-skirt, she made haste to leave us,
but found the door guarded by Tom Allen. When she saw
that she was really a prisoner among us, alarm seized her,

and woman-like, she began to cry, but not passionately or humbly. Her spirit was still equal to the occasion, and she faced us with the tears running over her cheeks.

"'If there is a man among you with a spark of honor, open this door! Mr. Kittredge, this is your house. Allow me to ask if I am to be retained a prisoner in it, or what you expect to gain by my forcible detention?"

"Tom Allen whispered something unheard by any save her, and she struck at him with her riding-whip. This caused both Darling and myself to interpose, and I turned door-keeper while Allen retreated to the other side of the room with rather a higher color than usual on his lumpish face. All this while—not a long while, at all—King had remained in sullen silence, scowling at the proceedings. At this juncture, however, he spoke:

"'Boys,' said he, 'this joke has gone far enough, and if you will permit us to take our leave, I will see Miss Bryant safe home.'

"Involuntarily she turned toward the only one who proffered help; but Darling and I were too angry at the ruse to allow him to succeed, and stood our ground by the door. 'You see, Teresa, how it is,' continued King, glancing at us defiantly: 'these fellows mean to keep you a prisoner in this house until they make you do and say as they please.'

"'What is it you wish me to do and say?" asked Teresa, with forced composure.

"'We wish you to state,' said I, hoarsely, 'whether or not you are or have been engaged to either of us. We want you to say it because we are all candidates for your favor, and because there is a dispute among us as to whose claim is the strongest. It will put an end to our quarrel, and secure to you the instant return of your liberty, if you will declare the truth.'

"At that she sank down on a chair and covered her face with her hands. After a little time she gathered courage and looked up at Darling and me. I observed, even then, that she took no notice of the others. 'If I am promised to either of you, you know it. But this I say now: if I were a hundred times promised, I would break that promise after such insult as you have all offered me this evening. Let me go!'

"What Charlie Darling suffered all through the interview had been patent to each of us. When she delivered his sentence in tones so determined, a cry that was a groan escaped his colorless lips. To say that *I* did not writhe under her just scorn would be false. Tears, few, but hot and bitter, blinded my eyes. She took no further notice of any of us, but sat waiting for her release.

"'You knew by this time,' I said, 'that you had been deceived.'

"I felt by this time that I had been a fool—a poor, coarse fool; there had been treachery somewhere, and that all together we were a villainous lot. I was only hesitating about how to get out of the scrape decently, when Darling spoke in a voice that was hardly recognizable:

"'Teresa, we *were* engaged; I told these others so before; but they would not believe me. On the contrary, each one claims to have received such encouragement from you as to entitle him to be considered your favored lover. Hard as it was for me to believe such falsehood possible to you, two of these claimants insisted upon their rights against mine, and they overruled my judgment and wishes to such a degree that I consented to this trial for you. It has resulted in nothing except shame to us and annoyance to you! I beg your pardon. More I will not say to-night.'

"Then she rose up and faced us all again with burning cheeks and flashing eyes. 'If any other man says I have given him a promise, or anything amounting to a promise, he lies. To Tom Allen I have always been friendly, and have romped with him at our little parties; but to-night he grossly insulted me, and I will never speak to him again.

As to Harry King, I was friendly with him, too, until about a fortnight ago he presumed to kiss me rudely, in spite of resistance, since which time I have barely recognized him. If Mr. Kittredge says I have made him any promises, he is unworthy of the great respect I have always had for him;' and with that last word she broke down, and sobbed as if her heart would break. But it was only for a few minutes that she cried—she was herself again before we had recovered our composure.

" 'What was it Tom Allen said to you?' asked Charlie, when her tears were dried.

" ' He said *he* would have me, if the rest did cast me off. Thank you,' with a mocking courtesy to Allen. 'It is fortunate for you—and for you all, that I have no "big brother." '

" 'I beg you will believe no "big brother" could add to my punishment,' Charlie answered; and I felt included in the confession. Then he offered to see her home without more delay, but she declined any escort whatever, only requesting us to remain where we were until she had been gone half an hour; and rode off into the moonlight and solitude unattended, with what feelings in her heart God knows. We all watched her until she was hidden from sight by the shadows of a grove of pines, and I still remember the shudder with which I saw her plunge recklessly into the gloom—manlike, careful about her beautiful body, and not regarding her tender girl heart.

" That must have been a pleasant half hour for you," I could not help remarking.

" Pleasant! yes; we were like a lot of devils chained. That night dissolved all friendships between any two of us, except between Darling and me; and *that* could never be quite the same again, for had I not shown him that I believed myself a favored rival? though I afterwards pretended to impute my belief to vanity."

" How did you account *to yourself* for the delusion? Had she not flirted, as it is called, with you?"

"She had certainly caused me to be deluded, innocently or otherwise, into a belief that she regarded me with peculiar favor; and I had been accustomed to take certain little liberties with her, which probably seemed of far greater importance to me than they did to her; for her passional nature was hardly yet awakened, and among our primitive society there was no great restraint upon any innocent familiarities."

"What became of her after that night?—did she marry Darling?"

The answer did not come at once. Thought and feeling were with the past; and I could not bring myself to intrude the present upon it, but busied myself with the leaves and vines and mosses that I had snatched from the banks in passing, while my friend was absorbed in his silent reminiscences.

"You have not heard the saddest part of the story yet," he said at last, slowly and reluctantly. "She kept her word with each of us; ignoring Allen and King entirely; and only vouchsafing a passing word to Charlie and me. Poor Charlie was broken-hearted. He had never been strong, and now he was weak, ill; in short, fell into a decline, and died in the following year."

"Did the story never get out?"

"Not the true story. That scoundrel King spread a rumor abroad which caused much mischief, and was most cruel after what we had done to outrage her feelings in the first instance; but that was his revenge for her slight—I never knew whether she regretted Darling or not. She was so sensitive and willfully proud that she would have died herself sooner than betray a regret for any one who had offended her. Her mother died, and her father took her away with him to the Sandwich Islands. It was said he was not kind to her, especially after her 'disgrace,' as he called it."

"She never forgave you? What do you know about her subsequent history?"

"Nothing of it. But she had her revenge for what went before. After she went to the Islands I wrote her a very full and perfect confession of my fault, and the extenuating circumstances, and offered her my love, with the assurance that it had always been hers. What do you think she wrote me in return? Only this: that once she *had* loved me; that she had but just made the discovery that she loved me, and not Charlie Darling, when we mutually insulted her as we did, and forced her to discard both of us; for which she was not now sorry."

"After all, she was not an angel," I said, laughing lightly, to his embarrassment.

"But to think of using a girl of sixteen like that!"

"You are in a self-accusing mood to-day. Let us talk of our neighbors. Bad as that practice is, I believe it is better than talking about ourselves:—Mrs. Sancy thinks so, I know?"

"Who is Mrs. Sancy?"

"I will introduce you to-morrow."

Next to being principal in a romantic *affaire de cœur* is the excitement of being an interested third party. In consonance with this belief I laid awake most of the night imagining the possible and probable "conclusion of the whole matter." I never doubted that Mrs. Sancy was Teresa, nor that she was more fascinating at thirty-one than she had been at sixteen: but fifteen years work great changes in the intellectual and moral person, and much as I desired to play the part of Fate in bringing these two people together, I was very doubtful about the result. But I need not have troubled myself to assume the prerogative of Fate, which by choosing its own instruments saved me all responsibility in the matter.

As Mr. Kittredge messed with a party of military officers, and was off on an early excursion to unknown localities, I saw nothing of him the following morning. We were to ride on the beach after lunch, returning on the turn of the tide to see the bathers. Therefore no opportunity seemed likely to present itself before evening for the promised introduction.

The afternoon proved fine, and we were cantering gaily along in the fresh breeze and sunshine, when another party appeared, advancing from the opposite direction, whom I knew to be Mrs. Sancy, her little daughter Isabelle, and the Kanaka servant. The child and servant were galloping hard, and passed us with a rush. But the lady seemed in a quieter mood, riding easily and carelessly, with an air of pre-occupation. Suddenly she too gave her horse whip and rein, and as she dashed past I heard her exclaim, "The quicksands! the quicksands!"

Instinctively we drew rein, turned, and followed. We rode hard for a few minutes, without overtaking her; then slackened our speed on seeing her come up with the child, and arrest the race which had so alarmed her.

"There are no quicksands in this direction;" was the first remark of Kittredge when we could speak.

"What should make her think so?"

"There *were* quicksands there a number of years ago, and by her manner she must have known it then."

"And by the same token," I replied, "she cannot have been here since the change."

"Who is she?"

"My friend, Mrs. Sancy."

"Where is she from?"

"From the quicksands;" I replied evasively, as I saw the lady approaching us.

"I fear you have shared my fright," she said, as soon as she came within speaking distance. "When I used to be familiar with these sands there was a dangerous spot out there; but I perceive time has effaced it, as he does so many things;" smiling, and bowing to my escort.

"There are some things time never effaces, even from the sands," returned Kittredge, growing visibly pale.

" That is contrary to the poets," laughingly she rejoined; "but I believe the poets have been superseded by the scientists, who prove everything for you by a fossil."

I could not help watching her to learn how much or how little recognition there was in her face. The color came and went, I could perceive; but whether with doubt or certainty I could not determine. I felt I ought to introduce them, but shrunk from helping on the denouement in that way. In my embarrassment I said nothing. We were now approaching the vicinity of the bathing-houses, and seeing the visitors collecting for the bath, an excuse was furnished for quickening our paces. Mrs. Saucy bowed and left us. Mr. Kittredge seemed to have lost the power of speech.

Fifteen minutes after I was sitting on some drift-wood, watching the pranks of the gayest of the crowd as they "jumped the rollers," when Mrs. Saucy came out of a dressing-room, followed by her Kanaka with a surf-board. Her bathing-dress was very jaunty and becoming, and her skill as a swimmer drew to her a great deal of attention. To swim out and float in on the rollers seemed to be to her no more of a feat than it would be to a sea-gull, she did it so easily and gracefully. But to-day something went wrong with her. Either she was too warm from riding, or her circulation was disturbed by the meeting with Kittredge, or both; at all events the second time she swam out she failed to return. The board slipped away from her, and she sank out of sight.

While I gazed horror-stricken, scarce understanding what had taken place, a man rushed past me in his bathing clothes, running out to where the water was deep enough to float him, and striking out rapidly from there. I could not recognize him in that dress, but I knew it was Kittredge. Fate had sent him. The incoming tide kept her where she sank, and he soon brought her to the surface and through the surf to the beach. I spread my cloak on

9

the sand, and, wrapping her in it, began rubbing and rolling her, with the assistance of other ladies, for resuscitation from drowning.

In three minutes more Kittredge was kneeling by my side with a brandy-flask, administering its contents drop by drop, and giving orders. "It is congestion," said he. "You must rub her chest, her back, her hands and feet; so, so. She will die in your hands if you are not quick. For God's sake, work fast!"

By his presence of mind she was saved as by a miracle. When she was removed to her lodgings, and able to converse, she asked me who it was that had rescued her.

"Mr. Kittredge," I said.

"The same I met on the beach?"

"The same."

She smiled in a faint, half-dreaming way, and turned away her face. She thought I did not know her secret.

I am not going to let my hero take advantage of the first emotion of gratitude after a service, to mention his wishes in, as many story-tellers do. I consider it a mean advantage; besides Mr. Kittredge did not do it. In fact, he absented himself for a week. When he returned, I introduced him formally to Mrs. Saucy, and we three walked together down to the beach, and seated ourselves on a white old cottonwood that had floated out of the Columbia river, and been cast by the high tides of winter above the shelving sands.

We were rather a silent party for a few minutes. In his abstraction, Mr. Kittredge reached down and traced a name in the sand with the point of my parasol stick—TERESA.

Then, seeing the letters staring at him, he looked up at her, and said, "I could not brush them out if I would. Time has failed to do that." Her gaze wandered away, out to sea, up towards the Capes, down toward the Head; and a delicate color grew upon her cheek. "It has scarcely changed in fifteen years," she said. "I did not count on finding all things the same."

With that I made a pretense of leaving them, to seek
shells along the beach; for I knew that fate could no longer
be averted. When I returned she was aware that I possessed the secret of both, and she smiled upon me a recognition of my right to be pleased with what I saw; what I
beheld seeming the prelude to a happy marriage. That
night I wrote in my diary, after some comments on my relations with Mr. Kittredge:

> "It is best to be off with the old love,
> Before you are on with the new."

AN OLD FOOL.

PART I.

THE annual rain-fall on the lower Columbia River is upward of eighty inches—often almost ninety; and the greater amount of this fall is during the winter months, from November to March, generally the least intermittent in December. I mention this climatic fact, the better to be understood in attempting to describe a certain December afternoon in the year 186–.

It lacked but two days of Christmas, and the sun had not shone out brightly for a single hour in three weeks. On this afternoon the steady pour from the clouds was a strong reminder of the ancient deluge. Between the rain itself and the mist which always accompanies the rain-fall in Oregon, the world seemed nearly blotted out. Standing on the wharf at Astoria, the noble river looked like a great gray caldron of steaming water, evaporating freely at 42°. The lofty highlands on the opposite shore had lost all shape, or certain altitude. The stately forest of firs along their summits were shrouded in ever-changing masses of whitish-gray fog. Nothing could be seen of the light-house on the headland at the mouth of the river; nothing of Tongue Point, two miles above Astoria; and only a dim presentment of the town itself, and the hills at the back of it. Even the old Astorians, used to this sort of weather and not disliking it, having little to do in the winter time, and being always braced up by sea-airs that even this fresh-water flood could not divest of their tonic flavor—these old sea-dogs, pilots, fishermen, and other *amphibia*, were constrained at last to give utterance to mild growls at the persistent character of the storm.

A crowd of these India-rubber clad, red-cheeked, and,

alas! too often red-nosed old men of the sea, had taken
shelter in the Railroad Saloon—called that, apparently, because there was no railroad then within hundreds of miles
—and were engaged in alternate wild railings at the
weather, reminiscences of other storms, and whisky-drink-
ing; there being an opinion current among these men that
water-proof garments alone did not suffice to keep out the
all-prevailing wet.

"If 'twant that we're so near the sea, with a good wide
sewage of river to carry off the water, we should all be
drownded; thet's my view on't," said Rumway, a bar pilot,
whose dripping hat-rim and general shiny appearance gave
point to his remark.

"You can't count on the sea to befriend you this time,
Captain. Better git yer ark alongside the wharf; fur we're
goin' to hev the Columbia runnin' up stream to-night, sure
as you're born."

"Hullo! Is that you, Joe Chillis? What brought you to
town in this kind o' weather? And what do you know about
the tides?—that's *my* business, I calculate."

"Mebbe it is; and mebbe a bar pilot knows more about
the tides nor a mountain man. But there'll be a rousin'
old tide to-night, and a sou'wester, to boot; you bet yer
life on that!"

"I'll grant you thet a mountain man knows a heap thet
other men don't. But I'll never agree thet he can tell *me*
anything about *my* business. Take a drink, Joe, and then
let's hear some o' your mountain yarns."

"Thankee; don't keer ef I do. I can't stop to spin
yarns, tho', this evenin'. I've got to git home. It won't
be easy work pullin' agin the tide an hour or two from
now."

"What's your hurry?" "A story—a story!" "Let's
make a night of it." "O, come, Joe, you are not wanted
at home. Cabin won't run away; wife won't scold."
"Stop along ov us till mornin';" were the various rather

noisy and ejaculatory remarks upon Chillis's avowed intention of abandoning good and appreciative company, without stopping to tell one of his ever-ready tales of Indian and bear fighting in the Rocky Mountains thirty years before.

"Why, you ain't goin' out again till you've shaken off the water, Joe. You're dripping like a Newfoundland;" said Captain Rumway, as Chillis put down his empty glass, and turned toward the door, which he had entered not five minutes before. This thoughtfulness for his comfort, however, only meant, "Stay till you've taken another drink, and then maybe you will tell us a story;" and Chillis knew the bait well enough to decline it.

"Thankee, Captain. One bucketful more or less won't make no difference. I'm wet to the skin now. Thank ye all, gentlemen; I've got business to attend to this evenin'. Have any of you seen Eb Smiley this arternoon?"—looking back, with his hand on the door-knob. "I'd like to speak to him afore I leave, ef you can tell me whar to find him."

"You'll find him in there," answered the bar-tender, crooking his thumb toward a room leading out of the saloon, containing a tumbled single-bed and a wooden settee, besides various masculine bijouterie in the shape of boots, old and new, clean and dirty; candle and cigar ends; dusty bits of paper on a stand, the chief ornament of which was a black-looking derringer; coats, vests, fishing-tackle; and cheap prints, adorning the walls in the wildest disregard of effect—except, indeed, the effect aimed at were chaos.

Into this apartment Chillis unceremoniously thrust himself through the half-open door, frowning as darkly as his fine and pleasant features would admit of, and muttering to himself, "Damme, I thought as much."

On the wooden settee reclined a man thirty years his junior—Chillis was over sixty, though he did not look it—sleeping the heavy, stupid sleep of intoxication. The old hunter did not stand upon ceremony, nor hesitate to invade the sleeper's privacy, but marched up to the settee, his ragged old blanket-coat dripping tiny streams from every separate tatter, and proceeded at once roughly to arouse the drunken man by a prolonged and vigorous shaking.

"Wha'er want? Lemme 'lone," grumbled Smiley, only dimly conscious of what was being said or done to him.

"Get up, I say. Get up, you fool! and come along home. Your wife is needin' ye. Go home and take care of her and the boy. Come along—d'ye hear?"

But the sleeper's brain was impervious to sound or sense. He only muttered, in a drowsy whisper, "Lemme 'lone," a few times, and went off into a deeper stupor than before.

"You miserable cuss," snarled Chillis, in his wrath, "be d—d to you, then! Drink yerself to death, ef you want to —the sooner the better;" and, with this parting adjuration, and an extra shake, the old mountain man, who had drank barrels of alcohol himself with comparative immunity from harm, turned his back upon this younger degenerate victim of modern whisky, and strode out of the room and the house, without stopping to reply to the renewed entreaties of his friends to remain and "make a night of it."

Making directly for the wharf, where his boat was moored, half filled with water, he hastily bailed it out, pushed off, and, dropping the oars into the row-locks, bent to the work before him; for the tide was already beginning to run up, and the course he had to take brought him dead against it for the first two or three miles, after which the tide would be with him, and, if there should not be too much sea, the labor of impelling the boat would be materially lessened.

The lookout from a small boat was an ugly one at three o'clock of this rainy December afternoon. A dense, cold fog had been rolling in from the sea for the last half hour, and the wind was rising with the tide. Under the shelter of the hills at the foot of which Astoria nestled, the wind did not make itself felt; but once past "The Point," and in the exposed waters of Young's Bay, the south-westers had a fair sweep of the great river, of which the bay is only an inlet. One of these dreaded storms was preparing to make itself felt, as Chillis had predicted, and as he now saw by the way in which the mist was being blown off the face of the river, and the "white-caps" came instead. Before he arrived off the Point he laid down his oars, and, taking out of his coat-pocket a saturated yellow cotton handkerchief, proceeded to tie his old soft felt hat down over his ears, and otherwise make ready for a struggle with wind and water—neither of them adversaries to be trifled with, as he knew.

Not a minute too soon, either; for, just when he had resumed the oars, the boat, having drifted out of her course, was caught by a wave and a blast on its broadside, and nearly upset.

"Steady, little gal," said Chillis, bringing his boat round, head to the wind. "None o' your capers now. Thar is serious work on hand, an' I want you to behave better'n ever you did afore. It's you an' me, an' the White Rose, this time, sure," and he pressed his lips together grimly, and peered out from under his bent old hat at the storm which was driving furiously against his broad breast, and into his white, anxious face, almost blinding and strangling him. His boat was a small one—too small for the seas of the lower Columbia—but it was trim and light, and steered easily. Besides, the old mountaineer was a skilled oarsman, albeit this accomplishment was not a part of the education of American hunters and trappers, as it was of the French *voyageurs.* Keeping his little craft head to the wind, he took each wave squarely on the prow, and with a powerful stroke of the oars cut through it, or sprang over it, and then made ready for the next. Meanwhile, the storm increased, the rain driving at an angle of 45°, and in sheets that flapped smotheringly about him like wet blankets, and threatened to swamp his boat without assistance from the waves. It was growing colder, too, and his sodden garments were of little service to protect him from the chill that comes with a south-wester; nor was the grip of the naked hands upon the oars stimulating to the circulation of his old blood through the swollen fingers.

But old Joe Chillis had a distinct comprehension of the situation, and felt himself to be master of it. He had gone over to Astoria that day, not to drink whisky and tell stories, but to do a good turn for the " White Rose." Failing in his purpose, he was going back again, at any cost, to make up for the miscarriage of that effort. Death itself could not frighten him; for what was the Columbia in a storm to the dangers he had passed through in years of hunting and trapping in the Rocky Mountains? He had seemed to bear a charmed life then; he would believe that the charm had not deserted him.

But, O, how his old arms ached! and the storm freshening every minute, with two miles further to row, in the teeth of it. The tide was with him now; but the wind was against the tide, and made an ugly sea. If he only could reach the mouth of the creek before dark. If he could? Why, he must. The tide would be up so that he could not find the entrance in the dark. He worked resolutely—worked harder than ever—but he did not accomplish so much, because his strength was giving out. When he first became aware of this, he heaved a great sigh, as if his heart were broken, then pressed his lips together as before, and peered through the thick gray twilight, looking for the creek's mouth while yet there was a little light.

He was now in the very worst part of the bay, where the current from Young's River was strongest, setting out toward the Columbia, and where the wind had the fairest sweep, blowing from the coast across the low Clatsop plains. Only the tide and his failing strength were opposed to these; would they enable him to hold his own? He set his teeth harder than ever, but it was all in vain, and directly the catastrophe came. His strength wavered, the boat veered round, a sudden gust and roll of water took it broadside, and over she went, keel up, more than a mile from land.

But this was not the last of Joe Chillis—not by any manner of means. He had trapped beaver too many years to mind a ducking more or less, if he only had his strength. So, when he came up, he clutched an oar that was floating past him, and looked about for the boat. She was not far off—the tide was holding her, bobbing up and down like a cork. In a few minutes she was righted, and Chillis had scrambled in, losing his oar while doing it, and regaining it while being nearly upset again.

It had become a matter of life and death now to keep afloat, with only one oar to fight the sea with; and, though hoping little from the expedient, in such a gale—blowing the wrong way, besides—Chillis shouted for assistance in every lull of the tempest. To his own intense astonishment, as well as relief, his hail was answered.

"Where away?" came on the wind, the sound seeming to flap and flutter like a shred of torn sail.

"Off the creek, about a mile?" shouted Chillis, with those powerful lungs of his, that had gotten much of their bellows-like proportions during a dozen years of breathing the thin air of the mountains.

"All right!" was returned on the snapping, fluttering gale. After this answer, Chillis contented himself with keeping his boat right side up, and giving an occasional prolonged "Oh-whoo!" to guide his rescuers through the thickening gloom. How long it seemed, with the growing darkness, and the effort to avoid another upset! But the promised help came at last, in the shape of the mail-carrier's plunger, her trim little mast catching his eyes, shining white and bare out of the dusk. Directly he heard the voices of the mail-carrier and another.

"Where be ye? *Who* be ye?"

"Right here, under yer bow. Joe Chillis, you bet your life!"

"Waal, come aboard here, mighty quick. Make fast. Mind your boat; don't let her strike us. Pole off—pole off, with yer oar!"

"Mind *your* oars," returned Chillis; "I'll mind mine"— every word spoken with a yell.

"What was the row, out there?" asks the mail-carrier, making a trumpet of his hand.

"Boat flopped over; lost an oar," answered Chillis, keeping his little craft from flying on board by main force.

"Guess I won't go over to-night," says the carrier. "'Taint safe for the mail"—The wind snatching the word "mail" out of his mouth, and scattering it over the water as if it had been a broken bundle of letters. "I'll go back to Skippanon"—the letters flying every way again.

"Couldn't get over noways, now," shouts back Chillis, glad in his heart that he could not, and that the chance, or mischance, favored his previous designs. Then he said no more, but watched his boat, warding it off carefully until they reached the mouth of the creek and got inside, with nothing worse to contend against than the insolent wind and rain.

"This is a purty stiff tide, for this time o' day. It won't take long to pull up to Skippanon, with all this water pushin' us along. Goin' home to-night, Joe?"

"Yes, I'm goin' home, ef I can borrer an oar," said Chillis. "My house ain't altogether safe without me, in sech weather as this."

"Safer 'n most houses, ef she don't break away from her moorin's," returned the mail-carrier, laughing. "Ef I can git somebody to take my place for a week, I'm comin' up to spend it with you, an' do some shootin'. Nothin' like such an establishment as yours to go huntin' in—house an' boat all in one—go where you please, an' stay as long as you please."

"Find me an oar to git home with, an' you can come an' stay as long as the grub holds out."

"Waal, I can do that, I guess, when we git to the landin'. I keep an extra pair or two for emergencies. But it's gittin' awful black, Chillis, an' I don't envy you the trip up the creek. It's crooked as a string o' S's, an' full o' shoals, to boot."

"It won't be shoal to-night," remarked Chillis, and relapsed into silence.

In a few minutes the boat's bow touched the bank. "Mind the tiller!" called out both oarsmen, savagely. But as no one minded it, and it was too dark to see what was the matter, the mail-carrier dropped his oar, and stepped back to the stern to *feel* what it was.

"He's fast asleep, or drunk, or dead, I don't know which," he called to the other oarsman, as he got hold of the steering gear, and headed the boat up-stream again. His companion made no reply, and the party proceeded in silence to the landing. Here, by dint of much shouting and hallooing, the inmates of a house close by became informed of something unusual outside, and, after a suitable delay, a man appeared, carrying a lantern.

"It's you, is it?" he said to the mail-carrier. "I reckoned you wouldn't cross to-night. Who ye got in there?"

"It's Joe Chillis. We picked him up outside, about a mile off the land. His boat had been upset, an' he'd lost an oar; an' ef we hadn't gone to his assistance it would have been the last of old Joe, I guess."

"Hullo, Joe! Why don't you git up?" asked the man, seeing that Chillis did not rise, or change his position.

"By George! I don't know what's the matter with him. Give me the lantern;" and the mail-carrier took the light and flashed it over Chillis's face.

"I don't know whether he's asleep, or has fainted, or what. He's awful white, an' there's an ugly cut in his shoulder, an' his coat all torn away. Must have hurt himself tryin' to right his boat, I guess. George! the iron on the row-lock must have struck right into the flesh."

"He didn't say he was hurt," rejoined the other oars-man.

"It's like enough he didn't know it," said the man with the lantern. "When a man's in danger he doesn't feel a hurt. Poor old Joe! he wasn't drunk, or he couldn't have handled his boat at all in this weather. We must take him in, I s'pose."

Then the three men lifted him upon his feet, and, by shaking and talking, aroused him sufficiently to walk with their support to the house. There they laid him on a bench, and brought him a glass of hot whisky and water; and the women of the house gathered about shyly, gazing compassionately upon the ugly wound in the old man's delicate white flesh, white and delicate as the fairest woman's.

Presently, Chillis sat up and looked about him. "Have you got me the oars?" he said to the mail-carrier.

"You won't row any more to-night, Joe, *I* guess," the carrier answered, smiling grimly. "Look at your shoulder, man."

"Shoulder be d—d!" retorted Chillis. "Beg pardon, ladies; I didn't see you. Been asleep, haven't I? Perhaps, sence you seem to think I'm not fit for rowin', one of these ladies will do me the favor to help me put myself in order. Have you a piece of court-plaster, or a healing salve, ma'am?"—to the elder woman. "Ladies mostly keep sech trifles about them, I believe."

Then he straightened himself up to his magnificent height, and threw out his broad, round chest, as if the gash in his shoulder were an epaulet or a band of stars instead.

"Of course, I can do something for you," said the woman he had addressed, very cheerfully and quickly. "I have the best healing salve in all the country;" and, running away, she quickly returned with a roll of linen, and the invaluable salve.

"I must look at the wound, and see if it wants washing out. Ugh! O, dear! it is a dreadful cut, and ragged. You will have to go to the doctor with that, I'm afraid. But I'll just put this on to-night, to prevent your taking cold in it; though you will take cold, anyway, if you do not get a change of clothes;" and the good woman looked round at her husband, asking him with her eyes to offer this very necessary kindness.

"You'll stop with us to-night, Joe," said the man, in answer to this appeal, "an' the sooner you git off them wet clothes the better. I'll lend you some o' mine."

"Yes, indeed, Mr. Chillis, you must get out of these wet things, and put on some of Ben's. Then you will let me get you a bit of hot supper, and go right to bed. You don't look as if you could sit up. There!" she added, as the salve was pressed gently down over the torn flesh, and heaving a deep sigh, "if you feel half as sick as I do, just looking at it, you will do well to get ready to lie down."

"Thankee, ma'am. It's worth a man's while to git hurt a leetle, ef he has a lady to take care o' him," answered Chillis, gallantly. "But I can't accept your kindness any furder to-night. Ef I can git the loan of a lantern an' a pair o' oars, it is all I ask, for home I must go, as soon as possible."

"Ben will lend you a lantern," said the mail-carrier, "an' I will lend you the oars, as I promised; but what on earth you want to go any further in this storm for, beats me."

"This storm has only jist begun, and its goin' to last three days," returned Chillis. "No use waitin' for it to quit; so, good-night to you all. I've made a pretty mess o' your floor," he added, turning to glance at the little black puddles that had drained out of his great spongy blanket coat, and run down through his leaky boots on to the white-scoured boards of the kitchen; then, glancing from them to the mistress of the house—"I hope you'll excuse me." And with that he opened the door quickly, and shut himself out into the tempest once more, making his way by the lantern's aid to the boat-house at the landing, where he helped himself to what he needed, and was soon pulling up the creek. Luckily there was no current against him, for it was sickening work making the oar-stroke with that hurt in his shoulder.

He could see by the light of the lantern, which he occasionally held aloft, that the long grass of the tide-marsh was already completely submerged, the immense flats looking like a sea, with the wind driving the water before it in long rolls, or catching it up and flirting it through the air in spray and foam. His only guide to his course was the scattering line of low willows whose tops still bent and shook above the flood, indicating the slightly raised banks of the creek, everything more distant being hidden in the profound darkness which brooded over and seemed a part of the storm. But even with these landmarks he wandered a good deal in his reckoning, and an hour or more had elapsed before his watchful eyes caught the gleam of what might have been a star reflected in the ocean.

"Thank God!" he whispered, and pulled a little faster toward that spark of light.

In ten minutes more, he moored his boat to the hitching-post in front of a tiny cottage, from whose uncurtained window the light of a brisk wood-fire was shining. As the chain clanked in the ring, the door opened, and a woman and child looked out.

"Is that you, Eben?" asked the woman, in an eager voice, made husky by previous weeping. · "I certainly feared you were drowned." Then seeing, as her eyes became accustomed to the darkness, that the figure still lingering about the boat was not her husband's she shrank back, fearing the worst.

"I'm sorry I'm not the one you looked for, Mrs. Smiley," answered Chillis, standing on the bit of portico, with its dripping honeysuckle vines swinging in the wind; " but

I'm better than nobody, I reckon, an' Smiley will hardly be home to-night. The bay's awful rough, an' ef I hadn't started over early, I shouldn't have ventured, neither. No, you needn't look for your husband to-night, ma'am."

"Will you not come in by the fire, Mr. Chillis?" asked the woman, hesitatingly, seeing that he seemed waiting to be invited.

"Thankee. But I shall spile your floor, ef I do. I'm a perfect sponge, not fit to come near a lady, nohow. I thought," he added, as he closed the door and advanced to the hearth, "that I would jest stop an' see ef I could do anything for you, seein' as I guessed you'd be alone, and mebbe afeard o' the storm an' the high tide. Ladies mostly is afeard to be alone at sech times"—untying the yellow cotton handkerchief and throwing his sodden hat upon the stone hearth.

"Do you think there is any danger?" asked Mrs. Smiley, embarrassed, yet anxious. She stood in the middle of the room, behind him, with that irresolute air an inexperienced person has in unexpected circumstances.

He turned around with his back to the blaze, while a faint mist of evaporation began to creep out all over him, and occasionally to dart out in slender streams and float up the wide chimney.

"There's no danger *now*, an' mebbe there won't *be* any. But the tide will not turn much afore midnight, an' it's higher now than it generally is when it is full."

"What's that?" cried Willie, the boy, his senses sharpened by the mention of danger.

"It's the wind rattlin' my boat-chains," returned Chillis, smiling at the little fellow's startled looks.

"Your boat-chain!" echoed his mother, not less startled. "Was it your boat that you were fastening to the hitching-post? I thought it was your horse. Is the water up so high, then, already?"—her cheeks paling as she spoke.

"I dragged it up a little way," returned Chillis, slowly,

and turning his face back to the fire. He was listening attentively, and thought he caught the sound of lapping water.

"Have you just come from Astoria?" asked Mrs. Smiley, approaching, and standing at one corner of the hearth. The fire-light shone full upon her now, and revealed a clear white face; large, dark-gray eyes, full of sadness and perplexity; a beautifully shaped head, coiled round and round with heavy twists of golden hair, that glittered in its high lights like burnished metal; and a figure at once full and lithe in its proportions, clad in a neat-fitting dress of some soft, dark material, set off with a tiny white collar and bright ribbon. It was easy to see why she was the "White Rose" to the rough old mountain man. She was looking up at him with an eager, questioning gaze, that meant, O, ever so much more than her words.

"Not quite direct. I stopped down at the landin', an' I lost a little time gittin' capsized in the bay. I left about three o'clock."

"Might not Eben have left a little later," the gray eyes added, "and have been capsized, too?"

"He wouldn't *try* to cross half an hour later—I'll wager my head on that. He can't get away from town to-night; an', what is worse, I don't think he can cross for two or three days. We've got our Christmas storm on hand, an' a worse one than we've had for twenty years, or I'm mistaken."

"If you thought the storm was going to be severe, why did you not warn Eben, Mr. Chillis?" The gray eyes watched him steadily.

"I did say, there would be a sou'-wester uncommon severe; but Rumway laughed at me for prophesyin' in his company. Besides, I was in a hurry to get off, myself, and wouldn't argue with 'em. Smiley's a man to take his own way pretty much, too."

"I wish you had warned him," sighed Mrs. Smiley, and

10

turned wearily away. She left her guest gazing into the fire
and still steaming in a very unsavory manner, lighted a
candle, set it in the window, and opened the door to look
out. What she saw made her start back with a cry of af-
fright, and hurriedly close the door.

"Your boat is this side of the hitching-post, and the
water is all around us!"

"An' it is not yet eight o'clock. I guessed it would be
so."

Just then, a fearful blast shook the house, and the boat's
chain clanked nearer. Willie caught his mother's hand,
and shivered all over with terror. "O, mamma!" he
sobbed," will the water drown our house?"

"I hope not, my boy. It may come up and wet our
warm, dry floor; but I trust it will not give us so much
trouble. We do not like wet feet, do we, Willie?"

Then the mother, intent on soothing the child, sat down
in the fire-light and held his curly head in her lap, whispering little cooing sentences into his ear whenever he grew
restless; while her strange, unbidden guest continued to
evaporate in one corner of the hearth, sitting with his hands
on his knees, staring at something in the coals. There was
no attempt at conversation. There had never, until this evening, been a dozen words exchanged between these neighbors, who knew each other by sight and by reputation well
enough. Joe Chillis was not a man whose personal appearance—so far as clothes went—nor whose reputation,
would commend him to women generally—the one being
shabby and careless, the other smacking of recklessness and
whisky. Not that any great harm was known of the man;
but that he was out of the pale of polite society even in this
new and isolated corner of the earth. He had had an Indian wife in his youth; being more accustomed to the ways
of her people than of his own. For nearly twenty years he
had lived a thriftless, bachelor existence, known among men,
and by hearsay among women, as a noted story-teller, and

genial, devil-may-care, old mountain man, whose heart was
in the right place, but who never drew very heavily upon
his brain resources, except to embellish a tale of his early
exploits in Indian-fighting, bear-killing and beaver-trapping.
It was with a curious feeling of wonder that Mrs. Smiley
found herself *tête-à-tête* with him at her own fireside; and,
in spite of her anxiety about other matters, she could not
help studying him a good deal, as he sat there, silent and
almost as motionless as a statue; nor keep from noticing
his splendid *physique,* and the aristocratic cut of his features; nor from imagining him as he must have been in his
youth. She was absorbed for a little while, picturing this
gallant young White among his Indian associates—trying
to fancy how he treated his squaw wife, and whether he
really cared for her as he would for a White woman; then,
she wondered what kind of an experience his present life
would be for any one else—herself, for instance—living
most of the year on a flat-boat housed in, and hiding in
sloughs, and all manner of watery, out-of-the-way places.
She loved forest and stream, and sylvan shades, well
enough; but not well enough for that. So a human creature who could thus voluntarily exile himself must be peculiar. But Joe Chillis did not look peculiar; he looked as
alive and human as anybody—in fact, particularly alive and
human just now; and it was not any eccentricity which had
brought him to her this night, but a real human reason.
What was the reason?

What with his mother's cooing whispers, and the passing
of her light hand over his hair, Willie had fallen asleep.
Mrs. Smiley lifted him in her arms and laid him on the
lounge, covering him carefully, and touching him tenderly,
kissing his bright curls at the last. Chillis turned to watch
her—he could not help it. Perhaps he speculated about
her way of living and acting, as she had speculated about
his. Meantime, the tempest outside increased in fury, and
the little cottage trembled with its fitful shocks.

Now that Willie was asleep, Mrs. Chillis felt a growing
nervousness and embarrassment. She could not bring
herself to sit down again, alone with Joe Chillis. Not that
she was afraid of him—there was nothing in his appearance to inspire a dread of the man; but she wanted to
know what he was there for. The sensitive nerves of the
man felt this mental inquiry of her, but he would not be
the first to speak; so he let her flutter about—brightening
the fire, putting to right things that were right enough as
they were, and making a pretense of being busied with
household cares. At length, there was nothing more to do
except to wind the clock, which stood on the mantel, over
the hearth. Here was her opportunity. "The evening
has seemed very long," she said, " but it is nine o'clock, at
last."

Chillis got up, went to the door, and opened it. The
boat was bumping against the floor of the tiny portico.
She saw it, too, and her heart gave a great bound. Chillis
came back, and sat down by the fire, looking very grave
and preoccupied. With a little shiver, she sat down opposite. It was clear that he had no intention of going; and,
strange as she felt the situation to be, she experienced a
sort of relief that he was there. She was not a cowardly
woman, nor was her guest one she would have been likely
to appeal to in any peril; but, since a possible peril had
come, and he was there of his own accord, she owned to
herself she was not sorry. She was a woman, any way,
and must needs require services of men, whoever they
might be. Having disposed of this question, it occurred
to her to be gracious to the man whose services she had
made up her mind to accept. Glancing into his face, she
noticed its pallor; and then remembered what he had said
about being capsized in the bay, and that he was an old
man; and then, that he might not have had any supper.
All of which inspired her to say, "I beg pardon, Mr.
Chillis. I presume you have eaten nothing this evening.

I shall get you something, right away—a cup of hot coffee, for instance." And, without waiting to hear his faint denial, Mrs. Smiley made all haste to put her hospitable intentions into practice, and soon had spread a little table with a very appetizing array of cold meats, fruit, bread, and coffee.

While her guest, with a few words of thanks, accepted and disposed of the refreshments, Mrs. Smiley sat and gazed at the fire in her turn. The little cottage trembled, the windows rattled, the storm roared without, and—yes, the water actually lapped against the house ! She started, turning to the door. The wind was driving the flood in under it. She felt a chill run through her flesh.

" Mr. Chillis, the water is really coming into the house !"

" Yes, I reckoned that it would," returned the old man, calmly, rising from the table and returning to the hearth. " That is the nicest supper I've had for these dozen years; and it has done me good, too. I was a little wore out with pullin' over the bay, agin the wind."

Mrs. Smiley looked at him curiously, and then at the water splashing in under the door. He understood her perfectly.

" A wettin' wouldn't hurt you, though it would be disagreeable, an' I should be sorry to have you put to that inconvenience. But the wind *and* the water may unsettle the foundation o' your house, the chimney bein' on the outside, an' no support to it. Even that would not certainly put you in danger, as the frame would likely float. But I knew, ef sech a thing should happen, an' you here alone, you would be very much frightened, an' perhaps lose your life a-tryin' to save it."

" And you came up from the landing in all this storm to take care of me?" Mrs. Smiley exclaimed, with flushing cheeks.

" I came all the way from Astoria to do it," answered Chillis, looking at the new-blown roses of her face.

"And Eben——" She checked herself, and fixed her eyes upon the hearth.

"He thought there was no danger, most likely."

"Mr. Chillis, I can never thank you!" she cried, fervently, as she turned to glance at the sleeping child.

"White Rose," he answered, under his breath, "I don't want any thanks but those I've got." Then, aloud to her: "You might have some blankets ready, in case we are turned out o' the house. The fire will be 'most sure to be put out, any way, an' you an' the boy will be cold."

Mrs. Smiley was shivering with that tenseness of the nerves which the bravest women suffer from, when obliged to wait the slow but certain approach of danger. Her teeth chattered together, as she went about her band-box of a house, collecting things that would be needed, should she be forced to abandon the shelter of its lowly roof; and, as she was thus engaged, she thought the place had never seemed so cosy as it did this wild and terrible night. She put on her rubber overshoes, tied snugly on a pretty woollen hood, got ready a pile of blankets and a warm shawl, lighted a large glass lantern (as she saw the water approaching the fireplace), and, last, proceeded to arouse Willie, and wrap him up in overcoat, little fur cap, and warm mittens; when all was done, she turned and looked anxiously at the face of her guest. It might have been a mask, for all she could learn from it. He was silently watching her, not looking either depressed or hopeful. She went up to him, and touched his sleeve. "How wet you are, still," she said, compassionately. "I had forgotten that you must must have been uncomfortable after your capsize in the bay. Perhaps it is not too late to change your clothes. You will find some of Eben's in the next room. Shall I lay them out for you?"

He smiled when she touched him, a bright, warm smile, that took away ten years of his age; but he did not move.

"No," said he, "it's no use now, to put on dry clothes.

It won't hurt me to be wet; I'm used to it; but I shall be sorry when this cheerful fire is out."

He had hardly spoken, when a blast struck the house, more terrific than any that had gone before it, and a narrow crack became visible between the hearth-stone and the floor, through which the water oozed in quite rapidly. Mrs. Smiley's face blanched.

"That started the house a leetle," said Chillis, lighting his lantern by the fire.

"Could we get to the landing, do you think?" asked Mrs. Smiley, springing instinctively to the lounge, where the child lay in a half-slumber.

"Not afore the tide begins to run out. Ef it was daylight, we might, by keepin' out o' the channel; but the best we can do now is to stick to the place we're in as long as it holds together, or keeps right side up. When we can't stay no longer, we'll take to the boat.''

"I believe you know best, Mr. Chillis; but it's frightful waiting for one's house to float away from under one's feet, or fall about one's head. And the tide, too! I have always feared and hated the tides, they have been a horror to me ever since I came here. It seems so dreadful to have the earth slowly sinking into the sea; for that is the way it appears to do, you know."

"Yes, I remember hearin' you say you were nervous about the tides, once, when I called here to see your husband. Curious, that I often thought o' that chance sayin' o' yours, isn't it?"

Mrs. Smiley's reply was a smothered cry of terror, as another blast—sudden, strong, protracted — pushed the house still further away from the fire-place, letting the storm in at the opening; for it was from that direction that the wind came.

"Now she floats!" exclaimed Chillis. "We'll soon know whether she's seaworthy or not. I had better take a look at my boat, I reckon; for that's our last resort, in case your ark is worthless, Mrs. Smiley." He laughed softly, and stepped more vigorously than he had done, as the danger grew more certain.

"All right yet—cable not parted; ready to do us a good turn, if we need it."

"We shall not be floated off to the bay, shall we?" asked Mrs. Smiley, trying to smile too.

"Not afore the tide turns, certain."

"It seems to me that I should feel safer anywhere than here. Unseen dangers always are harder to battle with, even in imagination. I do not wish to put you to any further trouble; but I should not mind the storm and the open boat so much as seeing my house going to pieces, with me in it—and Willie."

"I've been a-thinkin'," replied Chillis, "that the house, arter all, ain't goin' to be much protection, with the water splashin' under foot, an' the wind an' rain drivin' in on that side where the chimney is took away. It's an awful pity such a neat, nice little place should come to grief, like this —a real snug little home!"

"And what else were you thinking?"—bringing him back to the subject of expedients.

"You mentioned goin' to the landin'. Well, we can't go there; for I doubt ef I could find the way in the dark, with the water over the tops of the bushes on the creek bank. Besides, in broad daylight it would be tough work, pullin' agin' the flood; an' I had the misfortin to hurt my shoulder, tryin' to right my boat in the bay, which partly disables me, I am sorry to say; for I should like to put my whole strength to your service."

"O, Mr. Chillis!—say no more, I beg. How selfish I am! when you have been so kind—with a bruise on your shoulder, and all! Cannot I do anything for you? I have liquor in the closet, if you would like to bathe with it."

"See—she moves again!" cried he, as the house swayed yet further away from the smouldering fire. "I've heard of ' abandoniu' one's hearth-stone;' but I'd no idea that was the way they done it."

"I had best get the brandy, any way, I think. We may need it, if we are forced to go into the boat. But do let me do something for you now, Mr. Chillis? It seems cruel, that you have been in your wet clothes for hours, and tired and bruised besides."

"Thankee—'tain't no use!"—as she offered him the brandy-flask. " The lady down at the landin' put on a plaster, as you can see for yourself"—throwing back the corner of a cloth cape the woman had placed over his shoulders, to cover the rent in his coat. " The doctor will have to fix it up, I reckon; for it is cut up pretty bad with the iron."

Mrs. Smiley turned suddenly sick. She was just at that stage of excitement when " a rose-leaf on the beaker's brim " causes the overflow of the cup. The undulations of the water, under the floor and over it, contributed still further to the feeling; and she hurried to the lounge to save herself from falling. Here she threw herself beside Willie, and cried a little, quietly, under cover of her shawl.

"There she goes! Well, this isn't pleasant, noways," said Chillis, as the house, freed with a final crash from impediments, swayed about unsteadily, impelled by wind and water. " I was sayin', a bit ago, that we could not git to the landin', at present. There are three ways o' choosin', though, which are these: to stay where we are; to git into the boat, an' let the house take its chances; or to try to git to my cabin, where we would be safe an' could keep warm."

"How long would it take us to get to your house?" asked Mrs. Smiley, from under her shawl.

"An hour, mebbe. We should have to feel our way."

Mrs. Smiley reflected. Sitting out in an open boat, without trying to do anything, would be horrible; staying where she was would be hardly less so. It would be six or seven hours still to daylight. There was no chance of the storm abating, though the water must recede after midnight.

"Let us go," she said, sitting up. "You will not desert me, I know; and why should I keep you here all night, in anxiety and peril? Once at home, you can rest and nurse yourself."

"So be it; an' God help us!"

"Amen!"

Chillis opened the door and looked out, placing a light first in the window. Then coming back for a basin, he waded out, bailed his boat, and, unfastening the chain, hauled it alongside the doorway. Mrs. Smiley had hastily put some provisions into a tin bucket, with a cover, and some things for Willie into another, and stood holding them, ready to be stowed away.

"You will have to take the tiller," said Chillis, placing the buckets safely in the boat.

"I meant to take an oar," said she.

"If you know how to steer, it will be better for me to pull alone. Now, let us have the boy, right in the bottom here, with plenty o' blankets under and over him; the same for yourself. The lanterns—so. Now, jump in!"

"The fire is dead on the hearth," she said, looking back through the empty house, and across the gap of water showing through the broken wall. "What a horrible scene! God sent you, Mr. Chillis, to help me live through it."

"I believe he did. Are you quite ready?"

"Quite; only tell me what I must do. I wish I could help you."

"You do?" he answered; and then he bent himself to the work before him, with a sense of its responsibility which exalted it into a deed of the purest chivalry.

PART II.

THE widow Smiley did not live on Clatsop Plains. Ever since the great storm at Christmas, when her house was carried off its foundations by the high tide, she had refused to go back to it. When the neighbors heard of her hus-

band's death, they took her over to Astoria to see him
buried, for there was no home to bring him to, and she had
never returned. Smiley, they say, was drowned where he
fell, in the streets of Astoria, that night of the high tide,
being too intoxicated to get up. But nobody told the
widow that. They said to her that he stumbled off the
wharf, in the dark, and that the tide brought him ashore,
and that was enough for her to know.

She was staying with the family at the landing when the
news came, two days after his death. Joe Chillis brought
her things down to the landing, and had them sent over to
Astoria, where she decided to stay; and afterward she sold
the farm and bought a small house in town, where, after
two or three months, she opened a school for young children. And the women of the place had all taken to making
much of Joe Chillis, in consideration of his conduct during
that memorable time, and of his sufferings in consequence;
for he was laid up a long while afterward with that hurt in
his shoulder, and the consequences of his exposure. Mrs.
Smiley always treated him with the highest respect, and did
not conceal that she had a great regard for him, if he *was*
nothing but an old mountain man, who had had a squaw
wife; which regard, under the circumstances, was not to be
wondered at.

Widow Smiley was young, and pretty, and *smart;* and
Captain Rumway, the pilot, was dreadfully taken up with
her, and nobody would blame her for taking a second husband, who was able and willing to provide well for her. If
it was to be a match, nobody would speak a word against it.
It was said that he had left off drinking on her account, and
was building a fine house up on the hill, on one of the prettiest lots in town. Such was the gossip about Mrs. Smiley,
a year and a half after the night of the high tide.

It was the afternoon of a July day, in Astoria; and, since
we have given the reader so dismal a picture of December,
let us, in justice, say a word about this July day. All day

long the air had been as bright and clear as crystal, and the sun had sparkled on the blue waters of the noblest of rivers without blinding the eyes with glare, or sickening the senses with heat. Along either shore rose lofty highlands, crowned with cool-looking forests of dark-green firs. Far to the east, like a cloud on the horizon, the snowy cone of St. Helen's mountain stood up above the wooded heights of the Cascade Range, with Mount Adams peeping over its shoulder. Quite near, and partly closing off the view up the river, was picturesque Tongue Point—a lovely island of green—connected with the shore only by a low and narrow isthmus. From this promontory to the point below the town, the bank of the river was curtained and garlanded with blossoming shrubs—mock-orange, honeysuckle, spirea, *aerifolia*, crimson roses, and clusters of elder-berries, lavender, scarlet, and orange—everywhere, except where men had torn them away to make room for their improvements.

Looking seaward, there was the long line of white surf which marks where sea and river meet, miles away; with the cape and light-house tower standing out in sharp relief against the expanse of ocean beyond, and sailing vessels lying off the bar waiting for Rumway and his associates to come off and show them the entrance between the sandspits. And nearer, all about on the surface of the sparkling river, snowy sails were glancing in the sun, like the wings of birds that skim beside them. It is hard, in July, to believe it has ever been December.

Perhaps Mrs. Smiley was thinking so, as from her rose-embowered cottage-porch on the hill, not far from Captain Rumway's new house, she watched the sun sinking in a golden glory behind the light-house and the cape. Her school dismissed for the week, and her household tasks completed, she was taking her repose in a great sleepy-hollow of a chair, near enough to the roses to catch their delicate fragrance. Her white dress looked fresh and dainty, with a rose-colored ribbon at the throat, and a bunch of spirea; sea-foam, Willie called it, in her gleaming, braided hair. Her great gray eyes, neither sad nor bright, but sweetly serious, harmonized the delicate pure tones that made up her person and her dress, leaving nothing to be desired, except, perhaps, a suggestion of color in the clear, white oval of her cheeks. And that an accident supplied.

For, while the sun yet sent lances of gold up out of the sea, the garden gate clicked, and Captain Rumway came up the walk. He was a handsome man, of fine figure, with a bronzed complexion, dark eyes, and hair always becomingly tossed up, owing to a slight wave in it, and a springy quality it had of its own. The sun and sea-air, while they had bronzed his face, had imparted to his cheeks that rich glow which is often the only thing lacking to make a dark face beautiful. Looking at him, one could hardly help catching something of his glow, if only through admiration of it. Mrs. Smiley's sudden color was possibly to be accounted for on this ground.

"Good evening, Mrs. Smiley," he said, lifting his hat gracefully. "I have come to ask you to walk over and look at my house. No, thank you; I will not come in, if you are ready for the walk. I will stop here and smell these roses while you get your hat."

"Is your house so nearly completed, then?" she asked, as they went down the walk together.

"So nearly, that I require a woman's opinion upon the inside arrangements; and there is no one whose judgment upon such matters I value more than yours."

"I suppose you mean to imply that I am a good housekeeper? But there is great diversity of taste among good housekeepers, Mr. Rumway."

"Your taste will suit me—that I am sure of. I did not see Willie at home; is he gone away?" he asked, to cover a sudden embarrassing consciousness.

"I let him go home with Mr. Chillis, last evening, but I expect him home to-night."

" Poor old Joe! He takes a great deal of comfort with the boy. And no wonder!—he is a charming child, worthy such parentage,"—glancing at his companion's face.

" I am glad when anything of mine gives Mr. Chillis pleasure," returned Mrs. Smiley, looking straight ahead. " I teach Willie to have a great respect and love for him. It is the least we can do."

Rumway noticed the inclusive *we*, and winced. " He is a strange man," he said, by way of answer.

" A hero!" cried Mrs. Smiley firmly.

" And never more so then when in whisky," added Rumway, ungenerously.

" Younger and more fortunate men have had that fault," she returned, thinking of Eben.

" And conquered it," he added, thinking of himself.

" Here we are. Just step in this door-way a bit and look at the view. Glorious, isn't it? I have sent for a lot of very choice shrubs and trees for the grounds, and mean to make this the prettiest place in town."

" It must be very pretty, with this view," replied Mrs. Smiley, drinking in the beauty of the scene with genuine delight.

" Please to step inside. Now, it is about the arrangement of the doors, windows, closets, and all that, I wanted advice. I am told that ladies claim to understand these things better than men."

" They ought, I am sure, since the house is alone their realm. What a charming room! So light, so airy, with such a view! and the doors and windows in the right places, too. And this cunning little porch towards the west! I'm glad you have that porch, Mr. Rumway. I have always said every house should have a sunset porch. I enjoy mine so much these lovely summer evenings."

And so they went through the house: she delighted with it, in the main, but making little suggestions, here and there; he palpitating with her praises, as if they had been bestowed on himself. And, indeed, was not this house a part of himself, having so many of his sweetest hopes built into it? For what higher proof does a man give of a worthy love then in constructing a bright and cheerful shelter for the object of it—than in making sure of a fitting home?

"It will lack nothing," she said, as they stood together again on the "sunset porch," talking of so grouping the shrubbery as not to intercept the view.

"Except a mistress," he added, turning his eyes upon her face, full of intense meaning. "With the right woman in it, it will seem perfect to me, without her, it is nothing but a monument of my folly. There is but one woman I ever want to see in it. Can you guess who it is? Will you come?"

Mrs. Smiley looked up into the glowing face bent over her, searching the passionate dark eyes with her clear, cool gaze; while slowly the delicate color crept over face and neck, as her eyes fell before his ardent looks, and she drew in her breath quickly.

"I, I do not know; there are so many things to think of."

"What things? Let me help you consider them. If you mean—"

"O, mamma, mamma!" shouted Willie, from the street. "Here we are, and I've had such a splendid time. We've got some fish for you, too. Are you coming right home?" And there, on the sidewalk, was Chillis, carrying a basket, with his hat stuck full of flowers, and as regardless as a child of the drollery of his appearance.

Mrs. Smiley started a little as she caught the expression of his face, thinking it did not comport with the holiday appearance of his habiliments, and hastened at once to obey its silent appeal. Rumway walked beside her to the gate.

"Have you no answer for me?" he asked, hurriedly.

"Give me a week," she returned, and slipped away from

him, taking the basket from Chillis, and ordering Willie to
carry it, while she walked by the old man's side.

"You have been lookin' at your new house? he remarked.
"You need not try to hide your secret from me. I see it
in your face;" and he looked long and wistfully upon the
rosy record.

"If you see something in *my* face, I see something in
yours. You have a trouble, a new pain of some kind.
Yesterday you looked forty, and radiant; this evening your
face is white and drawn by suffering."

"You do observe the old man's face sometimes, then?
That other has not quite blotted it out? O, my lovely lady!
How sweet an' dainty you look, in that white dress. It does
my old eyes good to look at you."

"You are never too ill or sad to make me pretty compliments, Mr. Chillis. Do you know, I think I have grown
quite vain since I have had you to flatter me. We consti-
tute a mutual admiration society, I'm sure."

Then she led him into the rose-covered porch, and seated
him in the "sleepy-hollow;" brought him a dish of strawberries, and told him to rest while she got ready his
supper.

"Rest!" he answered; "*I'm* not tired. Willie an' I
cooked our own supper, too. So you jest put Willie to
bed—he's tired enough, I guess—an' then come an' talk to
me. That's all I want to-night—is jest to hear the White
Rose talk."

While Mrs. Smiley was occupied with Willie—his wants
and his prattle—her guest sat motionless, his head on his
hand, his elbow resting on the arm of the chair. He had
that rare repose of bearing which is understood to be a
sign of high breeding, but in him was temperament, or a
quietude caught from nature and solitude. It gave a posi-
tive charm to his manner, whether animated or depressed;
a dignified, introspective, self-possessed carriage, that
suited with his powerfully built, symmetrical frame, and

regular cast of features. Yet, self-contained as his usual expression was, his face was capable of vivid illuminations, and striking changes of aspect, under the influence of feelings either pleasant or painful. In the shadow of the rose-vines, and the gathering twilight, it would have been impossible to discern, by any change of feature, what his meditations might be now.

"The moon is full to-night," said Mrs. Smiley, bringing out her low rocker and placing it near her friend. "It will be glorious on the river, and all the 'young folks' will be out, I suppose."

"Did not Rumway ask you to go? Don't let me keep you at home, ef he did."

"No; I am not counted among young folks any longer," returned she, with a little sigh, that might mean something or nothing. Then a silence fell between them for several minutes. It was the fashion of these friends to wait for the spirit to move them to converse, and not unfrequently a silence longer than that which was in heaven came between their sentences; but to-night there was thunder in their spiritual atmosphere, and the stillness was oppressive. Mrs. Smiley beat a tattoo with her slipper.

"Rumway asked you to marry him, did he?" began Chillis, at last, in a low and measured tone.

"Yes."

"An' you accepted him?"

"Not yet"—in a quavering adagio.

"But you will?"

"Perhaps so. I do not know "—in a firmer voice.

"Rumway is doin' well, an' he is a pretty good fellow, as men go. But he is not half the man that I was at his age —or, rather, that I might have been, ef I had had sech a motive for bein' a man as he has."

"It is not difficult to believe that, Mr. Chillis. There is heroic material in you, and, I fear, none in Mr. Rumway." She spoke naturally and cheerfully now, as if she had no

11

sentiment too sacred to be revealed about the person in question. "But why was there no motive?"

"Why? It was my fate; there was none—that's all. I had gone off to the mountains when a lad, an' couldn't git back—couldn't even git letters from home. The fur companies didn't allow o' correspondence—it made their men homesick. When I came to be a man, I did as the other men did, took an Indian wife, an' became the father o' half-breed children. I never expected to live any other way than jest as we lived then—roamin' about the mountains, exposed to dangers continually, an' reckless because it was no use to think. But, after I had been a savage for a dozen years—long enough to ruin any man—the fur companies began to break up. The beaver were all hunted out o' the mountains. The men were ashamed to go home—Indians as we all were—an' so drifted off down here, where it was possible to git somethin' to eat, an' where there was quite a settlement o' retired trappers, missionaries, deserted sailors, and such-like Whites."

"You brought your families with you?"

"Of course. We could not leave them in the mountains, with the children, to starve. Besides, we loved our children. They were not to blame for bein' half-Indian; an' we could not separate them from their mothers, ef we had a-wished. We did the only thing we could do, under the circumstances—married the mothers by White men's laws, to make the children legitimate. Even the heads of the Hudson's Bay Company were forced to comply with the sentiment of the White settlers; an' their descendants are among the first families of Oregon. But they had money an' position; the trappers had neither, though there were some splendid men among them—so our families were looked down upon. O, White Rose! didn't I use to have some bitter thoughts in those days? for my blood was high blood, in the State where I was raised."

"I can imagine it, very easily," said Mrs. Smiley, softly.

"But I never let on. I was wild and devil-may-care. To hide my mortification, I faced it out, as well as I could; but I wasn't made, in the beginnin', for that kind o' life, an' it took away my manhood. After the country began to settle up, an' families—real White families—began to move in, I used to be nearly crazy, sometimes. Many's the day that I've rode through the woods, or over the prairies, tryin' to git away from myself; but I never said a cross word to the squaw wife. Why should I?—it was not her fault. Sometimes she fretted at me (the Indian women are great scolds); but I did not answer her back. I displeased her with my vagabond ways, very likely—her White husband, to whom she looked for better things. I couldn't work; I didn't take no interest in work, like other men."

"O, Mr. Chillis! was not that a great mistake? Would not some kind of ambition have helped to fill up the blank in your life?"

"I didn't have any—I couldn't have any, with that old Indian woman sittin' there, in the corner o' my hearth. When the crazy fit came on, I jest turned my back on home, an' mounted my horse for a long, lonely ride, or went to town and drank whisky till I was past rememberin' my trouble. But I never complained. The men I associated with expected me to amuse them, an' I generally did, with all manner o' wild freaks an' incredible stories— some o' which were truer than they believed, for I had had plenty of adventures in the mountains. White Rose, do you imagine I ever loved that squaw wife o' mine?"

"I remember asking myself such a question, that night of the storm, as you stood by the fire, so still and strange. I was speculating about your history, and starting these very queries you have answered to-night."

"But you have never asked me."

"No; how could I? But I am glad to know. Now I understand the great patience — the tender, pathetic patience—which I have often remarked in you. Only those who have suffered long and silently can ever attain to it."

"An' so people say, 'Poor old Joe!' an' they don't know what they mean, when they say it. They think I am a man without the ambitions an' passions of other men; a simple, good fellow, without too much brain, an' only the heart of a fool. But they don't know me—they don't know me!"

"How could they, without hearing what you have just told me, or without knowing you as I know you?"

"They never will know. I don't want to be pitied for my mistakes. 'Poor old Joe' is proud, as well as poor."

Mrs. Smiley sat silent, gazing at the river's silver ripples. Her shapely hands were folded in her lap; her whole attitude quiet, absorbed. Whether she was thinking of what she had heard, or whether she had forgotten it, no one could have guessed from her manner; and Chillis could not wait to know. The fountains of the deep had been stirred until they would not rest.

"Was there no other question you asked yourself about the old mountain man which he can answer? Did you never wonder whether he ever had loved at all?"

"You have made me wonder, to-night, whether, at some period of your life, you have not loved some woman of your own race and color. You must have had some opportunities of knowing white women."

"Very few. An' my pride was agin seekin' what I knew was not for me; for the woman I fancied to myself was no common white woman. White Rose, I carried a young man's heart in my bosom until I was near sixty, *an' then I lost it.*" He put out a hand and touched one of hers, ever so lightly. "I need not tell you any more."

A silence that made their pulses seem audible followed this confession. A heavy shadow descended upon both hearts, and a sudden dreary sense of an unutterable and unalterable sorrow burdened their spirits.

After a little, "Mr. Chillis! Mr. Chillis!" wailed the woman's pathetic voice; and "O, my lovely lady!" sighed the man's.

"What shall I do? what shall I do? I am so sorry. What shall I do?"

"Tell me to go. I knew it would have to end so. I knew that Rumway would drive me to say what I ought not to say; for he is not worthy o' you—no man that I know of is. Ef I was as young as he, an' had his chance, I would *make* myself worthy o' you, or die. But it is too late. Old Joe Chillis may starve his heart, as he has many a time starved his body in the desert. But I did love you so! O, my sweet White Rose, I did love you so! always, from the first time I saw you."

"What is that you say?" said Mrs. Smiley, in a shocked voice.

"Always, I said, from the first time I saw you. My love was true; it did not harm you. I said, ' *There* is such a woman as God designed for me. But it is too late to have her now. I will jest worship her humbly, a great ways off, an' say " God bless her!" when she passes; an' think o' her sweet ways when I am ridin' through the woods, or polin' my huntin'-boat up the sloughs, among the willows an' pond-lilies. She would hardly blame me, ef she knew I loved her that way.'

"But it grew harder afterwards, White Rose, when you were grateful to me, in your pretty, womanly way, an' treated me so kindly before all the world, an' let your little boy love me, an' loved me yourself—I knew it—in a gentle, friendly fashion. O, but it was sweet!—but not sweet enough, sometimes. Ef I have been crazed for the lack o' love in my younger days, I have been crazed with love since then. There have been days when I could neither work nor eat, nights when I could not sleep, for thinkin' o' what might have been, but never could be; times when I have been tempted to upset my boat in the bay, an' never try to right it. But when I had almost conquered my madness, that you might never know, then comes this Rumway, with his fine looks, an' his fine house, an' his fine professions, an'

blots me out entirely; for what will old Joe be worth to
Madame Rumway, or to Madame Rumway's fine husband?"

Mrs. Smiley sat thoughtful and silent a long time after
this declaration of love, that gave all and required so little.
She was sorry for it; but since it was so, and she must know
it, she was glad that she had heard it that night. She could
place it in the balance with that other declaration, and decide upon their relative value to her; for she saw, as he did,
that the two were incompatible—one must be given up.

"It is late," she said, rising. "You will come up and
take breakfast with Willie and me, before you go home?
My strawberries are in their prime."

"I thought you would a-told me to go, an' never come
back," he said, stepping out into the moonlight with the
elastic tread of twenty-five. He stopped and looked back
at her, with a beaming countenance, like a boy's.

She was standing on the step above him, looking down
at him with a pleasant but serious expression. "I am going to trust you never to repeat to me what you have said
to-night. I know I can trust you."

"So be it, White Rose," he returned, with so rapid and
involuntary a change of attitude, voice, and expression,
that the pang of his hurt pierced her heart also. But "I
know I can trust you," she repeated, as if she had not seen
that shrinking from the blow. "And I am going to try to
make your life a little pleasanter, and more like other people's. When you are dressed up, and ordered to behave
properly, and made to look as handsome as you can, so that
ladies shall take notice of you and flatter you with their
eyes and tongues, and you come to have the·same interest
in the world that other men have—and why shouldn't you?
—then your imagination will not be running away with
you, or making angels out of common little persons like
myself—how dreadfully prosy and commonplace you have
no idea! And I forbid you to allow Willie to stick your
hat full of flowers, when you go fishing together; and order

you to make that young impudence respectful to you on all occasions—asserting your authority, if necessary. And, lastly, I prefer you should not call me Madame Rumway until I have a certified and legal claim to the title. Good-night."

He stood bareheaded, his face drooping and half-concealed, pulling the withered flowers out of his hat. Slowly he raised it, made a military salute, and placed it on his head. "It is for you to command and me to obey," he said.

"Breakfast as seven o'clock precisely," called out the tuneful voice of Mrs. Smiley after him, as he went down the garden-path with bent head, walking more like an old man than she had ever seen him. Then she went into the house, closed it carefully, after the manner of lone women, and went up to her room. But deliciously cool and fragrant as was the tiny chamber, Mrs. Smiley could not sleep that night. Nor did Chillis come to breakfast next morning.

A month passed away. Work was suspended on Mr. Rumway's house, the doors and windows boarded up, and the gate locked. Everybody knew it could mean but one thing—that Mrs. Smiley had refused the owner. But the handsome captain put a serene face upon it, and kept about his business industriously and like a gentleman. The fact that he did not return to his wild courses was remarked upon as something hardly to be credited, but greatly to his honor; for it was universally conceded, that such a disappointment as his was enough to drive almost any man to drink who had indulged in it previously; such is the generally admitted frailty of man's moral constitution.

Toward the last of August, Mrs. Smiley received a visit from Chillis. He was dressed with more than his customary regard to appearances, and looked a little paler and thinner than usual. Otherwise, he was just the same as ever; and, with no questions asked or answered on either

side, their old relations were re-established, and Willie
was rapturously excited with the prospect of more Saturday excursions. Yet there was this difference in their
manner toward each other—that he now seldom addressed
her as " White Rose," and never as " my lovely lady;"
while it was she who made graceful little compliments to
him, and was always gay and bright in his company, and
constantly watchful of his comfort or pleasure. She prevailed upon him, too, to make calls with her upon other
ladies; and gave him frequent commissions that would
bring him in contact with a variety of persons. But she
could not help seeing, that it was only in obedience to her
wishes that he made calls, or mingled with the town-people;
and when, one evening, returning together from a visit
where he had been very much patronized, he had remarked,
with a shrug and smile of self-contempt, " It is no use,
Mrs. Smiley—oil an' water won't mix," she had given it up,
and never more interfered with his old habits.

So the summer passed, and winter came again, with its
long rains, dark days, and sad associations. Although
Mrs. Smiley was not at all a " weakly woman," constant
effort and care, and the absence of anything very flattering
in her future, or inspiring in her present, wore upon her,
exhausting her vitality too rapidly for perfect health, as
the constantly increasing delicacy of her appearance testi-
fied. In truth, when the spring opened, she found herself
so languid and depressed as to be hardly able to teach, in
addition to her house-work. Then it was that the gossips
took up her case once more, and declared, with considerable unanimity, that Mrs. Smiley was pining for the handsome Captain, after all, and, if ever she had refused him,
was sorry for it—thus revenging themselves upon a woman
audacious enough to refuse a man many others would have
thought " good enough for them," and " too good for " so
unappreciative a person.

With the first bright and warm weather, Willie went to

spend a week with his friend, and Mrs. Smiley felt forced to take a vacation. A yachting-party were going over to the cape, and Captain Rumway was to take them out over the bar. Rumway himself sent an invitation to Mrs. Smiley—this being the first offer of amity he had felt able to make since the previous July. She laughed a little, to herself, when the note came (for she was not ignorant of the town-tattle—what school-teacher ever is?) and sent an acceptance. If Captain Rumway were half as courageous as she, the chatterers would be confounded, she promised herself, as she made her toilet for the occasion—not too nice for sea-water, but bright and pretty, and becoming, as her toilets always were.

So she sailed over to the cape with the "young folks," and, as widows can—particularly widows who have gossip to avenge—was more charming than any girl of them all, to others beside Captain Rumway. The officers of the garrison vied with each other in showing her attentions; and the light-house keeper, in exhibiting the wonders and beauties of the place, always, if unconsciously, appealed to Mrs. Smiley for admiration and appreciation. Yet she wore her honors modestly, contriving to share this homage with some other, and never accepting it as all meant for herself. And toward Captain Rumway her manner was as absolutely free from either coquetry or awkwardness as that of the most indifferent acquaintance. Nobody, seeing her perfectly frank yet quiet and cool deportment with her former suitor, could say, without falsehood, that she in any way concerned herself about him; and if he had heard that she was pining for him, he was probably undeceived during that excursion. Thus she came home feeling that she had vindicated herself, and with a pretty color in her face that made her look as girlish as any young lady of them all.

But, if Captain Rumway had reopened an acquaintance with Mrs. Smiley out of compassion for any woes she might be suffering on his account, or out of a design to show how

completely he was master of himself, or, in short, for any
motive whatever, he was taken in his own devices, and
compelled to surrender unconditionally. Like the man in
Scripture, out of whom the devils were cast only to return,
his last estate was worse than the first, as he was soon compelled to acknowledge; and one of the first signs of this
relapse into fatuity was the resumption of work on the un-
finished house, and the ornamentation of the neglected
grounds.

"I will make it such a place as she cannot refuse," he
said to himself, more or less hopefully. "She will have to
accept the house and grounds, with me thrown in. And
whatever she is pining for, she *is* pining, *that* I can see. It
may be for outdoor air and recreation, and the care which
a husband only can give her. If it be that she can take
them along with me."

Thus it was, that when Chillis brought Willie home from
his long visit to the woods and streams, he saw the work-
men busy on the Captain's house. He heard, too, about
the excursion to the cape, and the inevitable comments upon Rumway's proceedings. But he said nothing about it to
Mrs. Smiley, though he spent the evening in the snug little
parlor, and they talked together of many things personally
interesting to both; especially about Willie's education and
profession in life.

"He ought to go to college," said his mother. "I wish
him to be a scholarly man, whatever profession he decides
upon afterward. I could not bear that he should not have
a liberal education."

"Yes, Willie must be a gentleman," said Chillis; "for
his mother's sake he must be that."

"But how to provide the means to furnish such an education as he ought to have, is what puzzles me," continued
Mrs. Smiley, pausing in her needle-work to study that
problem more closely, and gazing absently at the face of
her guest. "Will ten years more of school-teaching do it,
I wonder?"

"'Ten years o' school-teachin', an' house-work, an' sew-in'!" cried he. "Yes, long before that you will be under the sod o' the grave-yard! *You* cannot send the boy to college."

"Who, then?"— smiling at his vehemence.

"*I* will."

"You, Mr. Chillis? I thought...." She checked herself, fearing to hurt his pride.

"You thought I was poor, an' so I am, for I never tried to make money. *I* don't want money. But there is land belongin' to me out in the valley—five or six hundred acres —an' land is growin' more valuable every year. Ten years from now I reckon mine would pay a boy's schoolin'. So you needn't work yourself to death for that, Mrs. Smiley."

The tears sprang to the gray eyes which were turned upon him with such eloquent looks. "It is like you," she said, in a broken voice, "and I have nothing to say."

"You are welcome to my land, White Rose, an' there is nothin' *to* be said."

Then she bent her head over her sewing, feeling, indeed, that there was little use for words.

"Do you know," he asked, breaking a protracted silence, "that you have got to give up teachin'?"

"And do what? I might take to gardening. That would be better, perhaps; I have thought about it."

"Let me see your hands. They look like gardenin': two rose-leaves! Don't it make me wish to be back in my prime? Work for you! Wouldn't I love to work for you?"

"And do you not, in every way you can? Am I to have no pride about accepting so much service? What a poor creature you must take me for, Mr. Chillis."

"There is nothin' else in the world that I think of; nothin' else that I live for; an' after all it is so little, that I cannot save you from spoilin' your pretty looks with care. An' you have troubled yourself about me, too; don't think I haven't seen it. You fret your lovely soul about the old man's trouble, when you can't help it—you, nor nobody. An', after all, what does it matter about *me?* *I* am nothin', and you are everything. I want you to remember that, and do everything for your own happiness without wastin' a thought on me. I am content to keep my distance, ef I only see you happy and well off. Do you understand me?"

Mrs. Smiley looked up with a suffused face. "Mr. Chillis," she answered, "you make me ashamed of myself and my selfishness. Let us never refer to this subject again. Work don't hurt me; and since you have offered to provide for Willie's education, you have lifted half my burden. Why should you stand at a distance to see me happier than I am, when I am so happy as to have such a friend as you? How am I to be happier by your being at a distance, who have been the kindest of friends? You are out of spirits this evening, and you talk just a little—nonsense." And she smiled at him in a sweetly apologetic fashion for the word.

"That is like enough," he returned gravely; "but I want you to remember my words, foolish or not. Don't let me stand in your light—not for one minute; and don't forgit this: that Joe Chillis is happy when he sees the White Rose bloomin' and bright."

Contrary to his command, Mrs. Smiley did endeavor to forget these words in the weeks following, when the old mountain-man came no more to her rose-embowered cottage, and when Captain Rumway invented many ingenious schemes for getting the pale school-teacher to take more recreation and fresh air. She endeavored to forget them, but she could not, though her resolve to ignore them was as strong as it ever had been when her burdens had seemed lighter! But in spite of her resolve, and in spite of the fact that it could not be said that any encouragement had been given to repeat his addresses, Rumway continued to work at his house and grounds steadily, and, to all appearance, hopefully. And although he never consulted Mrs. Smiley now concerning the arrangement of either, he showed that he remembered her suggestions of the year before, by following them out without deviation.

Thus quietly, without incident, the June days slipped away, and the perfect July weather returned once more, · when there was always a chair or two out on the sunset porch at evening. At last Chillis re-appeared, and took a seat in one of them, quite in the usual way. He had been away, he said, attending to some business.

"An' I have fixed that matter all right about the boy's schoolin', he added. "The papers are made out in the clerk's office, an' will be sent to you as soon as they are recorded. There are five hundred and forty acres, which you will know how to manage better than I can tell you. You can sell by and by, ef you can't yet the money out of it any other way. The taxes won't be much, the land being unimproved."

"You do not mean that you have *deeded* all your land to Willie?" asked Mrs. Smiley. "I protest against it: he must not have it! Would you let us rob you," she asked wonderingly. "What are *you* to do, by and by, as you say?"

"Me? I shall do well enough. Money is o' no use to me. But ef I should want a meal or a blanket that I couldn't get, the boy wouldn't see me want them long. Ef he forgot old Joe Chillis, his mother wouldn't, I reckon."

"You pay too high a price for our remembrance, Mr. Chillis; we are not worth it. But why do you talk of forgetting? You are not going away from us?"

"Yes; I am goin' to start to-morrow for my old stampin' ground, east o' the mountains. My only livin' son is over there, somewhar. He don't amount to much—the Indian in him is too strong; but, like enough, he will be glad to see his father afore I die. An' I want to git away from here."

" You will come back? Promise me you will come back?"
For something in his voice, and his settled expression of
melancholy and renunciation, made her fear he was taking
this step for a reason that could not be named between
them.

" It is likely," he said; " but ef I come or no, don't fret
about me. Just remember this that I am tellin' you now.
The day I first saw you was the most fortunate day of my life.
Ef I hadn't a-met you, I should have died as I had lived—
like a creature without a soul. An' now I have a soul, in
you. An' when I come to die, as I shall before many
years, I shall die happy, thinkin' how my old hands had
served the sweetest woman under heaven, and how they
had been touched by hers so kindly, many a time, when
she condescended to serve *me*."

What could she say to a charge like this? Yet say something she must, and so she answered, that he thought too
highly of her, who was no better than other women; but,
that, since in his great singleness of heart, he did her this
honor, to set her above all the world, she could only be
humbly grateful, and wish really to be what in his vivid imagination she seemed to him. Then she turned the talk
upon less personal topics, and Willie was called and informed of the loss he was about to sustain; upon which
there was a great deal of childish questioning, and boyish
regret for the good times no more to be that summer.

" I should like to take care of your boat," said he—"your
hunting-boat, I mean. If I had it over here, I would take
mamma down to it every Saturday, and she could sew and
do everything there, just as she does at home; and it would
be gay, now, wouldn't it?"

" The old boat is sold, my boy; that an' the row-boat, and
the pony, too. You'll have to wait till I come back for
huntin', and fishin', and ridin'."

Then Mrs. Smiley knew almost certainly that this visit was
the last she would ever receive from Joe Chillis, and,

though she tried hard to seem unaffected by the parting, and to talk of his return hopefully, the effort proved abortive, and conversation flagged. Still he sat there silent and nearly motionless through the whole evening, thinking what thoughts she guessed only too well. With a great sigh, at last he rose to go.

"You will be sure to write at the end of your journey, and let us know how you find things there, and when you are coming back?"

"I will write," said he; "an' I want you to write back and tell me that you remember what I advised you some time ago." He took her hands, folded them in his own, kissed them reverently, and turned away.

Mrs. Smiley watched him going down the garden-walk, as she had watched him a year before, and noted how slow and uncertain his steps had grown since then. At the gate he turned and waved his hand, and she in turn fluttered her little white handkerchief. Then she sat down with the handkerchief over her head, and sobbed for full five minutes.

"There are things in life one cannot comprehend," she muttered to herself, "things we cannot dare to meddle with or try to alter; Providences, I suppose, they are. If God had made a man like that for me, of my own age, and given him opportunities suited to his capacities, and he had loved me as this man loves, what a life ours would have been!"

The summer weather and bracing north-west breezes from the ocean renewed, in a measure, Mrs. Smiley's health, and restored her cheerful spirits; and, if she missed her old friend, she kept silent about it, as she did about most things that concerned herself. To Willie's questioning she gave those evasive replies children are used to receive; but she frequently told him, in talks about his future, that Mr. Chillis had promised to send him to college, and that as long as he lived he must love and respect so generous a friend. "And, Willie," she never failed to add, "if ever you see an old man who is in need of anything; food, or clothes, or shelter; be very sure that you furnish them, as far as you are able." She was teaching him to pay his debt: "for, inasmuch as ye have done it unto the least of these," he had done it unto his benefactor.

September came, and yet no news had arrived from beyond the mountains. Captain Rumway's house was finished up to the last touch of varnish. The lawn, and the shrubbery, and fence were all just as they should be; yet, so far as anybody knew, no mistress had been provided for them, when, one warm and hazy afternoon, Mrs. Smiley received an invitation to look at the completed mansion, and pass her judgment upon it.

"I am going to furnish it in good style," said its master, rather vauntingly, Mrs. Smiley thought, "and I hoped you would be so good as to give me your assistance in making out a list of the articles required to fit the house up perfectly, from parlor to kitchen."

"Any lady can furnish a list of articles for each room, Mr· Rumway, more or less costly, as you may order; but only the lady who is to live in the house can tell you what will please *her;*" and she smiled the very shadow of a superior smile.

Mr. Rumway had foolishly thought to get his house furnished according to Mrs. Smiley's taste, and now found he should have to consult Mrs. Rumway's, present or prospective, and the discovery annoyed him. Yet, why should he be annoyed? Was not the very opportunity presented that he had desired, of renewing his proposal to her to take the establishment in charge? So, although it compelled him to change his programme, he accepted the situation, and seized the tide at flood.

"It is that lady—the one I entreat to come and live in it—whose wishes I now consult. Once more will you come?"

Mrs. Smiley, though persistently looking aside, had caught the eloquent glance of the Captain's dark eyes, and something of the warmth of his face was reflected in her own. But she remained silent, looking at the distant highlands, without seeing them.

"You must have seen," he continued, "that notwithstanding your former answer, I have been bold enough to hope you might change your mind; for, in everything I have done here, I have tried to follow your expressed wishes. I should in all else strive to make you as happy as by accepting this home you would make me. You do not answer; shall I say it is 'yes?'" He bent so close that his dark, half-curling mop of hair just brushed her golden braids, and gave her a little shock like electricity, making her start away with a blush.

"Will you give me time to decide upon my answer, Mr. Rumway?"

"You asked for time before," he replied, in an agitated voice, "and, after making me suffer a week of suspense, refused me."

"I know it," she said simply, "and I was sorry I had asked it; but my reasons are even more imperative than they were then for wishing to delay. I want to decide right, at last," she added, with a faint attempt at a smile.

"That will be right which accords with your feelings, and certainly you can tell me now what they are—whether you find me the least bit lovable or not."

The gray eyes flashed a look up into the dark eyes, half of mirth and half of real inquiry. "I think one might learn to endure you, Mr. Rumway," she answered, demurely. "But"—changing her manner—"I can not tell you whether or not I can marry you, until—until—well," she concluded desperately—"it may be a day, or a week, or a month. There is something to be decided, and until it is decided, I can not give an answer."

Captain Rumway looked very rebellious.

12

"I do not ask you to wait, Mr. Rumway," said Mrs. Smiley, tormentingly. "Your house need not be long without a mistress."

"Of course, I must wait, if you give me the least ground of hope. This place was made for you, and no other woman shall ever come into it as my wife—that I swear. If you will not have me, I will sell it, and live a bachelor."

Mrs. Smiley laughed softly and tunefully. "Perhaps you would prefer to limit your endurance, and tell me how long you *will* allow me to deliberate before you sell and retire to bachelorhood?"

"You know very well," he returned, ruefully, "that I shall always be hoping against all reason that the wished-for answer was coming at last."

"Then we will say no more about it at present."

"And I may come occasionally to learn whether that 'something' has been decided?"

"Yes, if you have the patience for it. But, I warn you, there is a chance of my having to say 'No.'"

"If there is only a chance of your having to say 'No,' I think I may incur the risk," said Rumway, with a sudden accession of hopefulness; and, as they walked home together once more, the gossips pronounced it an engagement. The Captain himself felt that it was, although, when he reviewed the conversation, he discovered that he founded his impression upon that one glance of the gray eyes, rather than upon anything that had been said. And Mrs. Smiley put the matter out of mind as much as possible, and waited.

One day, about the last of the month, a letter came to her from over the mountains. It ran in this wise:

"MY LOVELY LADY: I am once more among the familyar seanes of 40 year ago. My son is hear, an' about as I expected. I had rather be back at Clatsop, with the old bote; but; owin' to circumstances I can't controll, think it better to end my dais on this side ov the mountains. You need not look for me to come back, but I send you an' the boy my best love, an' hope you hav done as I advised.

"Yours, faithfully, til deth,

"JOE CHILLIS."

Soon after the receipt of this letter, Captain Rumway called to inquire concerning the settlement of the matter on which his marriage depended. That evening he staid later than usual, and, in a long confidential talk which he had with Mrs. Smiley, learned that there was a condition attached to the consummation of his wishes, which required his recognition of the claims of "poor old Joe" to be considered a friend of the family. To do him justice, he yielded the point more gracefully than, from his consciousness of his own position, could have been expected.

The next day, Mrs. Smiley wrote as follows:

"DEAR MR. CHILLIS: I shall move into the new house about the last of October, *according to your advice.* We—that is, myself, and Willie, and the present owner of the house—shall be delighted if you will come and stay with us. But if you decide to remain with your son, believe that we think of you very often and very affectionately, and wish you every possible happiness. R. agrees with me that the land ought to be deeded back to you; and *I* think you had best return and get the benefit of it. It would make you very comfortable for life, properly managed, and about that we might help you. Please write and let us know what to do about it.

"Yours affectionately,

"ANNIE SMILEY."

No reply ever came to this letter; and, as it was written ten years ago, Mrs. Rumway has ceased to expect any. Willie is about to enter College.

HOW JACK HASTINGS SOLD HIS MINE.

THE passenger train from the East came thundering
down the head of the Humboldt Valley, just as morning brightened over the earth—refreshing eyes wearied with
yesterday's mountains and cañons, by a vision of green
willows and ash trees, a stream that was not a torrent, and
a stretch of grassy country.

Among the faces oftenest turned to the flitting views was
that of a young, gracefully-formed, neatly-dressed, deli-
cate-looking woman. The large brown eyes often returned
from gazing at the landscape, to scan with seriousness some
memoranda she held in her hand. "Arrive at Elko at eight
o'clock A. M." said the memorandum. Consulting a tiny
watch, whose hands pointed to ten minutes of eight, the
lady began making those little preparations which betoken
the journey's end at hand.

"What a strange looking place it is!" she thought, as
the motley collection of board shanties and canvas houses
came in sight;—for the famous Chloride District had been
discovered but a few months before, and the Pacific Railroad was only four weeks open. "I wish Jack had come
to meet me! I'm sure I don't see how I am to find the
stage agent to give him Jack's letter. What a number of
people!"

This mental ejaculation was called forth by the sight of
the long platform in front of the eating-house, crowded
with a surging mass of humanity just issuing from the dining-room. They were the passengers of the eastward-
bound train, ready to rush headlong for the cars when the
momently-expected "All aboard!" should be shouted at
them by the conductor. Into this crowd the freshly-ar-
rived passengers of the westward-bound train were a mo-

ment after ejected—each eyeing the other with a natural and pardonable interest.

The brown-eyed, graceful young lady conducted herself in a very business-like manner—presenting the checks for her baggage; inquiring out the office of Wells, Fargo & Co., and handing in her letter, all in the briefest possible time. Having secured a seat in a coach to Chloride Hill, with the promise of the agent to call for her when the time for departure arrived, the lady repaired to the dining-room just in time to see her acquaintances of the train departing. Sitting down alone to a hastily-cooked and underdone repast, she was about finishing a cup of bitter black coffee with a little shudder of disgust, when a gentleman seated himself opposite her at table. The glance the stranger cast in her direction was rather a lingering one; then he ordered his breakfast and ate it. Meanwhile the lady retired to the ladies' sitting-room.

After an hour of waiting, one, two, three, coaches rolled past the door, and the lady began to fear she had been forgotten, when the polite agent appeared to notify " Mrs. Hastings " that " the stage was ready." This was Mrs. Alice Hastings, then—wife of Mr. Jack Hastings, of Deep Cañon, Chloride District. The agent thought Mr. Hastings had a very pretty wife, and expressed his opinion in his manner, as men will.

When, just before starting, there entered three of the roughest-looking men she had ever encountered, Mrs. Hastings began to fear that in his zeal to obey instructions, the agent had exceeded them, and in packing the first three coaches with first-comers, had left this one to catch up the fag end of travel. If the first impression, gained from sight, had made her shrink a little, what was her dismay when, at the end of ten minutes, one of her fellow-travelers—the only American of the three—produced a bottle of brandy, which, having offered it first to her, he passed to the bullet-headed Irishman and very shabby Jew: repeating the courtesy once in twenty minutes for several times.

Mrs. Hastings was a brave sort of woman, where courage was needful; and she now began to consider the case in hand with what coolness she could command. One hundred and thirty miles—eighteen or twenty hours of such companionship—with no chance of change or intermission; a wilderness country to travel over, and all the other coaches a long way ahead. The dainty denizen of a city home, shuddering inwardly, showed outwardly a serene countenance. Her American friend, with wicked black eyes and a jolly and reckless style of carrying himself, continued to offer brandy at short intervals.

"Best take some, Madame," said he; "this dust will choke you if you don't."

"Thanks," returned the lady, with her sweetest smile, "I could not drink brandy. I have wine in my traveling-basket, should I need it; but much prefer water."

At the next station, although hardly four minutes were lost in changing horses, the men procured for her a cup of water. Mrs. Hastings' thanks were frank and cordial. She even carefully opened a conversation about the country they were passing over, and contrived to get them to ask a question or two about herself. When they learned that she had come all the way from New York on the newly-opened railroad, their interest was at its height; and when they heard that she was going to join her husband in the Chloride District, their sympathy was thoroughly enlisted.

"Wonderful—such a journey! How she could be six days on the cars, and yet able to take such a stage-ride as this, is astonishing."

Such were the American's comments. The Jew thought of the waiting husband—for your Israelite is a man of domestic and family affections. "Her husband looking for her, and she behind time! How troubled he must be! Didn't *he* know how it was? Wasn't his wife gone away on a visit once, and didn't write; and he a running to the express office every morning and evening for a letter, and get-

ting so anxious as to telegraph? Such an expense and loss
of time!—and all because he felt so uneasy about his wife!"

The bullet-headed young Irishman said nothing. He
was about half asleep from brandy and last night's travel;
too stupid to know that his hat had flown out of the window,
and was bowling along in the wind and dust half a mile
behind—all the better for his head, which looked at a red
heat now.

The lady had lifted the rude men up to her level, when
directly they were ashamed of their brandy and other vices,
and began to show instinctive traits of gentlemen. By the
time they arrived at the dinner station, where half an hour
was allowed for food and rest out of the eighteen or twenty,
she had at least two humble servitors, who showed great
concern for her comfort.

The day began to wane. They had traveled continuously
over a long stretch of plain between two mountain ranges,
over a country entirely uninhabited except by the stage
company's employees, who kept the stations and tended
the stock. This lone woman had seen but one other woman
on the road. Plenty of teams—great "prairie schooners,"
loaded with every conceivable thing for supplying the
wants of an isolated non-producing community, and drawn
by ten or fourteen mules—had been passed through the
day.

As night fell, Mrs. Hastings saw what she had never before seen or imagined—the camps of these teamsters by the
roadside; horses and mules staked, or tied to the wagons;
the men lying prone upon the earth, wrapped in blankets,
their dust-blackened faces turned up to the frosty twinkling
stars. Did people really live in that way?—how many superfluous things were there in a city!

The night was moonless and clear, and cold as at that
altitude they always are. Sleep, from the roughness of the
road, was impossible. Her companions dozed, and woke
with exclamations when the heavy lurchings of the coach

disturbed them too roughly. Mrs. Hastings never closed her eyes. When morning dawned, they were on the top of a range of mountains, like those that had been in sight all the day before. Down these heights they rattled away, and at four in the morning entered the streets of Chloride Hill—a city of board and canvas houses. Arrived at the stage office, the lady looked penetratingly into the crowd of men always waiting for the stages, but saw no face she recognized. Yes, one—and that the face of the gentleman who sat down opposite her at table in Elko.

"Permit me," he said; "I think you inquired for Mr. Hastings?"

"I did; he is my husband. I expected to find him here," she replied, feeling that sense of injury and desire to cry which tired women feel, jostled about in a crowd of men.

Leaving her a moment to say something to an employee of the office, the stranger returned immediately, saying to the man: "Take this lady to Mrs. Robb's boarding-house." Then to her: "I will inquire for your husband, and send him to you if he is in town. The hack does not go over to Deep Cañon for several hours yet. Meanwhile you had better take some rest. You must be greatly fatigued."

Fatigued! her head swam round and round; and she really was too much exhausted to feel as disappointed as she might at Jack's non-appearance. Much relieved by the prospect of a place to rest in, she followed the man summoned to escort her, and fifteen minutes after was sound asleep on a sofa of the boarding-house.

Three hours of sleep and a partial bath did much to restore tired nature's equilibrium; and, although her head still felt absurdly light, Mrs. Hastings enjoyed the really excellent breakfast provided for her, wondering how such delicacies ever got to Chloride Hill. Breakfast over, and no news of Jack, the time began to drag wearily. She was more than half inclined to be angry—only relenting when she remembered that she was two or three days behind

time, and of course Jack could not know when to expect
her. She had very full directions, and if she could not
find her way to Deep Cañon she was a goose, that was all!

So she sent for the driver of the hack, told him to get her
baggage from the express office; and started for Deep Cañon. Who should she find in the hack but her friend of the
morning!

"I could not hear of your husband," said he; "but you
are sure to find him at home."

Mrs. Hastings smiled faintly, and hoped she should.
Then she gave her thoughts to the peculiar scenery of the
country, and to the sharpness of the descent, as they whirled
rapidly down the four miles of cañon at the bottom of which
was the town of that name—another one of those places
which had "come up as a flower" in a morning. She
longed to ask about her husband and his "home"; but as
there were several persons in the stage, she restrained her
anxiety, and said never a word until they stopped before
the door of a saloon where all the other passengers alighted.
Then she told the driver she wanted to be taken to Mr.
Hastings' house.

He didn't know where that was, he said, but would inquire.

Did he know Dr. Earle?

"That's him, ma'am;" pointing out her friend of the
morning.

"How can I serve you?" he asked, raising his hat politely.

Mrs. Hastings blushed rosily, between vexation at Jack's
invisibility and confusion at being so suddenly confronted
with Dr. Earle.

"Mr. Hastings instructed me to inquire of you, if I had
any difficulty in finding him," she said, apologetically.

"I will show you his place with pleasure," returned the
Doctor pleasantly; and, jumping on the box, proceeded to
direct the driver.

Had ladies of Mrs. Hastings' style been as plenty in Deep Cañon as in New York, the driver would have grumbled at the no road he had to follow along the stony side of a hill and among the stumps of mahogany trees. But there were few like her in that mountain town, and his chivalry compelled him to go out of his way with every appearance of cheerfulness. Presently the stage stopped where the sloping ground made it very uncertain how long it could maintain its balance in that position; and the voice of Dr. Earle was heard saying " This is the place."

Mrs. Hastings, who had been looking out for some sign of home, was seized with a doubt of the credibility of her senses. It was on the tip of her tongue to say " This must be the house of some other Mr. Hastings," when she remembered prudence, and said nothing. Getting out and going toward the house to inquire, the door opened, and a man in a rough mining suit came quickly forward to meet her.

" Alice!"

" Jack!"

Dr. Earle and the driver studiously looked the other way while salutations were exchanged between Mr. and Mrs. Hastings. When they again ventured a look, the lady had disappeared within the cabin, the first glimpse of which had so dismayed her.

That afternoon, Jack initiated Alice into the mysteries of cooking by an open fire, and expatiated largely on the merits of his outside kitchen. Alice hinted to him that she was accustomed to sleep on something softer than a board, and the two went together to a store to purchase materials out of which to make a mattrass.

After that, for two or three weeks, Mrs. Hastings was industriously engaged in wondering what her husband meant when he wrote that he had built a house, and was getting things ready to receive her. Reason or romance as she might, she could not make that single room of rough boards, roofed with leaky canvas and unfurnished with a single comfort of life, into a house or home. At last, Jack seemed to guess her thoughts, for she never spoke them.

"If I could sell my mine," he then often said, "I could fix things up."

"If you sold your mine, Jack, you would go back to New York, and then there would be no need of fixing up this place." Alice wanted to say "horrid" place, but refrained.

At length, from uncongenial air, water, food, and circumstances in general, the transplanted flower began to droop. The great heat and rarified mountain air caused frantic headaches, aggravated by the glare which came through the white canvas roof. Then came the sudden mountain tempests, when the rain deluged everything, and it was hard to find a spot to stand in where the water did not drip through. She grew wild, looking forever at bare mountain sides simmering in the sun by day, and at night over their tops up to the piercing stars. A constant anxious fever burnt in her blood, that the cold night air could not quench, though she often left her couch to let it blow chilly over her, in her loose night robes. Then she fell really ill.

Sitting by her bedside, Jack said: "If I could sell my mine!" And she had answered, "let the mine go, Jack, and let us go home. Nothing is gained by stopping in this dreadful place."

Then Mr. Hastings had replied to her, "I have no money, Alice, to go home with, not a cent. I borrowed ten dollars of Earle to-day to buy some fruit for you."

That was the last straw that broke the camel's back. By night Mrs. Hastings was delirious, and Dr. Earle was called.

"She has a nervous fever," he said, "and needs the carefullest nursing."

"Which she cannot have in this d—d place," Mr. Hastings replied, profanely.

"Why don't you try to get something to do?" asked Earle of the sad-visaged husband, a day or two after.

"What is there to do? Everything is flat; there is neither business nor money in this cursed country. I've stayed here trying to sell my mine, until I'm dead broke; nothing to live on here, and nothing to get out with. What I'm to do with my wife there, I don't know. Let her die, perhaps, and throw her bones up that ravine to bleach in the sun. God! what a position to be in!"

"But you certainly must propose to do something, and that speedily. Couldn't you see it was half that that brought this illness on your wife; the inevitable which she saw closing down upon you?"

"If I cannot sell my mine soon, I'll blow out my brains, as that poor German did last week. Alice heard the report of the shot which killed him, and I think it hastened on her sickness."

"And so you propose to treat her to another such scene, and put an end to her?" said Earle, savagely.

"Better so than to let her starve," Jack returned, growing pale with the burden of possibilities which oppressed him. "How the devil I am to save her from that last, I don't know. There is neither business, money, nor credit in this infernal town. I've been everywhere in this district, asking for a situation at something, and cannot get anything better than digging ground on the new road."

"Even that might be better than starving," said Dr. Earle.

Jack was a faithful nurse; Dr. Earle an attentive physician; young people with elastic constitutions die hard: so Alice began to mend, and in a fortnight was convalescent. Jack got a situation in a quartz mill where the Doctor was part owner.

Left all day alone in the cabin, Alice began staring again at the dreary mountains whose walls inclosed her on every side. The bright scarlet and yellow flowers which grew out of their parched soil sometimes tempted her to a brief walk; but the lightness of the air fatigued her, and she did not care to clamber after them.

One day, being lonely, she thought to please Jack by dressing in something pretty and going to the mill to see him. So, laying aside the wrapper which she had worn almost constantly lately, she robed herself in a delicate linen lawn, donned a coquettish little hat and parasol, and set out for the mill, a mile away. Something in the thought of the pleasant surprise it would be to Jack gave her strength and animation; and though she arrived somewhat out of breath, she looked as dainty and fresh as a rose, and Jack was immensely proud and flattered. He introduced her to the head of the firm, showed her over the mill, pointed out to her the mule-train packing wood for the engine fires, got the amalgamator to give her specimens, and in every way showed his delight.

After an hour or so she thought about going home; but the walk home looked in prospect very much longer than the walk to the mill. In truth, it was harder by reason of being up-hill. But opportunely, as it seemed, just as Jack was seeing her off the door-stone of the office, Dr. Earle drove up, and, comprehending the situation, offered to take Mrs. Hastings to her own door in his carriage, if she would graciously allow him five minutes to see the head man in.

When they were seated in the carriage, a rare luxury in Deep Cañon, and had driven a half mile in embarrassed silence—for Mrs. Hastings somehow felt ashamed of her husband's dependence upon this man,—the Doctor spoke, and what he said was this:

"Your life is very uncongenial to you; you wish to escape from it, don't you?"

"Yes, I wish to escape; that is the word which suits my feeling—a very strange feeling it is."

"Describe it," said the Doctor, almost eagerly.

"Ever since I left the railroad, in the midst of a wilderness and was borne for so many hours away into the heart of a still more desert wilderness, my consciousness of things has been very much confused. I can only with difficulty

realize that there is any such place as New York; and San
Francisco is a fable. The world seems a great bare mountain plane; and I am hanging on to its edge by my finger-
tips, ready to drop away into space. Can you account for
such impressions?"

"Easily, if I chose. May I tell you something?"

"What is it?"

"I've half a mind to run away with you."

Now, as Dr. Earle was a rather young and a very handsome man, had been very kind, and was now looking at her
with eyes actually moistened with tears, a sudden sense of
being on the edge of a pitfall overcame Mrs. Hastings;
and she turned pale and red alternately. Yet, with the in-
stinct of a pure woman, to avoid recognizing an ugly
thought, she answered with a laugh as gay as she could
make it.

"If you were a witch, and offered me half of your broom-
stick to New York, I don't know but I should take it;—
that is, if there was room on it anywhere for Jack."

"There wouldn't be," said the Doctor, and said no
more.

The old fever seemed to have returned that afternoon.
The hills glared so that Mrs. Hastings closed the cabin
door to shut out the burning vision. The ground-squirrels,
thinking from the silence that no one was within, ran up
the mahogany tree at the side, and scampered over the
canvas roof in glee. One, more intent on gain than the
rest, invaded Jack's outside kitchen, knocking down the
tin dishes with a clang, and scattering the dirt from the
turf roof over the flour-sack and the two white plates.
Every sound made her heart beat faster. Afraid of the
silence and loneliness at last, she reopened the door; and
then a rough-looking man came to the entrance, to inquire
if there were any silver leads up the ravine.

Leads? she could not say: prospectors in plenty there
were.

Then he went his way, having satisfied his curiosity; and the door was closed again. Some straggling donkeys wandered near, which were mistaken for "Diggers;" and dreading their glittering eyes, the nervous prisoner drew the curtain over the one little sliding window. There was nothing to read, nothing to sew, no housekeeping duties, because no house to keep; she was glad when the hour arrived for preparing the late afternoon meal.

That night she dreamed that she was a skeleton lying up the cañon—the sunshine parching her naked bones; that Dr. Earle came along with a pack-train going to the mill, and picking her up carefully, laid her on top of a bundle of wood; that the Mexican driver covered her up with a blanket, which so smothered her that she awakened, and started up gasping for breath. The feeling of suffocation continuing, she stole softly to the door, and opening it, let the chilly night air blow over her. Most persons would have found Mr. Hastings' house freely ventilated, but some way poor Alice found it hard to breathe in it.

The summer was passing; times grew, if possible, harder than before. The prospectors, who had found plenty of "leads," had spent their "bottom dollar" in opening them up and in waiting for purchasers, and were going back to California any way they could. The capitalists were holding off, satisfied that in the end all the valuable mines would fall into their hands, and caring nothing how fared the brave but unlucky discoverers. In fact, they overshot themselves, and made hard times for their own mills, the miners having to stop getting out rock.

Then Jack lost his situation. Very soon food began to be scarce in the cabin of Mr. Hastings. Scanty as it was, it was more than Alice craved; or rather, it was not what she craved. If she ate for a day or two, for the next two or three days she suffered with nausea and aversion to anything which the outside kitchen afforded. Jack seldom mentioned his mine now, and looked haggard and hopeless. The conversation between her husband and Dr. Earle, recorded elsewhere, had been overheard by Alice, lying half conscious; and she had never forgotten the threat about blowing out his brains in case he failed to sell his mine. Trifling as such an apprehension may appear to another, it is not unlikely that it had its effect to keep up her nervous condition. The summer was going—was gone. Mrs. Hastings had not met Dr. Earle for several weeks; and, despite herself, when the worst fears oppressed her, her first impulse was to turn to him. It had always seemed so easy for him to do what he liked !

Perhaps *he* was growing anxious to know if he could give the thumb-screw another turn. At all events, he directed his steps toward Mr. Hastings' house on the afternoon of the last day in August. Mrs. Hastings received him at the threshold and offered him the camp-stool—the only chair she had—in the shade outside the door; at the same time seating herself upon the door-step with the same grace as if it had been a silken sofa.

She was not daintly dressed this afternoon; for that luxury, like others, calls for the expenditure of a certain amount of money, and money Alice had not—not even enough to pay a Chinaman for "doing up" one of her pretty muslins. Neither had she the facilities for doing them herself, had she been skilled in that sort of labor; for even to do your own washing and ironing pre-supposes the usual conveniences of a laundry, and these did not belong to the furniture of the outside kitchen. She had not worn her linen lawn since the visit to the mill. The dust which blew freely through every crack of the shrunken boards precluded such extravagance. Thus it happened that a soiled cashmere wrapper was her afternoon wear. She had faded a good deal since her coming to Deep Cañon; but still looked pretty and graceful, and rather too *spirituelle*.

The Doctor held in his hand, on the point of a knife, the flower of a cactus very common in the mountains, which he presented her, warning her at the same time against its needle-like thorns.

"It makes me sick," said Alice hastily, throwing it away. "It is the color of gold, which I want so much; and of the sunshine, which I hate so."

"I brought it to you to show you the little emerald bee that is always to be found in one: it is wonderously beautiful,—a living gem, is it not?"

"Yes, I know," Alice said, "I admired the first one I saw; but I admire nothing any longer—nothing at least which surrounds me here."

"I understand that, of course," returned the Doctor. "It is because your health is failing you—because the air disagrees with you."

"And because my husband is so unfortunate. If he could only get away from here—and I!" The vanity of such a supposition, in their present circumstances, brought the tears to her eyes and a quiver about her mouth.

"Why did you ever come here! Why did he ever ask you to come;—how *dared* he?" demanded the Doctor, setting his teeth together.

"That is a strange question, Doctor!" Mrs. Hastings answered with dignity, lifting her head like an antelope. "My husband was deceived by the same hopes which have ruined others. If I suffer, it is because we are both unfortunate."

"What will he do next?" questioned the Doctor curtly. The cruel meaning caused the blood to forsake her cheeks.

"I cannot tell what he will do,"—her brief answer rounded by an expressive silence.

"You might help him: shall I point out the way to you?" —watching her intently.

"Can you? *can* I help him?"—her whole form suddenly inspired with fresh life.

Dr. Earle looked into her eager face with a passion of jealous inquiry that made her cast down her eyes:

13

" Alice, do you *love* this Hastings?"

He called her Alice; he used a tone and asked a question which could not be misunderstood. Mrs. Hastings dropped her face into her hands, her hands upon her knees. She felt like a wild creature which the dogs hold at bay. She knew now what the man meant, and the temptation he used.

" Alice," he said again, " this man, your husband, possesses a prize he does not value; or does not know how to care for. Shall you stay here and starve with him ? Is he worth it ?"

" He is my husband," she answered simply, lifting up her face, calm, if mortally pale.

" And I might be your husband, after a brief interval," he said quickly. " There would have to be a divorce;—it could be conducted quietly. I do not ask you to commit yourself to dishonor. I will shield you; no care shall fall upon you, nor any reproach. Consider this well, dearest darling Alice! and what will be your fate if you depend upon him."

"Will it help *him* then, to desert him?" she asked faintly.

" Yes, unless by remaining with him you can insure his support. Maintain you he cannot. Suppose his mine were sold, he would waste that money as he wasted what he brought here. I don't want his mine, yet I will buy it to-morrow if that will satisfy you, and I have your promise to go with me. I told you once that I wanted to run away with you, and now I mean to. Shall I tell you my plan? "

" No, not to-day," Mrs. Hastings answered, struggling with her pain and embarrassment; "I could not bear it to-day, I think."

" How cruel I am while meaning to be kind! You are agitated as you ought not to be in your weak state. Shall I see you to-morrow—a professional visit, you know? "

" You will buy the mine?"—faintly, with something like a blush.

"Certainly; I swear I will — on what conditions, you know."

"On none other?"

"Shall I rob myself, not of money only, but of what is far dearer?—On *none other.*" He rose, took her cold hand, clasped it fervently, and went away.

When Jack came home to his very meagre dinner, he brought a can of peaches, which, being opened, looked so deliciously cool and tempting that Alice could not refrain from volubly exulting over them. "But how did you get them, Jack?" she asked; "not by going into debt, I hope."

"No. I was in Scott's store, and Earle, happening to come in just as Scott was selling some, and praising them highly, paid for a can, and asked me to take them to you and get your opinion. They are splendid, by Jove!"

"I do not fancy them," said Alice, setting down her plate; "but don't tell the Doctor," she added hastily.

"You don't fancy anything, lately, Alice," Mr. Hastings replied, rather crossly.

"Never mind, Jack; my appetite will come when you have sold your mine;" and upon that the unreasonably fastidious woman burst into tears.

"As if my position is not trying enough without seeing you cry!" said Jack, pausing from eating long enough to look injured. Plastic Jack! your surroundings were having their effect on you.

The *Mining News* of the second of September had a notice of the sale of Mr. Hastings' mine, the "Sybil," bearing chloride of silver, to Dr. Eustance Earle, all of Deep Cañon. The papers to be handed over and cash paid down at Chloride Hill on the seventh; at which time Dr. Earle would start for San Francisco on the business of the mining firm to which he belonged. Mr. Hastings, it was understood, would go east about the same time.

All the parties were at Chloride Hill on the morning of the seventh, promptly. By eleven o'clock, the above-mentioned transaction was completed. Shortly after, one of the Opposition Line's stages stopped at Mrs. Robb's boarding-house, and a lady, dressed for traveling, stepped quickly into it. Having few acquaintances, and being closely veiled, the lady passed unrecognized at the stage-office, where the other passengers got in.

Half an hour afterwards Mr. Jack Hastings received the following note:

"DEAR JACK: I sold your mine for you. Dr. Earle is running away with me, per agreement; but if you take the express this afternoon, you will reach Elko before the train leaves for San Francisco to-morrow. There is nothing worth going back for at Deep Cañon. If you love me, save me.   Devotedly,
                                    "ALICE."

It is superfluous to state that Jack took the express, which, arriving at Elko before the Opposition, made him master of the situation. Not that he felt very masterful: he didn't. He was thinking of many things that it hurt him to remember; but he was meaning to do differently in future. He had at last sold his mine—no, he'd be d——d if *he* had sold it; but—Hallo! there's a big dust out on the road there!—it must be the other stage. Think what you'll do and say, Jack Hastings!

What he did say was: "Ah, Doctor! you here? It was lucky for my wife, was n't it, since I got left, to have you to look after her? Thanks, old fellow; you are just in time for the train. Alice and I will stop over a day to rest. A thousand times obliged: good-bye! Alice, say good-bye to Doctor Earle! you will not see him again."

Their hands and eyes met. He was pale as marble: she flushed one instant, paled the next, with a curious expression in her eyes which the Doctor never forgot and never quite understood. It was enough to know that the game was up. He had another mine on his hands, and an ugly pain in his heart which he told himself bitterly would be obstinate of cure. If he only could be sure what that look in her eyes had meant!

WHAT THEY TOLD ME AT WILSON'S BAR.

THE mining season was ended in the narrow valley of one of the Sacramento's northern tributaries, as, in fact, it was throughout the whole region of "placer diggings;" for it was October of a dry year, and water had failed early in all the camps. The afternoon of a long, idle day at Wilson's Bar was drawing to a close. The medium through which the sun's hot rays reached the parched earth was one of red dust, the effect of which was that of a mellow Indian summer haze, pleasing to the eye, if abhored by the skin and lungs, compelled to take it in, whether brute or human. In the landscape was an incongruous mingling of beauty and deformity; the first, the work of nature; the last, the marring of man.

To the east and to the west rose hills, whose ruggedness was softened by distance to outlines of harmonious grandeur. Scattered over the valley between them, the stately "digger," or nut-pines, grew at near intervals, singly or in groups of three or five, harmonizing by their pale gray-green with the other half-tints of earth, air, and sky. Following the course of the dried up river was a line, more or less continuous, of the evergreen oaks, whose round, spreading tops are such a grateful relief to the eye in the immense levels of the lower Sacramento and upper San Joaquin valleys. Depending from these, hung long, venerable-looking beards of gray moss, as devoid of color as everything else in the landscape; everything else, except the California wild grape, which, so far from being devoid of color, was gorgeous enough in itself to lighten up the whole foreground of the picture. Growing in clumps upon the ground, it was gay as a bed of tulips. Clambering up occasional tall trees, it flaunted its crimson and party-colored foliage with true bacchanalian jollity, each leaf seeming drunk with its own red wine. There is truly nothing that grows in the Golden State more beautiful than the *Vitus Californica* in October.

That was Nature's side of the picture. The reverse was this: the earth everywhere torn and disfigured by prospectors, whose picks had produced the effect of some huge snout of swine, applied with the industry characteristic of that animal in forbidden grounds. Rude cabins were scattered about, chiefly in the neighborhood of the stream. Rockers, sluice-boxes, and sieves strewed its borders. Along the dusty road which led to Wilson's Bar toiled heavily laden trains of freight-wagons, carrying supplies for the coming winter. At each little deviation from the general level, the eight-mule teams strained every muscle; the dust-enswathed drivers swore franticly and whipped mercilessly; the immense wagons groaned and creaked, and—the world moved on, however much the pained observer might wish to bring it to a stand-still.

A rosy sunset beyond the western mountains was casting its soft glamour over the scene—happily not without one appreciative beholder—when Bob Matheny's wagon drew up in front of the Traveler's Rest, the principal hotel of Wilson's Bar. From the commotion which ensued immediately thereupon, it would appear that Matheny was a person widely and also somewhat favorably known; such ejaculations as "Hulloa! thar's Bob Matheny," "How-dy, old feller!" and many other similar expressions of welcome greeting him on all sides, as he turned from blocking the wheels of his wagon, which else might have backed down the slight incline that led to Traveler's Rest.

At the same moment that the hand-shaking was progressing, a young woman, mounted on a handsome filly, rode up to the rude steps of the hotel and prepared to dismount; and Bob Matheny instantly broke away from his numerous friends, to lift her from the saddle, which act occasioned a sympathetic smile in that same numerous circle, and a whisper ran round it, half audible, to the effect that Bob had " bin gittin' married," " A dog-goned purty gal," "The old cock's puttin' on frills," and similar appropriate remarks, *ad infinitum.* In the meantime—the young woman disappearing within the hotel, and Matheny occupying himself firstly with the wants of his team, and lastly with his own and those of his traveling companion—gossip had busily circulated the report among the idlers of Wilson's Bar that Bob Matheny had taken to himself a young wife, who was accompanying him on his monthly trip to the mountains. This report was published with the usual verbal commentaries, legends, and annotations; as relevant and piquant as that sort of gossip usually is, and as elegant as, from the dialect of Wilson's Bar, might be expected.

Late that evening, a group of honest miners discussed the matter in the Star Empire Saloon.

" He's the last man I'd a-suspected ov doin' sech a act," said Tom Davis, with a manly grief upon his honest countenance, as he hid the ace and right-bower under the brim of his ragged old *sombrero*, and proceeded to play the left upon the remainder of that suit—with emphasis, " the very last man!"   .

" It's a powerful temptation to a feller in *his* shoes," remarked the tall Kentuckian on his right. " A young gal is a mighty purty thing to look at, and takes a man's mind off from his misfortin's. You mind the verse, don't ye:

> 'Sorrows I divide, and joys I double?'"

" And give this world a world o' trouble," subjoined Davis's partner, with a good natured laugh at his own wit. " It's your deal, Huxly. Look and see if all the cards are in the pack. Deuced if I don't suspect somebody's hidin' them."

" Every keerd's thar thet I hed in my hands, ef you mean *me*," said the Kentuckian, sharply.

"Waal, I *don't* mean you. A feller may have his little joke, I suppose."

"Depends on the kind o' jokes. Here's the two missin' keerds on the floor. Now, ef you say I put 'em thar, it's a little joke I reckon I won't stand. *Sabe?*"

"Come, I'll pay for the drinks, old fel', if you'll allow me to apologize. Waiter, drinks all round. What'll you take, gentlemen?"

"Now, that's what I call blarsted 'an'some," remarked Huxley, who was an Englishman from Australia:

> 'Friend of me soul, this goblet sip,
> 'Twill dry the starting tear;
> 'Tis not so bright as woman's lip,
> But oh, 'tis more sincere!'

Here's to ye, me hearties."

"Which brings us back to our subject," responded Davis's partner, commonly called "Gentleman Bill," as the glasses were drained and sent away. "Do you believe in curses, Kentuck?"

"B'lieve in cusses? Don't the Bible tell about cussin'? Wasn't thar an old man in the Bible—I disremember his name—that cussed one of his sons, and blessed t'other one? I reckon I *do* b'lieve in cussin'."

His interlocutor laughed softly at the statement and argument. "Did you ever know any body to be cursed in such a manner that it was plain he was under a ban of unintermitting vengeance?"

"Ef you mean did I ever know a man as was cussed, I ken say I did, onct. He was a powerful mean man—a nigger-driver down in Tennessee. He was orful to swear, and cruel to the niggers, an' his wife besides. One day she died an' left a mite of a baby; an' he was so mad he swore he 'wouldn't bury her; the neighbors might bury her, an' the brat, too, if they liked.' As he was a-swearin' an' a-tearin' with all his might, an' a-callin' on God to cuss him ef he didn't do so an' so, all of a suddent, just as his mouth opened with a oath, he was struck speechless, an' never has spoke a word till this day!—leastways, not that I ever heard ov."

"That is what I should call a special example of Divine wrath," said Gentleman Bill, deftly dealing the cards for a new game. "What I meant to ask was, whether any one, yourself especially, had ever known one man to curse another man so as to bring ruin upon him, in spite of his will to resist it."

"Waal, I've heern tell of sech things; can't say as I know such a man, without it's Bob Matheny. *He* says he's cussed; an' I reckon he *is*. Everybody in Wilson's Bar has heern about that."

"Not everybody, for I am still ignorant of his story. Was that why Mr. Davis objected so strongly to his marriage? I begin to be interested. Count me another game, partner. I should like to hear about Mr. Matheny."

"You may tell the story, Davis," said Kentuck, magnanimously. "I want ter chaw terbacker fur awhile, an' I can't talk an' chaw."

Tom Davis gladly took up the theme, as it gave him an opportunity to display his oratorical and rhetorical abilities, of which he was almost as proud as he was of his skill in hiding cards in his sleeves, his hat, his hair, his boots.

"Gentlemen," he began, hesitating an instant—while, attention being fixed on what he was about to say, he stocked the cards—"gentlemen, it's one of the curusest things you ever heerd in yer life. It seems thar was a woman at the bottom of it—I believe thar allers is at the bottom of everything. Waal, he stole another man's sunflower—I've heerd Bob say so, hisself—an' the other feller got mad—as mad as thunder—an', when he found his gal had vamosed with Bob, he cursed him; an' his curse was this: that as long as he lived all that he did should prosper

for a little while, an' jest when he begun to enj'y it, a curse
should come onto it. Ef it wor business, when he thought
he was sure of a good thing, it should fail. Ef it wor love,
the woman he loved should die. Ef it wor children, they
should grow up, and turn agin' him; or, if they stuck to
him, the same curse should be on them; what they undertook should fail; what they loved should die."

"Did the woman he loved die? did his children desert
him?" asked the Englishman, eagerly.

"His wife died seven year arter he married her; one ov
his boys was killed by his horse fallin' on him; the other
got into bad company down to Red Bluffs, an', arter leadin'
the old man a devil of a life for two year or more, run off,
an' got taken by the lynchers—so folks said. I b'lieve he
has a gal, back in the States; but his wife's folks won't let
her come to Californy. They're a-eddicatin' her quite
grand, an' she writes a powerful nice letter. The old man
showed me one, last time he was up to the Bar. Han'some
as any school-marm's ever ye saw. But Bob says he don't
see what's the use; somethin's sure to happen her; somethin' allers does happen to him an' to his chillern."

"Is that why he thinks he's cursed—because ' something
always happens?'" asked Gentleman Bill, indifferently.

"Sart'in; an' it's so, as sure as yer born. Nothin' never
pans out long with Bob Matheny. His beginnin's is all
good, an' his endin's all bad. I reckon thar never was a
man to Wilson's Bar has been cleaned eout, down to the
bed-rock, as often as Matheny."

"Is he a good man?" asked the Englishman, interested.

"Never had a better man to Wilson's Bar," responded
Kentuck, decidedly, as he cast his quid under the table.
"He ain't a lucky feller, an' he's mighty superstitious an'
the like; but I make a heap o' Bob Matheny. His luck an'
his cuss don't hurt him none for me. It's jest a notion,
mebbe."

"Notion or no notion," said Davis, with a knowing leer,

"he's not the man to marry a nice gal like that 'un he's got up to the Rest. Better let her be for some lucky young feller as could make her happy. Don't you say so, boys?"

While the laugh went round, the crowd that had been gradually collecting and listening to the story, began to move, and then to part, as the man so much talked of forced his way toward the group of speakers.

"Hold yer tongue, Tom Davis," said Kentuck. "Hulloa, Bob! take my hand, won't ye? I'll introduce ye to my friends. My pardner is Huxly—a tip-top feller, as you'll diskiver fur yerself. Davis' pardner is Randolph—Gentleman Bill, we call him fur short, he's so nice and perlite. He's from yer State, too, I reckon."

"Randolphs of Booneville," said Gentleman Bill; rising and extending his hand.

Matheny, who was a mild-looking man of about fifty, with a hesitating manner and rather care-worn countenance, half concealed under a wide-brimmed, dusty black hat, instead of meeting half-way the extended hand of his friend's friend, thrust his own into his pockets and gazed fixedly at young Randolph. "Be ye Boone Randolph, or be ye his sperrit?" he asked, hoarsely.

"Neither, quite," said the young man, smiling, yet a little flushed. "I am son of Boone Randolph of Booneville, if you know who he was."

Matheny turned and hurried out of the crowd, followed by Kentuck, who wanted to have explained this singular conduct of Bob's towards his friends. As there was no witness of their conversation, its meaning can only be guessed at by another which took place two hours later, after Matheny had turned in at the Traveler's Rest. It was late, even for him, when Kentuck started for his lodgings at the other end of the long, densely crowded street—crowded not only with buildings of wood and canvas, but choked up with monstrous freight wagons, and their numerous horse and mule-teams, for which there was not stable-room enough in all Wilson's Bar. Stumbling along the uneven sidewalk, often touching with his feet some unhoused vagabond, Kentuck was about to mount the stairs which led to his bedroom, when some one touched him on the shoulder, and the voice of Gentleman Bill addressed him:

"I beg your pardon, Kentuck; but you've been with Matheny, haven't you? I want to know why he wouldn't shake hands. He told you, of course?"

"Waal, I'm a friend of Bob's, ye know, Bill; an' he is mighty rough on you, sure. Better not say nothin' about it."

"That wouldn't suit me, Kentuck. I want to understand something about the matter which concerns me so evidently. Come, out with it, and I'll leave you to go to bed."

"Waal, you heerd Tom Davis' blab this evenin'; an' you know that Bob's got the idee into his intelleck that the cuss of a sart'in man as he onct wronged is a-stickin' to him yit, an' never will let loose till he passes in his checks?"

"Who was the man?"

"Boone Randolph, of Booneville."

"My father?"

"Yaas, yer pap. He's down powerful on your pap, that's sart'in. Sez he to me: 'Loh! that's the ornary whelp ov the devil that cussed me. Old's I am I'd like to fight him, fur the sake o' the man that I knowed onct. I feel my young blood a-risin'; he looks so mighty like Boone Randolph.' But I tole him he war a fool to talk ov fightin' yer; ye'd whip him all ter flinders."

"I wouldn't fight him, of course: he's too old for me. And then he's just married, too, isn't he? I have no wish to make that young woman a widow."

"A widow!" said Kentuck, laughing. "That girl's name is Anne Matheny; but she ain't Bob's wife, not by a long shot. Why, she's Bob's darter, as has just come out to see her old pap."

"Well, I like that. I am less than ever inclined to fight the man who owns such a daughter. I must find a way to make friends with him, even if I have to quarrel with him to do it. Good-night, Kentuck. Pleasant dreams to you."

Gentleman Bill felt more than ordinarily wide-awake, whether it was from the novel excitement of the brief encounter with Matheny or not. When Kentuck had left him, he stood for some time irresolute, with no wish for rest, and no desire to go anywhere in particular. He looked up to the sky. It was murky with filmy fog-clouds and dust not yet settled to the earth. Not a star was visible in the whole arch of heaven. He looked down the street, and his eyes, accustomed to the darkness, could just faintly distinguish the outlines of the wagons that crowded it. Every sound was hushed, except the occasional movement of a restless animal, or the deep sighing of a sleeping one. Not a light was burning anywhere along the street. While gazing aimlessly into the gloom he saw, all at once, as if lighted by a flash from the sky, a sudden illumination spring up, and a column of flame stand erect over the Traveler's Rest.

Now, Wilson's Bar did not boast a fire company. At some seasons of the year, had a fire broken out, there would have been a chance of its extinguishment, inflammable as were the materials of which the place was built; but just after the long, hot summer, when the river was all but dried up, and every plank in houses, fences, and sidewalks so much tinder, a fire that should get under headway would have everything its own way. Seeing the danger, Gentleman Bill started down the street on a run, shouting, in his clarion tones, that ever-thrilling cry of "Fire! fire! fire!" till it seemed to him he must wake the dead. But it was that hour of the night, or rather morning, when sleep is heaviest, and the watchful senses off their guard. The teamsters, who slept in their wagons, were the first to be aroused; but they, seeing the peril which might come to their teams, and destruction to their property, kept by their own. The inhabitants of the dwellings awoke more slowly, and came pouring into the street only in time to see the roof of the Traveler's Rest falling in, although the lower story was not yet consumed.

Nobody knew much about the details of the scene that ensued. The current of heated air produced the usual rush of cold wind, which spread and fed the flames, until, in half an hour, all hope of saving any part of the principal street in the Bar was abandoned, and people were flying for safety to the outskirts of the town.

On a little eminence, overlooking the burning buildings, together stood Gentleman Bill and a young woman he had rescued from smoke and flame just in time to save her from suffocation. Together they looked down upon the conflagration, and together listened to the horrible medley of sounds proceeding from it.

"If I could only know that my father is safe!" was the repeated moan of Anne Matheny, as she gazed intently upon the scene of distress.

Seeing the fright and trouble in her eyes, her companion cunningly diverted her attention for one moment to the weird landscape stretching away toward the western mountains. It was the same scene she had beheld for the first time with such interest twelve hours before; but in what a different aspect! The murky heavens reflected the red glare of the flames upon every object for miles around, tinging each with a lurid gleam like nothing in nature. The dark neutrals of the far-off mountains, the gray-green of the pines, the sere colors of the parched valley, the dark dull-green of the oaks, garlanded with hoary moss, and the gay foliage of the wild grape; all came out distinctly in this furnace-glow, but with quite new effects. In the strong and strange fascination of the scene, both these young people, so singularly situated, forgot for three minutes their mutual anxiety. Longer it would be impossible to forget it.

"Do not you think I might go to look for my father now, Mr. —— ?"

"Randolph"—supplied that gentleman.

"Oh, thank you!—Mr. Randolph?"

"I do not see how you could, really;" and, without intending it in the least, but simply through his embarrassment, Randolph glanced hastily at her scanty dress, which thereby she blushingly understood to be his objection.

"If I could get only a blanket from father's wagon! Do you think it would be possible? Would you be running a risk to try for a blanket, do you think, Mr. Randolph? If there is any risk, please do not go ; but I am so anxious— so terribly anxious."

He knew she was, and knew the reason she had for her apprehensions; so, although he mistrusted the result of his errand, he answered simply: "Certainly; I will go, if you are not afraid to be left alone. *I* shall be in no danger."

"O, thank you—thank you! You will bring me a message from my father?"

"I hope so, indeed, since you desire it so much. I think you had better sit down on this newspaper, and let me cover your shoulders with my coat."

"No, indeed. If you are going near the fire, you will need it to protect you from cinders."

But Randolph quickly divested himself of his upper garment, and laid it lightly over her shivering form; then quietly charging her to feel no alarm, and as little anxiety as possible, strode rapidly away toward the fire. Fifteen minutes afterward he returned more slowly, with a blanket, which Anne rose up to receive.

"My father? Did you see my father?"

"I did not see him. He must have taken his horses off a little distance for safety, and you may not see him for several hours. Do not indulge in apprehensions. In the morning we shall find him: it is almost daylight now."

He pointed to a faint light along the eastern horizon; but her eyes were blinded with tears.

"It is not like my father to leave me so long—at such a time, too! He would not care for his horses, nor for anything but me. O, can he have perished!"

She spoke as though the awful significance of her loneliness had just dawned upon her. Randolph, from whom the thought had never been absent from the moment he saw the pillar of flame shooting up over the Traveler's Rest, was startled by the suddenness of her anguish; and an expression of profound grief came over his face, noticeable even to her inattentive eyes, and which comforted her by its sympathy, even in the midst of her alarm and distress.

The day had dawned when Anne Matheny lifted her tear-swollen face from her knees, and looked upon the smoking ruins of Wilson's Bar. It was but a blackened heap of rubbish; yet somewhere in its midst, she felt assured, were buried the charred remains of her father. Each moment that he came not deepened her conviction, until at last her companion ceased his efforts to inspire hope, and accepted her belief as his own. Then, with the inconsistency of sorrow, she violently repudiated the suspicion of her father's death, and besought him piteously to seek and bring him to her side.

It was while obeying this last command that Gentleman Bill encountered Kentuck, who, after the confusion of the fire was over, was, like himself, looking for Matheny. When they had consulted together, the two returned to the place where Anne was awaiting them.

"There is one request I have to make, Kentuck: which is, that you will not inform Miss Matheny of the enmity of her father toward my father and myself. It would only distress her. Besides, I should like to befriend her, poor girl! and I could not, if she looked upon me with her father's eyes."

" No, 'tain't no use to tell her nothin' about that, sure
enough. It's mighty curus, though, 'bout that fire: not
another man got hurt, not a mite; and Bob Matheny dead!
I'll be hanged if it ain't mighty curus. I hope *ye* won't
hurt the gal, bein' yer the son of yer father."

" Hurt her! I'd——"

Gentleman Bill did not say what he would do: but Kentuck, glancing his way, caught a perfectly comprehensible
expression, and muttered softly to himself:

" Waal, if that ain't the dog-gondest curusest sarcum-
stance I ever seed. Hit, the first pop! Waal, I'm not the
feller to come atween 'em ef thet's ther notion. Far play's
my rule."

To Bill, aloud, he said: "Reckon you'll hev' to let *me*
be her uncle for awhile yet. Yer most too young a feller
to offer to take car' of a gal like that. Bob Matheny's darter has a right to what leetle dust pans out o' Kentuck's
claim. Thet's my go."

Just at this moment Anne, who had been watching for
the return of her friend, seeing two figures approaching,
uttered a cry of joy and ran forward to meet them. The
shock of her disappointment at seeing a stranger in place
of her father, caused her nearly to swoon away in Kentuck's
arms.

" Neow, don't ye, honey," he said, soothingly, in his
kind Kentucky dialect. " Sho! don't ye take on. We's
all got to die, sometime or 'nother. Don't mind me: I'm
yer pap's oldest friend on this coast—hev' prospected an'
dug an' washed up with him sence '49; and a kinder
comrade a man never hed. In course, I consider it my
dooty an' privilege to see that you're took car' ov. The
Bar's purty much cleaned eout—thet's so; but I'll soon hev'
a cabin up somewhere; an' ye can jest run my shebang anyway ye like. Reckon I can find some nice woman to stay
along with ye, fur comp'ny."

This was just the kind of talk best calculated to engage

14

the attention of one in Anne's situation—half soothing and half suggestive—and by degrees her father's old friend succeeded in arousing her to face her loss, and the prospects of her future.

They told me at Wilson's Bar, only last October—it must have been about the anniversary of the fire—that in two or three months Anne had recovered her spirits and health so far as to essay teaching the little flock of children at the Bar, with flattering success; and that in two or three more it began to be observed that Gentleman Bill—now more commonly called Mr. Randolph, out of respect to Miss Matheny—generally happened to be in the neighborhood of the school-house about the hour of closing, in order that he might walk home with the teacher. In truth, the young people had taken to looking and sighing after each other in a way that provoked remark, and augured a wedding. As Anne insisted on completing her term of teaching, as well as on taking a little time for preparation, the wedding did not come off until the first part of September.

On this occasion—the only one of the kind Kentuck had ever had anything to do with—the rude, but generous-hearted Kentuckian made a point of displaying his hospitality on a scale commensurate with his ideas of its importance; and the *élite* of Wilson's Bar were invited to eat, drink, and dance from dusk till dawn of that memorable day. As for the bride, she looked as lovely as it is the right and duty of all brides to look—even lovelier than the most; and the groom was the very prince of bridegrooms—so all the maiden guests declared.

On the following morning, when the young couple were to go away, Annie kissed and cried over Kentuck, her second father, in a truly gratifying fashion; and Randolph behaved very gentlemanly and kindly—as, in fact, he always did; and Kentuck put on paternal airs, blessing his children in all the honeyed epithets of a true Kentuckian.

Alas, that the legend does not end here! If the reader is of my mind, he will wish that it had. But if he is of that sanguinary sort who always insist upon seeing the grist the gods send to their slow-grinding mills, he will prefer to know the sequel. As I have already told you, it was in September they were married. On the morning they left Kentuck the weather was extremely hot, with queer little clouds hanging about the mountains. They took the road up the cañon, toward McGibeney's ranch—laughing and chatting, as they rode along side by side, Anne replying to every lark singing by the roadside in a voice almost as musical.

Well, if it must be told, there was a cloud-burst on the mountains about noon that day. Not four hours after they had taken leave of him, Kentuck received their poor bruised bodies at his very threshold, brought there without the interposition of human hands. Wilson's Bar will long remember that day. The fire took chiefly that which could be replaced; but the flood washed out claims, ruined aqueducts, and destroyed lives of men and brutes, carrying away with it the labors and hopes of years.

MISS JORGENSEN.

I AM a plain, elderly, unmarried man, and I board at Mrs.
Mason's. A great deal of what I am about to relate
came under my own observation; and the remainder was
confided to me from time to time by my landlady, with
whom I am upon terms of friendship and intimacy, having
had a home in her house for a period of seven years.

Mrs. Mason lives in her own tenement, in a quiet part of
the city; and besides myself, has usually three or four other
boarders, generally teachers, or poor young authors—some
person always of the class that, having few other pleasures,
makes it a point to secure rooms with a fine view of the
bay. When Miss Jorgensen came to us, we were a quiet,
studious, yet harmonious and happy family; so well satisfied with our little community that we did not take kindly
to the proposed addition to our circle when Mrs. Mason
mentioned it. Neither did our landlady seem to desire any
change; but she explained to us that the young person ap-
plying had made a strong appeal; that her classes (she was
a teacher of French) were principally in our part of the
city; and that she would be satisfied with a mere closet for
a room. The only privilege for which she stipulated was
the use of the common parlor twice a week to receive her
company in.

"But I cannot agree to give up the parlor any single
evening," Mrs. Mason replied, "because it is used by all
the family, every evening. You will be entitled to the same
privileges with the others." After some hesitation this was
agreed to, and our new boarder was installed in the upper
hall bed-room, which, when it had received the necessary
furniture and a saratoga trunk, with numerous boxes and
baskets, would scarcely allow space enough to dress in.

However, Mrs. Mason reported that the tenant professed real satisfaction with her quarters; and we all were on tip-toe with curiosity to see the new inmate.

"Miss Jorgensen," said Mrs. Mason, that evening, as she escorted to the dinner-table a small, pale, dark-eyed young person, in deep mourning; and we being severally and separately presented afterward, endeavored to place this little lonely scrap of humanity at ease with ourselves. But in this well-intentioned effort Miss Jorgensen did not seem to meet us half way. On the contrary, she repelled us. She was reserved without being diffident; mercilessly critical, and fierily disputatious—all of which we found out in less than a week. She never entered or left a room without somehow disturbing the mental atmosphere of it, and giving the inmates a little shock; so that Mr. Quivey, our dramatic writer, soon took to calling her the "Electrical Eel," substituting "E. E." when the person indicated was within ear-shot possibly or probably. In return, as we afterward discovered, Miss Jorgensen told Miss Flower, our other young lady boarder, that she had christened Mr. Quivey " I. I."—"Incurable Idiot." How the "E. E." came to her knowledge was never made plain. Before three months were past, she had quarreled with every one in the house except Mrs. Mason and myself; though, to her credit be it said, she always apologized for her temper when they were over, with a frankness that disarmed resentment. Nevertheless, she was so frequently in a hostile attitude toward one or another in the family, that the mere mention of Miss Jorgensen's name was sure to arrest attention and excite expectations. Thus, when I only chanced to whisper to Mrs. Mason at breakfast one morning, " Miss Jorgensen keeps late hours," every one at the table glanced our way inquiringly, as much as to ask, " What has the little woman done now?" And when she appeared at the close of the meal with pale face and swollen eyes, explaining her tardiness by saying she had a headache, no one gave her sympathizing looks except the landlady.

That kind-hearted person confided to me, later in the day, that her new boarder troubled and puzzled her very much. "She will sit up until one or two o'clock every night, writing something or other, and that makes her late to breakfast. She goes out teaching every morning, and comes back tired and late to luncheon; and you see she is never in her place at dinner until the soup is removed, and every one at the table helped. When I once suggested that she ought not to sit up so long at night, and that her classes should be arranged not to fatigue her so much, with other bits of friendly advice, she gave me to understand, very promptly, that her ways were her own, and not to be interfered with by any one. And directly afterward the tears came into her eyes. I confess I did not understand her at all."

"What about the young man who calls here twice a week?" I inquired.

"She is engaged to him, she says."

"What sort of a person does he seem to be?"

"He looks well enough, only rather shabby, is very quiet, very attentive to her, and what you might call obedient to her requirements. She often seems displeased with him, but what she says to him at such times is unknown to me, for she does her scolding all in French; and he usually then invites her out to walk, by way of diversion, I suppose."

"Do you know that he comes every morning and carries her books for her? He certainly cannot be employed, or he would not have time for such gallantries."

"Perhaps he is engaged on one of the morning papers, and so is off duty in the forenoon. I cannot think so industrious a person as she would take up with a man both poor and idle. But you never know what a woman will do," sighed Mrs. Mason, who had known something of heart-troubles in her youth, and could sympathize with other unlucky women. "Excuse me; I must not stand here gossiping." And the good lady went about her house affairs.

A few moments later I was hurrying down town to my office, when I overtook Miss Jorgensen and Mr. Hurst. As usual, she was leaning upon his arm, and he was carrying her books. She was talking excitedly, in French, and I thought her to be crying, though her face was covered with a black veil. The few words I caught before she recognized me reminded me of my conversation with Mrs. Mason.

"You *must* get something to do, Harry," she was saying. " You know that I work every instant of the time, yet how little I can save if I have to supply you with money. It is a shame to be so idle and helpless, when there is so much to be done before——"

She perceived me and stopped short. " So," I thought, " this precious scamp is living off the earnings of the little French teacher, is he? A pretty fellow, truly! I'll get him his *congé* if I have to make love to her myself." Which latter conceit so amused me, that I had forgotten to be indignant with Mr. Hurst before I reached my office and plunged into the business of the day.

But I never made love to Miss Jorgensen. She was not the kind of person even a flirtish man would choose to talk sentiment with, and I was always far enough from being a gallant. So our affairs went on in just the usual way at Mrs. Mason's for three or four months. Miss Jorgensen and Mr. Quivey let fly their arrows of satire at each other; Miss Flower, the assistant high-school teacher, enacted the amiable go-between; our "promising young artist" was wisely neutral; Mrs. Mason and myself were presumed to be old enough to be out of the reach of boarding-house tiffs, and preserved a prudent unconsciousness. Mr. Hurst continued to call twice a week in the evening, and Miss Jorgensen kept on giving French lessons by day, and writing out translations for the press at night. She was grow-

ing very thin, very pale, and cried a good deal, as I had
reason to know, for her room adjoined mine, and more than
a few times I had listened to her sobbing, until I felt almost forced to interfere; but interfered I never had yet.

One foggy July evening, on coming home to dinner, I
encountered Miss Jorgensen in the hall. She appeared to
be just going out, a circumstance which surprised me somewhat, on account of the hour. I however opened the door
for her without comment, when by the fading daylight I
perceived that her face was deathly pale, and her black eyes
burning. She passed me without remark, and hurried off
into the foggy twilight. Nor did she appear at dinner; but
came in about eight o'clock and went directly to her own
room. When Mrs. Mason knocked at her door to inquire
if she was not going to take some refreshments, the only
reply that could be elicited was, that she had a headache,
and could not be induced to eat or drink—spoken through
the closed door.

"She's been having a row with that sunflower of her's,"
was Mr. Quivey's comment, when he overheard Mrs.
Mason's report to me, made in an undertone. Truth to tell,
Mr. Quivey, from associating so much with theatrical people in the capacity of playwright, had come to be rather
stagy in his style at times. "By the way, he was not on
escort duty this morning. I saw her proceeding along
Powell street alone, and anxiously peering up and down all
the cross streets, evidently on the lookout, but he failed to
put in an appearance."

"Which was very unkind of him, if she expected that
he would," put in Miss Flower, glancing from under her
long lashes at the speaker.

"That is so," returned Quivey; "for the fellow does
nothing else, I do believe, but play lackey to Miss Jorgensen; and if that is his sole occupation, he ought to perform
that duty faithfully. I do not see, for my part, how he
pays his way."

" Perhaps it pays him to be a lackey," I suggested, remembering what I had once overheard between them. Mrs. Mason gave me a cautioning glance, which she need not have done, for I had no intention of making known Miss Jorgensen's secrets.

" Well," said Miss Flower, as if she had been debating the question in her mind for some time previous, " I doubt if a woman can love a man who submits to her will as subserviently as Mr. Hurst seems to, to Miss Jorgensen. I know *some women* could not."

" By which you mean *you* could not," Mrs. Mason returned, smiling. " I do not see that the case need be very different with men. Subserviency never won anybody's respect or love either. Neither does willful opposition, any more. Proper self-respect and a fair share of self-love is more sure of winning admiration, from men or women, than too little self-assertion or too much."

" But where the self-assertion is all on one side, and the self-abasement all on the other—as in the case of Miss Jorgensen and Mr. Hurst—then how would you establish an equilibrium, Mrs. Mason?"

" It establishes itself in that case, I should say," clipped in Mr. Quivey. " Oil and water do not mix, but each keeps its own place perfectly, and without disturbance."

I do not know how long this conversation might have gone on in this half-earnest, half-facetious style, with Miss Jorgensen for its object, had not something happened just here to bring it abruptly to a close; and that something was the report of a pistol over our very heads.

" Great heaven !" ejaculated Miss Flower, losing all her color and self-possession together.

" E. E., as I live—she has shot herself !" cried Quivey, half doubting, half convinced.

I caught these words as I made a rapid movement toward the staircase. They struck me as so undeniably true that I never hesitated in making an assault upon her door. It was locked on the inside, and I could hear nothing except a faint moaning sound within. Fearing the worst, I threw my whole weight and strength against it, and it flew open with a crash. There lay Miss Jorgensen upon the floor, in the middle of her little room, uttering low moaning sobs, though apparently not unconscious. I stooped over and lifted her in my arms to lay her upon the bed, and as I did so, a small pocket-pistol fell at my feet, and I discovered blood upon the carpet.

" Yes, Miss Jorgensen had certainly shot herself, I told Mrs. Mason, and the rest who crowded after us into the little woman's room; but whether dangerously or not, I could not say, nor whether purposely or accidentally. Probably not dangerously, as she was already making signs to me to exclude people from the apartment.

" You had better bring a surgeon," I said to Quivey, who turned away muttering, followed by Miss Flower.

With Mrs. Mason's assistance, I soon made out the location of the wound, which was in the flesh of the upper part of the left arm, and consequently not so alarming as it would be painful during treatment.

" Could she have meant to shoot herself through the heart, and failed through agitation?" whispered Mrs. Mason to me, aside.

" No, no; it was an accident," murmured the victim, whose quick ear had caught the words. " I did not mean to shoot myself."

" Poor child, I am very sorry for you," returned Mrs. Mason gently, whose kind heart had always leaned toward the little French teacher, in spite of her singular ways. " It is very unfortunate; but you shall receive careful nursing until you recover. You need not worry about yourself, but try to bear it the best you can."

" O, I cannot bear it—I *must* be well to-morrow. O, what shall I do!" moaned Miss Jorgensen. " O, that this should have happened to-night!" And momently, after this thought occurred to her, her restlessness seemed to increase, until the surgeon came and began an examination of the wound.

While this was going on, notwithstanding the sickening pain, the sufferer seemed anxious only about the opinion to be given upon the importance of the wound as interfering with her usual pursuits.

When, in answer to a direct appeal, she was told that it must be some weeks before she could resume going out, a fainting fit immediately followed, which gave us no little trouble and alarm.

Before taking leave, the doctor accompanied me to my own apartment and proceeded to question me.

"What is the history of the case?" said he. "Is there anything peculiar in the life or habits of Miss Jorgensen, to account for her great anxiety to get well immediately?"

"She fears to lose her classes, I presume; and there may be other engagements which are unknown to us." I still had a great reluctance to saying what I suspected might be troubling Miss Jorgensen.

"Neither of which accounts for all that I observe in her case," returned the doctor. "What are her connections?— has she any family ties—any lover, even?"

"I believe she told Mrs. Mason she was engaged to a young man who calls here twice a week."

"Ah! Do you know where this young man is to be found? It might be best to communicate with him, in the morning. Possibly he may be able to dispel this anxious fear of hers, from whatever cause it arises."

I promised the Doctor to speak to Mrs. Mason about it, and he soon after took leave, having first satisfied himself that the unlucky pistol was incapable of doing further mischief, and safely hidden from Miss Jorgensen.

Naturally, the next morning, the table-talk turned upon the incident of the evening previous.

"She need not tell me that it was an accident," Mr.

Quivey was saying, very decidedly. "She is just the sort of woman for desperate remedies; and she is tired of living, with that vampire friend of hers draining her life-blood!"

I confess I felt startled by the correspondence of Quivey's opinion with my own; for I had heretofore believed that myself and Mrs. Mason were the only persons who suspected that Hurst was dependent upon Miss Jorgensen for the means of living. In my surprise I said: "You know that he does this?"

"I know that Craycroft paid him yesterday for a long translation done by Miss Jorgensen, and I do not believe he had an order for it, other than verbal. Craycroft seeing them so much together, paid the money, and took a receipt."

"Perhaps he paid the money to Mr. Hurst by her instructions, for her own use," suggested Miss Flower. "But then he did not see her last evening, did he? I hope he does not rob Miss Jorgensen. Such a delicate little woman has enough to do to look out for herself, I should think."

"One thing is certain," interposed Mrs. Mason, "Miss Jorgensen does what she does, and permits what she permits, intelligently; and our speculations concerning her affairs will not produce a remedy for what we fancy we see wrong in them." Which hint had the effect of silencing the discussion for that time.

Before I left the house that morning, I had a consultation with Mrs. Mason, who had passed the night in attendance upon Miss Jorgensen, and who had informed me that she had been very restless, in spite of the quieting prescription left by the doctor. "I wish you would go up and speak to her," Mrs. Mason said. "Perhaps you can do something for her which I could not; and I am sure she needs some such service."

Thus urged, I obeyed an impulse of my own, which had been to do this very thing. When I tapped softly at her door, she said, "Come in!" in a pained and petulant tone, as if any interruption was wearisome to her; but when she saw who it was, her countenance assumed an eager and animated expression, which rewarded me at once for the effort I was making.

"Thank you for coming to see me," said she quickly. "I was almost on the point of sending for you." Pausing for a moment, while her eyes searched my face, she continued: "I am in trouble, which cannot be all explained, and which will force you, if you do a service for me, to take me very much upon trust; but I will first assure you that what you may do for me will not involve *you* in any difficulty. More than this I cannot now say. Will you do this service for me, and keep your agency in the matter secret? The service is slight, the importance of secrecy great."

I expressed my willingness to do anything which would not compromise me with myself, and that, I told her, I did not fear her requiring.

She then proceeded, with some embarrassment, to say that she wished a note conveyed to Mr. Hurst; upon which I smiled, and answered, "I had conjectured as much."

"But you must not conjecture anything," she replied, with some asperity; "for you are sure to go wide of the truth. You think I have only to send for Mr. Hurst to bring him here; but you are mistaken. He cannot come, because he *dare* not. He is in hiding, but I cannot tell you why. Only do not betray him; I ask no more. You are not called upon to do any more—to do anything against him, I mean." Seeing me hesitate, she continued: "I need not tell you that I believe my life is in your hands. I have been living a long time with all my faculties upon a severe strain, so severe that I feel I shall go mad if the pressure is increased. I entreat you not to refuse me."

"Very well," I answered, "I will do what you require."

"It is only to take this"—she pulled a note from beneath her pillow, addressed to "Mr. Harry Hurst," and handed it to me—"to the address, which you will have no difficulty in finding, though I am sorry to have to send you on a walk so out of your way. And please take this also"—handing me a roll of coin, marked $100. No answer is expected. Of course, you will not give these things to any one but Mr. Hurst. That is all." And she sunk back wearily upon her pillow, with closed eyes, as if she had no further interest in the affair.

I know as well as if she had told me that this note was a warning to fly, and this money the means to make flight good. I had promised to deliver them on her simple entreaty and assurance that I should not dishonor myself. But might I not wrong society? Might not she be herself deceived about Hurst? The assertion of Quivey that he had collected money from her employers the day before occurred to me. Did she know it or not? I questioned, while regarding the thin, pale, weary face on the pillow before me. While I hesitated she opened her eyes with a wondering, impatient gaze.

" Do you repent !" she asked.

" I deliberate, rather," I replied. " I chanced to learn yesterday, that Mr. Hurst had drawn money from Craycroft & Co., and was thinking that if you knew it, you might not wish to send this also."

For an instant her black eyes blazed with anger, but whether at me or at Mr. Hurst I could not tell, and she seemed to hesitate, as I had done.

" Yes, take it," she said, with hopeless sadness in her tone, " He may need it; and for myself, what does it matter now ?"

" I shall do as you bid me," I replied, " but it is under protest; for it is my impression that you are doing yourself an injury, and Mr. Hurst no good."

" You don't understand," she returned, sharply. " Now go, please."

" Very well; I am gone. But I promise you that if you exact services of me, I shall insist on your taking care of

your health, by way of return. You are in a fever at this
moment, which I warn you will be serious if not checked.
Here comes the doctor. Good-morning."

I pass over the trifling incidents of my visit to the resi-
dence of Mr. Hurst. Suffice to say that Mr. Hurst had de-
parted to parts unknown, and that I had to carry about all
day Miss Jorgensen's letter and money. On returning
home to dinner that afternoon, I found a stranger occupying
Miss Jorgensen's place at table. He was a shrewd-looking
man of about forty years, talkative, versatile, and what you
might call "jolly." Nothing escaped his observation; nothing was uttered that he did not hear, often replying most
unexpectedly to what was not ihtended for him—a practice
that would have been annoying but for a certain tact and
good humor which disarmed criticism. The whole family,
while admitting that our new day-boarder was not exactly
congenial, confessed to liking his amusing talk immensely.

"He quite brightens us up; don't you think so, Mr.
Quivey?" was Miss Flower's method of indorsing him.

"He does very well just now," replied Quivey, "though
I'd lots rather see E. E. back in that place. When one
gets used to pickles or pepper, one wants pickles or pepper; honey palls on the appetite."

"I thought you had almost too much pepper sometimes,"
said Miss Flower, remembering the "I. I."

"It's a healthful stimulant," returned Quivey, ignoring
the covert reminder.

"But not always an agreeable one."

I suspected that Miss Flower, who had an intense admiration for dramatic talent, entertained her own reasons
for jogging Mr. Quivey's memory; and being willing to
give her every opportunity to promote her own views, I
took this occasion to make my report to Miss Jorgensen.
As might have been expected, she had been feverishly an-
ticipating my visit. I had no sooner entered the room than
she uttered her brief interrogation:

" Well ? "

I laid the note and the money upon the bed. " You see how it is ? " I said.

" He is gone ? "

" Yes."

"I am so very glad!" she said, with emphasis, while something like a smile lighted up her countenance. "This gives me a respite, at least. If he is prudent "—she checked herself, and giving me a grateful glance, exclaimed, " I am *so* much obliged to you."

"Nobody could be more welcome, I am sure, to so slight a service. I shall hope now to see you getting well."

" O, yes," she answered, " I must get well; there is so much to do. But my classes and my writing must be dropped for a while, I presume, unless the doctor will let me take in some of my scholars, for, of course, I cannot go out."

" Your arm must begin to heal before you can think of teaching, ever so little. I have an idea, Miss Jorgensen, from what you have said of yourself, that this necessity for repose, which is forced upon you, will prove to be an excellent thing. Certainly, you were wearing out very fast with your incessant labor."

"Perhaps so—I mean, perhaps inforced rest will not be bad for me; but, O, there is such need to work! I can so poorly afford to be idle."

" What you say relieves my mind of a suspicion, which at first I harbored, that the firing of that mischievous pistol was not wholly accidental. I now see you wish to live and work. But why had you such a weapon about you? Are you accustomed to fire-arms?"

" The mischief this one did me shows that I am not; and my having it about me came from a fear I had of its doing worse mischief in the hands of Mr. Hurst."

" Are affairs so desperate with him ?"

" Please don't question me. I cannot answer you satisfactorily. Mr. Hurst is in trouble, and the least that is said or known about him is the best. And yet you wonder, no doubt, that I should interest myself about a man who is compelled to act the part of a culprit. Well, I cannot tell you why at present; and it would be a great relief to know that you thought nothing more about it." This last she uttered rather petulantly, which warned me that this conversation was doing her no good.

" Believe, then," I said, " that I have no interest in your affairs, except the wish to promote your welfare. And I think I may venture to affirm that everybody in the house is equally at your service when you wish to command him or her."

" Thank you all; but I do not deserve your kindness; I have been so ill-tempered. The truth is I cannot afford to have friends; friends pry into one's affairs so mercilessly. Mrs. Mason tells me there is a new boarder," she said, suddenly changing the subject.

I assented, and gave what I intended to be an amusing account of the new-comers's conversation and manners.

" Was there anything said about me at dinner ?" she asked, with a painful consciousness of the opinion I might have of such a question.

"I do not think there was. We were all so taken up with the latest acquisition that we forgot you for the time."

" May I ask this favor of you, to keep the conversation away from me as much as possible? I am morbidly sensitive, I presume," she said, with a poor attempt at a smile, " and I cannot keep from fancying, while I lie here, what you are saying about me in the dining-room or parlor."

Of course, I hastened to disavow any disposition on the part of the family to make her a subject of conversation, and even promised to discountenance any reference to her whatever, if thereby she would be made more comfortable; after which I bade her good-night, having received the as-

15

surance that my visit had relieved her mind of several torturing apprehensions.

The more I saw and thought of Miss Jorgensen, the more
she interested and puzzled me. I should have inclined to
the opinion that she was a little disturbed at times in her
intellect, had it not been that there was apparent so much
"method in her madness;" this reflection always bringing
me back at last to the conclusion that her peculiarities
could all be accounted for upon the hypothesis she herself
presented; too much work and some great anxiety. The
spectacle of this human mite fighting the battle of life, not
only for herself but for the strong man who should have
been her protector, worked so upon my imagination and
my sympathy that I found it difficult to keep the little woman out of my thoughts.

I kept my word to her, discountenancing, as far as I
could, the discussion of her affairs, and in this effort Mrs.
Mason co-operated with me; but it was practically impossible to prevent the inquiries and remarks of those of the
family who were not so well informed concerning her as we
were. The new boarder, also, with that quick apprehension he had of every subject, had caught enough to become
interested in the patient up-stairs, and daily made some inquiries concerning her condition, and, as it appeared to me
—grown a little morbid, like Miss Jorgensen—was peculiarly
adroit in extracting information.

Three weeks slipped away, and Miss Jorgensen had
passed the most painful period of suppuration and healing
in her arm, and had promised to come down-stairs next day
to dine with the family. Mrs. Mason had just communicated the news to us in her cheeriest tones, as if each individual was interested in it, and was proceeding to turn
out our coffee, when a servant brought in the letters for the
house and laid them beside the tray, directly under the eye
of the new boarder, who sat on the landlady's left.

"'Miss Jorgensen," said he, reading the address of the

topmost one. "A very peculiar handwriting." Then taking up the letter, as if to further examine the writing, I observed that he was studying the postmark as well, which, being offended at his unmannerly curiosity, I sincerely hoped was illegible. But that it was only too fatally plain will soon appear.

With an air of *hauteur* I seldom assumed, I recalled the servant, and ordered the letter to be taken at once to Miss Jorgensen. Before leaving the house I was informed that Miss Jorgensen wished to speak to me.

" Mr. Hurst has done a most imprudent thing!" she exclaimed, the moment I was inside the door. " I ought to have published a ' personal,' or done something to let him know I could not go to the post-office, and to account for his not hearing from me."

" He has returned to the city?"

"Yes!" She fairly ground her teeth with rage at this " stupidity," as she termed it. " He always does the very thing he ought never to have done, and leaves undone the things most important to do. Of course he cannot come here, and I can not go to him without incurring the greatest risk. I really do not know what to do next."

Tears were now coursing down her pale cheeks—tears, it seemed, as much of anger as of sorrow.

"Let him take care of himself," I said, rather hotly. " It is not your province to care for him as you do."

She gave me an indescribable look. "What can you, what can any one know about it? He may want money; how can he take care of himself in such circumstances without money? I sent for you to contrive some plan by which he can be communicated with. Do tell me at once what to do."

" How can I tell you, when, as you say, I do not know what is required. You wish to see him, I presume?"

" How can I—O, I dislike so much to ask this of you— but *will* you take a message to him?" She asked this desperately, half expecting me to decline, as decline I did.

" Miss Jorgensen, you are now able to ride. Shall I send a carriage for you ?"

" There may be those on the lookout who would instantly suspect my purpose in going out in that way. On the contrary, nobody would suspect you."

" Still, I might be observed, which would not be pleasant, I can imagine, from what you leave me to surmise. No, Miss Jorgensen, much as I should like to serve you personally, you must excuse me from connecting myself in any way with Mr. Hurst; and if I might be allowed to offer advice, I should say that, in justice to yourself, you ought to cut loose from him at once."

Miss Jorgensen covered her face with one little emaciated hand, and sat silent a few seconds. " Send me the carriage," she said, " and I will go."

"You forgive me?"

" You have been very good," she said. "I ought not have required more of you. I will go at once; the sooner the better."

When I had reached the head of the stairs, I turned back again to her door.

" Once more let me counsel you to free yourself from all connection with Mr. Hurst. Why should you ruin your chances of happiness for one so undeserving, as I must think he is? Keep away from him; let him shift for himself."

" You don't know what you are talking about," she replied, with a touch of the old fierceness. "I have no chances of happiness to lose. Please go."

On my way down to the office I ordered a carriage.

What happened afterward I learned from Mrs. Mason and the evening papers. Miss Jorgensen, dressed in deep black, with her face veiled, entered the carriage, directing the driver to take her to the houses of some of her pupils. At the corner of the street, a gentleman, who proved to be our day-boarder, got upon the box with the driver, and remained there while Miss Jorgensen made her calls. Finding him constantly there, and becoming suspicious, she ordered the carriage home, and gave directions to have it return an hour later to take her down town for some shopping. At the time set, the carriage was in attendance, and conveyed her to one of the principal stores in the city. After re-entering the carriage, and giving her directions, our day-boarder once more mounted the box, though unobserved by her, and was conveyed with herself to the hiding-place of Mr. Hurst, contriving, by getting down before the door was opened, to elude her observation.

Another carriage, containing officers of the police, was following in the wake of this one, and drew up when Miss Jorgensen had entered the house where Hurst was concealed. After waiting long enough to make it certain that the person sought was within, the officers entered to search and capture.

At the moment they entered Hurst's apartment, he was saying, with much emotion, "If I can only reach China in safety, a way will be opened for me ——"

"Hush!" cried Miss Jorgensen, seeing the door opened, and by whom.

"All is over!" exclaimed Hurst. "I will never be taken to prison!" And, drawing a revolver, he deliberately shot himself through the head.

Miss Jorgensen was brought back to Mrs. Mason's in a fainting condition, and was ill for weeks afterward. That same evening our day-boarder called, and while settling his board with Mrs. Mason, acknowledged that he belonged to the detective police, and had for months been "working up" the case of a bank-robber and forger who had escaped from one of the eastern cities, and been lost to observation for a year and a half.

And we further learned in the same way, and ultimately from the lady herself, that Miss Jorgensen was a myth, and that the little French teacher was Madame ——, who had

suffered, and toiled, and risked everything for her unworthy husband, and who deserved rather to be congratulated than condoled with upon his loss.

It is now a year since all this happened, and it is the common gossip of our boarding-house that Mr. Quivey is devoted to the little dark-eyed widow; and although Miss
Flower still refers to " E. E." and "I. I.," nobody seems
to be in the least disturbed by the allusion.   When I say
to Quivey, "Make haste slowly, my dear fellow;" he returns: "Never fear, my friend; I shall know when the
time comes to speak."

THE coach of Wells, Fargo & Co. stood before the door of Piney-woods Station, and Sam Rice, the driver, was drawing on his lemon-colored gloves with an air, for Sam was the pink of stage-drivers, from his high white hat to his faultless French boots. Sad will it be when his profession shall have been altogether superseded; and the coach-and-six, with its gracious and graceful "whip," shall have been supplanted, on all the principal lines of travel, by the iron-horse with its grimy "driver" and train of thundering carriages.

The passengers had taken their seats—the one lady on the box—and Sam Rice stood, chronometer held daintily between thumb and finger, waiting for the second hand to come round the quarter of a minute, while the grooms slipped the last strap of the harness into its buckle. At the expiration of the quarter of a minute, as Sam stuck an unlighted cigar between his lips and took hold of the box to pull himself up to his seat, the good-natured landlady of Piney-woods Station called out, with some officiousness:

"Mr. Rice, don't you want a match?"

"That's just what I've been looking for these ten years," responded Sam; and at that instant his eyes were on a level with the lady's on the box, so that he could not help seeing the roguish glint of them, which so far disconcerted the usually self-possessed professor of the whip that he heard not the landlady's laugh, but gathered up the reins in such a hasty and careless manner as to cause Demon, the nigh-leader, to go off with a bound that nearly threw the owner of the eyes out of her place. The little flurry gave opportunity for Mrs. Dolly Page—that was the lady's name—to drop her veil over her face, and for Sam Rice to show his genteel handling of the ribbons, and conquer the unaccountable disturbance of his pulses.

Sam had looked at the way-bill, not ten minutes before, to ascertain the name of the pretty black-eyed woman seated at his left hand; and the consciousness of so great a curiosity gratified, may have augmented his unaccustomed embarrassment. Certain it is, Sam Rice had driven six horses, on a ticklish mountain road, for four years, without missing a trip; and had more than once encountered the "road-agents," without ever yet delivering them an express box; had had old and young ladies, plain and beautiful ones, to sit beside him, hundreds of times: yet this was the first time he had consulted the way-bill, on his own account, to find a lady's name. This one time, too, it had a *Mrs.* before it, which prefix gave him a pang he was very unwilling to own. On the other hand, Mrs. Dolly Page was clad in extremely deep black. Could she be in mourning for Mr. Page? If Demon had an unusual number of starting fits that afternoon, his driver was not altogether guiltless in the matter; for what horse, so sensitive as he, would not have felt the magnetism of something wrong behind him?

But as the mocking eyes kept hidden behind a veil, and the rich, musical voice uttered not a word through a whole half-hour, which seemed an age to Sam, he finally recovered himself so far as to say he believed he would not smoke, after all; and thereupon returned the cigar, still unlighted, to his pocket.

"I hope you do not deprive yourself of a luxury on my account," murmured the soft voice.

"I guess this dust and sunshine is enough for a lady to stand, without my smokin' in her face," returned Sam, politely, and glancing at the veil.

"Still, I beg you will smoke, if you are accustomed," persisted the cooing voice behind it. But Sam, to his praise be it spoken, refused to add anything to the discomforts of a summer day's ride across the mountains. His chivalry had its reward; for the lady thus favored, feeling constrained to make some return for such consideration, began to talk, in a vein that delighted her auditor, about horses—their points and their traits—and, lastly, about their drivers.

"I have always fancied," said Mrs. Dolly Page, "that if I were a man I should take to stage-driving as a profession. It seems to me a free and manly calling, one that develops some of the best qualities of a man. Of course, it has its drawbacks. One cannot always choose one's society on a stage, and there are temptations to bad habits. Besides, there are storms, and upsets, and all that sort of thing. I've often thought," continued Mrs. Dolly, "that we do not consider enough the hardships of drivers, nor what we owe them. You've read that poem—the Post-boy's Song:

> " ' Like a shuttle thrown by the hand of Fate,
> Forward and back I go.'

Well, it is just so. They do bring us our letters, full of good and ill news, helping to weave the web of Fate for us; yet not to blame for what tidings they bring, and always faithful to their duties, in storm or shine."

"I shall like my profession better after what you have said of it," answered Sam, giving his whip a curl to make it touch the off-leader's right ear. "I've done my duty mostly, and not complained of the hardships, though once or twice I've been too beat out to get off the box at the end of my drive; but that was in a long spell of bad weather, when the roads was just awful, and the rain as cold as snow."

"Would you mind letting me hold the lines awhile?" asked the cooing voice, at last. "I've driven a six-in-hand before."

Though decidedly startled, and averse to trusting his team to such a pair of hands, Sam was compelled, by the psychic force of the little woman, to yield up the reins. It

was with fear and trembling that he watched her handling
of them for the first mile; but, as she really seemed to
know what she was about, his confidence increased, and he
watched her with admiration. Her veil was now up, her
eyes were sparkling, and cheeks glowing. She did not
speak often, but, when she did, it was always something
piquant and graceful that she uttered. At last, just as the
station was in sight, she yielded up the lines, with a deep-
drawn sigh of satisfaction, apologizing for it by saying that
her hands, not being used to it, were tired. "I'm not
sure," she added, "but I shall take to the box, at last, as a
steady thing."

"If you do," responded Sam, gallantly, "I hope you
will drive on my line."

"Thanks. I shall ask you for a reference, when I apply
for the situation."

There was then a halt, a supply of fresh horses, and a
prompt, lively start. But the afternoon was intensely hot,
and the team soon sobered down. Mrs. Page did not offer
again to take the lines. She was overwarm and weary, perhaps, quiet and a little sad, at any rate. Mr. Rice was quiet,
too, and thoughtful. The passengers inside were asleep.
The coach rattled along at a steady pace, with the dust so
deep under the wheels as to still their rumble. At intervals, a freight-wagon was passed, drawn to one side, at a
"turn-out," or a rabbit skipped across the road, or a solitary horseman suggested alternately a "road-agent," or
one of James's heroes. Grand views presented themselves
of wooded cliffs and wild ravines. Tall pines threw
lengthening shadows across the open spaces on the mountain-sides. And so the afternoon wore away; and, when
the sun was setting, the passengers alighted for their
supper at the principal hotel of Lucky-dog—a mining-
camp, pretty well up in the Sierras.

"We both stop here," said Sam, as he helped the lady
down from her high position; letting her know by this remark that her destination was known to him.

"I'm rather glad of that," she answered, frankly, with a little smile; and, considering all that had transpired on that long drive, Sam was certainly pardonable if he felt almost sure that her reason for being glad was identical with his own.

Lucky-dog was one of those shambling, new camps, where one street serves for a string on which two or three dozen ill-assorted tenements are strung, every fifth one being a place intended for the relief of the universal American thirst, though the liquids dispensed at these beneficent institutions were observed rather to provoke than to abate the dryness of their patrons. Eating-houses were even more frequent than those which dispensed moisture to parched throats; so that, taking a cursory view of the windows fronting on the street, the impression was inevitably conveyed of the expected rush of famished armies, whose wants this charitable community were only too willing to supply for a sufficient consideration. The houses that were not eating and drinking-houses were hotels, if we except occasional grocery and general merchandise establishments. Into what out-of-the-way corners the inhabitants were stowed, it was impossible to conjecture, until it was discovered that the men lived at the places already inventoried, and that women abode not at all in Lucky-dog—or if there were any, not more than a half a dozen of them, and they lived in un-accustomed places.

The advent of Mrs. Page at the Silver Brick Hotel naturally made a sensation. As assemblage of not less than fifty gentlemen of leisure crowded about the entrance, each more intent than the other on getting a look at the arrivals, and especially at this one arrival—whose age, looks, name, business, and intentions in coming to Lucky-dog, were discussed with great freedom. Sam Rice was closely questioned, but proved reticent and non-committal. The landlord was besieged with inquiries—the landlady, too—and all without anybody being made much the wiser. There was the waybill, and there was the lady herself; put that and that together, and make what you could of it.

Mrs. Dolly Page did not seem discomposed in the least by the evident interest she inspired. With her black curls smoothly brushed, her black robes immaculately neat, with a pretty color in her round cheeks, and a quietly absorbed expression in her whole bearing, she endured the concentrated gaze of fifty pairs of eyes during the whole of dinner, without so much as one awkward movement, or the dropping of a fork or teaspoon. So it was plain that the curious would be compelled to await Mrs. Page's own time for developments.

But developments did not seem likely to come overwhelmingly. Mrs. Page made a fast friend of the landlady of the Silver Brick, by means of little household arts peculiarly her own, and, before a fortnight was gone, had become as indispensable to all the boarders as she was to Mrs. Shaughnessy herself. If she had a history, she kept it carefully from curious ears. Mrs. Shaughnessy was evidently satisfied, and quite challenged criticism of her favorite. Indeed, there was nothing to criticise. It was generally understood that she was a widow, who had to get on in the world as best she could, and thus the public sympathy was secured, and an embargo laid upon gossip. To be sure, there were certain men in Lucky-dog, of a class which has its representatives everywhere, who regarded all unappropriated women, especially pretty women, very much as the hunter regards game, and the more difficult the approach, the more exciting the chase. But these moral Nimrods had not half the chance with self-possessed Mrs. Dolly Page that they would have had with a different style of woman. The grosser sort got a sudden *congé;* and with the more refined sportsmen she coquetted just enough to show them that two could play at a game of "make-believe," and then sent them off with a lofty scorn edifying to behold—to the mingled admiration and amusement of Mrs. Shaughnessy.

The only affair which seemed to have a kernel of seriousness in it, was that of Mr. Samuel Rice. Regularly, when
the stage was in, on Sam's night, he paid his respects to
Mrs. Page. And Mrs. Page always received him with a
graceful friendliness, asking after the horses, and even
sometimes going so far as to accompany him to their sta-
bles. On these occasions she never failed to carry several
lumps of sugar in her pocket, which she fed to the handsome brutes off her own pink palm, until there was not one
of them she could not handle at her will.

Thus passed many weeks, until summer was drawing to a
close. Two or three times she had gone down to Piney-
woods Station and back, on Sam's coach, and always sat on
the box, and drove a part of the way, but never where her
driving would excite remark. It is superfluous to state,
that on these occasions there was a happy heart beneath
Sam's linen-duster, or that the bantering remarks of his
brother-drivers were borne with smiling equanimity, not to
say pride; for Sam was well aware that Mrs. Dolly Page's
brunette beauty, and his blonde-bearded style, together furnished a not unpleasing *tableau* of personal charms. Besides, Sam's motto was, "Let those laugh who win;" and
he seemed to himself to be on the road to heights of happiness beyond the ken of ordinary mortals—especially ordinary stage-drivers.

"I don't calkelate to drive stage more than a year or two
longer," Sam said to Mrs. Page, confidentially, on the return from their last trip together to Piney-woods Station.
"I've got a little place down in Amador, and an interest
in the Nip-and-tuck gold-mine, besides a few hundreds in
bank. I've a notion to settle down some day, in a cottage
with vines over the porch, with a little woman to tend the
flowers in the front-garden."

As if Sam's heightened color and shining eyes had not
sufficiently pointed this confession of his desires, it chanced
that at this moment the eyes of both were attracted to a

way-side picture: a cottage, a flower-bordered walk, a fair
young woman standing at the gate, with a crowing babe in
her arms lifting its little white hands to the sun-browned
face of a stalwart young farmer who was smiling proudly on
the two.   At this sudden apparition of his inmost thoughts,
Sam's heart gave a great bound, and there was a simultane-
ous ringing in his ears.   His first instinctive act was to
crack his whip so fiercely as to set the leaders off prancing;
and when, by this diversion, he had partly recovered self-
possession to glance at the face of his companion, a new
embarrassment seized him when he discovered two little
rivers of tears running over the crimsoned cheeks.   But a
coach-box is not a convenient place for sentiment to display itself; and, though the temptation was great to inquire
into the cause of the tears, with a view of offering consolation, Sam prudently looked the other way, and maintained
silence.   The reader, however, knows that those tears sank
into the beholder's soul, and caused to germinate countless
tender thoughts and emotions, which were, on some future
occasion, to be laid upon the alter of his devotion to Mrs.
Dolly Page.   And none the less, that, in a few minutes,
the eyes which shed them resumed their roguish brightness, and the lady was totally unconscious of having
heard, seen, or felt any embarrassment.   Sentiment between them was successfully *tabooed*, so far as utterance
was concerned, for that time.   And so Sam found, somewhat to his disappointment, it continued to fall out, that
whenever he got upon delicate ground, the lady was off
like a humming-bird, darting hither and yon, so that it was
impossible to put a finger upon her, or get so much as a
look at her brilliant and restless wings.   But nobody ever
tired of trying to find a humming-bird at rest; and so Sam
never gave up looking for the opportune moment of speaking his mind.

Meanwhile, Lucky-dog Camp was having a fresh sensation.   An organized band of gamblers, robbers, and " road-

agents" had made a swoop upon its property, of various
kinds, and had succeeded in making off with it. The very
night after the ride just mentioned, the best horses in Sam
Rice's team were stolen, making it necessary to substitute
what Sam called " a pa'r of ornery cayuses." To put the
climax to his misfortunes, the "road-agents" attacked him
next morning, when, the "orney cayuses" becoming un-
manageable, Sam was forced to surrender the treasure-box,
and the passengers their bullion. The excitement in Lucky-
dog was intense. A vigilance committee, secretly organized,
lay in waiting for the offenders, and, after a week or two,
made a capture of a well-known sporting-man, whose presence in camp had for some time been regarded with suspicion. Short shrift was afforded him. That same afternoon his gentlemanly person swung dangling from a
gnarled pine-tree limb, and his frightened soul had fled
into outer darkness.

When this event became known to Mrs. Dolly Page, she
turned ghostly white, and then fainted dead away. Mrs.
Shaughnessy was very much concerned for her friend; berating in round terms, the brutishness of people who could
talk of such things before a tender-hearted lady like that.
To Mr. Rice, particularly, she expatiated upon the coarseness of certain people, and the refined sensitiveness of
others; and Sam was much inclined to agree with her, so
far as her remarks applied to her friend, who was not yet
recovered sufficiently to be visible. Indeed, Mrs Page was
not visible for so many days, that Sam's soul began to long
for her with a mighty longing. At length, she made her
appearance, considerably paler and thinner than was her
wont; but doubly interesting and lovely to the eyes of so
partial an observer as Sam, who would willingly have
sheltered her weakness in his strong, manly arms. Sam,
naturally enough, would never have hinted at the event
which had so distressed her; but she relieved him of all
embarrassment on that subject, by saying to him almost at
once:

"Mr. Rice, I am told they have not buried the man they hung, so shockingly, the other day. They certainly will not leave him *there?*" she added, with a shudder.

"I don't know—I suppose," stammered Sam, "it is their way, with them fellows."

"But you will not allow it? You *cannot* allow it!"—excitedly.

"I couldn't prevent them," said Sam, quite humbly.

"Mr. Rice," and her voice was at once a command and an entreaty, "you *can* and *must* prevent it. You are not afraid? I will go with you—this very night—and will help you. Don't say you will not; for I cannot sleep until it is done. I have not slept for a week."

She looked so white and so wild, as she uttered this confession, that Sam would have been the wretch he was not, to refuse her. So he said:

"Don't you fret. I'll bury him, if it troubles you so. But you needn't go along. You couldn't; it's too far, and you're too weak,"—seeing how she trembled.

"I am not weak—only nervous. I prefer to go along. But we must be secret, I suppose? Oh!"—with a start that was indeed "nervous."

"Yes, we must be secret," said Sam; and he looked as if he did not half like the business, but would not refuse.

"You are a good man, Mr. Rice, and I thank you." And with that, Mrs. Dolly Page caught up one of his hands, and kissing it hastily, began to cry, as she walked quickly away.

"Don't cry, and don't go until I have promised to do whatever you ask, if it will make you well again," Sam said, following her to the door.

"Then call for me to take a walk with you to-night. The moon is full, but no one will observe us. They would not think of our going *there*,"—with another shudder—and she slipped away from his detaining hand.

That evening Mr. Samuel Rice and Mrs. Page took a walk by moonlight. Laughing gossips commented on it after their fashion; and disagreeable gossips remarked that they came home very late, after *their* fashion. But nobody, they believed, saw where they went, or what they did. Yet those two came from performing an act of Christian charity, each with a sense of guilt and unworthiness very irritating to endure, albeit from very different causes. One, because an unwelcome suspicion had thrust itself into his mind; and the other——

The ground of Sam's suspicion was a photograph, which, in handling the gambler's body somewhat awkwardly, by reason of its weight—Mrs. Page had found, at the last, she could not render any assistance—had slipped from some receptacle in its clothing. A hasty glance, under the full light of the moon, had shown him the features of the lady who sat twelve paces away, with her hands over her face. It is not always those that sin who suffer most from the consciousness of sin; and Sam, perhaps, with that hint of possible—nay, almost certain—wickedness in his breast-pocket, was more burdened by the weight of it than many a criminal about to suffer all the terrors of the law; for the woman that he loved stood accused, if not·convicted, before his conscience and her own, and he could not condemn, because his heart refused to judge her.

When the two stood together under the light of the lamp in the deserted parlor of the Silver Brick Hotel, the long silence which, by her quick perceptions, had been recognized as accusing her, upon what evidence she did not yet know, was at length broken by Sam's voice, husky with agitation.

" Mrs. Page," he said, assuming an unconscious dignity of mien and sternness of countenance, " I shall ask you some questions, sometime, which you may not think quite polite. And you must answer me: you understand. I'm bound to know the truth about this man."

"About this man!" Then he suspected her of connection with the wretched criminal whose body had only just

16

now been hidden from mocking eyes? How much did he suspect? how much did he *know?* Her pale face and frightened eyes seemed to ask these questions of him; but not a sound escaped her lips. The imploring look, so strange upon her usually bright face, touched all that was tender in Sam's romantic nature. In another moment he would have recalled his demand, and trusted her infinitely; but in that critical moment she fainted quite away, to his mingled sorrow and alarm; and Mrs. Shaughnessy being summoned, Sam received a wordy reprimand for having no more sense than to keep a sick woman up half of the night; smarting under which undeserved censure, he retired, to think over the events of the evening.

The hour of departure from Luckydog, for Sam's coach, was four o'clock in the morning; and its driver was not a little surprised, when about to mount the box, to discover Mrs. Page waiting to take a seat beside him. After the adventure of the previous night, it was with some restraint that he addressed her; and there was wanting, also, something of his cheerful alacrity of manner, when he requested the stranger who had taken the box-seat, to yield it to a lady. The stranger's mood seemed uncongenial, for he declined to abdicate, intimating that there was room for the lady between himself and the driver, if she insisted upon an outside seat.

But Mrs. Page did not insist. She whispered Sam to open the coach-door, and quietly took a seat inside; and Sam, with a sense of irritation very unusual with him, climbed reluctantly to his place, giving the "cayuses" the lash in a way that set them off on a keen run. By the time he had gotten his team cooled down, the unusual mood had passed, and the longing returned to hear the sweet voice, and watch the bright eyes that had made his happiness on former occasions. Puzzled as he was, and pained by the evidence he possessed of her connection, in some way, with the victim of lynch-law, *that* seemed like a dream in the

clear, sunny air of morning, while the more blissful past
asserted its claim to be considered reality. Not a lark,
warbling its flute-notes by the way-side, not a pretty bit of
the familiar landscape, nor glimpse of brook, that leaped
sparkling down the mountain, but recalled some charming
utterance of Mrs. Dolly Page, as he first knew her; as he
could not now recognize her in the pale, nervous, and evidently suffering woman, sitting, closely veiled, inside the
coach.

Occupied with these thoughts, Sam felt a disagreeable
shock when the outside passenger—in a voice that con-
trasted roughly with that other voice which was murmuring
in his ear—began a remark about the mining prospects of
Lucky-dog.

"Some rich discoveries made in the neighborhood, eh?
Did you ever try your luck at mining?"

"Waal, no. I own a little stock, though," answered
Sam, carelessly.

"In what mine?"

"In the Nip-and-tuck."

"Good mine, from all I hear about it. Never did any
prospecting?" asked the stranger, in that tone which de-
notes only a desire to make talk, with a view to kill time.

"No," in the same tone.

"That's odd," stuffing a handful of cut tobacco into his
mouth. "I'd have sworn 'twas you I saw swinging a pick
in the cañon east of camp last night."

"I'm not much on picks," Sam returned, with a slowness
that well counterfeited indifference. "I was visting a lady
last evening, which is a kind of prospecting more in my
line."

"Yes, I understand; that lady inside the coach. She's a
game one."

"It strikes me you're devilish free in your remarks," said
Sam, becoming irritated again.

"No offense meant, I'm sure. Take a cigar? We may

as well talk this matter over calmly, Mr. Rice. You see it's ten to one that you are implicated in this business. Been very attentive to Mrs. Page. Made several trips together. Let her handle your horses, so she could take them out of the stable for them thieves. Buried her thieving, gambling husband for her. You see the case *looks* bad, anyway; though I'm inclined to think you've just been made a tool of. I know she's a smart one. Tain't often you find one smarter."

Sam's eyes scintilliated. He was strangly minded to pitch the outside passenger off the coach. The struggle in his breast‚between conviction and resistance to conviction amounted to agony. He could not, in that supreme moment, discriminate between the anger he felt at being falsely accused, and the grief and rage of being so horrible disillusioned. Their combined anguish paled his cheeks, and set his teeth on edge: of all of which the outside passenger was coolly cognizant. As they were, at that moment, in sight of the first station, he resumed.

"Let her get up here, if she wants to; I can ride inside. I don't want to be hard on her; but mind, if you breathe a word to her about my being an officer, I'll arrest you on suspicion. Let every tub stand on its own bottom. If she's guilty, you can't help her, and don't want to, either; if she's innocent, she'll come out all right, never fear. Are you on the square, now?"

"Have you got a warrant?" asked Sam, in a low tone, as he wound the lines around the break, previous to getting down.

"You bet! but I'm in no hurry to serve it. Piney-woods station 'ill do just as well. Telegraph office there."

Mr. Rice was not in any haste this morning, being, as he said, ahead of time. He invited Mrs. Page to take her usual place on the box, telling her the gentleman had concluded to go inside; and brought her a glass of water from the bar. While he was returning the glass, the passengers,

including him of the outside, being busied assuaging their
thirst with something stronger than water, a rattle of wheels
and a clatter of hoofs was heard, and, lo! Mrs. Dolly Page
was discovered to be practicing her favorite accomplishment
of driving six-in-hand!

When the "outside" recovered from his momentary surprise, he clapped his hand on the shoulder of Mr. Rice, and
said, in a voice savage with spite and disappointment:

"I arrest you, sir."

"Arrest and be d——d!" returned Sam. "If you had
done your duty, you'd have arrested *her* while you had the
chance."

"That's so—your head is level; and if you'll assist me in
getting on to Piney-woods station in time to catch the run-
away—for she can't very well drive beyond that station—I'll
let you off."

"You'll wait till I'm on, I reckon. My horses can't go
on that errand, and you darsn't take the up-driver's team.
Put that it your pipe and smoke it, old smarty!"—and Sam's
eyes emitted steel-blue lightnings, though his face wore a
fixed expression of smiling.

Upon inquiry, it was ascertained that horses might be
procured a mile back from the station; and, while the
baffled officer, and such of the passengers as could not wait
until next day, went in pursuit of them, Sam mounted one
of the "cayuses," and made what haste he could after the
coach and Wells, Fargo & Company's express-box. Within
a mile or less of Piney-woods Station, he met the keeper,
the grooms, and an odd man or two, that chanced to have
been about the place, all armed to the teeth, who, when they
saw him, halted in surprise.

"Why, we reckoned you was dead," said the head man,
with an air of disappointment.

"Dead?" repeated Sam. "Have you seen my coach?"

"That's all right, down to the station; and the plucky
gal that druv it told us all about the raid the 'road-agents'
made on you. Whar's the passengers? any of 'em killed?"

"Passengers are all right.   Where is Mrs. Page?"

"She cried, an' tuk on awful about ye; an' borrered a hoss to ride right on down the road to meet the other stage, an' let 'em know what's up."

"She did, did she?" said Sam, very thoughtfully. "Waal, that *is* odd.   Why, she ran away with my team— that's what she did; and it's all a hoax about the 'road-agents.'   The passengers are back at the other station."

Sam had suddenly become "all things to all men," to a degree that surprised himself.   He was wrong about the horse, too, as was proven by its return to its owner four days after.   By the same hand came the following letter to Mr. Samuel Rice:

DEAR MR. RICE: It was so good of you! I thank you more than I can say.   I wish I could set myself right in your eyes, for I prize your friendship dearly—dearly; but I know that I cannot.   It has not been all my fault.   I was married to a bad, bad man, when I was only fifteen.   He has ruined my life; but now he is dead, and I need not fear him.   I *will* hereafter live as a good woman should live.   The tears run down my cheeks as I write you this farewell—as they did that day when I saw that sweet woman and her babe at the farm-house gate; and knew what was in your thought. Heaven send you such a wife.   Good-bye, dear Mr. Rice, good-bye.   "DOLLY PAGE!"

There are some men, as well as women, in this world, who could figure in the *role* of *Evangeline*, who have tender, loyal, and constant hearts.   Such a one was the driver of the Lucky-dog stage.   But, though he sat on that box for two years longer, and scrutinized every dark-eyed, sweet-voiced lady-passenger who rode in his coach during that time, often with an intense longing for a sight of the face he craved—it never came.   Out of the heaven of his life that star had vanished forever, and nothing was left him but a soiled photograph, and a tear-stained letter, worn with frequent folding and unfolding.

EL TESORO.

"WIMMEN nater is cur'us nater, that I'll allow. But a feller kind o' hankers arter 'em, fur all that. They're a mighty handy thing to hev about a house."

The above oracular statement proceeded from the parched and puckered lips of Sandy-haired Jim—one of the many "hands" employed on the immense Tesoro Rancho, which covered miles of valley, besides extending up on to the eastern flank of the Coast Range, and taking in considerable tracts of woodland and mountain pasture. Long before, when it acquired its name, under Spanish occupancy, there had been a rumor of the existence of the precious metals in the mountains which formed a portion of the grant; hence, its name, Tesoro, signifying *treasure*. All search for, or belief in, gold mines, had been abandoned, even before the land came into the possession of American owners, and now was only spoken of in the light of a Spanish legend; but the name was retained, partly as a geographical distinction of a large tract of country, though it was sometimes called the Edwards Ranch, after its present proprietor, and after the American fashion of pronunciation.

John Edwards had more than once said, in hearing of his men, that he would give half the proceeds of the mine and an interest in the ranch, to any one who would discover it and prove it to be of value; a remark which was not without weight, especially with the herders and shepherds, whose calling took them into the mountains a considerable portion of the year. But as the offer of the proprietor never seemed to assume the air of a business proposition, the men who might have been inflamed by it with a prospecting fever, held in check their desire to

acquire sudden riches, and never looked very sharp at the
"indications," which it was easy sometimes to imagine
they had found. But that is neither here nor there with
Sandy-haired Jim, who was not a cattle-herder, nor yet a
shepherd, but farmer or teamster, as the requirement was,
at different seasons of the year.

He was expressing himself concerning John Edwards'
sister, who, just one year ago, had come to set up domes-
ticity in the house of her brother; whereas, previous to her
advent, John had "bach'd it" on the ranch, with his men,
for four or five years. Jim, and the chum to whom his
remarks were addressed, were roosting on a fence, after the
manner of a certain class of agriculturists, hailing usually
from Missouri, and most frequently from the county of
Pike.

The pale December sunshine colored with a soft gold the
light morning haze which hung over the valley in which
lay the Tesoro Rancho. In spite of the year of drought
which had scorched up the grain-fields, and given a character of aridity to the landscape, it had a distinctive soft
beauty of tint and outline, seen in the favoring light we
have mentioned. Of all the fascinating pictures we remember to have seen, the most remarkable was one of a
desert scene, with nothing but the stretches of yellow sand
and the golden atmosphere for middle distance and back-
ground, and, for a foreground, a white tent, with camels
and picturesquely costumed Arabs grouped before it.
There was the sense of infinite distance in it which is so
satisfying to the mind, which the few figures and broken
lines intensified; and there was that witching warmth and
mellowness of coloring which does not belong to landscapes where green and gray hues predominate.

Having said thus much about a picture, we have explained why Californian views, even in our great, almost
treeless valleys, grow so into our hearts and imaginations,
after the first dash of disappointment at not finding them

like the vernal vales of New England or central New York. But Tesoro Rancho was not treeless. Great spreading oaks furnished just the necessary dark-green tones in the valley landscape; and the mountain-sides had multifarious shades of color, furnished by rocks and trees, by shadows, and by the atmosphere itself.

It was no wonder, then, that sandy-haired Jim, sitting on a rail-fence, in an attitude more curious than graceful, cast his glance often unconsciously over the far valley-reaches, and up the mountain-sides, with a dim perception of something pleasant in the view which his thought took no cognizance of. In fact, for the last minute or two, his gaze had been a silent one; and any observer might have pondered, considering the sharpness of the perch beneath him, whether he might not be making up his mind to descend from it as soon as his slow-working mentality had had time to convey the decision of his brain to his muscles.

At all events, that was what he did in answer to our mental query, taking up the thread of his discourse where it was broken off, as follows:

"Miss Edwards, neow (thar she is, a-comin down from the mount'in, with her arms full of them 'zalias she's so fond of), she's a mighty peart kind of a gal, and wuth a heap more to keep a man's house in good shape than one o' them soft-lookin' Chinee. Them's my sentiments."

"That's *so*," responded his chum, seeming constitutionally disinclined to a longer sentence.

"John Edwards has tuk to dressin' hisself nicer, and fixin' up the place as he didn't used to when he bach'd it, I can tell ye! When I see her bringin' her pianny, and her picturs, and books, and sich like traps, I just told myself, 'Neow, John Edwards has got a pretty passel of trash on his hands, I veow.' And I ment *her* as well as the other fol-de-rols. But, you bet your life, she's got more sense, two to one, than ary one of us! It was a lucky day for Edwards when she came onto this ranch, sure's you're born."

What further this equally philosophical and devoted admirer of Miss Edwards might have said on this, to him, evidently interesting topic, had he not been interrupted, will never be known. For the lady herself appeared upon the scene, putting an end to her own praises, and discovering to us, upon nearer view, that she added youth and grace, if not absolute beauty, to her other qualities.

Checking the rapid lope of her horse, as she came near where the men were standing, in attitudes of frank, if awkward, deference, she saluted them with a cheerful "Good-morning," and drew rein beside them.

"Take Brownie by the head, and walk a little way with me, if you please, James. I have something I wish to say to you," was the lady's low-voiced command. A certain flush and pleased expression on honest Jim's ruddy countenance reminded her instantly of the inherent vanity of man, and when she next addressed her attendant it was as "Mr. Harris," for such, indeed, was the surname of our lank Missourian, though not many of his associates had ever heard it.

"How long have you been on this place, Mr. Harris?"

"Near onto six year, Miss Edwards," replied Jim.

"Did you know Mr. Charles Erskine, my brother's former partner?"

"Just as well as I know your brother, Miss."

"What became of him, after he left this place?"

"I couldn't rightly say, miss. Some said he went to the mines, up in Idaho, and other folks said they'd seen him in 'Frisco: but I don't know nary thing about him."

"He must be found, Mr. Harris. Do you think you could find him, if I were to send you on such a mission? It is a very important one, and it is not every one I would intrust it to."

The flush and the pleased look returned to Jim's face. "I'd do the best I could, miss; and, mebbe, I'd do as well as another."

"That is what I was thinking, Mr. Harris. You have been a long time here, and you are prompt and capable about your own business; so I concluded I could trust you with mine. I am sure I was quite right."

Jim was going on to "swar she was," when Miss Edwards interrupted him, to enlighten him further as to the requirements of "her business:" "I do not wish my brother to know what errand I send you on. They had a dreadful quarrel once, I believe; and he might not agree with me as to the wisdom of what I am about to do. It will, therefore, be necessary for you to ask John's permission to go on a visit to San Francisco, as if it was for yourself you were going. The drought has left so little to do that you can be spared, without embarrassment, until the rains begin. I am going to have a grand festival at Christmas, and I would like you to be home before that time. I will explain further when you have got John's consent to your absence. Come to the house after, and ask if I have any commission for you."

When Miss Edwards cantered off, leaving him alone in the road, Jim was in a state of pleased bewilderment, not unmixed with an instinctive jealousy.

" I do wonder, neow, what she wants with Charlie Erskine. He was a powerful nice feller, and smart as lightnin'; but, somehow, he an' Edwards never could hitch hosses. Erskine allus went too fast for steady John, an' I doubt ef he didn't git him into some money troubles. I'd like to know, though, what that girl's got to do about it. Wonder ef she knowed him back in the States. Wimmen is cur'us, sure enough."

Jim's suggestion was the true one. Miss Edwards had known Charles Erskine " back in the States," and when they parted last, it had been as engaged lovers. When she left her home in the East to join her brother, a speedy marriage with him had been in contemplation. But how often did it happen, in old " steamer times," that wives left

New York to join husbands in San Francisco, only to find, on arrival at the end of a long voyage, the dear ones hidden from sight in the grave, or the false ones gone astray! And so it happened to Mary Edwards, that, when she set foot on California soil, no lover appeared to welcome her, and her trembling and blushing were turned to painful suspense and secret bitter tears.

Her brother had vouchsafed very little explanation; only declaring Charles Erskine a scoundrel, who had nearly ruined him, and swearing he should never set foot on Tesoro Rancho until every dollar of indebtedness was paid. Poor Mary found it hard settling into a place so new, and duties so unaccustomed; but her good sense and good spirits conquered difficulties as they arose, until now she was quite inclined to like the new life for its own sake. Her brother was kind, and gathered about her every comfort and many luxuries; though, owing to embarrassments into which Erskine had drawn him, and to the losses of a year of drought, his purse was not overflowing. Such was the situation of affairs on the December morning when our story opens.

Miss Edwards mentioned to her brother, during the day, that James Harris had spoken of going to the city, and that she had some commissions for him to perform. She had made up her mind to discountenance the heathen habits into which everybody on the ranch had fallen. She had done all she could to keep the men from going to bull-fights on the Sabbath, and had offered to read the morning service, if the men would attend; and now she was going to celebrate Christmas, though she really did believe that the people who never saw snow forgot that Christ was ever born! Yet was he not born in a country very strongly resembling this very one which ignored him?

John smiled, and offered no opposition; only bidding her remember not to make her commissions to the city very expensive ones, and suggesting, that, since she meant to be gay, she had better send some invitations to certain of their friends.

"By the way John, do you know where Charles Erskine is?" Miss Edwards asked, with much forced composure.

"The last I heard of him he was in San Francisco, lying dangerously ill," answered John coldly.

"Oh, John!"

"Mary, you must hope nothing from that man. Don't waste your sympathies on him, either; he'll never repay you the outgo."

"Tell me just one thing, John: Was Charles ever false to me? Tell me the truth."

"I think he kept good faith with you. It is not that I complain of in his conduct. The quarrel is strictly between us. He can never come here, with my consent."

"But I can go to him," said Miss Edwards, very quietly.

And she did go—with Sandy-haired Jim for an escort, and her brother's frowning face haunted her.

"If all is right," she said to him, at the very last, "I will be back to keep Christmas with you. Think as well as you can of me, John, and—good-by."

It will be seen, that, whatever Miss Edwards' little, womanly plan of reconciliation had been, it was, as to details, all changed by the information John had given her. What next she would do depended on circumstances. It was, perhaps, a question of life and death. The long, wearying, dusty stage-ride to San Francisco, passed like a disagreeable dream; neither incident of heat by day, nor cold by night, or influence of grand or lovely scenes, seemed to touch her consciousness. James Harris, in his best clothes and best manners—the latter having a certain gentle dignity about them that was born of the occasion—sat beside her, and ministered assiduously to those personal wants which she had forgotten in the absorption of her painful thoughts.

What Jim himself thought, if his mental processes could be called thinking, it would be difficult to state. He was dimly conscious that in his companion's mind there was a heavy trouble brooding; and conscious, also, of a desire to alleviate it, as far as possible, though in what way that might be done, he had not the remotest idea. There seemed an immense gulf between her and him, over which he never could reach to proffer consolation; and while he blindly groped in his own mind for some hint of his duty, he was fain to be content with such personal attentions as defending her from heat and cold, dust and fatigue, and reminding her that eating and drinking were among the necessary inconveniences of this life. After a couple of days spent in revolving the case hopelessly in his brain, his thoughts at length shaped themselves thus:

"Waal, neow, 'taint no concern of mine, to be sure; but I'm beound to see this gal threough. She's captain of this train, an' only got ter give her orders. I'll obey 'em, ef they take me to thunder. That's so, I veow!" After which conclusion of the whole matter, Jim appeared more at his ease in all respects. In truth, the most enlightened of us go to school to just such mental struggles, with profit to our minds and manners.

Arrived at San Francisco, Miss Edwards took quarters at at a hotel, determined before reporting herself to any of her acquaintance to first find whether Charles Erskine was alive, and, if so, where he could be found. What a wearisome search was that before traces of him were discovered, in a cheap boarding-house, in a narrow, dirty street. And what bitter disappointment it was to learn that he had gone away some weeks before, as soon as he was able to be moved. To renew the search in the city, to send telegrams in every direction, was the next effort, which, like the first, proved fruitless; and, at the end of ten days Miss Edwards made a few formal calls on her friends, concluded some necessary purchases, and set out on her return to Tesoro Rancho, exhausted in mind and body.

If Jim was careful of her comfort before, he was tender

toward her now; and the lady accepted the protecting care
of the serving-man with a dull sense of gratitude. She even
smiled on him faintly, in a languid way, but in a way that
seemed to him to lessen the distance between them. Jim's
education had been going on rapidly during the last ten
days. He seemed to himself to be quite another man than
the one who sat on the fence with Missouri Joe, less than
two weeks agone.

Perhaps Miss Edwards noticed the change, and innocently encouraged him to aspire. We must not blame her
if she did. This is what woman's education makes of her.
The most cultured women must be grateful and flattering
toward the rudest men, if circumstances throw them together. Born to depend on somebody, they must depend
on their inferiors when their superiors are not at hand;
must, in fact, assume an inferiority to those inferiors. If
they sometimes turn their heads with the dangerous deference, what wonder!

Secure in the distance between them, Miss Edwards assumed that she could safely defer to Sandy-haired Jim, if,
as it seemed, he enjoyed the sense of being her protector.
Even had he been her equal, she would have said to herself,
"He knows my heart is breaking for another, and will respect my grief." In this double security, she paid no heed
to the devotion of her companion, only thinking him the
kindest and most awkward of good and simple-minded
men. That is just what any of us would have thought
about Sandy-haired Jim, gentle readers.

John Edwards received his sister with a grave kindliness,
which aggravated her grief. He would not ask her a question, nor give her the smallest opportunity of appealing to
his sympathies. She had undertaken this business without
his sanction, and without his sympathy she must abide the
consequences. Toward her, personally, he should ever
feel and act brotherly; but toward her foolish weakness for
Erskine, he felt no charity. He was surprised and pleased

to see that his sister's spirit was nearly equal to his own; for, though visibly "pale and pining," after the absurd fashion of women, she went about her duties and recreations as usual, and prosecuted the threatened preparations for Christmas with enthusiasm.

In some of these, it was necessary to employ the services of one of the men, and Miss Edwards, without much thought of why, except that she was used to him, singled out Jim as her assistant. To her surprise, he excused himself, and begged to substitute Missouri Joe.

"You see, Miss Edwards, I've been a long time meanin' to take a trip into the mount'ins. I allow it'll rain in less nor a week, an' then it'll be too late; so ef you'll excuse me this onct, I'll promise to be on hand next time, sure."

"Oh, certainly, Mr. Harris; Joe will do very well, no doubt; and there is no need for you to make excuses. I thought you would like to assist about these preparations, and I am sure you would, too; but go, by all means, for, as you say, it must rain very soon, when it will be too late."

"Thar's nothing I'd like better nor stayin' to work for you, Miss Edwards," answered Jim, with some appearance of confusion; "but this time I'm obleeged to go—I am, sure."

"Well, good-by, and good luck to you, Mr. Harris," Miss Edwards said, pleasantly.

"Ef she only knowed what I'm a goin' fur!" muttered Jim to himself, as he went to "catch up" his horse, and pack up two or three days' rations of bread and meat. "But I ain't goin' to let on about it to a single soul. It's best to keep this business to myself, I reckon. 'Peared like 'twas a hint of that kind she give me, the other day, when she said, 'The gods help them that help themselves, Mr. Harris.' Such a heap o' sense as that gal's got! She's smarter'n John Edwards and me, and Missouri Joe, to boot: but I'm a-gainin' on it a leetle—I'm a-gainin' on it a leetle," concluded Jim, slowly, puckering his parched and sunburnt lips into a significant expression of mystery.

What it was he was "gainin' on," did not appear, for the weight of his thoughts had brought him to a dead-stand, a few feet from the fence, on the hither side of which was the animal he contemplated riding. At this juncture of entire absence of mind, the voice of John Edwards, hailing him from the road, a little way off, dissolved the spell:

"I say, Jim," hallooed Edwards; "if you discover that mine, I will give you half of it, and an interest in the ranch."

The words seemed to electrify the usually slow mind to which the idea was addressed. Turning short about, Jim, in a score of long strides, reached the fence separating him from Edwards.

"Will you put that in writin'?"

"To be sure, I will," answered John, nodding his head, with a puzzled and ironical smile.

"I'll go to the house with ye, an' hev it done to onct," said Jim, sententiously. "I hev about an hour to spar, I reckon."

John Edwards was struck by the unusual manner of the proverbially deliberate man, who had served him with the same unvarying "slow and sure" faithfulness for years; but he refrained from comments. Jim, in his awkward way, proved to be more of a man of business than could have been expected.

"I want a bond fur a deed, Mr. Edwards. That's the best way to settle it, I reckon."

"That is as good a way as any; the discovery to be made within a certain time."

"An' what interest in the ranch, Mr. Edwards?"

"Well, about the ranch," said John, thoughtfully, "I don't want to run any risk of trading it off for nothing, and there will have to be conditions attached to the transfer of any portion of that more than the one of discovery of the mine. Let it be this way: that on the mine proving by actual results to be worth a certain sum—say $50,000—the

17

deed shall be given to half the mine and one-third interest in the ranch; the supposition being, that, if it is proved to be worth $50,000, it is probably worth four times or ten times that amount."

"That's about it, I should say," returned Jim. "It's lib'ral in you, any way, Mr. Edwards."

"The truth is, Harris," said Edwards, looking him steadily in the eye, "I am in a devil of a pinch, that's the truth of it; and I am taking gambling chances on this thing. I only hope you may earn your third of the ranch. I'll not grudge it to you, if you do."

"Thank ye, sir. An' when them papers is made eout, I'll be off."

John handed him his papers half an hour afterward, which Jim prudently took care to have witnessed. Miss Edwards being called in, signed her name.

"So, this is what takes you to the mountains, Mr. Harris? I'm sure I wish you good luck."

"You did that afore, miss; an' it came, right on the spot."

"I must be your 'wishing fairy,'" said she, laughing.

"I'll bring you a Christmas present, Miss Edwards, like as not," Jim answered, coloring with delight at the thought.

"I hope you may. Thank you for the intention, any way."

"Are you going all alone, Harris?" asked Edwards, as he accompanied him a short distance from the house. "It is not quite safe going alone, is it? Have you any heirs, supposing you lose yourself or break your neck?"

Once more Jim was electrified with an idea. His light, gray eyes turned on his questioner with a sudden flash of intelligence:

"I mought choose my heir, I reckon."

"Certainly."

"Mought we go back to the house, an' make a will?"

"Aren't you afraid turning back so often may spoil your luck?" asked Edwards, laughing.

"Ef you think so, I'll never do it," answered Jim, soberly. "But I'll tell you, onct fur all, who it is shall be my heir if any thing chance me, an' I'll expect you'll act on the squar: that person is Miss Mary Edwards, your own sister, an' you'll not go fur to dispute my will?"

"I've no right to dispute your will, whether I approve of it or not. There will be no proof of it, however, and I could not make over your property to my sister, should there be other heirs with a natural and rightful claim to it. But you are not going to make your will just yet, Harris; so, good-by. You'll be home on Christmas?"

"I reckon I will."

John Edwards turned back to the house, and to banter his sister on Jim Harris's will, while that individual went about the business of his journey. His spirits were in a strange state of half-elation, half-depression. The depression was a natural consequence of the talk about a will, and the elation was the result of a strong and sudden faith which had sprung up in him in the success of his undertaking, and of the achievements of every kind it would render possible.

"She's my 'wishin' fairy,' she said, an' she wished me luck twice. I got the first stroke of it when John Edwards called to me across the field. I've got him strong on that; an' I war a leetle surprised, too. He wanted to make me look sharp, that's clar as mud. I'll look sharp, you bet, John Edwards! Didn't her hand look purty when she wrote her name? I've got her name to look at, any way." And at this stage of his reverie, Jim drew from an inner breast-pocket the bond which Miss Edwards had witnessed, and, after gazing at the signature for a moment with moveless features, gave a shy, hasty glance all round him, and pressed his parched and puckered lips on the paper.

The sentiment which caused this ebullition of emotion in

Sandy-haired Jim was one so dimly defined, so little understood, and so absolutely pure in its nature, that had Miss
Edwards been made aware of it, she could only have seen
in it the touching tribute which it was to abstract womanli-
ness—to the " wimmen nater," of which Jim was so frank
an admirer. The gulf which was between them had never
yet been crossed, even in imagination, though it is pre-
sumable; that, unknown to himself, Jim was trembling on
the verge of it at this moment, dragged thither by the excitement of prospective wealth and the possibilities involved
in it, and by the recollection of the pleasant words and
smiles of this, to him, queen of women.

After this gush of romance—the first and only one Jim
had ever been guilty of—he returned the document to his
pocket, and, with his customary deliberation, proceeded to
catch and mount his horse, and before noon was on his way
across the valley, toward that particular gorge in the mountain where *el tesoro* was supposed to be located. John Edwards stood in the house door watching him ambling over
the waste, yellow plain, until Jim and his horse together
appeared a mere speck in the distance, when he went to
talk over with his sister the late transaction, and make some
jesting remarks on the probability of the desired discovery.

The days sped by, and there remained but two before
Christmas. John and his sister were consulting together
over the arrangement of some evergreen arches and wreaths
of bay-leaves. Miss Edwards was explaining where the
floral ornaments should come in, where she would have this
picture, and where that, and how it would be best to light
the rooms.

"I confess, John," she said, sitting down to braid the
scarlet berries of the native *arbutus* into a wreath with the
leaves of the California nutmeg, " that I can not make it
seem like winter or like Christmas, with these open doors,
these flowers, and this warm sunlight streaming in at the
windows. I do wish we could have a flurry of snow, to
make it seem like the holidays."

"Snow is out of the question; but I should be thankful for a good rain-storm. If it does not rain soon, there will be another failure of crops next year in all this part of the country."

"And then we should have to 'go down into Egypt for corn,' as the Israelites used so. Do you feel very apprehensive, John?"

Before John could reply, his attention was diverted by a strange arrival. Dismounting from Jim's horse was a man whom he did not at once recognize, so shabby were his clothes, so worn and haggard his appearance. With a feeling of vague uneasiness and curiosity, he sauntered toward the gate, to give such greeting as seemed fit to the stranger who came in this guise, yet riding a well-conditioned horse belonging to one of his own men.

Miss Edwards, who had also recognized the animal, ran, impulsively, to the door. She saw her brother advance to within a few feet of the stranger, then turn abruptly on his heel and return toward the house. The man thus contemptuously received, reeled, as if he would have fallen, but caught at the gate-post, where he remained, leaning, as if unable to walk.

"Who is it, John?" asked Miss Edwards, anxiously regarding her brother's stern countenance; but he passed her, without a word.

A sudden pallor swept over her face, and she looked, for one moment, as if she might have fainted; then, with a cry of, "Oh, John, John, be merciful!" she ran after him, and threw her arms about him.

"Let me go, Mary," said he, hoarsely. "If you wish to see Charles Erskine, you can do as you please. _I_ wash my hands of him."

"But, John, he is ill; he is suffering; he may die—and at your gate!"

"Let him die!"

It was then that the soul of Miss Edwards "stood up in

her eyes, and looked at" her brother. She withdrew her arms and turned mutely toward the door, out of which she passed, with a proud, resolute, and rapid tread. Without hesitation she did that which is so hard for a woman to do —make advances toward the man with whom she had once been in tender relations, but whose position has, for any reason, been made to appear doubtful. She went to him, took him by the hand, and inquired, more tremulously than she meant, what she could do for him.

"Mary!" answered the sick man, and then fainted quite away.

Miss Edwards had him conveyed to her own room, by the hands of Missouri Joe and the Chinese cook, where she dispensed such restoratives as finally brought back consciousness; and some slight nourishment being administered, revealed the fact that exhaustion and famine, more than disease, had reduced the invalid to his present condition; on becoming aware of which fact, Miss Edwards grew suddenly embarrassed, and, arranging everything for his comfort. was about to withdraw from the apartment, when Erskine beckoned to her, and, fumbling in his pockets, brought out several pieces of white quartz, thickly studded with yellow metal, but of the value of which she had little conception.

"Take these to John," he said, "and tell him they are a peace-offering. They came from *el tesoro.*"

"You have seen James Harris; and he has discovered the mine!"

"I have seen no one. I discovered the mine myself."

"But the horse? It was Harris' horse you were riding."

"I did not know it; I found him, fortunately, when I could no longer walk."

"Poor Charlie," whispered Miss Edwards, moved by that womanly weakness which is always betraying the sex. She never knew how it was, but her head sank on the pillow; and, when she remembered it afterward, she was certain that, in the confusion of her ideas, he kissed her.

Then she fled from the room, and sought her brother every-where, saying, over and over, to herself, "Poor Jim! I wonder what has happened to him;" with tears streaming from her eyes, which she piously attributed to apprehensions for James Harris.

When John was found, and the "specimens" placed in his hands, he was first incredulous, and then indignant; for it hurts a proud man to be forced to change an opinion, or forgive an injury. The pressure of circumstances being too strong for him, he relented so far as to see Erskine, and talk over the discovery with him. What more the two men talked of, never transpired; but Miss Edwards concluded that everything was settled, as her brother gave orders concerning the entertainment of his former partner, and looked and spoke with unusual vivacity for the remainder of the day.

Many conjectures were formed concerning the fate of Sandy-haired Jim, by the men on the ranch, who generally agreed that his horse would not leave him, and that, if he were alive, he would be found not far from the spot where Charles Erskine picked up the animal. From Erskine's account, it appeared that he had been several weeks in the mountains, prospecting, before he discovered the mine; by which time he was so reduced in strength, through hardship and insufficient food, that it was with difficulty he made his way down to the valley. Just at a time when to proceed further seemed impossible, and when he had been absent two days from the mine, he fell in with a riding-horse, quietly grazing, at the foot of the mountain. Catching and mounting him, he rode, first along the edge of the valley for some distance, to find, if possibly a party were encamped there; but finding no one, started for his old home, riding as long as his strength allowed, and dismounting quite often to rest. In this way, three days and a half had passed, since the discovery of the mine. Judging from where the horse was found, Harris must have gone up on

the other side of the ridge or spur, in which *el tesoro* was
located. At all events, it was decided to send a party to
look for him, as, whether or not any accident had befallen
him, he was now without the means of reaching home; and,
to provide for any emergencies, John ordered the light
wagon to be taken along, with certain other articles, so suggestive of possible pain and calamity, that Miss Edwards
felt her blood chilled by the sight of them.

"He will be so disappointed," she said, "not to have
been the discoverer of the mine. John, you must make
him a handsome present, and I will see what I can do, to
show my gratitude for his many kindnesses."

And then, happy in the presence of her lover, and the
returning cheerfulness of her brother, Miss Edwards forgot to give more than a passing thought to James Harris,
while she busied herself in the preparations for a holiday,
which, to her, would be doubly an anniversary, ever afterward.

The clouds, which had been gathering for a storm, during the past week, sent down a deluge of rain, on Christmas Eve, making it necessary to light fires in the long-
empty fire-places, and giving a truly festive glow to the
holiday adornments of the Edwards Rancho. The ranch
hands were dancing to the music of the "Arkansas Traveler," in their separate quarters. John Edwards's half-
dozen friends from the city, with two or three of his sister's,
and the now convalescent Charles Erskine, clothed in a suit
of borrowed broadcloth, were making mirth and music,
after their more refined fashion, in Miss Edwards's parlor.

At the hour when, according to tradition, the Bethlehem
Babe was born, Missouri Joe appeared at the door, and
made a sign to the master of the house.

"It's a pity, like," said Joe, softly, "to leave him out
thar in the storm."

"'Him!' Do you mean Harris? How is he?"

"The storm can't hurt him none," continued Joe; "an'

it do not look right to fetch him in yer, nor to 'tother house, no more."

" What is it, John?" Miss Edwards asked anxiously, looking over his shoulder into the darkness. " Has Harris returned?"

" They have brought him," answered John; "and we must have him in here."

She shrank away, frightened and distressed, while the men brought what remained of Sandy-haired Jim, and deposited it carefully on a wooden bench in the hall. There was little to be told. The men had found him at the foot of a precipice where he had fallen. Beside him was a heavy nugget of pure gold, which he was evidently carrying when he fell. He had not died immediately, for in his breast-pocket was found the bond, with this indorsement, in pencil:

" I hev lit onto the mine foller mi trail up the kenyon miss Mary edwards is mi air so help me God goodby.
                                        JAMES HARRIS."

They buried him on Christmas Day; and Miss Edwards, smiling through her quiet-flowing tears, adorned his coffin with evergreen-wreaths and flowers. " I am glad to do this for him," she whispered to her lover, "for if ever there was a heart into which Christ was born at its birth, it was poor Jim's."

POEMS.

POEMS.

A PAGAN REVERIE.

Tell me, mother Nature! tender yet stern mother!
In what nomenclature (fitlier than another)
Can I laud and praise thee, entreat and implore thee;
Ask thee what thy ways be, question yet adore thee.

Over me thy heaven bends its royal arches;
Through its vault the seven planets keep their marches:
Rising, shining, setting, with no change or turning;
Never once forgetting—wasted not with burning.

On and on, unceasing, move the constellations,
Lessening nor increasing since the birth of nations:
Sun and moon unfailing keep their times and seasons,—
But man, unavailing, pleads to thee for reasons.

Why the great dumb mountains, why the ocean hoary—
Even the babbling fountains, older are than story,
And his life's duration 's but a few short marches
Of the constellations through the heavenly arches!

Even the oaks of Mamre, and the palms of Kedar,
(Praising thee with psalmry) and the stately cedar,
Through the cycling ages, stinted not are growing,—
While the holiest sages have not time for knowing.

Mother whom we cherish, savage while so tender,
Do the lilies perish mourning their lost splendor?
Does the diamond shimmer brightlier that eternal
Time makes nothing dimmer of its light supernal?

Do the treasures hidden in earth's rocky bosom,
Cry to men unbidden that they come and loose them?
Is the dew of dawntide sad because the Summer
Kissed to death the fawn-eyed Spring, the earlier comer?

Would the golden vapors trooping over heaven,
Quench the starry tapers of the sunless even?
When the arrowy lightnings smite the rocks asunder,
Do they shrink with frightenings from the bellowing thunder?

Inconceivable Nature! these, thy inert creatures,
With their sphinx-like stature, are of man the teachers;
Silent, secret, passive, endless as the ages,
'Gainst their forces massive fruitlessly he rages.

Winds and waves misuse him, buffet and destroy him;
Thorns and pebbles bruise him, heat and cold annoy him;
Sting of insect maddens, snarl of beast affrights him;
Shade of forest saddens, breath of flowers delights him.

O thou great, mysterious mother of all mystery!
At thy lips imperious man entreats his history.—
Whence he came—and whither is his spirit fleeing:
Ere it wandered hither had it other being:

Will its subtile essence, passing through death's portal,
Put on nobler presence in a life immortal?
Or is man but matter, that a touch ungentle,
Back again may shatter to forms elemental?

Can mere atoms question how they feel sensation?
Or dust make suggestion of its own creation?
Yet if man were better than his base conditions,
Could things baser fetter his sublime ambitions?

What unknown conjunction of the pure etherial,
With the form and function of the gross material,
Gives the product mortal? whose immortal yearning
Brings him to the portal of celestial learning.

To the portal gleaming, where the waiting sphinxes,
Humoring his dreaming, give him what he thinks is
Key to the arcana—plausible equation
Of the problems many in his incarnation.

Pitiful delusion!—in no nomenclature—
Maugre its profusion—O ambiguous nature!
Can man find expression of his own relation
To the great procession of facts in creation?

Fruitless speculating! none may lift the curtain
From the antedating ages and uncertain
When what is was not, and tides of pristine being
Beat on shores forgot, and all, as now, unseeing.

Whence impelled or whither, or by what volition;
Borne now here, now thither, in blind inanition.
Out of this abysmal, nebulous dim distance,
Haunted by a dismal, phantomic existence,

Issued man?—a creature without inspiration,
Gross of form and feature, dull of inclination?
Or was his primordial self a something higher?
Fresh from test and ordeal of elemental fire.

Were these ages golden while the world was younger,
When the giants olden knew not toil nor hunger?
When no pain nor malice marred joy's full completeness,
And life's honeyed chalice rapt the soul with sweetness?

When the restless river of time loved to linger;
Ere flesh felt the quiver of death's dissolving finger;
When man's intuition led without deflection,
To a sure fruition, and a full perfection.

Individual man is ever new created:
What his being's plan is, loosely predicated
On the circumstances of his sole condition,
Colored by the fancies borrowed from tradition.

His creation gives him clue to nothing older:
Naked, life receives him—wondering beholder
Of the world about him—and ere aught is certain,
Time and mystery flout him; and death drops the curtain.

Man, the dreamer, groping after what he should be,
Cheers himself with hoping to be what he would be:
When he hopes no longer, with self-adulation,
Fancies he was stronger at his first creation:

Else—in him inhering powers of intellection—
Death, by interfering with his mind's perfection,
Itself gives security to restore life's treasure,
Freed from all impurity and in endless measure.

Thou, O Nature, knowest, yet no word is spoken.
Time, that ever flowest, presses on unbroken:
All in vain the sages toil with proof and question—
The immemorial ages give no least suggestion.

PASSING BY HELICON.

My steps are turned away;
    Yet my eyes linger still,
    On their beloved hill,
    In one long, last survey:
Gazing through tears that multiply the view,
    Their passionate adieu!

O, joy-empurpled height,
    Down whose enchanted sides
    The rosy mist now glides,

How can I loose thy sight?
How can my eyes turn where my feet must go,
   Trailing their way in woe?

Gone is my strength of heart;
   The roses that I brought
   From thy dear bowers, and thought
To keep, since we must part—
Thy thornless roses, sweeter until now,
   Than round Hymettus' brow.

The golden-vested bees
   Find sweetest sweetness in—
   Such odors dwelt within
The moist red hearts of these—
Alas, no longer give out blissful breath,
   But odors rank with death.

Their dewiness is dank;
   It chills my pallid arms,
   Once blushing 'neath their charms;
And their green stems hang lank,
Stricken with leprosy, and fair no more,
   But withered to the core.

Vain thought! to bear along,
   Into this torrid track,
   Whence no one turneth back
With his first wanderer's song
Yet on his lips, thy odors and thy dews,
   To deck these dwarfed yews.

No more within thy vales,
   Beside thy plashing wells,
   Where sweet Euterpe dwells
With songs of nightingales,
And sounds of flutes that make pale Silence glow,
   Shall I their rapture know.

18

Farewell, ye stately palms!
  Clashing your cymbal tones,
  In thro' the mystic moans
Of pines at solemn psalms:
Ye myrtles, singing Love's inspired song,
  We part, and part for long!

Farewell, majestic peaks!
  Whereon my listening soul
  Hath trembled to the roll
Of thunders that Jove wreaks—
And calm Minerva's oracles hath heard
  All more than now unstirred !

Adieu, ye beds of bloom !
  No more shall zephyr bring
  To me, upon his wing,
Your loveliest perfume;
No more upon your pure, immortal dyes,
  Shall rest my happy eyes.

I pass by; at thy foot,
  O, mount of my delight !
  Ere yet from out thy sight,
I drop my voiceless lute:
It is in vain to strive to carry hence
  Its olden eloquence.

Your sacred groves no more
  My singing shall prolong,
  With echoes of my song,
Doubling it o'er and o'er.
Haunt of the muses, lost to wistful eyes,
  What dreams of thee shall rise !

Rise but to be dispelled—
    For here where I am cast,
    Such visions may not last,
By sterner fancies quelled:
Relentless Nemesis my doom hath sent—
    This cruel banishment!

LOST AT SEA.

A fleet set sail upon a summer sea:
    'Tis now so long ago,
I look no more to see my ships come home;
But in that fleet sailed all 't was dear to me.

Ships never bore such precious freight as these,
    Please God, to any woe.
His world is wide, and they may ride the foam,
Secure from danger, in some unknown seas.

But they have left me bankrupt on life's 'change;
    And daily I bestow
Regretful tears upon the blank account,
And with myself my losses rearrange.

Oh, mystic wind of fate, dost hold my dower
    Where I may never know?
Of all my treasure ventured what amount
Will the sea send me in my parting hour!

'TWAS JUNE, NOT I.

"Come out into the garden, Maud;"
    In whispered tones young Percy said:
    He but repeated what he'd read
That afternoon, with soft applaud:
A snatch, which for my same name's sake,
    He caught, out of the sweet, soft song,
A lover for his love did make,
    In half despite of some fond wrong:—
And more he quoted, just to show
    How still the rhymes ran in his head,
    With visions of the roses red
That on the poet's pen did grow.

The poet's spell was on our blood;
    The spell of June was in the air;
We felt, more than we understood,
    The charm of being young and fair.
Where everything is fair and young—
    As on June eves doth fitly seem:
The Earth herself lies in among
    The misty, azure fields of space,
A bride, whose startled blushes glow
    Less flame-like through the shrouds of lace
That sweeter all her beauties show.

We walked and talked beneath the trees—
    Bird-haunted, flowering trees of June—
    The roses purpled in the moon;
We breathed their fragrance on the breeze—
Young Percy's voice is tuned to clear
Deep tones, as if his heart were deep:
This night it fluttered on my ear
As young birds flutter in their sleep.
My own voice faltered when I said

How very sweet such hours must be
With one we love.   At that word he
Shook like the aspen overhead:
"Must be!" he drew me from the shade,
To read my face to show his own:
" Say *are*, dear Maud!"—my tongue was stayed;
My pliant limbs seemed turned to stone.

He held my hands I could not move—
The nerveless palms together prest—
And clasped them tightly to his breast;
While in my heart the question strove.
The fire-flies flashed like wandering stars—
I thought some sprang from out his eyes:
Surely some spirit makes or mars
At will our earthly destinies!
"Speak, Maud!"—at length I turned away:
He must have thought it woman's fear;
For, whispering softly in my ear
Such gentle thanks as might allay
Love's tender shame; left on my brow,
And on each hand, a warm light kiss—
I feel them burn there even now—
But all my fetters fell at this.

I spoke like an injured queen:
It's our own defence when we're surprised—
The way our weakness is disguised;
I said things that I could not mean,
Or ought not—since it was a lie
That love had not been in my mind:
'T was in the air I breathed; the sky
Shone love, and murmured it the wind.
It had absorbed my soul with bliss;
My blood ran love in every vein,
And to have been beloved again

Were heavenly!—so I thought till this
Unlooked for answer to the prayer
My heart was making with its might.
Thus challenged, caught in sudden snare,
Like two clouds meeting on a height,
And, pausing first in short strange lull,
Then bursting into awful storm,
Opposing feelings multiform,
Struggled in silence: and then full
Of our blind woman-wrath, broke forth
In stinging hail of sharp-edged ice,
As freezing as the polar north,
Yet maddening. O, the poor mean vice
We women have been taught to call
By virtue's name! the holy scorn
We feel for lovers left love-lorn
   By our own coldness, or by the wall
   Of other love 'twixt them and us!

The tempest past, I paused. He stood
Silent,—and yet "Ungenerous!"
Was hurled back, plainer than ere could
His lips have said it, by his eyes
   Fire-flashing, and his pale, set face,
   Beautiful, and unmarred by trace
Of aught save pain and pained surprise.
—I quailed at last before that gaze,
   And even faintly owned my wrong:
I said I "spoke in such amaze
   I could not choose words that belong
To such occasions." Here he smiled,
   To cover one low, quick-drawn sigh:
   "June eves disturb us differently,"
He said, at length; "and I, beguiled
By something in the air, did do
   My Lady Maud unmeant offence;

And, what is stranger far, she too,
Under the baleful influence
of this fair heaven "—he raised his eyes,
And gestured proudly toward the stars—
" Has done me wrong. Wrong, lady, mars
God's purpose, written on these skies,
Painted and uttered in this scene:
Acknowledged in each secret heart;
We both are wrong, you say; 'twould mean
That we too should be wide apart—
And so, adieu !"—with this he went.

I sat down whitening in the moon,
With heat as of a desert noon,
Sending its fever vehement
Across my brow, and through my frame—
The fever of a wild regret—
A vain regret without a name,
In which both love and loathing met.

Was this the same enchanted air
I breathed one little hour ago?
Did all these purple roses blow
But yestermorn, so sweet, so fair?
Was it *this* eve that some one said
" Come out into the garden, Maud?"
And while the sleepy birds o'erhead
Chirped out to know who walked abroad,
Did *we* admire the plumey flowers
On the wide-branched catalpa trees,
And locusts, scenting all the breeze;
And call the balm-trees our bird-towers?
Did *we* recall the " black bat Night,"
That flew before young Maud walked forth—
And say this Night's wings were too bright
For bats'—being feathered, from its birth,

Like butterflies' with powdered gold:
Still talking on, from gay to grave,
And trembling lest some sudden wave
Of the soul's deep, grown over-bold,
Should sweep the barriers of reserve,
And whelm us in tumultuous floods
Of unknown power? What did unnerve
Our frames, as if we walked with gods?
Unless they, meaning to destroy,
Had made us mad with a false heaven,
Or drunk with wine and honey given
Only for immortals to enjoy.

Alas, I only knew that late
I'd seemed in an enchanted sphere;
That now I felt the web of fate
Close round me, with a mortal fear.
If only once the gods invite
To banquets that are crowned with roses;
After which the celestial closes
Are barred to us; if in despite
Of such high favor, arrogant
We blindly choose to bide our time,
Rejecting Heaven's—and ignorant
What we have spurned, attempt to climb
To heavenly places at our will—
Finding no path thereto but one,
Nemesis-guarded, where atone
To heaven, all such as hopeful still,
Press toward the mount,—yet find it strewn
With corses, perished by the way,
Of those who Fate did importune
Too rashly, or her will gainsay.
If *I* have been thrust out from heaven,
This night, for insolent disdain,
Of putting a young god in pain,

How shall I hope to be forgiven?
Yet let me not be judged as one
Who mocks at any high behest;
My fault being that I kept the throne
Of a JOVE vacant in my breast,
And when APOLLO claimed the place
I was too loyal to my Jove;
Unmindful how the masks of love
Transfigure all things to our face.

Ah, well! if I have lost to fate
The greatest boon that heaven disposes;
And closed upon myself the gate
To fields of bliss; 'tis on these roses,
On this intoxicating air,
The witching influence of the moon,
The poet's rhymes that went in tune
To the night's voices low and rare;
To all, that goes to make such hours
Like hasheesh-dreams. These did defy,
With contrary fate-compelling power,
The intended bliss;—*'twas June, not I.*

LINES TO A LUMP OF VIRGIN GOLD.

Dull, yellow, heavy, lustreless—
With less of radiance than the burnished tress,
Crumpled on Beauty's forehead: cloddish, cold,
Kneaded together with the common mold!
Worn by sharp contact with the fretted edges
Of ancient drifts, or prisoned in deep ledges;
Hidden within some mountain's rugged breast
From man's desire and quest—
Would thou could'st speak and tell the mystery
That shrines thy history!

Yet 'tis of little consequence,
To-day, to know how thou wert made, or whence
Earthquake and flood have brought thee: thou art here,
At once the master that men love and fear—
Whom they have sought by many strange devices,
In ancient river-beds; in interstices
Of hardest quartz; upon the wave-wet strand,
Where curls the tawny sand
By mountain torrents hurried to the main,
And thence hurled back again:—

Yes, suffered, dared, and patiently
Offered up everything, O gold, to thee!—
Home, wife and children, native soil, and all
That once they deemed life's sweetest, at thy call;
Fled over burning plains; in deserts fainted;
Wearied for months at sea—yet ever painted
Thee as the shining Mecca, that to gain
Invalidated pain,
Cured the sick soul—made nugatory evil
Of man or devil.

Alas, and well-a-day! we know
What idle dreams were these that fooled men so.
On yonder hillside sleep in nameless graves,
To which they went untended, the poor slaves
Of fruitless toil; the victims of a fever
Called home-sickness—no remedy found ever;
Or slain by vices that grow rankly where
Men madly do and dare,
In alternations of high hope and deep abysses
Of recklessnesses.   .

Painfully, and by violence:
Even as heaven is taken, thou wert dragged whence
Nature had hidden thee—whose face is worn
With anxious furrows, and her bosom torn

In the hard strife—and ever yet there lingers
Upon these hills work for the " effacing fingers"
Of time, the healer, who makes all things seem
A half forgotten dream;
Who smooths deep furrows and lone graves together,
By touch of wind and weather.

Thou heavy, lustreless, dull clod!
Digged from the earth like a base common sod;
I wonder at thee, and thy power to hold
The world in bond to thee, thou yellow gold!
Yet do I sadly own thy fascination,
And would I gladly show my estimation
By giving house-room to thee, if thou'lt come
And cumber up my home;—
I'd even promise not to call attention
To these things that I mention!

" The King can do no wrong," and thou
Art King indeed to most of us, I trow.
Thou'rt an enchanter, at whoso sovereign will
All that there is of progress, learning, skill,
Of beauty, culture, grace—and I might even
Include religion, though that flouts at heaven—
Comes at thy bidding, flies before thy loss;—
And yet men call thee dross!
If thou art dross then I mistaken be
Of thy identity.

Ah, solid, weighty, beautiful!
How could I first have said that thou wert dull?
How could have wondered that men willingly
Gave up their homes, and toiled and died for thee?
Theirs was the martyrdom in which was planted
A glorious State, by precious memories haunted:
Ours is the comfort, ease, the power, the fame
Of an exalted name:

Theirs was the struggle of a proud ambition—
Ours is the full fruition.

Thou, yellow nugget, wert the star
That drew these willing votaries from afar,
'Twere wrong to call thee lustreless or base
That lightest onward all the human race,
Emblem art thou, in every song or story,
Of highest excellence and brightest glory:
Thou crown'st the angels, and enthronest Him
Who made the cherubim:
My reverend thought indeed is not withholden,
O nugget golden!

MAGDALENA.

You say there's a Being all-loving,
  Whose nature is justice and pity;
Could you say where you think he is roving?
  We have sought him from city to city,
But he never is where we can find him,
  When outrage and sorrow beset us;
It is strange we are always behind him,
  Or that He should forever forget us.

But being a god, he is thinking
  Of the masculine side of the Human;
And though just, it would surely be sinking
  The God to be thoughtful for woman.
For him and by him was man made:
  Sole heir of the earth and its treasures;
An after-thought, woman—the handmaid,
  Not of God, but of man and his pleasures.

Should you say that man's God would reprove us,
  If we found him and showed him our bruises?

It is dreary with no one to love us,
  Or to hold back the hand that abuses:
Man's hand, that first led and caressed us,
  Man's lips, that first kissed and betrayed;—
If his God could know how he's oppressed us,
  Do you think that we need be afraid?

For we loved him—and he who stood nearest
  To God, who could doubt or disdain?
When he swore by that God, and the dearest
  Of boons that he hoped to obtain
Of that God, that he truly would keep us
  In his heart of hearts precious and only:
Say, how could we think he would steep us
  In sorrow, and leave us thus lonely?

But you see how it is: he has left us,
  This demi-god, heir of creation;
Of our only good gifts has bereft us,
  And mocked at our mad desolation:
Says that we knew that such oaths would be broken—
  Says we lured him to lie and betray;
Quotes the word of his God as a token
  Of the law that makes woman his prey.

And now what shall we do? We have given
  To this master our handmaiden's dower:
Our beauty and youth, aye, and even
  Our souls have we left in his power.
Though we thought when we loved him, that loving
  Made of woman an angel, not demon;
We have found, to our fond faith's disproving,
  That love makes of woman a leman!

Yes, we gave, and he took: took not merely
  What we gave, for his lying pretences:
But our whole woman world, that so dearly

We held by till then: our defences
Of home, of fair fame; the affection
  Of parents and kindred; the human
Delight of child-love; the protection
  That is everywhere owed to a woman.

You say there's a Being all-loving,
  Whose nature is justice and pity:
Could you say where you think he is roving?
  We have sought him from city to city.
We have called unto him, our eyes streaming
  With the tears of our pain and despair:
We have shouted unto him blaspheming,
  And whispered unto him in prayer.

But he sleeps, or is absent, or lending
  His ear to man's prouder petition:
And the black silence over us bending
  Scorches hot with the breath of perdition.
For this fair world of man's, in which woman
  Pays for all that she gets with her beauty,
Is a desert that starves out the human,
  When her charms charm not squarely with duty.

For man were we made, says the preacher,
  To love him and serve him in meekness,
Of man's God is man solely the teacher
  Interpreting unto our weakness:
He the teacher, the master, dispenser
  Not only of law, but of living,
Breaks his own law with us, then turns censor,
  Accusing, but never forgiving.

Do you think that we have not been nursing
  Resentment for wrong and betrayal?
From our hearts, filled with gall, rises cursing,
  To our own and our masters' dismayal.

'T is for this that we seek the all-loving,
   Whose nature is justice and pity;
And we'll find Him, wherever he 's roving,
   In country, in town, or in city.

He must show us his justice, who made us;
   He must place sin where sin was conceived;
We must know if man's God will upbraid us
   Because we both loved and believed.
We must know if man's riches and power,
   His titles, crowns, sceptres and ermine,
Weigh with God against womanhood's dower,
   Or whether man's guilt they determine.

It would seem that man's God should restrain him,
   Or else should avenge our dishonor:
Shall the cries of the hopeless not pain him,
   Or shall woman take all guilt upon her?
Let us challenge the maker that made us;
   Let us cry to Christ, son of a woman;
We shall learn if, when man has betrayed us,
   Heaven's justice accords with the human.

We must know if because we were lowly,
   And kept in the place man assigned us,
He could seek us with passions unholy
   And be free, while his penalties bind us.
We would ask if his gold buys exemption,
   Or whether his manhood acquits him;
How it is that we scarce find redemption
   For sins less than his self-law permits him.

Do we dare the Almighty to question?
   Shall the clay to the potter appeal?
To whom else shall we go with suggestion?
   Shall the vase not complain to the wheel?
God answered Job out of the groaning

Of thunder and whirlwind and hailing;
　Will he turn a deaf ear to our moaning,
　　Or reply to our prayers with railing?

Did you speak of a Christ who is tender—
　A deity born of a woman?
Of the sorrowful, God and defender,
　And brother and friend of the human?
Long ago He ascended to heaven,
　Long ago was His teaching forgotten;
The lump has no longer the leaven,
　But is heavy, unwholesome and rotten.

The gods are all man's, whom he praises
　For laws that make woman his creature;
For the rest, theological mazes
　Furnish work for the salaried preacher.
In the youth of the world it was better,
　We had deities then of our choosing;
We could pray, though we wore then a fetter,
　To a GODDESS of binding and loosing.

We could kneel in a grove or a temple,
　No man's heavy hand on our shoulder:
Had in Pallas Athene example
　To make womanhood stronger and bolder.
But the temples are broken and plundered,
　Sacred altars profanely o'erthrown;
Where the oracle trembled and thundered,
　Are a cavern, a fount, and a stone.

Yet we would of the Christ hear the story,
　'Twas familiar in days that are ended;
His humility, purity, glory,
　Are they not into heaven ascended?
We see naught but scorning and hating;
　We hear naught but threats and contemning;
For your Christian is good and berating,
　And your sinner is first in condemning.

Should you say that the Christ would reprove us,
  If we found him and told him our trouble?
It is fearful with no one to love us,
  And our pain and despair growing double.
It is mad'ning to feel we're excluded
  From the homes of the mothers that bore us;
And that man, by no false arts deluded,
  May enter unchallenged before us.

It is hard to be humble when trodden;
  We cannot be meek when oppressed;
Nor pure while our souls are made sodden
  With loathing that can't be confessed;
Or true, while our bread and our shelter
  By a lying pretence is obtained—
Deceived, in deception we welter;
  By a touch are we evermore stained.

O hard lot of woman! the creature
  Of a creature whose God is asleep,
Or gone on a journey.   You teach her
  She was made to sin, suffer, and weep;
We wait for a new revelation,
  We cry for a God of our own;
O God unrevealed, bring salvation,
  From our necks lift the collar of stone!

REPOSE.

I lay me down straight, with closed eyes,
  And pale hands folded across my breast,
Thinking, unpained, of the sad surprise
  Of those who shall find me thus fall'n to rest;
And the grief in their looks when they learn no endeavor,
Can disturb my repose—for my sleep is forever.

19

I know that a smile will lie hid in my eyes,
  Even a soft throb of joy stir the pulse in my breast,
When they sit down to mourning, with tears and with sighs,
  And shudder at death, which to me is but rest.

So sweet to be parted at once from our pain;
  To put off our care as a robe that is worn;
To drop like a link broken out of a chain,
  And be lost in the sands by Time's tide overborne:
And to know at my loss all the wildest regretting,
Will be as a foot-print, washed out in forgetting.
To be certain of this—that my faults perish first;
  That when they behold me so calmly asleep,
They can but forgive me my errors at worst,
  And speak of my praises alone as they weep.

" Whom the gods love die young," they will say;
  Though they should think it, they will not say so:
"Whom the world pierces with thorns pass away,
  Grieving, yet asking and longing to go!"
No, when they see how divine my repose is,
They'll forget that my-life-path is not over roses;
And they'll whisper together, with hands full of flowers,
  How always I loved them to wear on my breast;
And strewing them over my bosom in showers,
  With hands shaken by sobs, leave me softly to rest.

There is one who will come when the rest are away;
  One bud of a rose will he bring for my hair;
He knows how I liked it, worn always that way,
  And his fingers will tremble while placing it there.
Yes, he'll remember those soft June-day closes,
When the sky was as flushed as our own crimson roses;
He'll remember the flush on the sky and the flowers,
  And the red on my cheek where his lips had been prest;
But the throes of his heart in the long, silent hours,
  Will disturb not my dreams, so profoundly I'll rest.

So, all will forget, what to think of mere pain,
    That the heart now asleep in this solemn repose,
Had contended with tempests of sorrow in vain,
    And gone down in the strife at the feet of its foes:
They will choose to be mute when a deed I have done,
Or a word I have spoke I can no more atone;
They'll remember I loved them, was faithful and true;
    They'll not say what a wild will abode in my breast;
But repeat to each other, as if they were new,
    Old stories of what did the loved one at rest.

Ah! while I lie soothing my soul with this dream,
    The terror of waking comes back to my heart;
Why is it not as I thus make it seem?
    Must I come back to the world, ere we part?
Deep was the swoon of my spirit—why break it?
Why bring me back to the struggles that shake it?
Alas, there is room on my feet for fresh bruises—
    The flowers are not dead on my brow or my breast—
When shall I learn " sweet adversity's uses,"
    And my tantalized spirit be truly at rest!

ASPASIA.

O, ye Athenians, drunken with self-praise,
    What dreams I had of you, beside the sea,
In far Milentus! while the golden days
    Slid into silver nights, so sweet to me;
For then I dreamed my day-dreams sweetly o'er,
    Fancying the touch of Pallas on my brow—
Libations of both heart and wine did pour,
    And offered up my being with my vow.

'Twas thus to Athens my heart drew at last
    My life, my soul, myself. Ah, well, I learn

To love and loathe the bonds that hold me fast,
　　Your captive and your conquerer in turn;
Am I not shamed to match my charms with those
　　Of fair boy-beauties? gentled for your love
To match the freshness of the morning rose,
　　And lisp in murmurs like the cooing dove.

O, men of Athens! by the purple sea
　　In far Miletus, when I dreamed of you,
Watching the winged ships that invited me
　　To follow their white track upon the blue;
'T was the desire to mate my lofty soul
　　That drew me ever like a viewless chain
Toward Homer's land of heroes, 'til I stole
　　Away from home and dreams, to you and pain.

I brought you beauty—but your *boys* invade
　　My woman's realm of love with girlish airs.
I brought high gifts, and powers to persuade,
　　To charm, to teach, with your philosophers.
But knowledge is man's realm alone, you hold;
　　And I who am your equal am cast down
Level with those who sell themselves for gold—
　　A crownless queen—a woman of the town!

Ye vain Athenians, know this, that I
　　By your hard laws am only made more free;
Your unloved dames may sit at home and cry,
　　But, being unwed, I meet you openly,
A foreigner, you cannot wed with me;
　　But I can win your hearts and sway your will,
And make your free wives envious to see
　　What power Aspasia wields, Milesian still.

Who would not be beloved of Pericles?
　　I could have had all Athens at my feet;
And have them for my flatterers, when I please;

Yet, one great man's great love is far more sweet!
He is my proper mate as I am his—
　You see my young dreams were not all in vain—
And I have tasted of ineffable bliss,
　If I am stung at times with fiery pain.

It is not that I long to be a wife
　By your Athenian laws, and sit at home
Behind a lattice, prisoner for life,
　With my lord left at liberty to roam;
Nor is it that I crave the right to be
　At the symposium or the Agora known;
My grievance is, that your proud dames to me
　Came to be taught, in secret and alone.
They fear; what *do* they fear? is't me or you?
　Am I not pure as any of them all?
But your laws are against me; and 'tis true,
　If fame is lowering, I have had a fall!
O, selfish men of Athens, shall the world
　Remember you, and pass my glory by?
Nay, 'til from their proud heights your names are hurled,
　Mine shall blaze with them on your Grecian sky.

Am I then boastful?　It is half in scorn
　Of caring for your love, or for your praise,
As women do, and must.　Had I been born
　In this proud Athens, I had spent my days
In jealousy of boys, and stolen hours
　With some Milesian, of a questioned place,
Learning of her the use of woman's powers
　Usurped by men of this patrician race.

Alas! I would I were a child again,
　Steeped in dream langours by the purple sea;
And Athens but the vision it was then,
　Its great men good, its noble women free:
That I in some winged ship should strive to fly

To reach this goal, and founder and go down!
O impious thought, how could I wish to die,
   With all that I have felt and learned unknown?

Nay, I am glad to be to future times
   As much Athenian as is Pericles;
Proud to be named by men of other climes
   The friend and pupil of great Socrates.
What is the gossip of the city dames
   Behind their lattices to one like me?
More glorious than their high patrician names
   I hold my privilege of being free!

And yet I would that they were free as I;
   It angers me that women are so weak,
Looking askance when ere they pass me by
   Lest on a chance their lords should see us speak;
And coming next day to an audience
   In hope of learning to resemble me:
They wish, they tell me, to learn eloquence—
   The lesson they should learn is *liberty*.

O Athens, city of the beautiful,
   Home of all art, all elegance, all grace;
Whose orators and poets sway the soul
   As the winds move the sea's unstable face;
O wonderous city, nurse and home of mind,
   This is my oracle to you this day—
No generous growth from starved roots will you find,
   But fruitless blossoms weakening to decay.

You take my meaning? Sappho is no more,
   And no more Sapphos will be, in your time;
The tree is dead on one side that before
   Ran with such burning sap of love and rhyme.
Your glorious city is the utmost flower
   Of a one-sided culture, that will spend

Itself upon itself, 'till, hour by hour,
  It runs its sources dry, and so must end.

That race is doomed, behind whose lattices
  Its once free women are constrained to peer
Upon the world of men with vacant eyes;
  It was not so in Homer's time, I hear.
But Eastern slaves have eaten of your store,]
  Till in your homes all eating bread are slaves;
They're built into your walls, beside your door,
  And bend beneath your lofty architraves.

A woman of the race that looks upon
  The sculptured emblems of captivity,
Shall bear a slave or tyrant for a son;
  And none shall know the worth of liberty.
Am I seditious ?—Nay, then, I will keep
  My lesson for your dames when next they steal
On tip-toe to an audience. Pray sleep
  Securely, and dream well: we wish your weal!

Why, what vain prattle: but my heart is sore
  With thinking on the emptiness of things,
And these Athenians, treacherous to the core,
  Who hung on Pericles with flatterings.
I would indeed I were a little child,
  Resting my tired limbs on the sunny sands
In far Miletus, where the airs blow mild,
  And countless looms throb under busy hands.

The busy hand must calm the busy thought,
  And labor cool the passions of the hour;
To the tired weaver, when his web is wrought,
  What signifies the party last in power?
But here in Athens, 'twixt philosophers
  Who reason on the nature of the soul;
And all the vain array of orators,
  Who strove to hold the people in control.

Between the poets, artists, critics, all,
　Who form a faction or who found a school,
We weave Penelope's web with hearts of gall,
　And my poor brain is oft the weary tool.
Yet do I choose this life.　What is to me
　Peace or good fame, away from all of these,
But living death?　I do choose liberty,
　And leave to Athens' dames their soulless ease.

The time shall come, when Athens is no more,
　And you and all your gods have passed away;
That other men, upon another shore,
　Shall from your errors learn a better way.
To them eternal justice will reveal
　Eternal truth, and in its better light
All that your legal falsehoods now conceal,
　Will stand forth clearly in the whole world's sight.

A REPRIMAND.

Behold my soul?　She sits so far above you
　Your wildest dream has never glanced so high;
Yet in the old-time when you said, " I love you,"
　How fairly we were mated, eye to eye.
How long we dallied on in flowery meadows,
　By languid lakes of purely sensuous dreams,
Steeped in enchanted mists, beguiled by shadows,
　Casting sweet flowers upon loitering streams,
My memory owns, and yours; mine with deep shame,
　Yours with a sigh that life is not the same.

What parted us, to leave you in the valley
　And send me struggling to the mountain-top?
Too weak for duty, even love failed to rally
　The manhood that should float your pinions up.

On my spent feet are many half-healed bruises,
  My limbs are wasted with their heavy toil,
But I have learned adversity's " sweet uses,"
  And brought my soul up pure through every soil;
Have I no right to scorn the man's dead power
  That leaves you far below me at this hour?

Scorn you I do, while pitying even more
  The ignoble weakness of a strength debased.
Do I yet mourn the faith that died of yore—
  The trust by timorous treachery effaced?
Through all, and over all, my soul mounts free
  To heights of peace you cannot hope to gain,
Sings to the stars its mountain minstrelsy,
  And smiles down proudly on your murky plain;
'Tis vain to invite you—yet come up, come up,
  Conquer your way toward the mountain-top !

TO MRS. ——.

I cannot find the meaning out
  That lies in wrong and pain and strife;
I know not why we grope through grief,
  Tear-blind, to touch the higher life.

I see the world so subtly fair,
  My heart with beauty often aches;
But ere I quiet this sweet pain,
  Some cross so presses, the heart breaks.

To-day, this lovely golden day,
  When heaven and earth are steeped in calm;
When every lightest air that blows,
  Sheds its delicious freight of balm.

If I but ope my lips, I sob;
　If but an eyelid lift, I weep;
I deprecate all good or ill,
　And only wish for endless sleep.

For who, I ask, has set my feet
　In all these dark and troubled ways?
And who denies my soul's desire,
　When with its might it cries and prays?

In my unconscious veins there runs
　Perchance, some old ancestral taint;
In Eve *I* sinned: poor Eve and I!
　We each may utter one complaint:—

One and the same—for knowledge came
　Too late to save *her* paradise;
And I my paradise have lost;
　Forsooth because *I* am not wise.

O vain traditions! small the aid
　We women gather from your lore:
Why, when the world was lost, did death
　Not come our children's birth before?

It had been better to have died,
　Sole prey of death, and ended so;
Than to have dragged through endless time,
　One long, unbroken trail of woe.

To suffer, yet not expiate;
　To die at last, yet not atone;
To mourn our heirship to a guilt,
　Erased by innocent blood alone!

You lift your hands in shocked surprise;
　You say enough I have not prayed:
Can prayer go back through centuries,
　And change the web of fate one braid?

Nay, own the truth, and say that we
 Are but the bonded slaves of doom;
Unconscious to the cradle came,
 Unwilling must go to the tomb.

Your woman's hands are void of help,
 Though my soul should be stung to death;
Could I avert one pang from you,
 Imploring with my latest breath?

And men!—we suffer any wrong
 That men, or mad, or blind, may do;—
Let me alone in my despair!
 There is no help for me or you.

I wait to find the meaning out
 That lies beyond the bitter end;
Comfort yourself with 'wearying heaven,
 I ask no comfort, oh my friend!

MOONLIGHT MEMORIES.

Do thy chamber windows open east,
 Beloved, as did ours of old?
And do you stand when day has ceased,
 Withdrawn thro' evening's porch of gold,
And watch the pink flush fade above
 The hills on which the wan moon leans,
Remembering the sweet girlish love
 That blest this hour in other scenes!

I see your hand upon your heart—
 I see you dash away the tears—
It is the same undying smart,
 That touched us in the long-gone years;
And cannot pass away. You stand

Your forehead to the window crest,
And stifle sobs that no command
　　Can keep from rising in your breast.

Dear, balm is not for griefs like ours,
　　Nor resurrection for dead hope:
In vain we cover wounds with flowers,
　　That grow upon life's western slope.
Their leaves tho' bright, are hard, and dry,
　　They have no soft and healing dew;
The pansies of past spring-times lie
　　Dead in the shadow of the yew.

You feel this in your heart, and turn
　　To pace the dimness of your room;
But lo, like fire within an urn,
　　The moonlight glows through all the gloom.
It sooths you like a living touch,
　　And spite of the slow-falling tears,
Sweet memories crowd with oh, so much,
　　Of all that girlhood's time endears.

On nights like this, with such a moon,
　　Full shining in a wintry sky;
Or on the softer nights of June,
　　When fleecy clouds fled thought-like by,
Within our chamber opening east,
　　With curtains from the window parted,
With hands and cheeks together prest,
　　We dreamed youth's glowing dreams, light-hearted.

Or talked of that mysterious love
　　That comes like fate to every soul:
And vowed to hold our lives above,
　　Perchance its sorrowful control.
Alas, the very vow we made,
　　To keep our lives from passion free,
To wiser hearts well had betrayed
　　Some future love's intensity.

How well that youthful vow was kept,
  Is written on a deathless page—
Vain all regrets, vain tears we've wept,
  The record lives from age to age.
But one who "doeth all things well,"
  Who made us differ from the throng,
Has it within his heart to quell
  This torturing pain of thirst, ere long.

And you, whose soul is all aglow
  With fire Prometheus brought from heaven,
Shall in some future surely know
  Joys for which high desires are given.
Not always in a restless pain
  Shall beat your heart, or throb your brow;
Not always shall you sigh in vain
  For hope's fruition, hidden now.

Beloved, are your tear-drops dried?
  The moon is riding high above:—
Though each from other's parted wide,
  We have not parted early love.
And tho' you never are forgot,
  The moonrise in the east shall be
The token that my evening thought
  Returns to home, and love and thee!

VERSES FOR M——.

  The river on the east
Ripples its azure flood within my sight;
  And, darting from the west,
Are "sunset arrows," feathered with red light.
  The northern breeze has hung
His wintry harp upon some giant pine;

And the pale stars among,
I see the star I love to name as mine:
    But toward the south I turn my eager eyes—
    Beyond its flushed horizon my heart lies.

    The snow-clad isles of ice,
Launched by wild Boreas from a northern shore,
    Journey the way my eyes
Turn with an envious longing evermore—
    Smiling back to the sky
Its own pink blush, and, floating out of sight,
    Bear south the softest dye
Of northern heavens, to fade in southern night:—
    My eyes but look the way my joys are gone,
    And the ice-islands travel not alone.

    The untrod fields of snow,
Glow with the rosy blush of parting day;
    And fancy asks if so
The snow is stained with sunset far away;
    And if some face, like mine,
Its forehead pressed against the window-pane,
    Peers northward, with the shine
Of the pole-star reflected in eyes' rain:
    "Ah yes," my heart says, "it is surely so;"
    And, like a bound bird, flutters hard to go.

    Sad eyes, that, blurred with tears,
Gaze into darkness, gaze no more in vain
    Whence no loved face appears,
And no voice comes to lull the heart's fond pain!
    Sad heart! restrain thy throbs,
For beauty, like a presence out of heaven,
    Rests over all, and robs
Sorrow of pain, and makes earth seem forgiven:—
    Twilight the fair eve ushers in with grace,
    And rose clouds melt for stars to take their place.

AUTUMNALIA.

The crimson color lays
As bright as beauty's blush along the West;
    And a warm golden haze,
Promising sheafs of ripe Autumnal days
    To crown the old year's crest.
Hangs in mid air, a half-pellucid maze,
    Through which the sun at set,
Grown round and rosy, looks with Bacchian blush,
    For an old wine-god meet—
Whose brows are dripping with the grape-blood sweet,
    As if his southern flush
Rejoiced him, in his northern-zone retreat.

    The amber-colored air
Musical is with hum of tiny things
    Held idly, struggling there,
As if the golden mist entangled were
    About the viewless wings,
That beat out music on their gilded snare.

    If but a leaf, all gay
With Autumn's gorgeous coloring, doth fall,
    Along its fluttering way
A shrill alarum wakes a sharp dismay,
    And, answering to the call,
The insect chorus swells and dies away
    With a fine piping noise.
As if some younger singing notes cried out,
    As do mischievous boys—
Startling their playmates with a pained voice,
    Or sudden thrilling shout,
Followed by laughters, full of little joys.

Perchance a lurking breeze
Springs, just awakened to its wayward play,
    Tossing the sober trees
Into a frolic maze of ecstasies,
    And snatching at the gay
Banners of Autumn, strews them where it please.

    The sunset colors glow
A second time in flame from out the wood,
    As bright and warm as though
The vanished clouds had fallen, and lodged below
    Among the tree-tops, hued
With all the colors of heaven's signal-bow.

    The fitful breezes die
Into a gentle whisper, and then sleep;
    And sweetly, mournfully,
Starting to sight, in the transparent sky,
    Lone in the upper deep,
Sad Hesper pours its beams upon the eye;
    And for one little hour,
Holds audience with the lesser lights of heaven;
    Then to its western bower
Descends in sudden darkness, as the flower
    That at the fall of Even
Shuts its bright eye, and yields to slumber's power.

    Soon, with a dusky face,
Pensive and proud as an East Indian queen,
    And with a solemn grace,
The moon ascends, and takes her royal place
    In the fair evening scene;
While all the reverential stars, apace,
Take up their march through the cool fields of space,
And dead is the sweet Autumn day whose close we've seen.

PALO SANTO.

In the deep woods of Mexico,
  Where screams the "painted paraquet,"
And mocking-birds flit to and fro,
  With borrowed notes they half forget;
Where brilliant flowers and poisonous vines
  Are mingled in a firm embrace,
And the same gaudy plant entwines
  Some reptile of a poisonous race;
Where spreads the *Itos'* icy shade,
  Benumbing, even in summer's heat,
The thoughtless traveler who hath laid
  Himself to noonday slumbers sweet;—
Where skulks unseen the beast of prey—
The native robber glares and hides,—
  And treacherous death keeps watch alway
On him who flies, or he who bides.

In these deep tropic woods there grows
A tree, whose tall and silvery bole
  Above the dusky forest shows,
  As shining as a saintly soul
Among the souls of sinful men;—
Lifting its milk-white flowers to heaven,
  And breathing incense out, as when
  The passing saints of earth are shriven.

The skulking robber drops his eyes,
  And signs himself with holy cross,
If, far between him and the skies,
  He sees its pearly blossoms toss.
The wanderer halts to gaze upon
  The lovely vision, far or near,
And smiles and sighs to think of one
  He wishes for the moment here.
20

The Mexic native fears not fang
    Of poisonous serpent, vine, nor bee,
If he may soothe the baleful pang
    With juices of this " holy tree."

How do we all, in life's wild ways,
    Which oft we traverse lost and lone,
Need that which heavenward draws the gaze,
    Some *Palo Santo* of our own!

A SUMMER DAY.

Fade not, sweet day!
Another hour like this—
So full of tranquil bliss—
May never come my way,
I walk in paths so shadowed and so cold:
    But stay thou, darling hour,
    Nor stint thy gracious power
To smile away the clouds that me enfold:
    Oh stay! when thou art gone,
    I shall be lost and lone.

Lost, lone, and sad;
And troubled more and more,
By the dark ways, and sore,
In which my feet are led;—
Alas, my heart, it was not always so!
    Therefore, O happy day,
    Haste not to fade away,
Nor let pale night chill all thy tender glow—
    Thy rosy mists, that steep
    The violet hills in sleep—

Thy airs of gold,
That over all the plain,
And fields of ripened grain,
A shimmering glory hold,—
The soft fatigue-dress of the drowsy sun;
Dreaming, as one who goes
To peace, and sweet repose,
After a battle hardly fought, and won:
Even so, my heart, to-day,
Dream all thy fears away.

O happy tears,
That everywhere I gaze,
Jewel the golden maze,
Flow on, till earth appears
Worthy the soft perfection of this scene:
Beat, heart, more soft and low,
Creep, hurrying blood, more slow:
Waste not one throb, to lose me the serene,
Deep, satisfying bliss
Of such an hour as this!

How like our dream,
Of that delightful rest
God keepeth for the blest,
This lovely peace doth seem;—
Perchance, my heart, He sent this gracious day,
That when the dark and cold,
Thy doubtful steps enfold,
Thou may'st remember, and press on thy way,
Nor faint midway the gloom
That lies this side the tomb.

All, all in vain,
Sweet day, do I entreat
To stay thy wingèd feet;
The gloom, the cold, the pain,

Gather me back as thou dost pale and fade;
  Yet in my heart I make
  A chamber for thy sake,
And keep thy picture in warm color laid:—
  Thy memory, happy day,
  Thou can'st not take away.

HE AND SHE.

Under the pines sat a young man and maiden,
"Love," said he; "life is sweet, think'st thou not so?"
Sweet were her eyes, full of pictures of Aidenn,—
"Life?" said she; "love is sweet; no more I know."

Into the wide world the maid and her lover
Wandered by pathways that sundered them far;
From pine-groves to palm-groves, he flitted a rover,
She tended his roses, and watched for his star.

Oft he said softly, while melting eyes glistened,
"Sweet is my life, love, with you ever near:"
Morning and evening she waited and listened
For a voice and a foot-step that never came near.

Fainting at last, on her threshold she found him:
"Life is but ashes, and bitter," he sighed.
She, with her tender arms folded around him,
Whispered—"But love is still sweet;" and so died.

O WILD NOVEMBER WIND.

O wild November wind, blow back to me
  The withered leaves, that drift adown the past;
Waft me some murmur of the summer sea,
  On which youth's fairy fleet of dreams was cast;

Return to me the beautiful No More—
  O wild November wind, restore, restore!

November wind, in what dim, loathsome cave,
  Languish the tender-plumed gales of spring?
No more their dances dimple o'er the wave,
  Nor freighted pinions song and perfume bring:
Those gales are dead—that dimpling sea is dark;
  And cloudy ghosts clutch at each mist-like bark.

O wild, wild wind, where are the summer airs
  That kissed the roses of the long-ago?
Taking them captive—swooned in blissful snares—
  To let them perish. Now no roses blow
In the waste gardens thou art laying bare:
  Where are my heart's bright roses, where, oh where?

Thou hast no answer, thou unpitying gale?
  No gentle whisper from the past to me !
No snatches of sweet song—no tender tale—
  No happy ripple of that summer sea;
Are all my dreams wrecked on the nevermore?
  O wild November wind, restore, restore!

BY THE SEA.

Blue is the mist on the mountains,
  White is the fog on the sea;
Ruby and gold is the sunset,—
  And Bertha is waiting for me.

Down on the loathsome sand-beach,
  Her eyes as blue as the mist;
Her brows as white as the sea-fog,—
  Bertha, whose lips I have kissed.

Bertha, whose lips are like rubies,
  Whose hair is like coiléd gold;
Whose sweet, rare smile is tenderer
  Than any legend of old.

One morn, one noon, one sunset,
  Must pass before we meet;
O wind and sail bear steady on,
  And bring me to her feet.

The morn rose pale and sullen,
  The noon was still and dun;
Across the storm at sunset,
  Came the boom of a signal-gun.

Who treads the loathsome sand-beach,
  With wet, disordered hair;
With garments tangled with sea-weed,
  And cheeks more pale than fair?

O blue-eyed, white-browed maiden,
  He will keep love's tryst no more;
His ship sailed safely into port—
  But on the heavenward shore.

POLK COUNTY HILLS.

November came that day,
And all the air was gray
With delicate mists, blown down
From hill-tops by the south wind's balmy breath;
  And all the oaks were brown
  As Egypt's kings in death;
  The maple's crown of gold
  Laid tarnished on the wold;
The alder and the ash, the aspen and the willow,
  Wore tattered suits of yellow.

The soft October rains
Had left some scarlet stains
Of color on the landscape's neutral ground;
  Those fine ephemeral things,
  The winged motes of sound,
  That sing the "Harvest Home"
  Of ripe Autumn in the gloam
Of the deep and bosky woods, in the field and
      by the river,
  Sang that day their best endeavor.

I said: "In what sweet place
Shall we meet face to face,
  Her loveliest self to see—
Meet Nature at her sad autumnal rites,
  And learn the mystery
  Of her unnamed delights?"
  Then you said: "Let us go
  Where the late violets blow
In hollows of the hills, under dead oak leaves
      hiding;—
  We'll find she's there abiding."

Do we recall that day?
Has its grace passed away?
  Its tenderest, dream-like tone,
Like one of Turner's landscapes limned on air—
  Has its fine perfume flown
  And left the memory bare?
  Not so; its charm is still
  Over wood, vale and hill—
The ferny odor sweet, the humming insect
      chorus,
  The spirit that before us

Enticed us with delights
To the blue, breezy hights.

O, beautiful hills that stand
Serene 'twixt earth and heaven, with the grace
Of both to make you grand,—
Your loveliness leaves place
For nothing fairer; fair
And complete beyond compare.
O, lovely purple hills, O, first day of November,
Be sure that I remember!

WAITING.

I cannot wean my wayward heart from waiting,
Though the steps watched for never come anear;
The wearying want clings to it unabating—
The fruitless wish for presences once dear.

No fairer eve e'er blessed a poet's vision;
No softer airs e'er kissed a fevered brow;
No scene more truly could be called Elysian,
Than this which holds my gaze enchanted now.

And yet I pine;—this beautiful completeness
Is incomplete, to my desiring heart;
'Tis Beauty's form, without her soul of sweetness—
The pure, but chiseled loveliness of art.

There is no longer pleasure in emotion.
I envy those dead souls no touch can thrill;
Who—"painted ships upon a painted ocean,"—
Seem to be moved, yet are forever still.

Where are they fled?—they whose delightful voices,
Whose very footsteps had a charmed fall:
No more, no more their sound my heart rejoices:
Change, death, and distance part me now from all.

And this fair evening, with remembrance teeming,
  Pierces my soul with every sharp regret;
The sweetest beauty saddens to my seeming,
  Since all that's fair forbids me to forget.

Eyes that have gazed upon yon silver crescent,
  'Till filled with light, then turned to gaze in mine,
Lips that could clothe a fancy evanescent,
  In words whose magic thrilled the brain like wine:

Hands that have wreathed June's roses in my tresses,
  And gathered violets to deck my breast,
Where are ye now? I miss your dear caresses—
  I miss the lips, the eyes, that made me blest.

Lonely I sit and watch the fitful burning
  Of prairie fires, far off, through gathering gloom;
While the young moon, and one bright star returning
  Down the blue solitude, leave Night their room.

Gone is the glimmer of the silent river;
  Hushed is the wind that sped the leaves to-day;
Alone through silence falls the crystal shiver
  Of the sweet starlight, on its earthward way.

And yet I wait, how vainly! for a token—
  A sigh, a touch, a whisper from the past;
Alas, I listen for a word unspoken,
  And wail for arms that have embraced their last.

I wish no more, as once I wished, each feeling
  To grow immortal in my happy breast;
Since not to feel will leave no wounds for healing—
  The pulse that thrills not has no need of rest.

As the conviction sinks into my spirit
  That my quick heart is doomed to death in life;
Or that these pangs must pierce and never sear it,
  I am abandoned to despairing strife.

To the lost life, alas! no more returning—
　In this to come no semblance of the past—
Only to wait!—hoping this ceaseless yearning
　May, 'ere long, end—and rest may come at last.

PALMA.

What tellest thou to heaven,
Thou royal tropic tree?
At morn or noon or even,
Proud dweller by the sea,
What is thy song to heaven?

The homesick heart that fainted
In torrid sun and air,
With peace becomes acquainted
Beholding thee so fair—
With joy becomes acquainted:

And charms itself with fancies
About thy kingly race—
With gay and wild romances
That mimic thee in grace—
Of supple, glorious fancies.

I feel thou art not tender,
Scion of sun and sea—
The wild-bird does not render
To thee its minstrelsy—
Fearing thou art not tender:

But calm, serene and saintly,
As highborn things should be:
Who, if they love us faintly,
Make us love reverently,
Because they are so saintly.

To be loved without loving,
O proud and princely palm!
Is to fancy our ship moving
With the ocean at dead calm—
The joy of love is loving.

Because the Sun did sire thee,
The Ocean nurse thy youth,
Because the Stars desire thee,
The warm winds whisper truth,
Shall nothing ever fire thee?

What is thy tale to heaven
In the sultry tropic noon?
What whisperest thou at even
To the dusky Indian Moon—
Has she sins to be forgiven?

Keep all her secrets; loyal
As only great souls are—
As only souls most royal,
To the flower or to the star
Alike are purely loyal.

O Palma, if thou hearest,
Thou proud and princely tree!
Thou knowest that my Dearest
Is emblemed forth in thee—
My kingly Palm, my Dearest.

I am his Moon admiring,
His wooing Wind, his Star;
And I glory in desiring
My Palm-tree from afar—
Glad as happier lovers are,
Am happy in desiring!

MAKING MOAN.

*I have learned how vainly given
Life's most precious things may be.*
—Landon.

O, Christ, to-night I bring
A sad, weak heart, to lay before thy feet;
   Too sad, almost, to cling
   Even to Thee; too suffering,
If Thou shouldst pierce me, to regard the sting;
Too stunned to feel the pity I entreat
Closing around me its embraces sweet.

   Shepherd, who gatherest up
The weary ones from all the world's highways;
   And bringest them to sup
   Of Thy bread, and Thy blessed cup;
If so Thou will, lay me within the scope
Only of Thy great tenderness, that rays
Too melting may not reach me from Thy face.

   Here let me lie, and press
My forehead's pain out on Thy mantle's hem;
   And chide not my distress,
   For this, that I have loved thee less,
In loving so much some, whose sordidness
Has left me outcast, at the last, from them
And their poor love, which I cannot contemn.

   No, cannot, even now,
Put Thee before them in my broken heart.
   But, gentle Shepherd, Thou
   Dost even such as I allow
The healing of Thy presence.   Let my brow
Be covered from thy sight, while I, apart,
Brood over in dull pain my mortal hurt.

CHILDHOOD.

A child of scarcely seven years,
   Light haired, and fair as any lily;
With pure eyes ready in their tears
   At chiding words, or glances chilly;
And sudden smiles, as inly bright
   As lamps through alabaster shining,
With ready mirth, and fancies light,
   Dashed with strange dreams of child-divining:
     A child in all infantile grace,
     Yet with the angel lingering in her face.

A curious, eager, questioning child,
   Whose logic leads to naive conclusions;
Her little knowledge reconciled
   To truth amid some odd confusions;
Yet credulous, and loving much
   The problems hardest for her reason,
Placing her lovely faith on such,
   And deeming disbelief a treason;
     Doubting that which she can disprove,
     And wisely trusting all the rest to love.

Such graces dwell beside your hearth,
   And bless you in a priceless pleasure,
Leaving no sweeter spot on earth
   Than that which holds your household treasure.
No entertainment ever yet
   Had half the exquisite completeness—
The gladness without one regret,
   You gather from your darling's sweetness:
     An angel sits beside the hearth
     Where e're an innocent child is found on earth.

A LITTLE BIRD THAT EVERY ONE KNOWS.

There's a little bird with a wondrous song---
A little bird that every one knows—
(Though it sings for the most part *under the rose*),
That is petted and pampered wherever it goes,
And nourished in bosoms gentle and strong.

This petted bird has a crooked beak
And eyes like live coals set in its head,
A gray breast dappled with glowing red—
DABBLED—not dappled, I should have said,
From a fancy it has of which I shall speak.

This eccentricity that I name
Is, that whenever the bird would sing
It darts its black head under its wing,
And moistens its beak in—darling thing!—
A human heart that is broken with shame.

Then this cherished bird its song begins—
Always begins its song one way—
With two little dulcet words, THEY SAY,
Carolled in such a charming way
That the listener's heart it surely wins.

This sweetest of songsters sits beside
Every hearth in this Christian land,
Ever so humble or never so grand,
Gloating o'er crumbs which many a hand
Gathers to nourish it, far and wide.

Over each crumb that it gathers up
It winningly carols those two soft words
In the dulcet notes of the sweetest of birds,
Darting its sharp beak under its wing
As it might in a ruby drinking-cup.

A delicate thing is our bird withal
And owns but a fickle appetite,
So that old and young take a keen delight
In serving it ever, day and night,
With the last gay heart now turned to gall.

Thus, though a dainty dear, it sings
In a very well-conditioned way
A truly wonderful sort of lay,
Whose burden is ever the same—THEY SAY—
Darting its dabbled beak under its wings.

WAYWARD LOVE.

I leant above your chair last night,
  And on your brow once and again,
I pressed a kiss as still and light
  As I would have your bosom's pain.
You did not feel the gentle touch,
  It gave you neither grief nor pleasure,
Though that caress held, oh, so much,
  Of love and blessing without measure.

Thus ever when I see you sad,
  My heart toward you overflows;
But when again you're gay and glad,
  I shrink back into cold repose,
I know not why I like you best,
  O'erclouded by a passing sorrow—
Unless because it gives a zest
  To the *insouciance* of to-morrow.

You're welcome to my light caress,
  And all the love that with it went;
To live, and love you any less,
  Would rob me of my soul's content.

Continue sometimes to be sad,
  That I may feel that pity tender,
Which grieves for you, and yet is glad
  Of an excuse for love's surrender.

A LYRIC OF LIFE.

Said one to me: "I seem to be—
Like a bird blown out to sea,
In the hurricane's wild track—
Lost, wing-weary, beating back
Vainly toward a fading shore,
It shall rest on nevermore."

Said I: "Betide, some good ships ride,
Over all the waters wide;
Spread your wings upon the blast,
Let it bear you far and fast:
In some sea, serene and blue,
Succor-ships are waiting you."

This soul then said: "Would I were dead—
Billows rolling o'er my head!
Those that sail the ships will cast
Storm-waifs back into the blast;
Omens evil will they call
What the hurricane lets fall."

For my reply: "Beneath the sky
Countless isles of beauty lie:
Waifs upon the ocean thrown,
After tossings long and lone,
To those blessed shores have come,
Finding there love, heaven, and home."

This soul to me: "The seething sea,
Tossing hungry under me,

I fear to trust; the ships I fear;
I see no isle of beauty near;
The sun is blotted out—no more
'T will shine for me on any shore."

Once more I said: "Be not afraid;
Yield to the storm without a dread;
For the tree, by tempests torn
From its native soil, is borne
Green, to where its ripened fruit
Gives a sturdy forest-root.

"That which we lose, we think we choose,
Oft, from slavery to use.
Shocks that break our chains, tho' rude,
Open paths to highest good:
Wise, my sister soul, is she
Who takes of life the proffered key."

FROM AN UNPUBLISHED POEM.

"Nay, Hylas, I have come
To where life's landscape takes a western slope,
And breezes from the occidental shores
Sigh thro' the thinning locks around my brow,
And on my cheeks fan flickering summer fires.
Oh, winged feet of Time, forget your flight,
And let me dream of those rose-scented bowers
That lapped my soul in youth's enchanted East!
It needs no demon-essence of Hasheesh
To flash *that* sunrise glory in my eyes!—
It needs no Flora to bring back those flowers—
No gay Apollo to sound liquid reeds—
No muse to consecrate the hills and streams—
No God or oracle within those groves

To render sacred all the emerald glooms:
For here dwelt such bright angels as attend
The innocent ways of youth's unsullied feet;
And all the beautiful band of sinless hopes,
Twining their crowns of pearl-white amaranth;
And rosy, dream-draped, sapphire-eyed desires
Whose twin-born deities were Truth and Faith
Having their altars over all the land.
Beauty held court within its vales by day,
And Love made concert with the nightingales
In singing 'mong the myrtles, starry eves."

  "You are inspired, Zobedia, your eyes
Look not upon the present summer world,
But see some mystery beyond the close
Of this pale blue horizon."

  "Erewhile I wandered from this happy land.
Crowned with its roses, wearing in my eyes
Reflections of its shining glorious heaven,
And bearing on my breast and in my hands
Its violets, and lilies white and sweet,—
Following the music floating in the air
Made by the fall of founts, the voice of streams
And murmur of the winds among the trees,
I strayed in reveries of soft delight
Beyond the bounds of this delicious East.

But oh, the splendors of that newer clime!
It was as if those oriental dreams
In which my soul was steeped to fervidness,
Were here transmuted to their golden real
With added glories for each shape or hue.
The stately trees wore coronals of flowers
That swung their censers in the mid-day sun:
The pines and palms of my delightful east
Chaunted their wild songs nearer to the stars;

Even the roses had more exquisite hues,
And for one blossom I had left behind
I found a bower in this fragrant land.
Bright birds, no larger than the costly gems
The river bedded in their golden sands,
Sparkle like prismal rain-drops 'mong the leaves;
And others sang, or flashed their plumage gay
Like rainbow fragments on my dazzled eyes.
The sky had warmer teints: I could not tell
Whether the heavens lent color to the flowers,
Or but reflected that which glowed in them.
The gales that blew from off the cloud-lost hills,
Struck from the clambering vines Eolian songs,
That mingled with the splashing noise of founts,
In music such as stirs to passionate thought:
This peerless land was thronged with souls like mine,
Straying from East to South, impelled unseen,
And lost, like mine, in its enchanted vales:—
Souls that conversed apart in pairs, or sang
Low breeze-like airs, more tender than sweet words;
Save here and there a wanderer like myself,
Dreaming alone, and dropping silent tears,
Scarce knowing why, upon the little group
Of Eastern flowers we had not yet resigned:—
'Till one came softly smiling in my eyes,
And dried their tears with radiance from his own.

At last it came—I knew not how it came—
But a tornado swept this sunny South,
And when I woke once more, I stood alone.
My senses sickened at the dismal waste,
And caring not, now all things bright were dead,
That a volcano rolled its burning tide
In fiery rivers far athwart the land,
I turned my feet to aimless wanderings.
The equatorial sun poured scorching beams,

On my defenceless head.   The burning winds
Seemed drying up the blood within my veins.
The straggling flowers that had outlived the storm
Won but a feeble, half-contemptuous smile;
And if a bird attempted a brief song,
I closed my ears lest it should burst my brain.
After much wandering I came at last
To cooler skies and a less stifling air;
And finally to this more temperate clime.
Where every beauty is of milder type—
Where the simoon nor tempest ever come,
And I can soothe the fever of my soul
In the bland breezes blowing from the West."

NEVADA.

Sphinx, down whose rugged face
The sliding centuries their furrows cleave
By sun and frost and cloud-burst; scarce to leave
Perceptible a trace
Of age or sorrow;
Faint hints of yesterdays with no to-morrow;—
My mind regards thee with a questioning eye,
To know thy secret, high.

If Theban mystery,
With head of woman, soaring, bird-like wings
And serpent's tail on lion's trunk, were things
Puzzling in history;
And men invented
For it an origin which represented
Chimera and a monster double-headed,
By myths Phenician wedded—

Their issue being this—
This most chimerical and wonderous thing

From whose dumb mouth not even the gods could wring
    Truth, nor antithesis:
    Then, what I think is,
This creature—being chief among men's sphinxes—
Is eloquent, and overflows with story,
    Beside thy silence hoary!

    Nevada!—desert waste!
Mighty, and inhospitable, and stern;
Hiding a meaning over which we yearn
    In eager, panting haste—
    Grasping and losing,
Still being deluded ever by' our choosing—
Answer us Sphinx: What is thy meaning double
    But endless toil and trouble?

    Inscrutable, men strive
To rend thy secret from thy rocky breast;
Breaking their hearts, and periling heaven's rest
    For hopes that cannot thrive;
    Whilst unrelenting,
Upon thy mountain throne, and unrepenting,
Thou sittest, basking in a fervid sun,
    Seeing or hearing none.

    I sit beneath thy stars,
The shallop moon beached on a bank of clouds—;
And see thy mountains wrapped in shadowed shrouds,
    Glad that the darkness bars
    The day's suggestion—
The endless repetition of one question;
Glad that thy stony face I cannot see,
    Nevada—Mystery!

THE VINE.

" Too many clusters weaken the vine "—
　　And that is why, on this morn in May,
She who should walk doth weakly recline
　　By the window whose view overlooks the Bay;
While I and the "clusters" dance in the sun,
　　Defying the breeze coming in from the sea,
　　Mocking the bird-song and chasing the bee,
Letting our fullness of mirth over-run,
　　　　While the " Vine " at the window smiles down on our
　　　　　　glee.

If I should vow that these " clusters " are fair,
　　So, you would say, are a million more;
Ah, even jewels a rank must share—
　　Not every diamond's a Koh-i-noor!
Thus when our LILLIAN, needing but wings,
　　Plays us the queen of the fairies, we deem
　　Grace such as hers a bewildering dream—
Her laughter, her gestures, a dozen things,
　　Furnish our worshiping fondness a theme.

Or when our ALICE, scarcely less tall,
　　And none the less fair, tries her slim baby feet,
Or a new has lisped, to the pride of us all,
　　Smiling, we cry, " was aught ever so sweet?"
Even wee BERTHA, turning her eyes,
　　Searching and slow from one face to another—
Wrinkling her brow in a comic surprise,
　　And winking so soberly at her pale mother,
For a baby, is wondrously pretty and wise!

Well, *let* the " vine " recline in the sun—
　　Three such rare " clusters " in three short years,
Have sapped the red wine in her veins that should
　　run—

For the choicest of species the gardener fears!
Lillian, queen of the lilies shall be,
    Fair, tall and graceful—queenly in will;
Alice a Provence rose—rarely sweet she;
    Bertha Narcissa—white daffodil—
And the "vine," once more strong, shall entwine
    around the three !

WHAT THE SEA SAID TO ME.

One evening as I sat beside the sea,
A little rippling wave stole up to me,
And whispered softly, yet impressively,
    The word Eternity:
I smiled, that anything so small should utter,
A word the ocean in its wrath might mutter;
And with a mirthful fancy, vainly strove,
To suit its cadence to some word of love—
But all the little wave would say to me,
Was, over and again, Eternity!

After a time, the winds, from their dark caves,
Arose, and wrestled with the swelling waves,
Shrieking as doth a madman when he raves;
    Yet still Eternity
Was spoken audibly unto my hearing;
While foaming billows, their huge crests up-rearing,
Rushed with a furious force upon the shore,
That only answered with a sullen roar;
As if it hoarsely echoed what the sea
Said with such emphasis—Eternity!

And by and by, the sky grew dun and dim;
Soon all was darkness, save the foam's white gleam;
And all was silence save the sea's deep hymn—
    That hymn Eternity:

While some dread presence, all the darkness filling,
Crept round my heart, its healthy pulses chilling;
Making the night, so awful unto me,
More fearful with that word Eternity.

So that my spirit, trembling and afraid,
Bowed down itself before its God, and prayed
For His strong arm of terror to be stayed;
   And sighed Eternity
From its white lips, as the dark sea, subsiding,
Sank into broken murmurs; and the gliding
Of the soothed waters seemed once more to me
The whisper I first heard, Eternity.

But now I mocked not what the ripple said:
I only reverently bent my head,
While the pure stars, unveiled, their lustre shed
   Upon the peaceful sea—
And the mild moon, with a majestic motion,
Uprose, and shed upon the murmuring ocean,
Her calm and radiant glory, as if she
Knew it the symbol of Eternity.

HYMN.

Down through the dark, my God,
 Reach me Thy hand;
Guide me along the road
 I fail to understand.
Blindly I grope my way,
 In doubt and fear,
Uncertain when I pray
 If Thou art near.

O, God, renew my trust,
 Hear when I cry;

Out of the cloud and dust
    Lift me to thee on high.
The crooked paths make plain,
    The burden light;
Touch me and heal my pain,
    And clear my sight.

O, take my hand in Thine,
    And lead me so
That all my steps incline
    In Thy right way to go.   .
Out of this awful night
    Some whisper send,
That I may feel my God,
    My loving friend.

O, let me feel and see
    Thy hand and face;
And let me learn of Thee
    My true right place.
For I am Thine, and Thou
    Art also mine.
Unto Thy will I bow,
    Helper divine!

DO YOU HEAR THE WOMEN PRAYING?

[Read before the Women's Prayer League of Portland, Oregon, May
27, 1874.]

Do you hear the women praying, oh my brothers?
    Do you hear what words they say?
These, this free-born nation's wives and mothers,
    Bowing, where you proudly stand, to pray!
Can you coldly look upon their faces,
    Pale, sad faces, seamed with frequent tears;

See their hands uplifted in their places—
　　Hands that toiled for all your boyhood's years?

Can you see your wives and daughters pleading
　　In the dust you spurn beneath your feet,
Baring hearts for years in secret bleeding,
　　To the scoffs and jestings of the street?
Can you hear, and yet not heed the crying
　　Of the children perishing for bread?
Born in fear, not love, and daily dying,
　　Cursed of God, they think, but cursed of *you* instead?

Do you hear the women praying, oh my brothers?
　　Hear the oft-repeated burden of their prayer—
Hear them asking for one boon above all others—
　　Not for vengeance on the wrongs they have to bear;
But imploring, as their Lord did, " God forgive them,
　　For they know not what they do;
Strike the sin, but spare the sinners—save them"—
　　Meaning, oh ye men and brothers, *you!*

For your heels have ground the women's faces;
　　You have coined their blood and tears for gold;
Have betrayed their kisses and embraces—
　　Returned their love with curses twentyfold;
Made the wife's crown one of thorns and not of honor,
　　Made her motherhood a pain and dread;
Heaped life's toil unrecompensed upon her;
　　Laid her sons upon her bosom, dead!

Do you hear the women praying, oh my brothers?
　　Have you not one word to say?
Will a *just* God be as gentle as these mothers,
　　If you dare to say them nay?
Oh, ye men, God waits for *you* to answer
　　The prayers that to him rise,
He waits to know if *you* are just ere *He* is—
　　There your deliverance lies!

Rise and assert the manhood of this nation,
  Its courage, honor, might—
Wipe off the dust of our humiliation—
  Dare nobly to do right!
Shall women plead from out the dust forever?
  Will you not work, men, if you cannot pray?
Hold up the suppliant hands with your endeavor,
  And seize the world's salvation while you may.

Yes, from the eastern to the western ocean,
  The sound of prayer is heard;
And in our hearts great billows of emotion
  At every breath are stirred.
From mountain tops of prayer down to sin's valley
  The voice of women sounds the cry, " Come up!"
O, men and brothers, heed that cry, and rally—
  Help us to dash to earth the deadly cup!

"OUR LIFE IS TWOFOLD."

Sweet, kiss my eyelids close, and let me lie,
On this old-fashioned sofa, in the dim
And purple twilight, shut out from the sky,
Which is too garish for my softer whim.
And while I, looking inward on my thought,
Tell thee what phantoms thicken in its air.
Twine thou thy gentle fingers, slumber-fraught,
With the loose shreds of my disheveled hair:
I shall see inly better if thou keep
My outer senses in a charmed sleep.

Sweet friend!—I love that pleasant name of friend—
We walk not ever singly, through the world;
But even as our shadow doth attend
Our going in the sunshine, and is furled

About us in the darkness—so that shade
Which haunts our other self, is faintly seen
Beside us in our gladness, and is made
To wrap us coldy life's bright hours between.
Unconsciously we court it.   In our youth,
While yet our morning sky is pink with joy,
We, curious if our happiness be truth,
Try to discern the shadow of alloy.
O, I remember well the earliest time
A sorrow touched me, and I nursed it then;
Tho' but few summers of our northern clime
Had sunned my growth among the souls of men.

In an old wood, reputed for its age,
And for its beauty wild and picturesque;
The bound and goal of each day's pilgrimage,
Where were all forms of graceful and grotesque;
And countless hues, from the dark stately pine
That whispered its wild mysteries to my ear,
To the smooth silver of the birch-trees shine,
Showing between the aspens straight and fair;
With forest flowers, and delicate vines that crept
From the rich soil far up among the trees,
Seeking that light their boughs did intercept,
And dalliance and caresses of the breeze.
In midst of these, sheltered from sun and wind
Glimmered a lake, in long and shining curves,
Like a bright fillet that should serve to bind
That scene to earth—if she the gem deserves!
For gem it was, as proud upon her brow
As jewels on the forehead of a queen;
And one thought as one turned from it, of how
Eve exiled, must have missed some just such scene.
O, there I type my life!   I used to sigh
Sitting on this side, with my lap piled up
With violets of the real sapphire dye,

For the gay gold of the bright buttercup
Spangling the green sod on the other side—
For the lake's breadth was but an arrow's flight,
And the brief distance did not serve to hide
What yet could not be reached except by sight.

Day after day I dreamed there, while my heart
Gathered up knowledge in its childish way,
Making fine pictures with unconscious art,
And learning beauty more and more each day.
Ever and ever haunted I that spot—
Sitting in dells scooped out between the hills,
That rising close around me, formed a grot
Fragrant with ferns, and musical with rills.
Far up above me grew the long-armed beech,
Dropping its branches down in graceful bent;
While farther up, beyond my utmost reach,
Stood dusky hemlocks, crowning the ascent.
And all about were sweeter sights and sounds
Than elsewhere, but in poet's dream, abounds.

Thus, and because my life was all too fair,
I sought to color it with thoughts I nursed
In sylvan solitudes: and in the air
Of these soft, silent influences, I first
Saw, or felt, rather, that the shadow fell
Upon my pathway from the light behind—
The light of youth's first joyousness. Ah, well,
If it had stayed there, nor been more unkind!
My earliest sorrow was a flower's death—
At which I wept until my swollen eyes
Refused to shed more tears—just that my wreath
One morn in autumn lacked its choicest dyes.
So, knowing what it was to have a loss,
I went on losing, and the shadow grew
Darker and longer, 'till it lies across

My pathway to the measure of my view.
We all remember sorrow's first impress—
No matter whether we had cause to grieve,
Or whether sad in very willfulness—
The leason is the same that we receive.
And afterwards, when the great shadow falls—
The tempest—when the lightning's flash reveals
The darkness brooding o'er us, and appals
Hope by the terror of thé stroke it deals—
Then, how the shadow hugs us in its fold!
We see no light behind, and none to come;
But dumbly shiver in the gloom and cold,
Or with despair lie down, and wait our doom.

Sweet, press thy cheek upon my own again—
Even now my life's dark ghost is haunting nigh:
Sing me to sleep with some old favorite strain—
Some gentle poet's loving lullaby;
For I would dream, and in my dream forget
Our twofold life is full of shadows set.

SOUVENIR.

You ask me, "Do you think of me?
 Dear, thoughts of thee are like this river,
Which pours itself into the sea,
 Yet empties its own channel never.

All other thoughts are like these sail
 Drifting the river's surface over;
They veer about with every gale—
 The *river* keeps its course forever.

So deep and still, so strong and true,
 The current of my soul sets thee-ward,
Thy river I, my ocean you,
 And all myself am running seaward.

I ONLY WISH TO KNOW.

Pray do not take the kiss again
  I risked so much in getting,
Nor let my blushes make you vain
  To your and my regretting.
I'm sure I've heard your sex repeat
  A thousand times or so,
That stolen kisses are most sweet—
  I only wished to know!

I own 'twas not so neatly done
  As you know how to do it,
And that the fright out-did the fun,
  But still I do not rue it.
I can afford the extra beat
  My heart took at your " Oh!"
Which plainly said *that* kiss was sweet—
  When I so wished to know!

Nay, I will not give back the kiss,
  Nor will I take a second;
Creme de la creme of pain and bliss
  This one shall e'er be reckoned.
The pain was mine, the bliss was—*ours,*
  You smile to hear it so;
But the same thought was surely yours,
  As I have cause to know.

LINES WRITTEN IN AN ALBUM.

The highest use of happy love is this;
  To make us loving to the loveless ones;
Willing indeed to halve our meed of bliss,
  If our sweet plenty others' want atones:
Of love's abundance may God give thee store,
To spend in love's sweet charities, LENORE.

LOVE'S FOOTSTEPS.

I sang a song of olden times,
   Sitting upon our sacred hill—
   Sang it to feel my bosom thrill
To the sweet pathos of its rhymes.

I trilled the music o'er and o'er,
   And happy, gazed upon the scene,
   Thinking that there had never been
So blue a sea, so fair a shore.

A vague half dream was in my mind;
   I hardly saw how sat the sun;
   I noted not the day was gone
The rosy western hills behind.

'Till, soft as if Apollo blew
   For me the sweet Thessalian flute,
   I heard a sound which made me mute,
And more than singing thrilled me through.

THY STEP—well known and well beloved!
   No more I dreamed on shore or sea;
   I thought of, saw but only thee,
Nor spoke, but blushed to be so moved.

THE POET'S MINISTERS.

POET.

Oh, my soul! the draught is bitter
   Yet it must be sweetly drunken:
Heart and soul! the grinding fetter
   Galls, yet have ye never shrunken:
Heart and soul, and pining spirit,
   Fail me not! no coward weakness

Such as ye are should inherit—
Be ye strong even in your meekness.

Born were ye to these strange uses,
  To brief joy and crushing ill,
To small good and great abuses;
  Yet oh, yield not, till they kill.
The stag wounded runneth steady
  With his blood in streams a-gushing;
Soul and spirit, be ye ready
  For the arrows toward ye rushing.

SPIRIT OF THE FLOWERS.

Now what ails our gentle friend?
  In his eye a meaning double,
Sorrow and defiance blend—
  Let us soothe him of his trouble.
Poet! do not pass us by :
  See how we are robed to meet you;
Heed you not our perfumed sigh?
  Heed you not how sweet we greet you?
Ever since the breath of morn
  We have waited for your coming,
Fearing when the bee's dull horn
  Round our quiet bower was humming:
We have kept our sweets for thee—
  Poet, do not pass us by :
Place us on thy breast, for see !
  By the sunset we must die.

SPIRIT OF THE MOUNTAIN STREAM.

Bathe thy pale face in the flood
  Which overflows this crystal fountain,
Then to rouse thy sluggish blood,
  Seek its source far up the mountain.
Note thou how the stream doth sing
  Its soft carol, low and light,

To the jagged rocks that fling
  Mildew shadows, black and blight.
Learn a lesson from the stream,
  Poet! though thy path may lie
Hid forever from the gleam
  Of the blue and sunny sky,—
Though thy way be steep and long,
  Sing thou still a cheerful song!

SPIRIT OF BEAUTY.

Come sister spirits, touch his eyelids newly,
  With that rare juice whose magic power it is,
To give the rose-hue to those things which truly
  Wear the sad livery of ugliness.
Oh, dignify the office of the meanest
  Of all God's manifold created things;
And sprinkle his heart's wounds with the serenest
  Waters of sweetness, from our fabled springs.
Oh, close him round with visions of all rareness,
  Make him see everything with smiling eye;
Let all his dreams be unsurpassed for fairness,
  And what we feign out-charm reality.
Come, sister spirits, up and do your duty;
When the Poet pines, feast his soul with beauty.

SPIRIT OF THE TREES.

Let us wave our branches gently
  With a murmur low and loving;
He will say we sang him quaintly
  Some old ballad, sweetly moving.
'Tis of all the ways the surest
  To awake a poet's fancies,
For he loves these things the purest—
  Sigh of leaves, and scent of pansies.
He has loved us, we will love him,
  And will cheer his hour of sadness,

Spirits, wave your boughs above him
To a measure of soft gladness.

SPIRIT OF LOVE.

Ye gentle ministers, ye have done well,
  But 'tis for love that most the poet pineth,
And till I spell him with my magic spell,
  In vain for him earth smiles or heaven shineth.
Behold I touch his heart, and there upspring
  Blooms to his cheeks, and flashes to his eyes;
His scornful lips upon the instant sing,
  And all his pulses leap with ecstasies.
'Tis love the poet wants; he cannot live
Without caressing and without caress,
  Which all to charity his fellows give;
But I will wrap his soul in tenderness,
  And straightway from his lips will burst a song
All loving hearts shall echo and prolong.

POET.

O Earth, and Sky, and Flowers, and Streams agushing,
  God made ye beautiful to make us blest:
O bright-winged Songsters through the blue air rushing;
  O murmuring Tree-tops, by the winds carest;
O Waves of Ocean, Ripples of the River,
  O Dew and Fragrance, Sunlight, and Starbeam,
O blessed summer-sounds that round me quiver,
  Delights impassable that round me teem—
    Oh all things beautiful! God made ye so
    That the glad hearts of men might overflow!

O Soul within me, whose wings sweep a lyre—
  God gave thee song that thou might'st give him praise;
O Heart that glows with the Promethean fire,
  O Spirit whose fine chords some influence plays:
O all sweet thoughts and beautiful emotions,
  O smiles and tears, and trembling and delight,

Have ye not all part in the soul's devotions,
   To help it swell its anthem's happy height?
      Spirit of Love, of God, of inspiration,
      The poet's glad heart bursts in acclamation !

CHORUS OF SPIRITS.

      Ring every flower-bell on the wind,
         And let each insect louder sing;
      Let elfin " joy be unconfined;"
         And let the laughing fairies bring
      A wreath enchanted, and to bind
         Upon the Poet's worthy brow
      Heartsease and laurel, and a kind
         Of valley lily, white as snow;
      And fresh May-roses, branching long—
         Braid all these in a garland gay,
      To crown the Poet for his song,
         Sung in our haunts this summer day !

SUNSET AT THE MOUTH OF THE COLUMBIA.

      There sinks the sun; like cavalier of old,
         Servant of crafty Spain,
      He flaunts his banner, barred with blood and gold,
         Wide o'er the western main,
      A thousand spear heads glint beyond the trees
         In columns bright and long:
      While kindling fancy hears upon the breeze
         The swell and shout of song.

      And yet, not here Spain's gay, adventurous host,
         Dipped sword or planted cross;
      The treasures guarded by this rock-bound coast,
         Counted them gain nor loss.
      The blue Columbia, sired by the eternal hills,

And wedded with the sea;
O'er golden sands, tithes from a thousand rills,
Rolled in lone majesty—

Through deep ravine, through burning, barren plain,
Through wild and rocky strait,
Through forest dark, and mountain rent in twain,
Toward the sunset gate.
While curious eyes, keen with the lust of gold,
Caught not the informing gleam;
These mighty breakers age on age have rolled
To meet this mighty stream.

Age after age these noble hills have kept,
The same majestic lines:
Age after age the horizon's edge been swept
By fringe of pointed pines.
Summers and Winters circling came and went,
Bringing no change of scene;
Unresting, and unhasting, and unspent,
Dwelt nature here serene.

Till God's own time to plant of Freedom's seed,
In this selected soil;
Denied forever unto blood and greed;
But blest to honest toil.
There sinks the sun. Gay Cavalier! no more
His banners trail the sea,
And all his legions shining on the shore
Fade into mystery.

The swelling tide laps on the shingly beach,
Like any starving thing;
And hungry breakers, white with wrath, upreach,
In vain clamoring.
The shadows fall; just level with mine eye
Sweet Hesper stands and shines,

And shines beneath an arc of golden sky,
  Pinked round with pointed pines.

A noble scene! all breadth, deep tone and power,
  Suggesting glorious themes;
Shaming the idler who would fill the hour
  With unsubstantial dreams.
Be mine the dreams prophetic, shadowing forth
  The things that yet shall be,
When through this gate the treasures of the North
  Flow outward to the sea.

THE PASSING OF THE YEAR.

      _   Worn and poor,
The Old Year came to Eternity's door.
Once, when his limbs were young and strong,
From that shining portal came he forth,
Led by the sound of shout and song,
To the festive halls of jubilant earth;—
Now, his allotted cycle o'er,
He waited, spent, by the Golden Door.

      Faint and far—faint and far,
Surging up soft between sun and star,
Strains of revelry smote his ear;
Musical murmurs from lyre and lute—
Rising in choruses grand and clear,
Sinking in cadences almost mute—
Vexing the ear of him who sate
Wearied beside the Shining Gate.

      Sad and low,
Flowed in an undertone of woe:
Wailing among the moons it came,
Sobbing in echoes against the stars;

Smothered behind some comet's flame,
Lost in the wind of the war-like Mars,
—Mingling, ever and anon,
With the music's swell a sigh or moan.

       " As in a glass,
Let the earth once before me pass,"
The Old Year said; and space untold
Vanished, till nothing came between;
Folded away, crystal and gold,
Nor azure air did intervene;
" As in a glass " he saw the earth
Decking a bier and waiting a birth.

" You crown me dead," the Old Year said,
" Before my parting hour is sped:
O fickle, false, and reckless world!
Time to Eternity may not haste;
Not till the last Hour's wing is furled
Within the gate my reign is past!
O Earth! O World! fair, false and vain,
I grieve not at my closing reign."

       Yet spirit-sore
The dead king noted a palace door;
He saw the gay crowd gather in;
He scanned the face of each passer by;
Snowiest soul, and heart of sin;
Tried and untried humanity:
Age and Youth, Pleasure and Pain,
Braided at chance in a motley skein.

      " Ill betide
Ye thankless ones!" the Old Year cried;
" Have I not given you night and day, .
Over and over, score upon score,
Wherein to live, and love, and pray,

And suck the ripe world to its rotten core?
Yet do you reek if my reign be done?
E're I pass ye crown the newer one!
At ball and rout ye dance and shout,
Shutting men's cries of suffering out,
That startle the white-tressed silences
Musing beside the fount of light,
In the eternal space, to press
Their roses, each a nebula bright,
More close to their lips serene,
While ye wear this unconscious mein!"

"Even so."
The revelers said: "We'll have naught of woe.
Why should we mourn, who have our fill?
Enough that the hungry wretches cry:
We from our plenty cast at will
Some crumbs to make their wet eyelids dry;
But to the rich the world is fair—
Why should we grovel in tears and prayer?"

In her innocent bliss,
A fair bride said with sweet earnestness,
"For the dead Year am I truly sad;
Since in its happy and hopeful days,
Every brief hour my heart was glad,
And blessings were strewn in all my ways:
Will it be so forevermore?
Will the New Years bring of love new store?"

Youth and maid.
Of their conscious blushes half afraid,
Shunning each other's tell-tale eyes,
Yet cherishing hopes too fond to own;
Speed the Old Year with secret sighs;
And smile that his time is overflown;
Shall they not hear each other say
"Dear Love!" ere the New Year's passed away?

"O, haste on!
The year or the pleasure is dead that is gone!"
Boasted the man of pomp and power;
"That which we hold is alone the good;
Give me new pleasures for every hour,
And grieve over past joys ye who would—
Joys that are fled are poor, I wis—
Give me forever the newest bliss!"

"Wish me joy,"
Girl-Beauty cried, with glances coy:
"In the New Year a woman I;
I'll then have jewels in my hair,
And such rare webs as Princes buy
Be none too choice for me to wear:
I'll queen it as a beauty should,
And not be won before I'm wooed!"

"Poor and proud—poor and proud!"
Sighed a student in the motley crowd—
"I heard her whisper that aside: ·
O fatal fairness, aping heaven
When earthly most!—I'll not deride—
God knows that were all good gifts given
To me as lavishly as rain,
I'd bring them to her feet again."

"Here are the fools we use for tools;
Bending their passion, ere it cools,
To any need," the cynic said:
"Lo, I will give him gold, and he
Shall sell me brain as it were bread!
His very soul I'll hold in fee
For baubles that shall buy the hand
Of the coldest woman in the land!"

Spirit sore,
The Old Year cared to see no more;
While, as he turned, he heard a moan—
Frosty and keen was the wintry night—
Prone on the marble paving-stone,
Unwatched, unwept, a piteous sight,
Starved and dying a poor wretch lay;
Through the blast he heard him gasping say:

"O, Old Year!
From sightless eyes you force this tear;
Sorrows you've heaped upon my head,
Losses you've gathered to drive me. wild,
All that I lived for, loved, are dead,—
Brother and sister, wife and child,
I, too, am perishing as well;
I shall share the toll of your passing bell!"

Grieved, and sad,
For the sins and woes the Human had,
The Old Year strove to avert his eyes;
But fly or turn wherever he would,
On his vexed ear smote the mingled cries
Of revel and new-made widowhood—
Of grief that would not be comforted
With the loved and beautiful lying dead.

Evermore, every hour,
Rising from hovel, hall and tower,
Swelling the strain of discontent;
Gurgled the hopeless prayer for alms,
Rung out the wild oath impotent;
Echoed by some brief walls of calms,
Straining the listener's shrinking ears,
Like silence when thunderbolts are near.

Across that calm, like gales of balm,
Some low, sweet household voices came;
Thrilling, like flute-notes straying out
From land to sea, some stormy night,
The ear that listens for the shout
Of drowning boatmen lost to sight—
And died away, again so soon
The pulseless air seemed fallen in a swoon.

          Once pure and clear,
Clarion strains fell on his ear:
The preacher shook the soulless creeds,
And pierced men's hearts with arrowy words,
Yet failed to stir them to good deeds:
Their new-fledged thoughts, like July birds,
Soared on the air and glanced away,
Before the eloquent voice could stay.

         "'Tis very sad the man is mad,"
The men and women gaily said;
As they, laughing, thread their homeward road,
Talking of other holidays;
Of last year, how it rained or snowed;
Who went abroad, who wed a blaze
Of diamonds with his shoddy bride,
On certain days—and who had died.

         "Would I were dead,
And vexed no more," the Old Year said:
"In vain may the preacher pray and warn;
The tinkling cymbals in your ears
Turn every gracious word to scorn;
Ye care not for the orphan's tears;
Your sides are fed, and your bodies clad
Is there anything heaven itself could add?"

And then he sighed, as one who died,
With a great wish unsatisfied;
Around him like a wintry sea,
Whose waves were nations, surged the world,
Stormy, unstable, constantly
Upheaved to be again down-hurled;
Here struggled some for freedom; here
Oppression rode in the high career.

In hot debate
Men struggled, while the hours waxed late;
Contending with the watchful zeal
Of gladiators, trained to die;
Yet not for life, nor country's weal,
But that their names might hang on high
As men who loved themselves, indeed,
And robbed the State to satisfy their need!

Heads of snow, and eyes aglow
With fires that youth might blush to know;
And brows whose youthful fairness shamed
The desperate thoughts that strove within;
While each his cause exulting named
As purest that the world had seen:
All names they had to tickle honest ears,
Reform, and Rights, and sweet Philanthropy's cares.

"Well-a-day! Well-a-day!"
The Old Year strove to put away
Sight and sound of the reckless earth;
But soft! from out a cottage door,
Sweet strains of neither grief nor mirth,
Upon his dying ear did pour;
"Give us, O God," the singers said,
As good a year as this one dead!"

Pealing loud from sod to cloud,
Earth's bell's rang out in a chorus proud;
Great waves of music shook the air
From organs pulsing with the sound;
Hushed was the voice of sob and prayer,
As time touched the eternal bound:
To the dead monarch earth was dimmed,
But the golden portals brighter beamed.

   Sad no more,
The Old Year reached the golden door,
Just as the hours with crystal clang
Aside the shining portals bent
And murmuring 'mong the spheres there rang
The chorus of earth's acknowledgment:
One had passed out at the golden door,
And one had gone in forevermore!